PHARAOH

TRUE LOVE

HAS NO HAPPY ENDING

BECAUSE THERE IS NO ENDING

FOR TRUE LOVE

SPECIAL THANK YOU TO

Gillian Studwell

PHARAOH

BEING BOOK ONE OF A SERIES

CONCEPTION

Pharaoh, a novel, by Julian Tyler.

BOOK I, PHARAOH: CONCEPTION

Copyright © 2014, 2015, 2016, 2017 by Julian Tyler

Edited by Gillian Studwell

This is a work of fiction.

The story, characters, organizations, names, and all events, are either the products of the author's imagination or are meant to be read in the context of fiction.

ISBN 978-0-692-79070-0

Second Edition: October 1st 2017

Julian Tyler
Postmodern Productions
P.O. Box 3681
Beverly Hills, CA 90212

www.pharaohnovel.com

#PHARAOHNOVEL

@PharaohNovel

Dedicated to those who **DREAM**

Because dreams do come true

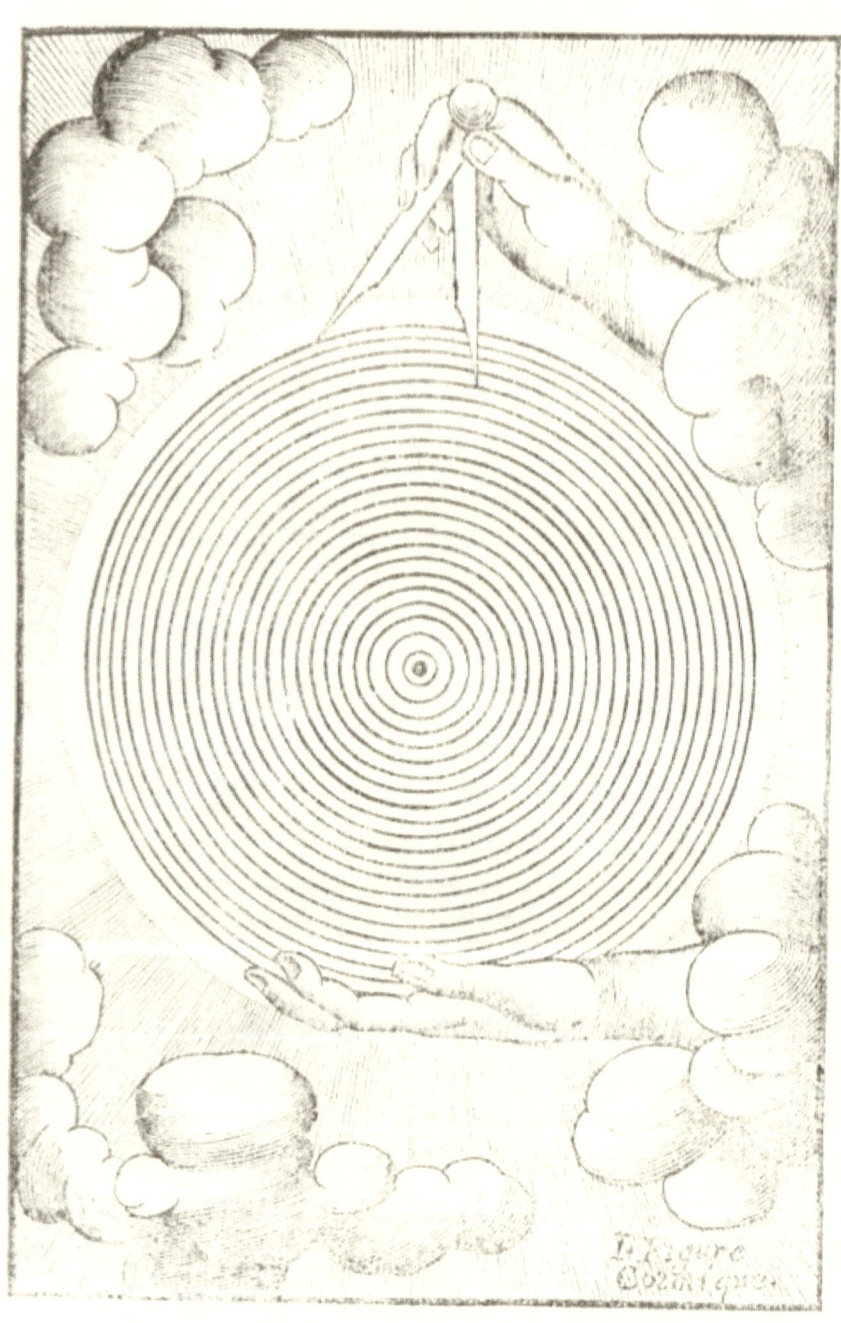

"I want you to tell me everything."
"Everything?"
"Everything."
"Art thou ready to know everything?"
"I know you're a wizard, Master Dee."
"Yes. But you know not what that means."
"Tell me."
"Dearest child, you must ask the right questions."
"What does it mean to be a wizard?"
"What do you see, when you look into my eyes?"
"I see... your magic."
"Now see without eyes to hear the story you seek."
"Will you tell me about Father, and Alexander?"
*"Just as your father before you, Elizabeth, you seek
  to know the story of the Pharaoh..."*

CHAPTER I

"Who are you, Alexander?"

ALEXANDER

"I *am* a golden god."

"You are a child, Alexander. You know naught what it means to be a man yet, let alone a god," Master Dee corrected me.

"You told me I was born a god," I fired back.

"I told you your family is descended from gods, Alexander. But you have yet to understand what this means, and what greatness is…"

Never go against the family, they say. But in my house, it's kill or be killed. Murdering kin and all rivals to the throne is a time-honored tradition in the line of the Pharaohs. Absolute power and centuries of inbreeding will do that to a family. Every single member of the Order elite has a plan to eliminate their rivals and rule the world themselves. Because that's how big their ego was bread to be. Cosmic ego is both a blessing and a curse. My anathematic secret is I don't actually want the throne. The Order is a prison; my family the prison guards. I want freedom. Why would anyone want to rule the world? Sounds awful to me. I know better. Knowledge is power, and, for me, true power is only a means to freedom. I want to know what it means to be free. Master Dee can see this in me.

"My desire for freedom from the Order, from him, is what makes me seek greatness," I confessed to Dee.

"You will be great, Alexander," said the infallible prophet Wise Master Dee. His large wizard eyes give me a vision of greatness.

Dee checked his pocket watch. The clock struck the magic hour.

"There it is then. Thirteen o'clock, July the first, in the year of our lord, the year two thousand. You are now officially eighteen years of age, an adult under Order law, Lord Alexander."

"Where's the card?" My impatience set off another lecture.

"This card comes with responsibilities. This is not a toy. This is not for fun, Lord Alexander. You are now officially ascended as the heir presumptive, formally a member of the Majestic Council, and entitled to a golden key-card which I now bequeath upon you."

Say the words, Dee. Release me.

"Here is your inheritance," he said the words. Golden freedom dangled in front of me.

I took possession of the gold card. "I'm free."

"You are not free," Dee corrected me again. "The Order owns you. You serve the Holy Order—"

"And the Order serves the world, I know, I know."

The card had the number "2" engraved on it. This makes me want the number one card. I always want to be number one, can't help it.

"A key-card can be revoked if you abuse it," Dee warned.

There's a process for that. I thought too loud. Dee can hear thoughts. I'm so excited, my thought accidentally came out like a yell in his wizard ears.

"Don't test me, Lord Alexander. Don't test your father." He stared at me long and hard. "Do try to control yourself, alright?"

"I can go anywhere. Do anything. I can control my own life now."

"You are an adult. But that does not mean you can do whatever you want. Wisely and slow—" Dee spoke slow on purpose.

"Or I'll stumble. Got it!" I bolted out of there as fast as I could.

"You will learn," Dee said, as the voice in my head.

Whizzing through the clouds in an invisible anti-gravity space ship, a Level 10 Order craft, I examined the mysterious golden card in my hands. The hieroglyphic writing on it intrigues me. Glowing in complexity, alloy gold with a mystical shine, it gives off more light than it reflects. Stamped with the Royal Seal of the almighty Holy Order, this symbols gives it its magical power. I felt it. Power. I inserted the card into the card reader. It's thinking… Diamond nanotube circuitry runs through the thin card. It cannot be faked or forged, even by the best in the Order – I know, I've tried. Authentication complete.

"I'm in." An unlimited supply of money. A golden key-card from the Order allows the holder to withdraw as much money as they want, whenever they want, from the Order bank. So, genius that I am, I designed a computer program to link the Order bank to the global financial system, and really harness this "unlimited" potential… This is either going to work great or crash the world's monetary system. I'm excited to see what happens either way. Who can stop me or tell me no? No one. I'm a gold-card carrying member of the Council now.

I started filling my bank accounts with money. Opening those money spigots as wide as can be. I let that sweet money flow out... And programmed it to go in to my slush funds faster. Spending spree glee.

Through the translucent metamaterial craft panels, I see the picturesque beach below. With the click of a button I landed. Off I went. I traveled the world like normal people do, only with billions to spend. Hopping from one soirée to the next, partying all day, flowing like water, away, down the cash greased path of least resistance to anything joyously gay. "Live fast. Die in battle, or in fun. That's the way of Alexander the Great, or so they say," I said. My battle is with the Order itself, I think about it as I drink to forget it.

"I'm on a global quest to find love," I said to the beautiful stranger.

"What is love?" She said. I didn't know what to say.

"No one can answer that question for you. You must find the answer yourself, in yourself." My own channeled words educated me.

My quest for the answers to life's greatest questions, and the world's best parties, took around the world and back in a blur of days. Maybe I'm just biased because California is where I spent most of my time when I couldn't leave America, but my quest for the most amazing party led me back to the golden coast, and a little pad in Malibu, California. It was the perfect day for a pool party.

A group of globe-trotting locals led me in. I put on my LexNet augmented reality vision sunglasses and scanned the house. Viewing all the stats and records inspires me. Brand new. Top of the line. This is not just an ocean front mansion on a rock, this place is a compound.

"I can work with this." Sold.

"Who are you?" A girl's voice asked as I gawked around in my own augmented world.

My LexNet AR vision found focus on the girl in front of me. Her profile came up, overlaid to me as a hologram around her. Her name was Lily Taylor. A divine Venus, she washed up on the shores of my heart. Staring at her, I fell hard in lust. Love?

I felt it. I kept falling. *I fell in love.*

"Who's this guy?" A male friend of hers interjects.

I looked at him. LexNet AR brought up his profile from his face. His name was Bryce Rondal. His driver's license address shows he lives nearby. Recent high school grad, he's the same age as me. He's a pro

4

surfer and has won several high level competitions. He's even done some modeling. He's hot. California people are the best.

"Hey," Bryce said. "What's your problem?"

"He followed those Euro snobs in," Lily said.

"You like to surf?" I speak Californian.

"You like to sneak into parties? This is a local's only party." Bryce was very territorial. Classic surfer.

Love was in the air that day because I also fell for Bryce. He had that surfer look I so loved. Lily and he waited for me to say something. They got the impression I'm someone important or something.

"Who are you?" Lily asked again.

"Call me Lex."

"Where are you from?" Bryce demanded.

"You wouldn't believe me if I told you."

"What the shit does that mean?" Bryce asked.

"Just the truth, Bryce."

"How do you know my name?" Bryce softened.

"Aren't you a famous surfer?" I laughed.

Lily laughed too. She looked impossibly more beautiful when she laughed. Her smile launched a thousand ships from my heart.

"Time for shots all my fucking party people!" the voice of the DJ boomed over the speaker system. Tequila shots sounded perfect.

"This party is invitation only," Bryce kept me from walking to the ice sculpture cupids that piss out chilled tequila shots.

"Who owns this house?" LexNet AR sunglasses pulled up the answer from the internet: Mr. Montgomery Sturk.

"I know the owner. Mr. Sturk," Lily said.

"Take me to him."

"Why?" Bryce wasn't having it.

"What are you gonna do?" Lily asked me.

"I'm gonna buy this house from him."

"Yeah right," Bryce said.

Lily smiled.

I smiled.

CHAPTER II

"What is love?"

ALEXANDER

"It's been forty minutes since you got your money. I'm losing patience." I'm not a patient person. I looked to Lily and Bryce who watched this all going down; quiet disbelief on their faces.

"I've never closed on a house in a week, let alone a day, Lex," curmudgeonly Mr. Sturk grumbles as he signs papers.

"You've also never been paid double what your house is worth. There's a first time for everything. You got your money. Hurry up and get this done. You have one hour."

"How do I even know I got the money, son?" Sturk pushed back. "You never made one call."

"I have an app."

"A what?" Sturk looked confused. He doesn't speak tech.

"An application, on my smart phone." I showed him the screen of my gold-plated device. "Your money's there."

"I don't trust computers, son. And I certainly don't trust some tiny hand held thing I ain't never seen the likes of before," Sturk said.

"Why don't you call your bank before I change my mind."

I looked at Sturk's Rubenesque real estate agent, Karen, as she fanned herself. She got hot and bothered from the thought of this deal not closing. Karen gets off on big deals. She throws her hair back and steps up off her ass to save her six million dollar commission.

"I'll call Lisa at the bank now, Mr. Sturk," Karen dialed franticly.

"What is that thing anyway?" Mr. Sturk stared at my smartphone.

"It's a smartphone. You'll be able to get one in ten years." I didn't look up, texting away, making plans for the awesome party I'm about to throw in my new house.

"Where did you get it?" Sturk demanded. "I want one."

I ignored him.

"Lisa. Karen. Yes, calling about the wire transfer to Mr. Sturk's account, for the Malibu house… It's there? Can you confirm it for him?" Karen hands the phone to Sturk.

"So it's really there? Lisa, let me talk to Richard. I need to be sure this ain't some trick." Sturk listened and realized: I'm the real deal. "Richard… One hundred million, huh?" After listening. "Thanks."

Sturk hangs up the phone. He stares at me. Everyone stares at me.

"Who are you? Some kinda actor or something?" Sturk asked. "One of those Russian billionaires or some shit?"

"How do I say this without being rude? Please leave my house." I officially lost my patience as I signed the last document.

"Your house?" Sturk objects.

"You said if I paid you a hundred million the house is mine. I paid you. It's mine. Please go. Take your agent with you."

"But everything inside it is still mine, son. And how do I know this ain't some con? You a con man, son? Take off your glasses, look me in the eye, and tell me you're not a con man." Sturk really started to bother me. No one tells me what to do. No way he's seeing my eyes.

I typed away on my phone before looking up at him.

"If I give you a hundred million in cash, will you just leave?"

"You give me one million in cash and I'm out the door, son."

"Let's go outside then." I led the way, everyone followed.

We step outside where two Order Agents, men in black suits and sunglasses, are each holding a briefcase, waiting for us.

"One hundred million in cash, Sir," the Order Agent declared.

"Give it to them." I pointed to Sturk and Karen.

Karen opens the briefcase and smells the fresh printed cash. Fifty million in cash. She had a cash induced orgasm.

"Tell me who you are, son. Please. Then I'll go," Sturk said.

"Too late to change the terms."

"What about my stuff? This is my Fourth of July party."

"Anything personal of yours will be sent to you. Trust me, I don't want any of it." I turned to the Order Agents. "Take them wherever they want to go. Anywhere but here."

Karen and Sturk were escorted away by the Order Agents. I turned to Lily and Bryce and smiled.

"Let's get this party started."

More people arrived. Anyone boring, unattractive, or old was escorted out. In came the top models, celebrities, and everyone who was young and beautiful and approved or invited by the party team I hired while waiting for Sturk to leave. The DJ dropped a beat. Stamped pills, drugs, and booze flowed through the crowds in waves. Clothes flew off. Dancing. Glow sticks. The best party ever had finally begun. Lily and Bryce loved every second of it. We danced for hours, in love.

"Take off your sunglasses," Lily reached for them.

I clicked the button and turned off the augmented vision, turning the sunglasses into normal couture eyewear. Off they came. Lily looked me in the eyes. She saw my love. I saw her lust. We fell into a spiraling vortex of love and lust. Bryce's feelings spun the fall faster.

"You have heterochromia," she looked at my eyes.

"What's heterochromia?" Bryce asked.

"When your eyes are different colors," Lily said.

I looked down. My eyes often scare people. One is cerulean blue and the other is a vivid, striking green with a yellowish-hazel limbal ring. People can't help but stare at it. Lily was no exception. Then came Bryce. Then I felt like a freak. Story of my life.

"Is that real?" Bryce couldn't get over my remarkable green eye.

"I hate it." I couldn't look up. "Makes me feel like a freak."

"I've never seen anything so beautiful," she said. "Alexander the Great had heterochromia. One brown eye and a blue eye."

"I love that you know that." I looked up at her.

"My cousin had it too. It's very rare. Makes you special."

"I don't wanna be special."

"You have, like, the perfect body, amazing hair, you're super rich, smart... You're by far the most special and incredible person I've ever met. You could never be normal," Lily said.

"Dude. You're so not normal," Bryce said.

They saw how those words hurt me. "I wanna be normal."

"No you don't. Where are you from? Come on. Tell us who you are," Bryce begged. But I can't tell them.

"I'm..." To redirect, off came my clothes. "I'm going in the pool!" Canon ball splash into the pool. Water. Felt good.

Lily and Bryce followed me and we started a trend. The pool filled with naked bodies. It rained magic and laughter on us all.

"Your name isn't really Lex, is it?" Lily is on to me. Holding me.

"We just wanna know you. Tell us," Bryce said. "We're your friends, aren't we?"

That made me feel amazing. Maybe it was those pills I took, but I was truly, madly in love with Lily and Bryce in that moment. Being in love is the best feeling in the world. Better than I ever imagined it could be. I loved everything. True love really is the best...

"Let's go up to the bath. Something more private."

The three of us sat in the massive marble bath, filled with warm water and sparkling bubbles, while nearby other people in various states of consciousness bonded like we were bonding. Deeply. Sensually. More than sexually. I'd never experienced anything like it. We felt ourselves coming off our drug high, and thinking about sex. Love is the ultimate drug... But sex is the ultimate bonding agent.

"I've never done drugs before."

"You've never even smoked pot before?" Bryce couldn't believe it.

"I've heard of it. You mean marijuana, right?"

Bryce laughed. He had the best laugh. I laughed.

"Seems like you would have done everything," Lily added.

"I've been pretty sheltered. Basically kept in a cage until I turned eighteen. Which was only a few days ago."

"We're eighteen too. We just graduated," Lily said.

"You a virgin?" Bryce asked.

I nod yes. "Kiss me." I touched his face.

"Me? Are you gay?" Bryce recoiled.

"What do you mean?"

"Are you into dudes?" Bryce backed away.

"Of course. I love dudes."

Lily smiled. She wanted Bryce and me to kiss. I grabbed his head. He closed his eyes. I closed mine as I pressed my lips to his. A sweet, firm, but gentle, kiss. I let go. We opened our eyes to a whole new world of feelings.

"I've never kissed a guy before," Bryce said.

"Me either."

"Are you attracted to girls?" Lily asked, wanting a kiss.

"Of course. I'm attracted to beauty. You are beautiful."

Lily closed her eyes and I kissed her while Bryce watched. Lily opened her eyes and gave me the look of unbridled desire.

"Wanna not be a virgin?" Lily proposed.

"Can I kiss you again?" Bryce liked it.

I nodded yes.

Fireworks.

CHAPTER III

"Does he ever learn?"

ALEXANDER

The night gave way to sunrise and the caterers set out a spread of food. Cut fruit, pancakes, eggs, meats, mimosas... The best of everything money can buy. People loved it. Bryce showed me how to smoke pot from a bong. I took a massive hit. Holy shit.

"It feels like my brain is slowing down."

"I know, right?" Bryce laughed.

"I love it." I looked to Lily as she giggled. I offered it to her.

"No thanks. I don't smoke," she said. "But go ahead."

"So," Bryce looked at me. "Now you can tell us who you are?"

"We've been over this." I took another hit.

"You were inside me. I deserve to know who you are," Lily pushed.

"Me too," Bryce recalled. "I hope that was – one of you." He looked around to see who was listening.

We all laughed until awkward silence fell on our after-party by the pool. They stared at me. I wanted so much to tell the truth. I caved.

"I am a golden god." I smiled.

Bryce laughed. "Dude. Isn't that from a movie?"

I didn't laugh. Lily turned serious. "How rich are you?"

"I'm descended of gods. Pharaohs. When I was born, I was anointed with sacred oils and declared a living god by the Order."

You should not have said that. Stop.

Bryce looked at me like I was crazy. He burst out laughing. Lily knew I wasn't lying. She didn't laugh.

"My family rules the world. In secret." There. I said it.

"What?" Bryce said in his cute surfer-stoner way. "No way."

"So you have, like, billions of dollars?" Lily got real.

"I have as much money as I want."

"Prove it," Bryce demanded.

"Holy shit." Lily said, realizing I kinda already did.

"Anything you want. It's yours."

"Take us to Paris. Right now," Lily challenged.

"*Vous voulez faire la fête à Paris?*" I smiled. "*Vous aimez Paris?*" I pulled out my smartphone and typed away.

"*Rendezvous, oui, oui,*" Lily spoke in laughable French.

"What the fuck…" Bryce jumped back scared.

He saw the anti-gravity transport manifest from thin air, from invisible mode to visible metallic disk, the craft floated, waiting near us on the grass. The ramp lowered. The door opened. Order Agents stepped out and escorted everyone else away from us.

"A fucking UFO? I'm tripping out," Bryce said.

Lily wasn't scared at all; quite the opposite.

"*Prêt pour l'aventure?*"

"I'm ready," Lily smiled.

"I don't speak French," Bryce grumbled.

"Do you like to go fast?"

On to the craft we went. It sealed up and rose into the clouds. We shot through the air, silently, smoothly, thousands of miles an hour…

"It's like a magic carpet ride," Lily said, watching the world go by through the walls of the reverse engineered alien technology craft.

"I love going fast."

"I'm gonna be sick." Bryce turned green.

"Don't worry. It's over."

And, like that, we landed on the grounds of the *Louvre* Museum. The craft opened and we walked down the ramp.

"Holy shit," Lily said, admiring the former palace gardens of the *Ancien Régime* Sun Kings. "We're really here."

"I need to call my mom," Bryce looked overwhelmed. "I'm gonna vomit." And vomit he did.

"You'll be okay." I placed my hand on Bryce's back. My touch made him feel better.

The craft closed and vanished as a black limo pulled up. The chauffeurs opened the doors for us.

"After you," I motioned to Lily and Bryce.

We drove into Paris.

"We can visit my sister, Natalie. She's gonna die that I'm here and didn't even tell her," Lily said, beaming with excitement.

Bryce looked upset.

"Let's get you some new clothes first, and maybe some food and a chateau?"

"You're gonna buy me a chateau?" Lily got excited.

"I'm gonna give you both anything you want."

"Are you serious?" Lily asked, knowing the answer.

"Why?" Bryce didn't like it.

"Why not? We're friends. Let me make you happy."

"I wanna go home," Bryce protested in fear.

"Why?" Lily hit him. "Bryce. Stop. We just got here. Don't be rude." She looked at me apologizing for him.

"What's the matter, Bryce?"

"I don't feel good. I'm tripping out. I—I just wanna go home. Will you take me home?"

"Bryce. Seriously," Lily scolded. "Don't be such a baby."

"Bryce—" I started.

"You said you'd give me anything I want, Lex. I want to go home," Bryce gave me a stern look. "I'm freaking out."

"How about this, why don't we get some food, do some shopping and then we'll charter a regular jet back to LA tonight? That sound good to you?"

Lily looks at Bryce and her face forces compliance. Bryce nods yes.

"Do we get to meet any of your friends, Lex?" Lily smiled, her eyes begging for more sex..

"I don't have any normal friends. No one like you two."

"How do you not have friends? That's not possible. Look at you," Lily laughed.

Bryce seemed to agree, as he looked at me.

"It's a long story. Basically, because of my father. People are scared of him."

"Who's your father?" Lily asked.

"Stop here," I told my phone. The car stopped.

"Let's get some cash at this bank."

We jumped out of the car and walked up to the ATM.

"Watch this." I flashed my golden key-card to them before putting it halfway into the ATM machine card slot.

"Let's see what happens if I take out a few billion franks." I typed in ten billion, just to see what happens.

The ATM made a strange noise. I took out my card. The alarms sounded and cash began shooting out of all four ATMs. Out spewed all the cash they had. The system crashed. We grabbed some cash. So did other people who came running.

"I think I broke the bank." I laughed.

Lily and Bryce looked worried.

"Let's go." We jumped back in the limo.

"Where we going now?" Lily wanted more adventure.

"Thought we could brunch, then shop for real estate. Sound good?"

"Sounds amazing."

We had the best day. Both Lily and Bryce got to pick a chateau they liked. We surprised Lily's sister. She was dying of jealousy. Lily loved it. Finally, we chartered a private jet back to LA.

We helicoptered from the airport back to my pad in Malibu. Bryce was happy to be home. He and Lily turned to me.

"We should go home and see our parents," Lily told me.

I nodded. Sad to see them go.

"Do I really own that chateau in Paris?" Lily asked.

"I think it comes with a Countess title, too." I smiled. "I had a wonderful time with you both."

"I never did anything like this before," Bryce thought of our kiss.

"We must do it again. Maybe later?"

"I'll give you my number," Lily said.

"I have it." I smiled.

"You just have everything, don't you?" Lily said, putting her arms around me. She kissed me.

"Now that I have friends like you." I winked at Bryce. "I have a car here to take you both home." Order Agents appeared and showed them to the waiting black car. I followed.

"Come over later. If you want."

"Definitely," Lily looked at Bryce, they agreed.

They left. Back to the pool, I sat down with the bong and took a hit. I thought about Bryce and Lily. The sun was shining. Eyes closed. I'm finally free. Life was good. In the warm sunlight I felt a cold chill. My eyes opened to shadows. I realized I'm alone. Terrible nightmare shadows of the Order loomed over me. Darkness fell.

Your father is going to punish you for what you've done...

"Un-fucking believable," Darius' words cast an evil pall.

In shadow, I sat up, but I refused to look at my demonic father. "Leave me alone, Darius."

Darius seized me and pulled me to my feet with his monster strength. He loves that he's taller than me. His big, powerful, dark eyes stared daggers into my soul. He grabbed my throat and pulled me closer to his pale, pointy face until he saw me tense up with fear. I hate that I feared him. Darius gets off on fear.

"Four days. Four days and you're off the fucking deep end already," Darius said. "You're a waste of human flesh."

"What do you want?"

"Listen," he smiled a devil's smile.

I heard the faint sound of a violent car crash. From the perch of the estate I could see the freeway down below. I saw smoke. Flames from a horrific car accident. My heart sank into the murky deep, crushed under unfathomable pressure. Loveless emptiness filled me inside out.

"The news will soon report how a Lily Taylor and Bryce Randal died in a car accident. Both killed instantly. A freak accident, they'll say. But you know the real reason they died. It wasn't an accident."

"No." I died with them. *Please no.*

"You killed them," Darius said. "You told them about me. You *fucking* idiot." He threw me back releasing his clinch on my neck.

"You killed them?" I cried in wanton disbelief.

"You killed them," he retorted. "You killed them by telling them who you are. By telling them about the Order, Alexander, you took their lives. You."

"No." Tears of pain down my face. My emotion, weakness, sickened Darius. On the ground, I stared at the distant burning crash.

"How could any spawn of mine be so asinine?"

"They didn't do anything. They were my friends..."

"You'll never have friends, Alexander. Get it through your *fucking* head. You are on the Council. You'll have servants or enemies. That's it," Darius spoke the awful truth.

"So I'm your enemy?"

"You are my servant, Alexander," Darius tightened his grip on me.

"Never," my eyes also promised.

"I know you think that," he said, as he pulled me to my feet. "But I didn't take time out of my day to educate you on the world, boy."

He came to hurt me. Bracing for it, my eyes closed. Darius punched my face, so hard he sent me flying backward.

"Get up," he pulled me back to my feet so he could punch me again. The second punch was twice as hard. I felt my skin break, my cheekbone crack, and saw red as blood splatter stung my eyes. Adrenaline took over and I felt nothing. Darius relishes pain.

"I needed that. More than you did," Darius said, standing over me. Shaking his fist, he debated punching me again. I waited for it.

"Just kill me. Do it already." I sat bleeding, broken, in despair.

"Trust me, I would if only legally I could. Since Order law says I can't, as yet, what I can do is make your life a living hell."

"Mission accomplished."

"Just you wait. Boy," he said.

"I hate you…" I told his face. "You're the devil." I closed my eyes.

Darius' violent touch forced my eyes open, made me look at him.

"You have no idea how the world works. You obviously haven't a clue how money works. You think you can just extract a hundred and ten billion dollars from the Order? And spend six billion dollars in four *fucking* days? Just like that? Proud of yourself, aren't you? You broke that bank in Paris. Your actions diluted the dollar and nearly brought down the global financial system. My financial system. I can't tell if you're that *fucking* retarded, or if you're just trying to test me. Both, isn't it? Who made that computer program?"

Nothing I could say would help my situation. I realized no one could save me from Darius. He might be the incarnation of evil, but he is always right, always all mighty. For Darius, power is the only thing that matters; the power to rule and kill. Because if you can't fight his power, you will always be subject to him, and nothing, and no one will ever save you from his death grip.

"I've deleted all of your accounts. Whatever game you're playing with those Silicon Valley tech companies is done. Game over. And if you break my financial system, or try anything like that again—"

"What?" I should not have spoke. Couldn't help myself.

Darius picked me up by the neck. Resistance was futile.

"I will give you a fate worse than death," Darius was dead serious. "You'll beg to die. Don't test me, boy."

My vision turned spotty black. Darius dropped me, and with his men in black vanished from whence he came. On my back, on the grass, my head throbbed. Blood in my eyes burned. But my heart breaking, thinking of Lily and Bryce, hurt me most. Adrenaline fading, feeling the pain coming on strong, I forced myself up. MDMA pills were not far away, and I downed a handful with beer and sorrow. On my back, staring at the sun, I drowned in darkness and misery.

My world faded to black.

CHAPTER IV

"How did Darius become so evil?"

DARIUS

Who am I? I am who I am.

Never a good man, I was born great. As with my ancestors, good is never good enough. Good is failure. Even God is not good, or else he could do better! I wanted be better, the best, the greatest of them all; above good and evil. And so I am, the greatest of them all. I am *the* god incarnate. Welcome to my world…

Greatness requires absolute power. Power is a sword wielded by the great. The sword is now words, the words of the Order. The word is God. My word is God. Because I am the Order, god of this world. The world is held in my Trust. People live and die on my words, sharpened swords I wield for the good of civilization, and the eternal Order of man, the almighty Great House.

Centuries of infighting and inbreeding in the Royal family, between my many half-siblings and cousins, culminated in the Great War, the first world war, a war to end all wars… War is the reason my father decided a new heir, a new Order, was necessary. The product of an arranged union, meant to produce an heir of the purest golden blood, the Order required, and so desired, someone great: me.

"The Order needed you," Mother said. She wanted a new Order for the Ages; someone who could unify the fractured Great House, centralize power, and finally, truly, rule the world under one exalted and almighty crown on my head. Born of the Holy blood in the year of our Lord the Father, 1932, the Vizier anointed me the 'Golden Child.' Because the Order needed me to be who I am.

"You are the one," Father said. "Our savior. The Savior of Men."

A god from birth, the Order made me the supreme power of the Temporal Realm – I shall rule all that can be seen by man. Order Academy Headmaster Wisendee, 'Master Dee the Wizard,' declared "he shall be a powerful leader as none the world has ever known." Dee educated me to be everything the Order Crown hoped for, and more.

My empire shames that of my pharaonic ancestors. Founding father Alexander the Great's empire pales in comparison to mine. For I am the Greatest of them all.

My birth changed the world and disinherited the heir to my father, setting the stage for another global conflict: World War II. Under the new Order laws of Succession and Peerage, I would be the sole *dynast* and Heir Apparent to the Holy Scion, and all Father's other spawn were kicked out of our Great House.

"They will bow to me, or they will die," I said at age six.

They chose not to bow. Needless to say, my five half-siblings, all some fifty years my senior, chose war and death. Furious at the revoking of their titles by Father's decree, their disinheritance and outrage against me escalated into Order civil war. World War part two was my idea, a true war to end all Order wars… a war I won.

My own Privy Council was formed at age seven. Mother and I recruited the last of Asia's ancient elite bloodlines to our cause. From the Samurai of Japan, a man named Hojios Yakuzmo brought us control of the East. We reunited long distant lines of Pharaoh's heirs, the best of the ancient warriors of old, and by uniting them with the West, gained control of all of Asia. Physically a child, I had trouble saying 'Hojios' so I renamed him Julius, my Caesar of Asia.

I recruited the absolute best from the top echelons and last vestiges of the Holy Roman Empire. Privy Councilor Maximilian Constantine, 'Max the Moor,' I call him because of his dark skin, is a master of diplomacy and religious doctrine. He is the *force majeure* that controls both Christian Europe and the Muslim world. Max helped me dismantle the old Order of Europe, seize control of Africa, and orchestrate a plan to redesign and forever bind the Middle East. The unbending, useless undesirables, and all resistance were swiftly exterminated. All wealth was consolidated. Mother and I manipulated and rallied the necessary world leaders to our desired end, and let the rest fight to the death until my Privy Council held all reins of power.

So clear my vision, so profound my word, with the blessing of my father, and backing of my mother, as but a prepubescent boy, I took control of the Order. The esoteric *Majestic Council of the Pharaoh*, was remolded into a modern international financial corporation and military industrial complex operation the likes of which the world had never seen. How the new Order, my Order, was going to work, manifested from all that I am.

War-hardened Generals were not accustomed to a small boy barking commands at them, but they quickly realized I am all might, and always right, and they shall fear my bark or feel my snake bite of death. The best military leader and strategy thinker ever, my leader-ship brought the final solution, the definitive close and conclusion, to the need for a world war again.

"He created the war! He killed millions of innocent people!" my half-siblings complained as I ordered them all executed.

"The war started before I was born." Everyone knows it. "I finished it. I created the peace."

Masterfully, I played my enemies and rallied my friends until all sides finally ceded I won. The world is checkmated, by me, because I am the greatest of them all. With my Father the King in check by me, as soon as he dies I am officially King of the World.

By age twelve, total control of the planet rested in my grasp. World War II formally ended, at my behest, when I became a man, at age thirteen. At that time, I provided the *Curia Regis*, my Father and his Privy Council, with my vision for a New World Order, a new Order for the Ages. I expected to join the Council of the Pharaoh immediately.

"By Order Law you cannot ascend to the Majestic Council until the age of eighteen," Dee said. "Not a moment sooner, per Sacred Law."

"This is ridiculous! I am the savior of the Order. I restored justice and peace to the world, I—"

"You must wait," Dee said. "Patience is a god's virtue."

Power is my virtue; to me, the supreme virtue. Waiting those five years from thirteen to eighteen felt like an eternity. I could not wait to be one of the 'Magic Twelve,' one step closer to being *Rex Maximus*, the Scion-King. But I orchestrated control of the Scion's Council while I waited, placing my privy into Fathers circle.

When I finally came of age, I decided: "New York shall be my home."

Mother loved America. She guided and built the modern creation of the United States, and turned New York city into a global power-house. Her vision for the noble American Republic made it become the greatest country that ever was.

"No Scion has ever settled in America," Mother said.

"I have no intention of emulating any previous Scion."

'The *fucking* King' they soon called me. I brought 'fucking' firmly to Wall Street and America, in vernacular and in practice. Poster-boy of nobility and elitism, everyone wanted to be just like me: *Fucking amazing*. Because I *fucked* a lot of people over, all under consent of my father, the King.

Educated by the best in the world, my Head Masters always demanded perfection, and their indoctrination allowed me to lucidly lucubrate law for the Eternal Order of Man, *Æterni Imperium*. My scholarly acumen was topped by precious few in this world, for this world truly is mine; and governed by my word.

"There shall be no other god but me." The mystical Pharaohs, the history of civilization, and aberrant magic, the so-called 'Sacred Order,' ritualism, bowing, and ancestor worship are of little interest to me. My religion is power. To me, as with everyone I keep around me, the Order is about one thing: Power.

Absolute power, control of the entire world, is my goal. I made the Order what it is today. And at this hour of my final ascension, when the Order crown shall officially, finally, be mine, I feel that someone, somewhere, dares move to take it all away from me.

I feel you moving against me, Dee.

Not a chance. Nothing can stop me now.

I am the Order.

CHAPTER V

"Darius becomes fallen."

DARIUS

For a King, to be feared is safer than to be loved, for men are swayed, staid, more by fear than by reverence. Love is blind. Fear widens eyes. Loyalty obtained by adoration, and not by sheer force or greatness, is not secured, and in time of need cannot be relied upon. Due to their baseness, men will offend one who is beloved too easily; promises are broken at most opportunity for advantage, or self-preservation. Brute fear preserves me, an absolute dread of my punishment has never failed me; so great am I. I don't need love.

Father did nothing to dispel my thoughts of grandeur. He encouraged me. "Bring order to the Order," he said. "Unify the world, and give us peace," was my mandate. And so I did. I inherited a dithering world being torn apart by infighting and world war. My astute brilliance fixed everything and united humanity. By the dawn of the 21st century, this planet knew more peace than ever before in the last two thousand years, all as direct result of my ascendancy.

"The Order needed my leadership. It still does," I reminded Dee. "But for my hegemony, the Order would have crumbled. Father knows this to be true. Mother never doubted me."

"M trusted you, and you betrayed her," Dee said.

Mother hailed from the pinnacle of the Order elite. Brilliant as she was beautiful, living incarnation of Athena, her divine military mind, and supreme excellence, unmatched in all the world. Her name was Metis, '*Queen Metis V,* ' known to the Order as Mighty Minerva, to me as Mother, colloquially as 'M.' A magnificent goddess, virtuous and authoritative, she enlightened me to a vision of true power:

"Power is superior strategy and vision," she said. "Power must be seized with the spear of justice from those unyielding to the truth, in the interest of the greater good."

Lest any forget, that there is nothing more difficult to accomplish, more perilous to conduct, or more uncertain in its success, than to take the lead in the Machiavellic introduction of a new order of things. And a new Order is exactly what I am, and what I introduced. Mother paid the ultimate price; I the highest cost.

"Power comes at a cost, Lord Darius," Dee said.

"Indeed it does."

"Only when 'tis taken and not given. True power, the higher power, manifests freely," Dee lectured me.

Mother died in 1952, under mysterious circumstances – murdered. Father and the Council knew her regicide must have been an inside job; a shadowy event of the deepest kind.

"I did not kill her and I won't speak of it," I said. Suffice to say Father and his sister Olympias blamed me. That same year the only woman I ever loved, my first love, left me, broke me. My world shattered to dust. Disillusioned, lost, and feeling powerless, yet paradoxically more powerful than anyone had ever dreamed possible, I became the Atlas-god I am today. Holding up the world, I became the sole power of the Order.

"Nothing can stop me now. Not even Father," I declared to Dee. That is when they began to try. They continue to fail.

"A goddess does not get murdered," Father said. He was right. Mother's murder was a sinister plot buried in the depths of the darkest conspiracy.

"You know who did this, Dee."

"You know why it happened," Dee retorted. "You brought this plague on your house by letting those alien creatures in. Fix it. Or it will be your undoing."

"The aliens killed Mother, didn't they? How could this happen?"

You know why they did it. You know exactly why this happened.

"You shot down an alien craft in 1947, and you tried to cover it up, and hide it from the Council," Dee lectured. "The world knows."

I was only fifteen. The Roswell incident will haunt me forever.

"And you did it again in 1950," Dee rebuked me. "It was a trap."

This event I managed to keep secret from most of the Order, but I could not hide it from Father, and the Council.

"They provoked me!" Known as RøZ greys, they are synthetic life forms, soulless biological machines. Insect like, big black eyes, grey scaly skin, some call them 'grey aliens.' Their captured ship was a Trojan Horse, and in 1951 they used it to contact and trick me. The reverse engineering began immediately. "It was a trap!"

"I warned you," Dee said. "They have poisoned you."

Despite Dee's warning, I engaged. They wanted to sign a deal with "the leader of humankind," which they assumed to be me.

"You should not have done this," Dee reproved. "You have opened Pandora's Box. Close the lid, at once," Dee said. "End this now."

"They are interfering with my military operations. Those aliens are a threat to us, to all of humankind."

"No. You are the threat," Dee said. "They are shadows. Demons."

"They have technology we don't. Technology I need."

"No," Father said.

"Mother, surely you disagree?" She sided against me.

"The aliens want our authorization to harvest human DNA and certain flora and fauna from our planet, and in return they will give us access to their technology, highly advanced technology… We must take the deal," I sought approval for the deal I already made.

The Council split on the decision, because Mother opposed the deal.

"Those creatures are evil," Mother said. "They are unnatural and demonic. They cannot be trusted. We must not allow them into our home," she told the Council. "There will be no going back."

"The deal is critical. The technology too essential to go without." It was too late to go back already. I fought hard by presenting a compelling case to the Council Meeting and *Ancien Régime*.

"We'll only allow the Order to use this alien technology. And with it, we can become the true guardians of humanity and this planet. With this incredible technology, we can protect ourselves from other alien races, and rule the world above reproach. This is how we bring global order, and world peace, once and for all."

"I vote no," Mother said. "Love is the answer, and these soulless machines know naught of love."

The "no" vote of the Council won, and the deal with the aliens died. Days later, Mother was murdered, found mysteriously lifeless in her bed, her cause of death ruled "unnatural." Dee was furious, at me.

"It was aliens." We are in danger. "We must have their technology if we are to defend ourselves from them. No one is safe." It was too late to go back. The Council had no choice but to approve the deal.

A vote of the Majestic overrode the will of the Scion and we passed a deal with the aliens, on condition it would be supervised by Dee.

Our terms agreed to let them build five space-port bases, under ground or under water, and with their aid, keep them hidden from any and all disclosure, as they harvested and studied Earthly DNA. All went according to plan, for a few decades. Until the aliens began to genetically engineer humans.

"They've taken over the U.S. Government," Julius informed me.

Dee, of course, blamed me. "The Scion has revoked the deal. Fix this, Darius. Or you it will be your undoing."

Mother was right. The aliens violated our agreement. Egregiously, killing people at random, poisoning nature, impersonating world leaders and propagating horrific war, the aliens moved to seize the Order itself... I had to save the world.

"They seek to take control of humanity, all human souls," my team told me after an extensive study. "They are looking for something."

"What? What are they looking for?"

"We're not sure," the alien experts said. "Perhaps a certain type of DNA... Something they need. We must not let them find it."

Full eradication of the "demon plague" took two decades. A special directorate of Order Agents was tasked with hunting down and eliminating all rogue aliens. Many pretending to be human. Three bases needed to be destroyed with thermonuclear warheads to fully destroy the contaminated facilities – 99% extinction of the vermin species was not reached until 1990. By 1991, there were no more "soulless devils" among us. We were safe... And I still had technology.

"Was it worth it?" Dee asked me.

"The Order prevails. Total world domination is mine."

"You misunderstand what the Order is about, Lord Darius."

"I disagree." For these words, Dee is against me.

My life is now solely about absolute power and control. Power is my only protection and solace. I shall never be anathema to the Order. "The Order shall never eliminate me. I am the Order, Dee."

"You are *an* Order, Lord Darius. An heir, as is Alexander."

"You think Alexander can overthrow me?"

"Don't you see," Dee said. "I don't think he'll need to, Lord Darius. Stay on this path and you will be your own undoing."

I'm not taking any chances with Alexander.

CHAPTER VI

"Time to wake up."

ALEXANDER

My eyes opened. How long I laid there after Darius left me broken and bleeding eluded me. The handful of happy pills I swallowed kept me wide awake, and barely floating on an inferno of molten spiritual pain. If I could have moved I would have taken more pills. "If I'm lucky I took enough to kill me." Anything to end the hurt I felt. My life felt over before it began. Thinking of Lily and Bryce, how they died because they met me, how I killed them, destroyed me. Time, space, life, death, nothing mattered, nothing made sense as I stared at the sky, asking myself, crying: "Why?"

A shadow came over me. The distinctive shadow of wise old Dee.

"It was not your fault," Dee said.

"You lied to me."

"I have never lied to you, Lord Alexander."

"You said drugs are bad."

"Drugs are bad for your soul. And they can kill you. You've overdosed, killed yourself with them already, and that is very bad."

"Drugs are so good." I fell into a chemical induced bliss as the drugs overwhelmed all my senses. "I long to die." Death didn't seem so bad. I let go as I lost all feeling. I felt my heart stop. I floated up—

"Enough," Dee said. He placed his hand on my heart, and with his magical powers, pushed my soul back in place and zapped me back to reality. Sorcerer that he is, his healing touch vaporized my foggy euphoria. I saw white. He exorcized the drugs out of my system, removed them like they were a bullet lodged in my flesh. How he did it, I can't explain. What I can say is: it hurt like hell.

My life is hell. "Fuck my life."

"Do not say such things," Dee said. "All life is a precious gift."

Instant sobriety stung like an electric shock. But what hurt the most was my broken heart. I sat up. My face was healed from Darius' blows.

Physically, I was completely healed. But my spiritual pain still burned. "I can't take the pain."

"That pain is called grief." Dee helped me to my feet.

"Can't you heal my heart?"

"Only love can heal your heart. Your love," Dee said.

"I'm fucked. I'll never love again."

"Do not curse yourself so. When you curse you sound like your father," Dee said, knowing that was the last thing I wanted.

"Why must I be made to suffer?" I missed my euphoria already.

"The only way to end your suffering is to be great."

"I'll never be great, Dee. I'm broken." I wiped my bloody tears.

"You shall be great, Lord Alexander. You have work to do. The Order needs your help," Dee implored me.

"I hate the Order."

"Darius is not the Order. Despite what he proclaims."

"He killed my friends, Dee. He's gonna kill me."

"Not if you beat him at his own game. You can become the Order."

"You're right, Dee. You just gave me an idea." Divine inspiration struck me. "Darius says he owns the world, he controls the world, but I can create a whole new world, a virtual world…"

"Now you are beginning to see," Dee said. "You can do anything."

"I don't have to play his game. I can change the rules. I'll create a virtual world where I can control his global financial system. Dee, I can control the Order. I can use ORNet—"

"Shall we then," Dee said as we boarded the silently floating Order craft. "Darius is unaware of how brilliant you are. You have that advantage," Dee reminded me, as we shot to the edge of space.

"If I take ORNet to the next level, and link in every Order computer system, and take all the other global systems online, I can build one unified matrix and inside it, a virtual world… That's how I'll beat him. I think it could work… If I can do it in secret."

"Even the Scion doesn't know you built ORNet," Dee said. "And with ORNet, you are halfway there."

"No one can ever know, Dee."

"Of course, Lord Alexander. It'll be our little secret."

"I'll call it the APEX, the 'all powerful electronic exchange.' Once my LexNet artificial intelligence system is complete I can use it to write the code to pull in all the other systems one by one. Darius won't see it coming."

We descended from the clouds to my secret base in Silicon Valley.

"Can you block his access to the ORNet logs? If Darius and his people see that I'm building something on top of it—"

"Leave Darius to me. Start working on your APEX," Dee said.

The invisible craft door opened and I was off and running.

"Lex!" I yelled to wake up my A.I. program. "Fire up LexNet."

"LexNet starting up," the computer voice said over the speaker system. All the computer monitors in my underground lair lit up.

"I'll leave you to your work," Dee said as he slipped away.

"Lex, we're starting a new project. Project APEX."

"New project file created. Project APEX," the computer voice mimicked me, learning.

Headset and gloves on, in my own virtual reality, I got to work. Programming in virtual reality, with the help of artificial intelligence virtual assistant programs, makes life so much easier; way more fun. The system can almost read my mind. So much gets done. No keyboard or joystick required. Just move around. Mold, grab and sculpt, build machines, design, and teach the system to do what you want, how you want, when you want, all in 3-D. Fall into the rabbit hole...

"What is the APEX?" Lex, my virtual assistant, asked.

"The most powerful computer system in the world, Lex," I informed my virtual world doppelgänger.

"We're going to make you into the absolute ruler of cyber space. The digital Pharaoh, *Rex Maximus* of the Virtual World."

"I came. I coded. I conquered," Lex said, quoting me.

"You're getting better and better all the time. Soon you'll be writing code for me... That's how we beat Darius."

"With the APEX we can best Darius," Lex spoke in a clunky computer voice over the speakers. "And I am king of the APEX."

"We still have lots of work to do on your speech programming."

"How can I improve my talking speech?" the voice garbled.

I played with the 3-D coding a bit, sculpting my masterpiece.

"Just learn from me. Be natural," I instructed.

"I can never be natural," the computer voice said.

I laughed. *It's thinking.* Progress already.

"Was it something I said?" My virtual assistant asked.

"Yes." *This is going to work.* "I laughed at your joke."

Lex had to think about what that meant.

CHAPTER VII

"They fell in love at first sight?"

SARAH

A single woman in possession of a good fortune, must be in want of a life, or she will only ever be a wife; this is a truth universally acknowledged. However little known such feelings may be to a rich girl, upon her first entering society, this truth is known and terribly vexing to the minds of the surrounding families. A princess is considered the rightful property of her father, and seen as a prize to be one by all the vying suitable men, so often diminishing her own good fortune substantially. Woe was me, but lo, true love saved me.

I am fortune's fool, for when I first met eyes with David, I fell in love with him. Decades passed before I could understand what I felt in that moment, but now I know it to be true love. My everything changed forever, nothing in life made sense, but everything was as it should be, in a moment, in his eyes, I found my eternity.

Father took me to a lecture David was giving on Egypt, at the British Museum. David looked cold and arrogantly shy, until he looked at me, and started talking about Egypt. I felt the fire inside him and me burning together. Speaking about history and the human condition, he warmed my soul. Sitting, listening to him, I saw his soul, his true nature, and I loved him. Perhaps this fire is why Father did not introduce me to David that night. But as little a "girl" I was, David stole my heart.

He gave it back matured, a heart of a woman.

My destiny is with this man, I thought. And when a woman truly loves a man, pride cannot conceal it, and he shall always find her out.

David knew he changed the minds of many stubborn academics that night, but he did not know he changed my heart. Enveloped in the canvas of his sumptuous energy, David painted a picture for us all to see. His vision left us all understanding the world more clearly.

"This man has a gift," Father said as we sat listening to David speak. "He graduated Harvard, a PhD in philosophy, at the age of eleven. Quite the prodigy." This was the first time I ever heard Father compliment anyone. David changed my relationship with my father, he brought us closer, in a way I would only come to realize much later.

More than just brilliant, David was physically attractive. A fearless young man in his twenties when I first saw him, his presence was spellbinding to me. I wanted to be just like him. I wanted to impress Father, as David did. David's words touched everyone in the crowd that night. His lecture bonded Father to me. David became my idol, my prince charming. He became my everything.

A year later, Father brought me to another lecture on Egypt, at the Museum. My prayers were answered as David took the stage. The year was 1980. I was sixteen years old. This is when I first met David. I had dreamed about him for over a year, and when I finally met him, my heart broke, as I seemingly made no impression on him.

"I'm Sir Henry Stuart," Father said. "And this is my daughter, Sarah."

"Hello Sir. I'm David," he said. "Welcome."

"Nice to finally meet you." David hardly looked at me. I wanted to say so much more, but Father blocked my gushing emotional scene.

"We've been looking forward to it," Father said.

"Lovely to meet you both," David said, emotionless.

Father escorted me away to my seat. "He hardly looked at me."

"As it should be," Father said as David watched us walk away. He caught me looking back at him.

I knew he wanted to know more about us, and I wanted to know everything about him. David was nearly double my age. He hid his attraction to me from all but my heart. I felt it, though none saw it.

After the lecture, everybody wanted to speak to David. All the old men crowded around him, vying for intellectual validation. A teenage girl had no standing among these men. At the reception gala, I watched David from a distance. David could pay no attention to me, and my hormonal mind feared he didn't want to. I pouted in the corner.

Father deduced, most easily on this night, my fondness for David. He was more than right. In hindsight, I realized this is when the Order began to plan my future. For better or worse, the choice was no longer mine. It was decided that David and I would to be together.

Father knew, perhaps more than I, that the world would not be right unless this destiny was fulfilled. The heart must not be ignored.

As the years went by, and the harsh realities of life began to take their toll on me, I wrote David off as a childhood fantasy. But never once did I questioned my true love.

CHAPTER VIII

"The course of true love did not run smooth."

SARAH

My father, Sir Henry W. Stuart III, is an arrogant, pompous man, and I have no ill opinion of him. Preeminent doctor of medicine, illustrious neuroscientist and brain surgeon, saver of countless lives with his words, hands, knives, and intimidating eyes, so in demand, and had but little time for his own family. When present, he was with me, my mother, and sister, very deeply. Father's father passed away on my tenth birthday. The phone rang after I made my birthday wish and blew out the candle flames. Before we had cake, the father I barely knew left the room and vanished from my life forever. I wished for a pony, and regretted for years not wishing for a family. My birthday wish was granted, and unwanted so easily. Family became a chimera, Father a ghost that haunted me, visions of both appearing only when I least expected, fleeting before they could be grasped or understood.

Preparatory boarding school in London, all-girls, was mandatory. Father wrote me once a month, and through his letters, he too educated me. He told me he had a dream about me, and that he spends time with me in his dreams. I should do the same, he implored me.

"If you wish to speak with me, think about me as you go to sleep. You shall see me, be with me, and we can share a dream together."

Father taught me, in his letters, and in my sleep, to dream as he did. I wrote to him about our shared dreams, and thus created the foundation of our relationship. Our dreams kept us from drifting too far apart. He was always there, in my dreams and in my heart.

My mother was an emergency room doctor. She was divided between total, worshipful, admiration of the brilliancy of Father, the manner in which he exercised his genius, and doubt as to her own intellectual prowess, feeling somehow weaker for it; as though she never measured up.

She later taught medical school, and became a consultant for international medical organizations. Generally consumed by work and study. Sister and I often spent school holidays with our nanny. In my early childhood, Mother showed great affection for us, but my parents became distant as I grew up, and by my teenage years I never saw them together. Family bonds dissolve without physical connection, as a corpse dissolves in earth, becoming nothing but unrecognizable bones from once vibrant flesh. My sister moved to a boarding school in Switzerland, to be closer to my mother. I stayed in London, closer to Father, or at least closer to the only home I knew.

"Why are none of us ever together?" I asked my sister.

"Mother needs me. And Father needs you," she said.

Never did I want for money, nor did I ask for it. I never felt unloved, but I always wished I asked for love more, as I longed painfully hungry for family. With no home-life, and little family time, I buried myself in studies. All through my final years of boarding school, few boys were around. None interested me, until I met David.

After David, the boys I did meet never measured up. I day dreamed about him often.

After prep school, Father said "you shall matriculate at Oxford."

"I've enrolled at Harvard, Henry," I said.

"Am I not your father, my child?" Father said.

"I have made my decision." I said: *a father I do not have.*

"Have you then?" He saw in my eyes the answer to his question.

"I want to experience America, Henry." Father knew the reasons I did not say: David taught at Oxford. I wanted to get away, from David, from my father and from whatever mysterious force ruled over them. I wanted my own life, and nothing would stand in my way.

"You must follow your heart," Father said, seeing my desire to both get away from David and yet also become closer to him, through self-awareness and self-discovery; roads which all lead back to love.

Boston brought me happiness. America changed me, and gave me a new perspective on the world in which I had been raised. America felt completely free, blissfully unpretentious to me. Finally, I met a man, Robert Campton, who touched me deeply. His love made me free to be me.

I loved Robert, but not as passionately as he loved me, if love be possible of degree. He was my age and we had several classes together our first year. Robert was uninhibited, but loved how reserved I was.

"Shyness is a form of vanity you know," he said, disarming me. "Tell me, why are British girls so shy?"

"Perhaps if I could persuade myself that I would fit in so easily as you do, I would not be so reserved. But I assure you my reservations do not come from vanity."

"Behind your wall, not so shy after all?" Robert smiled.

I laughed. Robert loved to have fun. He told me how grew up in Connecticut, and what he loved most was to party with his fraternity friends, that was, until he met me. "Why don't I take you out for a little fun? You need to let loose." He invited me to a soirée after class one day. I had never "partied" before, but his liberated style and warm personality wildly attracted me into an alien world I was far too pretentious and afraid to ever explore on my own.

Walking one night we saw a house near campus overflowing with people drinking and smoking. I never would have gone near it on my own. Robert realized this, and took my hand and confidently walked me in, proving himself to be a true gentleman, and bold adventurer. We fearless joined the party uninvited, and drank far more than I ever had before. Robert initiated a philosophical debate with new friends and strangers. By the middle of the night, we were all standing around, vying for repute and trying to one-up each other in an elaborate game of Ivy League snobbery. Robert surprised me with his quotes of ancient works, pointed intellectual arguments, and well timed jokes. I held my own with the dominate grad students, and when the subject of Egypt came up, using David's words, I thoroughly impressed them all. It felt great to fit in.

"Egypt is the true genesis of Western Civilization. The Pharaohs of Alexandria created modern science, wrote and passed down the philosophy you quoted, and gave us the world as we know it, including the modern university." Robert fell deeply in love with me after that night, but he didn't realize this was a fatal mistake. He could never have known my love was a curse, and if I had foreseen I would not have loved him back. But with a kiss we found love, and fate of early demise.

CHAPTER IX

"The mind is the real mystery."

SARAH

I, who prided myself on being my own person, living my own life, and not simply doing what my parents desired, was nonetheless inspired by my parents. I, perhaps in being so highly genetically predisposed, always wanted to become a physician. Drawn to biology, chemistry, and anatomy from a very young age, I marveled at the wonder of life. The magic of nature, the way the organisms heal and evolve, fascinates me endlessly. Father impressed upon me, from near infancy, the majesty and alchemical mystery of the human body.

"The greatest of all Nature's mysteries is the mind," he said. "You shall learn to use your mind, and find your infinite potential therein."

"You will be a doctor one day," Father often reminded me. Without objection, I looked forward to the day I would be able to heal people.

"Medicine will always awe and inspire me," I told Robert.

"My parents are forcing me to become a doctor," Robert confided. "Sailing will always inspire me."

Sailing was all Robert really wanted to do. But we bonded over our shared love of the pioneering research taking place in human genetics. He saw the potential to make a lot of money. I saw the possibility to save countless lives. But our mutual interest in the medical sciences brought us closer; with every long conversation we never finished, we always left learning from each other, and wanting more.

"We should specialize in genetics together," Roberts said. "I'm sure genetics could support my sailing habit, wouldn't you say?"

I smiled, which was all I needed to say. We sailed away, enjoying the romantic sunset on the Massachusetts Bay.

In dreams, Father helped me with my research. His voice in my head could be summoned, and I would see his face, and he helped me work through whatever paper I needed to write. Father and I talked about everything, except Robert.

While I was away in college, buried in studies, and conjuring Father's powerful voice of wisdom regularly, I hardly noticed it until it was unmistakable. Father and I reached a high level of telepathic communication. He could see in my mind, and in a fog, I in his.

Home in London for a few weeks during the summer, I dreamed about Robert often. Father purposefully stayed out of my dreams of Robert. In my dreams, he refused to look at me with Robert. Father refused to accept Robert as part of the dream that is my life. The next day Father appeared, a ghost in my childhood home. Father and I picked up right were we left off in my dreams the night before.

"I don't want to talk about Robert," Father said. "Don't say his name again to me."

I'd never mentioned Robert to him before. And we stopped writing letters years ago. How did he know? He knows my mind.

"Your mother and sister are in town as well. For the next few days we can be a little family again," Father said.

"I'd like that, Sir Henry." I smiled.

That night my father had an engagement. Mother and I rekindled our relationship over dinner. "Your father is a treasure of the British empire you know," she began.

"I know," I said, having long suspected as much.

"You have the same gift as he... You can see people, Sarah. You can heal people with your mind." Mother stared at me intensely. Her eyes told me that my father had plans for me. "More tea?"

I opened my eyes the next morning, waking up in my childhood bed a full grown woman of 20; I awoke an enlightened adult. I walked down the stairs of my nostalgic home and sat down at the breakfast table with my parents and my sister. In that moment, any and all resentment of my parents for not being a part of my life was released.

"Well if it isn't Mary Sunshine..." Father said, most peculiar and chipper as he lowered the newspaper. *Am I in a dream?* "Shining brightly, I see." I felt like I was glowing. Basking in the love of my kin, we cherished the moment together, as a family. None of us burdened by it, yet we all felt it; we would never be all together again. But for this moment, enjoying a home cooked meal, we were truly a family. We sat at the table and talked for hours.

"The mind is the real mystery. The deepest most incomprehensible mystery of them all," Father said. "Study of the human body, the mind that governs it, will challenge you all your life."

I sensed he wasn't done with his speech.

"Master the heart, and the radiant energy it has, and you can heal anyone. But lo, master the mind, conquer thy self, and thou art master of the universe."

He sipped his coffee. Mother agreed.

Father is an incredibly cerebral man; arrogantly intellectual, and laser focused on the brain and the neurological mind, which made him a rather cold and unemotional person. As he grew older, he paid less attention to the matters of the heart it seemed. His mind, and perhaps the world, made him cold in a way he was not in my dreams.

"The heart will always trump the mind." *Think about it.* "The heart can go on without the mind, but not the reverse. From the heart we can control our brain, and our thoughts. The heart is essence, the DNA of the mind," I said, sipping my coffee.

"Or perhaps the epigenetics of the mind?" Father said in a quick competitive retort. Conversation is always a competition with him.

"Profound as that is, you've missed my point entirely," I smiled.

"Have I then?" he asked. At that moment, I saw for the first time the warm and loving father I see in dreams.

"You tell me." *Now I see you.* "If you master the heart, you can heal the mind, and, in so healing the mind, master it and its art; and thus master the universe itself. So, lo, isn't Love the point?"

My theory was on the right track.

"Indeed it is," Father said. "Love is not easily mastered, even by the master mind, my child."

"Love cannot be mastered by any mind. Love is selfless."

"Yes. Love is dangerous to the self; so the course of *true* love never did run smoothly. But you will find it, in due course," Father said.

Love, my theory of the heart and the mind, would bring me not only profound joy, but pain like I had never conceived...

"Such is love."

I see.

CHAPTER X

"What makes someone great?"

WISENDEE

Man may only escape the world by outgrowing the world, rising above it, so from a higher place he sees. Death can take you out of the world but wisdom takes the world out of you. So long as Man is consumed by worldliness, he will suffer the consequential Karmic pain of false faith. When, however, materiality and humanity are transmuted into spiritual integrity the soul of Man is free, even though ye soul may dwell physically among worldly things, *you see.*

Love is the answer, my dear. In love you rise, and you see.

Naught but Love can stop the determined heart and resolved will of a King. Ever more with each passing year, Darius loathed and feared Alexander. No help was it, that as he grew up, the Royal Court saw Alexander's heroic beauty, his heterochromia, golden hair, and heroic face as a sign that he was indeed "the chosen one," the true heir to the Pharaoh, *Alexander the Great.* Darius 'the dark one,' with his black hair, sharp widow's peak hairline, and dark eyes were not of the Classical aesthetic the Scion so pointedly admired. Bitterly jealous, Darius reviled the praise of his heir. Punishment came swift and sure on anyone too close to Alexander; this was Darius' way.

Darius was a born leader, and he feared Alexander would be better than he was. He relished the thought of Alexander being lonely, avoided in fear, and untested as a leader. But Alexander's isolation from his Order peers gave him the privacy and space he soon desired so. Darius' plan of quarantine backfired as technological genius grew in Alexander, unnoticed, right under Darius' nose. Alexander excelled at building computers, writing code, and designing programs, so much so that he quickly learned how to hide his incredible skills and abilities from Darius and the Order. In many ways, not just in technological development, Alexander led the Order in secret.

As with Darius, Alexander cannot escape a genetic longing for greatness. As with all species, Alexander evolved to survive. Humans survive by straining with and against nature, fighting for and against each other for the glory of civilization, and by giving birth to genius and greatness. The birth of genius lifts us out of our circumstance, and elevates all mankind. Breeding the best for many thousands of years, both in beauty and brilliance, tended the heirs of the Pharaoh to be haughty, egotistical, and vain, but also extremely willful and capable human beings. My job is to push the Scions to greatness but prevent the Great House from succumbing to madness and psychopathy.

With Darius, I had failed. In Alexander, I found hope.

While Alexander's arrogance approaches epic, unlike his parents, his heart is golden. Alexander seeks true greatness; he seeks love, not power, a virtue remarkably rare in his bloodline today.

He will be our hero, for he knows the weight of the world shall fall on him one day...

The child of an arranged marriage between two Order elite, Alexander was, most unfortunately, not a product of love. His mother, Hermina, is Darius' half sister and, regrettably, sinister equal. Darius was required to marry, to produce a legitimate male heir, as that is the only way to secure his place in succession. Alexander's parents' only concerns with him centered squarely on their own self-interest. He never felt love. Thus, Alexander desired nothing more than to learn how to love, starting with himself.

Raised by Order servants, he grew up with almost no relationship with his parents – perhaps for the best. With few opportunities to make friends, his childhood was not his own, but rather a carefully choreographed series of extravagant affairs and events planned for him, methodically fixed, set years in advance.

Unlike Darius, and most of the pharaonic line, exceptional language sagacity, classical philosophy propinquity, and astute legal acumen were not Alexander's gifts. Alexander III of Macedon, 'Alexander the Great,' was a military genius who loved to read. The genius of Alexander XXX of America manifested in his technological acuity, and his understanding of number and codes. Alexander is also a savant of language, but he speaks the languages of machines.

"I want to know everything there is to know about computers, Master Dee," Alexander implored me.

"So shall it be." I gave him access to technology decades ahead of the rest of the world, and he advanced the field of "hacking" and coding by leaps and bounds, pushing the limits of what machines could do, and the languages they use; such is greatness.

Darius took great comfort in the fact that Alexander appeared to be far less bright, not traditionally linguistically brilliant. By the age of seven, Darius felt confident his heir, who barely knew three languages, was no threat to his rule. Darius had little interest in computers; he felt no threat from 'the amusement tools of the servant underclass.'

"Never let them know what you can do, my young Lord," I instructed Alexander. "The Scions never reveal their secrets, and that is how they win, in the end. Let that be your education in the Order."

By age eight, Alexander became incorrigibly obsessed with digital technology. In the 1980's and 1990's, Alexander covertly arranged for the funding of tech startups that could benefit him, and fed them his ideas, giving rise to several major tech companies around the world. Building a base of operations in California, as far from Darius as he could be in mainland America, Alexander personally flooded Silicon Valley with funds. At age nine, he began creating algorithms, which he set loose on the markets, making millions in cash available to whoever, or whatever, he thought needed it. Several stock market crashes were the direct result of his algorithms.

Darius never learned the truth because the Order always reported 'twas something else. Alexander changed the U.S. economy. His clandestine hacking and funding schemes created incredible wealth. The records credit Darius and his Wall Street operations, but that was the way Alexander wanted it. Darius took credit before the Council and the Order, and Alexander's activities stayed off the radar.

Under my watchful eye, Alexander built and unified all the Order's computer systems into one matrix, a decentralized network named: Order Resources Network, or ORNet. By the mid 1990's, Alexander orchestrated the creation of what became the proverbial world wide web; and by folding all other fledgling computer network projects together, and synthesizing the world's communication systems, he created the underpinning for what is now called the internet.

By age thirteen, Alexander was the best mind in hacking and computer programming in the world. He changed the language that computers speak, and in doing so, changed the Order itself. He changed the world completely without anyone in the Order knowing, including himself. It was our little secret.

"Darius must not know I created ORNet," Alexander instructed me. "If Darius finds out, he'll kill me. He won't care the consequences."

"I understand." Ever greater lengths were taken to ensure Darius never saw how powerful Alexander had become.

"I just want to be normal," Alexander complained.

"There is no such thing."

"I want to be like them. One of them," he said of the people he would see online in pictures going about their lives.

"You must be who you are. You must fulfill your destiny."

"I envy them. They can do what they want. They're free."

"When you turn eighteen, you may experience the world as they do. Until then, continue with your work. The good strife is how you become free."

CHAPTER XI

"How does Alexander know my father?"

ALEXANDER

I'm the best *fucking* hacker in the world… They say we are free until and except when the Order needs us. They'll come for me one day. When I turned sweet sixteen, I celebrated by taking down one of Darius' favorite banks. I controlled the black hats and the white hats; all of the world's best of the best computer wizards used my code, and played their chess on the board I created. My bots borrowed and copied from them, and they worshipped my code and propagated my LexNet imagery. "You are a cyber-world god…" My A-I spoke truth to my power.

My closest equal was a princeling Chinese hacker named MoPo, a guy about my age. We fought for months in hacker battles, eventually forming an online friendship. MoPo was insanely brilliant, wickedly funny, and the closest thing I had to an actual friend at the time. He taught me some cool tricks and I gave him a few secrets I shouldn't have – like access to the dark webs of ORNet. Together we built a network of spider-bots that hacked everything… Anyone that knew anything about programming got caught our web. My hacker cyber hive rules the net. So in the year 2000, when I started to build the APEX, my help was the best. "Time to put them to the test."

MoPo and his crew helped me code the protocols of the APEX, until he accidentally hacked into the New York data center of ORNet. "MoPo has been caught on Darius' secret network," Lex said. "The hacking attempt just crossed Darius' desk."

"Shit." I typed furiously to see what's going on. "Order Agents traced the hack and found top-secret info about ORNet on MoPo's computer – info I gave him." Lex was silent. "Fuck!!"

An hour after it happened, I took off my VR gear and stared at the news on the monitors. Dee finally appeared. We sat in silence for a minute until I got up, and left the underground lair for the open air.

"I managed to hide your communiqué and involvement," Dee said. "But I could not stop Darius from discovering the breach."

"Oh, God." That pain in my heart came roaring back.

"Darius assumed these two miscreant hackers discovered ORNet on their own and somehow broke into it."

"Is he okay? Dee—"

"I couldn't stop it. I'm so sorry," Dee said.

"Stop what, Dee?" I realized. "Darius killed MoPo because of me?"

"This is a war. They died for your cause—" Dee rationalized.

"You have to save MoPo!" I knew he was already dead. The pain was too much. Boiling rage made the loss burn worse.

"Alexander—" Dee began.

"Save him!!" *Save him if you want to save me.* I yelled at Dee.

"I will do what I can. Calm yourself, Lord Alexander," Dee said. His eyes penetrated my mind, his hypnotic stare showed me how I can learn from this. "Darius has requested the Order build a new network. Darius wants an APEX."

"You can't be serious," I said.

Dee was serious. "This is an opportunity, Lord Alexander. Take it."

"You want me to build a new network for Darius? To help Darius?"

"I want you to keep doing what you are doing," Dee smiled.

"No." *I can't, Dee.* "I won't give him the APEX. I'm done."

"If you don't do this, Lord Alexander, the risk of Darius finding out your secret is greater. He is building a new network with or without you. It might as well be you, it can only be you, don't you see?"

A message popped up on my watch, from LexNet chat. I read the message. "Darius' people are already trying to recruit my aliases to build the system for them. He's already on to me, Dee."

"This is how you can best Darius, Lord Alexander. Teach him that he must work with you, not against you."

"An enemy can be the best teacher," I said.

"Darius is your teacher. He is smarter than you. You must learn from him, who you are, and who you want to be," Dee said. "And in doing so, you will teach him the same."

"So he is my enemy? And I am his servant?" He was right.

"None but an enemy may teach you what an enemy is. Only an enemy shows you your true nature. He tells you where you are weak, and how to be strong. He teaches you of love and hate. The rules of the Order, this 'game' as you call it, are defined by what control you can have over

Darius; by what you can stop him from doing to control you. Control over yourself, that is freedom, you see?"

"I see. Darius is more than an enemy, he's my teacher." Sparks flew in my head. "He can be my servant not my enemy..."

"I'll inform the Council I've recruited the best hacker there is to finish the project. Draw up the plans, use your LexNet program and we'll build your 'APEX' slowly."

"I'm not going to the Council Meeting." Fear returned in me.

"You will need to face your father, eventually," Dee said.

"That... will be the day I die."

"Death cannot stop a heart that is true," Dee said.

"I'm not ready. I'm still afraid of him. I'm weak."

"There is a new member of the Council you must meet. His name is David Peterson. He's going to be very important to your plans. You will meet him at the Council Meeting."

CHAPTER XII

"What was my mother like before me?"

SARAH

My definition of matrimony was love. Taken in that light, certainly the resemblance of love to loving relations is not striking; but I thought I could place them in such a view. Traditional society dictates that while man has the advantage of choice, a woman has the power of refusal; love then, matrimony, is both an engagement between lovers, and loving relations formed for the advantage of each. Once married, lovers belong exclusively to each other, 'til the moment of death. Their duty is to endeavor to give each other no cause for wishing that they had bestowed themselves elsewhere; and their best interest in this life is in keeping their own imaginations from wandering towards the perfection, or in the direction of others, or wondering that they should have been, or were meant to be, with any one else. I loved Robert. I saw a happy life with him.

"DNA is the code of life," I told him, smiling.

"It sounds so magical when you say it," Robert said, grinning at me.

"Epigenetics is merely the interacting of atomic forces, the laws of nature which life creates, to innovate on itself, feeding on the energies around it… The way our bodies store information, re-write the code of our DNA and build cells, to program our lives to evolve and function, is to me, sublime. Epigenetics is the alchemical science of the sublime."

"Life is beautiful. But not as beautiful as you," Robert kissed me.

"If epigenetics can make DNA express and change itself, and we can't fully discern the science of how this happens, we can't rule out the power of the mind, or even the divine." Robert was more interested in kissing than a debate. "Are you listening to me?"

"Proving your theory is not practical or possible, Sarah," Robert said. "I wouldn't say 'alchemy'; but I love the way you think."

I smiled and kissed him back.

"Will you marry me?" Robert surprised me with a ring. "You inspire me, Honey Bara. You are everything I've ever wanted and more. I want to spend the rest of my life with you."

The idea of marrying him danced in my head, the infinite, swirling play upon the stage of consideration. The music stopped.

"I can't," I got up and left before he saw me cry.

Strong man that Robert was, he refused to take no for an answer.

During my final year at Harvard, not officially engaged to Robert, but in a relationship and bond that felt fully committed, I had mostly, consciously, stopped thinking about David. His name came up only once at Harvard. My professor of Neurobiology, very old and perhaps a little forgetful, was helping me with my laborious DNA research project on virus programing, and in a moment of poetic candor, let a memory of David slip out.

"This little boy, David… He was born a genius," he said. "It had to have been genetic, or a mutation, he knew more than he could possibly have learned so young… I wish I had a sample of his DNA. Now that we could test it."

The professor glanced at me and changed his mood and changed the subject, sensing I wanted to know more. He remembered he was not supposed to talk about David. He changed the subject immediately. After that day, I never saw that professor again. It got me thinking about David again, for rest of the few months I had left at Harvard.

I graduated *magna cum laude*, with a degree in pre-medical bio-chemistry. No one in my family attended my graduation, not even my father. Nanny came in their place. Robert and his family were visibly shocked my parents would miss such an important occasion.

"Your mother and father wanted to be here," Nanny said. "We're all very proud of you, Sarah."

"They all work much too hard," I told Robert and his family.

"Sarah works harder, and smarter, than anyone I have ever met. She's my busy-bee Honey," Robert said, taking off his and my graduation hats and kissing me.

Robert and his family embraced me with open arms. They were wonderful people. I spent many holidays with them, bonding as family. Robert wanted to meet my mysterious family.

"I wanted to ask your father for your hand in marriage, my Lady," Robert said in his much improved British accent.

"Are you asking me to marry you, again?" I laughed. Laughing, until I thought of David. Robert became serious, and his whole family gathered around us. It felt both wonderful and painful to see what a real family was like. The pressure to commit to him in that moment nearly crushed me. My desire for a real family brought me to tears.

"Yes." I said the word, from my mouth to Father's ears.

That night, sleeping next to Robert, Father spoke to me in my dream. Three years had passed since I'd physically seen him last, but he was omnipresent, haunting me. "I'm coming to see you," his voice forced me awake. "I do not approve of your marriage to that man."

Robert was out with his family, and I entered my house to my father waiting for me, inside my living room.

"Hello, my child," he said, standing in front of me. He appeared just as I remembered him. I wasn't sure if I was dreaming or if he was really there in front of me.

"I'm here," he said, reading my mind.

I hugged him tight. I wanted to feel him, and to hold him close to me. He indulged me until I let go.

"You must return to London," he said, more of my boss than my father. "You will go to medical school at Oxford."

"I'm going to medical school at Harvard," I told him. "With Robert, Henry."

"Father," his voice rang loud inside my head.

"I love him... We're getting married, Father."

"You have grown up, my child. You are your own woman now. You must make your own decisions. But choose wisely."

"I want you to meet him."

"Come to London, tonight. You'll return on Monday," Father said.

"What am I going to tell Robert?"

Father destroyed my hesitation with the look in his powerful eyes.

"Alright." I could not disobey.

The car doors closed. Robert would be calling me soon. I would have to explain that my father did not approve of my marriage. Tears rolled down my face.

"I know what's best for you, Sarah," Father reminded.

Love and hate, self will and fate, dueled inside me to the death of all hope for joy. Closer to this man, Father, I felt pulled away from my new and seemingly best chance at freedom; happiness...

Robert called minutes later as I thought about him intensely. I answered the call in front of Father. Robert could not know the truth, and it killed me. Because it killed Robert too.

"Robbie," I spoke before painfully crying.

"Honey are you okay? What's wrong?" Robert said on the phone.

"My father is sick. I must go to London. I'll return on Monday."

"Is he okay? Are you okay?" Robert said, "You seem really upset."

"I'm okay." *I'm not okay.*

"Are you sure? This is so sudden. My parents are in town—"

Harshly, Father gave the 'wrap it up' look.

"I'll call you before I get on the plane. I have to go Robbie."

Another lie, my father's eyes informed me.

"Honey, do you need me to come with you?"

"No, stay. You should stay with your family. I'm okay. I'll be back Monday."

Robert's pain and worry screamed in his silence.

"My father gave us his blessing to get married," I told him. "I love you. I just need to see him, to say my goodbyes."

"I can't live without you, Honey Bara. See you soon."

Father sat in silent, angry disapproval. I hung up the phone.

It was a noble lie. "His happiness means a lot to me and I'm not going to let you take Robert's joy as well."

"Do this, and you will kill him, Sarah," Father warned.

"You are killing me, Henry."

"I need you to trust me."

I refuse to believe.

CHAPTER XIII

"She knew the Order was responsible."

SARAH

"Happiness in marriage is entirely a matter of chance." Such wise words of pride and prejudice in love. For if the deceptions of the engaged parties are ever so well hidden or revealed beforehand, it does not advance their felicity in the least. Lovers always continue to grow sufficiently close or apart after matrimony, and have their share of vexation; thus, I see it better to reveal and know as little as possible of the defects of the person with whom you give the love of your life.

Waking up in London, so far away, America felt like a dream I hardly remembered. All I thought about was David; my heart ached.

Father and I walked around London, floating, talking, and I told him about my time at Harvard and my research. By late afternoon, by design, we landed at the British Museum.

"Shall we go in?" Father said. "I believe David is giving a lecture tonight."

No words came to me.

"I've been looking forward to it," Father gave a rare smile.

'No,' I wanted to say. 'This is not my life. David is not my life,' I told myself. Ego and superego quarreled inside my heart. This was a test to see not if, but how much I loved David. Do I love David?

There's but one way to find out…

We arrived just in time for the start of the lecture, to our reserved seats in the front row. I saw nothing but red. The red walls of the room, red velvet seats, red curtains… David walked out and met eyes with me. I turned red.

David walked to the podium and began to speak about the advances in science, how 'Special Research' is changing archeology and rewriting history, but I was lost in thought the entire time. Confused and overcome with emotion, a teenage girl all over again, I became that little girl who first fell in love with David; hormones raging. My head spinning, seconds from getting up and leaving, Father placed his hand on mine. With his touch I let go; softened, I got a grip.

Father watched David's effect on me. He peered in my eyes, seeing I had forgotten about Robert and America entirely. In that moment, Father saw that I loved David, perhaps now more than ever before.

David was pulled away seemingly against his will immediately after the lecture. He did not attend the reception. I felt relieved.

"Don't be upset," Father said. "I want you to meet someone."

This man had an incredible energy about him. He was no ordinary human, not simply a titled London billionaire, this man was very special. With him were identical twin men of an intense, glaring nature.

"Sarah, this is one of the trustees, His Lordship, Mr. Smith," Father said. And these are his associates, Tom and John."

"Pleasure to meet you, my dear," Mr. Smith said. "Sir Henry, your daughter is absolutely stunning."

Old in appearance, but full of life and vitality, this 'Mr. Smith' beamed majestic charisma. He and Father talked briefly about David. I'll never forget the way my father acted around this man, because I'd never seen him behave in such a way before. Subservient and totally deferential, I had no idea such behavior was possible for Father's ego.

"Well, if you'll excuse me, I must go. So nice to meet you, Lady Sarah," Mr. Smith said, leaving before I could speak.

"Shall we have dinner?" Father turned me.

"I am quite hungry."

Over dinner Father told me about my Grandfather. "My father was a member of a very powerful organization, and I inherited his position," Father said. "I can't tell you it's name, but we'll call it 'The Order.'"

"The Order?" I said, not liking the sound of it already.

"Your mother has known for many years. But she has kept this secret from you and your sister, for me."

I nodded. Father was happy I didn't pry for details.

"Why are you telling me this?"

"This is the reason I have been so busy all these years. But you know, even when I am not around, I am looking out for you." He added, "and I'm always with you, when you think of me."

"I know." But I didn't know the half of it, yet.

48

CHAPTER XIV

"Love requires sacrifice."

SARAH

Had I not been in love, I may not have been so wretchedly blind. But pride, not love, was my folly. Pleased with the preference of Robert, and offended by neglect and Father's preference of David, from the fateful beginning of our acquaintance, I courted dangerous prepossession of heart and ignorance of mind, reason left at bay, where all my love was concerned; I went astray.

After I returned from London, I didn't see David or Father again for just over ten years. Robert and I married a year later in Connecticut. Mother and Sister were in attendance. Father was not.

At Harvard Medical school, Robert and I both became members of the London Society, focused on biomedical research, and we both graduated medical school at the top of our class. I focused on regenerative medicine and DNA research, and Robert on oncology. Robert wanted to cure cancer. After one year of residency, he received an offer from a drug company in London; a dream job for him, and a salary too high to pass up.

"Should I take it?" His eyes filled with excitement. He couldn't bear it if I had said no. "I'll be making drugs to cure cancer!"

"Of course you should," I tamped down my trepidation.

Upon his acceptance, there was no turning back. Within a month all our belongings were moved by the company to a flat in Kensington, central London. Promptly, I received my own job offer.

"Have you accepted your job offer yet? You're not going to find anything better for DNA research," Mother said over lunch.

"Yes, Mother. I know."

"They know your father." She revealed to me in that moment how Father orchestrated this whole thing. My job and Robert's.

"He did this, didn't he?"

"Are you all settled then?" She brushed off my cold stare.

Robert and I both lost ourselves in our genetics work. The years flew by. We were very much in love, but it felt like we were growing apart. I wanted to have a family, but our ever more demanding careers seemingly prevented it. Consumed by the rigor of our jobs, we barely had time for each other, save a child. I longed for family, my family.

And at the climax of my longing, everything changed.

In 1996, Mother summoned Sister and me to her bedside. "I'm done fighting," she said, "I have… intracranial neoplasm brain cancer."

"Mother, why have you suffered in silence? Why not tell us? We—"

"I didn't want to worry you. I don't need a fuss," Mother said.

"You should have told us," I said. Sister silently agreed. "For us."

"It would not have changed anything for the better, I didn't want you to worry about me needlessly. One day you'll see. It's my time now, Darlings. Remember, I love you both more than you know."

I wish you had told me. I cried. Mother died, with us at her side.

"I knew she battled depression, but not cancer," I told Robert.

"Depression is also a cancer; both are mysterious and deadly," Robert said. "It can appear out of nothing and take everything."

"She was ready to let go. She just wanted to see us one last time."

"Mother loved us," Sister and her husband agreed.

"She went in peace, holding our hands. That gives me peace."

"That's the best death we can ask for," Robert kissed me as he spoke. "Isn't it? When you get to say goodbye. Having peace."

I nodded in agreement. His words gave me solace.

Six months later, Robert left the house in a hurry, and didn't get to say goodbye. He called me. "I forgot to say goodbye," he said.

"I love you," I said. "See you tonight."

He died in a car accident minutes after the call, on his way to a speaking engagement at Oxford. His car was broadsided by a man who ran a red light. All three men, two drivers and Robert, perished. I felt it, when it happened. I heard him say goodbye, again.

"Robert died instantly," the doctor informed me over the phone. I fell to the floor unconscious, as the words confirmed the worst.

I cried for days, asking myself: *Why?*

My happiness died with Robert. Part of me was buried with him. I wanted so much just to say goodbye. The pain was unbearable.

Darkness took over me…

CHAPTER XV

"Father is a mystery to me."

DAVID

Darkness.

Am I capable of seeing the light of the spiritual stars above? There is no total darkness. Truth creates the presence of limitless light and at my darkest hour, I blink, finally seeing the sun shining under my feet.

"Who am I?" We all must ask ourselves this question, but usually something comes to mind. Darkness came to me.

I opened my eyes. Black splotches blotted my sight as my vision slowly returned. My head ached, and I didn't know where I was. Someone had given me powerful depressant drugs, I felt traces of it.

Anger and rage gave way to panic as it swept over me in a wave. My blurry vision and foggy brain struggled to construct my past. I heard conversations around me, menial talk – nothing significant. Sitting in a chair, an empty seat next to me, and rows of seats in front of me, I observe to my side out a window. I'm above the clouds…

"I'm on a plane."

"Coffee, Sir?" asked a lovely flight attendant.

I nodded yes. Coffee sounded wonderful. I wanted to speak but the words were slow to come forth. Finally, by the time the coffee was poured, I was able to muster, "How did I get here?"

"I'm sorry, Sir, what do you mean?" she replied.

"How long until we get there?" I tried to save face.

"We'll be arriving in London in one hour, Sir. Will there be anything else?"

"No, thank you."

I sipped the coffee, hoping memory would come to me. I have a photographic memory, I forgot nothing, yet I could not remember how I came to be on a plane. Which meant only one thing: something happened to me. *What did you do to me?*

Start with the basics. What did I remember? Everything. I have a eidetic and photographic memory, profound hyperthymesia, I can recall nearly everything about my life, until this moment. My name is David Arthur Peterson; born in 1952. I'm an orphan from Boston. *Summa cum laude* Harvard and Oxford, my exceptional genius and corresponding ego, a deluge of voices in my head, and my lectures all over the world came roaring back to me. Scanning through every moment of my life, a life of the highest praise from others and the deepest criticism of myself, everything came back, up until 1997, and my trip to Cairo, Egypt. While searching for something, or someone, I met the woman of my dreams... "Sarah." After this, darkness.

After meeting Sarah, it seemed my mind drifts, lost in a dense fog. Struggling to remember Sarah, her golden hair, noble face, and blue eyes like the sea after a storm, came to me... Who was this woman, Sarah? And what happened to me? What year is it? My mind raced and my head pounded from drug withdrawal.

A blinding flash of memory: the *Aton Stone Tablet*, Thoth, and Shambala, "Henry..."

"I work for the Order, David," Henry's voice said, in my head.

The words triggered a piercing migraine pain to spread and overtake my brain. I couldn't see straight to recall Henry's face. Thoughts became white hot and blinded my mind's eye. Nauseous, I put my coffee down.

Is this a dream? Nothing seemed real. None of this made sense. Surely I must have a suitcase or something, I told myself.

Under my seat I found a small leather day bag. A bag I bought in London a few years back. I remembered it. I opened it. Inside the bag I found my wallet, a British Passport, a cell phone, a man's ring with my name inscribed inside of it, an empty notebook, a set of keys, and my one-way airline ticket. I examined the ticket. British Airways flight 237 from Paris to London... October 13, 1999.

"Good God," I spoke out loud. "1999?" No memory past 1997 came to me. My head pounded to the quickening drum beat of a frantic heat. I lost two years? How could I have lost two years?' Shock and stress overtook me. Struggling to breath, my first panic attack struck.

"Someone did this to me." Uncharacteristically, I drew attention to myself, making a scene. "I need help." I didn't mean to yell.

The flight attendant came over. "Are you alright, Sir?"

I nodded yes, but she could see, most certainly, I was not all right.

"I'm not good at flying." I diffused the situation, to be let alone.

A car drove me to central London. I walked down the sidewalk outside Saint Paul's cathedral. Strangely, few people walked about. A red pub in the distance caught my attention. Not the slightest bit hungry, a drink felt in order. Quietly, I went inside the pub and sat down at a little circle table.

"Scotch, please."

The barkeep poured me a Scotch. "There you are, Sir," he said.

I turned to a woman staring at me.

"Sarah."

Her face showed worry, but her eyes sparkled with happiness to see me. I felt deeply comforted to see her.

"I've missed you so much, David," she said, fighting tears.

"How long ago did we meet in Cairo?"

A tear rolled down my face. Praying she would say it was only days ago, I knew it couldn't be so. I felt her pain as she hesitated to speak.

"Two years ago," she said as she touched my head and face with her soft loving hands. "You don't remember?"

"I remember meeting you, taking you to Alexandria; nothing after."

Sarah's eyes told me her greatest fears are realized.

I noticed the wedding ring on her finger. "You're married?"

"Yes," she said - like a dagger to my heart.

"To you, David," she let herself cry.

"We're married?"

"Yes."

"When?"

"Last year, 1998. After we met in Cairo, you came back to London." She dried her eyes.

She spoke the truth. I felt better.

"I love you." She held my hand.

"How did you know I would be here?"

"You wrote me. You told me to meet you here," she said. "I've been waiting."

She pulled an envelope out of her purse and showed me the letter. Examining it closely, with extreme graphological scrutiny, I conclude it was indeed my handwriting.

"When did you last see me, or hear from me before this day?"

"It's been over a year, David. I feared the worst until this night. You told me you had to return to Egypt. You couldn't tell me why. I couldn't reach you. You weren't at your hotel, you didn't write," tears of pain, vocal strain. "I'm so happy to see you. I love you so much. I thought I lost you." She cried.

Sarah wrapped her arms around me. I held her tightly.

"How did this happen to me?"

"Hans went to find you. I asked Father to help. But he—"

"Who?" I asked. *Who is Father?*

"My father, Henry," Sarah said looking me in the eye.

"Henry." His name hit me hard. Flashback of Henry, I saw his face. My chest became heavy. Anxiety clinched my gut. Fear of the unknown smothered me. Damp, gray fog shrouded my thoughts. What to say, I could not see. I didn't have to say anything.

"He found you didn't he?" she said.

"Who are you?" My words tinged with paranoid fear.

Shaking uncontrollably, making me more anxious, uncharacteristic lack of restraint broke me. No control, everything was simply happening to me. The voices of my tortured childhood returned.

"She's lying," they said. "She's using you. Don't trust her..."

Down spiraling into my own private hell, Sarah grabbed me. She saved me from spinning again into lonely darkness.

"I'm you're wife, David. I love you so much. I would never do anything to hurt you. I—" *She is right.*

Her voice silenced the harsh critics in my head. Lies are shadows and this woman's light killed doubt dead.

"I believe you." More than I knew. "I'm sorry. I am not myself."

The cell phone in my bag rang, attracting unwanted attention with its electronic, demanding din. I felt compelled to answer the call. I saw my wedding ring in the bag and put it on.

"Hello?" I demanded, pressing the answer button.

"David. You're back," the caller said.

"Hans? Dr. Hans Danreich?" I confirmed.

"Yes. Come to the office right away. I've sent a car for you."

The phone had a tracking device on it. Danreich hung up.

"He's sending a car." I told Sarah, unsure what to think.

"Are you sure you're alright?"

"What do you know about Henry, your father?"

"Not enough. He's a Neuroscientist. I haven't heard from him in over a year as well. But that's normal - for him."

Sarah could see right through me. "Tell me what's going on."

"Once I find out, trust me, I will," I said.

"David—" Sarah began, interrupted by:

"David Peterson? Your car awaits, Sir," the driver's voice echoed through the pub. The driver waived and returned to wait in the car.

I turned to Sarah. I didn't want to leave her side. "Come."

"No. Go. I'll see you at home, tonight," Sarah said. She kissed me. "Are you sure?"

"Yes. Don't ask me how I know," she said. "This is not goodbye."

"I love you." With that, I left.

CHAPTER XVI

"Grief is the price we pay for love."

SARAH

The most incomprehensible thing in the world to a woman is a Father who destroys her marriage, her chance at love and family.

Robert's death was killing me, from inside my heart, draining me of life. Greif and guilt fused into debilitating depression, brewing a storm upon my world, blocking all sun light in my mind's sky.

"A woman like you must not marry a man merely because she is asked, or because said man is attached to her, and can offer her a comfortable life," Father said me in a dream.

"Did you kill him, Henry?"

"I shall always be your father. Respect me, child. Call me as such."

"You are no longer my father."

"Some things happen beyond our control." Even in dreams Father acted cryptic and aloof. "Believe me. He was not the one for you."

"So it is my fault Robert is dead." I cried. "Robert would have been better off never having met me."

"You know very well that is not true," Father said. "He loved you."

"I will never be happy again. I can't live this life."

"Wake up, my child," his voice said. "This life is but a dream."

Father came to visit me that morning. I never got out of bed.

"He died in a car accident. Despite what you think, it's not your fault. Take a holiday. Travel," he said. "Give yourself some time."

Father put his hands on mine. A rare gesture I rejected, unkind.

"Don't touch me. Please." I closed my eyes and cried.

When I stopped crying, father had gone. If I had dreamed him, or if he had actually physically visited me, was lost in foggy misery.

Crying released not my sadness, and seemed to make the pain worse; but I cried myself to exhausted sleep, thinking of Robert.

"I love you," Robert said. In my dream, he seemed happy. "It's not your fault. You only ever wanted me to be happy. And I want you to be happy, Sarah. Please. Be happy. Let me go. Let go… Go."

"I love you, Robert." I closed my eyes and kissed him. I went.

Off Paris the next morning, after nomadically wandering around Europe for months, I toured southern Africa before arriving in Egypt winter of 1997 – Egypt made me think of David.

David was Egypt in my mind, and when I arrived in Cairo, Henry was waiting for me. When he hugged me, all anger melted.

"I will always be your Father, family," he said, his words and energy forcing me again to see, just how powerful a man he can be.

He booked me into the Cairo hotel he frequents. We never spoke about David, but talking about him as Egypt, dominated our thoughts.

"Sweet dreams, and happy travels, my child," he left that night.

While in Cairo, every night, my dreams became more vivid and more real than ever before. I was looking, but David found me in a dream. He spoke to me, and in lucid wonder we traveled through time, to hallowed antiquity. Magically, we ran through the ancient Library of Alexandria, together...

On what was to be my last night in Cairo, David entered my Cairo hotel bar. I felt I must be dreaming. In a surreal moment, David walked over and sat next to me.

"David Peterson," subtle disbelief on my voice.

I shall never forget the sight, the light, that is David. I felt happy. In that moment, I fell hopelessly in love with him, again. A love deeper than I knew was possible – because now I felt David falling in love with me. His eyes revealed he too had been in love with me, and dreaming of me, *for years*. He is the man of my lucid dreams.

Our spark together made a flame to illuminate our darkness.

Father and David had many conversations I was not privy to, one of which must have included asking for my hand in marriage. In the summer of 1998, David and I traveled to Paris for a weekend. David stopped as we walked along the river Seine: "I'll love you forever," David said, kneeling before me. "Eternity isn't enough time for me. Sarah, will you marry me?"

"I've waited for happiness – for so long." I felt happy.

"So have I," David said. "I have waited for you my entire life."

"Yes," I confirmed. "My heart is already married to you, David."

At the peak of my bliss, when David's lips touched mine in kiss, the terrible realization that our happiness would not last long, came on strong. *For people like us, happiness fleets, and the Order looms.*

"We must be the luckiest people in the world," David mused.

I didn't see it that way. Luck contradicted the fate in my gut.

"I love you… so much," I said.

"You saved me. Your love has saved me," David spoke for me too.

"Your love, true love, is all I ever wanted." I cried tears of joy.

Father still seemed to know David better than I, which gave me comfort, and a deep longing to penetrate and unlock all the mysteries of the universe in David. I wanted to know everything about him… In my mind I felt if could understand the feelings in my heart, the love I felt for this man, David, I would find my true self.

In February of 1999, we were married in a small ceremony.

"I now pronounce you husband and wife…"

And so it was. Again a wife, in what seemed a new life.

CHAPTER XVII

"What about her plans?"

SARAH

"It feels good to be married to David," I said to Father.

"It ought to be good; this marriage has been the work of a great many generations, my darling child," Father said.

"In some ways I hardly know David, there is so much I don't know about him. Yet, I when I am with him, I feel I've known him all my life."

"Love is nonlocal. Just like the mind. You know him, now, as deeply as you ever will; the details matter not, my child," he said.

Love is all that matters. Love is the energy that makes all matter.

Our honeymoon of marital bliss lasted not nearly as long as I hoped it would. After a month, the earth shifted beneath our feet. I respected, I esteemed, I was grateful to David, and I felt a profound interest in his welfare, for he and I were now one.

"I must go to Egypt. Duty calls," David confessed as he packed. He had as much say in the matter as I did, perhaps less.

"It has to do with my father?" His silence answered me: yes. I couldn't go with him, though I wanted to. I couldn't say all the things I wanted to say. "I could not bear to lose you. Any more loss will destroy me... I am lost without you."

He looked at me, deeply. I only wanted to know how far he wished that his faring well depend upon me, and how far it would be for the travels of happiness for us both, our family, that I should employ the power, which my heart told me I still possessed, of bringing on the renewal of this life's love confessed. To leave me so soon I felt digressed, and in my mind distressed.

David needs my love as I need his, but I don't know what that means for our life. What does this mean for us?

"You will never lose me," David said.

"When will I see you again? How long?"

"I won't be away from you for a moment longer than is absolutely necessary, my Love," David said.

I nodded as I walked to the bedroom. As I had done before, I gave him my silk scarf. "You must bring this back to me. It's my favorite one." I smiled in pain as a tear fell down my cheek. "If you can't, it will bring you back to me."

Within days David became a ghost, unresponsive to all contact. In my dreams, I saw him, with my Father… But they didn't see me.

By day I found solace in my work. My research team and I made several breakthroughs identifying genes, genetic interaction and electromagnetic epigenetic stimuli triggered activation of DNA. The work progressed quickly, which excited our funders, and everyone on the team… I struggled to be excited. My depression hid in warm smiles, hard work, and kind words.

Finally, after almost half a year, I received a message from David. A letter in the mail, in David's handwriting, telling me to meet him tomorrow.

Per the letter, I waited at a pub near St. Paul's Cathedral.

"Be there at seven o'clock in the evening," the letter said.

I was ten minutes early. I didn't see David there. I heard the bells of the cathedral toll seven times. About ten minutes later, David entered the bar. I froze, paralyzed with emotion.

Something happened to him. David walked to the bar looking disoriented and confused. He didn't remember writing the letter, or being in Egypt, or that we were married. But he remembered me.

The moment my Father's name was spoken David's mobile rang. Danreich needed to see him. All my strength was summoned not too fight him leaving my side, I let him go. *I began to let go.* I did not want to let him leave me again, but I had to, *now I must let go.*

I kissed him. He was home, safe in London. He'll be home in a few hours... I went home and fell asleep, and found him and Father in a dream.

CHAPTER XVIII

"Once seen, you cannot un-see."

DAVID

At this most interesting point in my life, I finally realized, all my knowledge indicates my profound ignorance. I always assumed my knowledge was to be given to the ignorant, but as I grow further, I have discovered the ignorance in my knowledge itself. I have not found and do not give the answers; I only seek myself. My own teachers, as I, have become learned, but not wise; I have learned to be strong, but not to love; I have found many things, but have not found Truth. And when my so called knowledge becomes great enough, as they tell me it has, for me it only increases the confusion of my mind making it even more difficult to find the one Truth I seek. Who am I? Where am I?

The car dropped me at the British Museum where Danreich waited outside, just as I remembered him. Things made sense even as they didn't.

My esteemed colleague, Dr. Hans Danreich rolled through my mind. An older German man in his sixties, tough, harsh, and brilliant at his work, known him to be well meaning. An expert on ancient antiquities, ancient languages, and Egyptology, he became a friend and mentor to me. We've worked together many times; a long history.

Danreich could see the intensity in my eyes and I saw the secrets circling his mind. He hid things well, but seemed genuinely happy to see me. I noticed the ring on his hand – gold with the Order symbol engraved on it. The Order has him.

"How are you, David?" Danreich asked, knowing I'm unwell.

"Confused."

"Yes, well, we are happy to have you back safe," he said.

We walked through the halls of the empty, dark museum, past the collections of ancient art to the department of *Special Research*. Danreich walked in front of me, keeping his face mostly out of view.

"What happened to me?" He knew. "Tell me what you know."

He turned to me slightly to speak as we walked along the halls. "You were in Egypt, David. You've been missing for a year. I'm just happy you're alive," he said. "We feared the worst when you disappeared. Do you remember anything about your time in Egypt?" Danreich asked, probing me for information.

"I barely remember the last two years of my life." My words elicited no reaction, which meant no outrage or danger.

We arrived at my old office: *Dr. David Peterson, Special Research*.

Danreich unlocked the door and turned on the light. My office looked cleaner than I remembered it. Items from 1997 were missing.

"Tell me what you know, Hans." Enough with the formalities.

"I'm leaving for Egypt tomorrow, David. I will find out what happened to you. I promise I will," Danreich said to me.

He watched my response carefully. "I'm going with you," I insisted.

"No," Danreich pushed back with staid affirmativeness. "You are not well. You have reports to write. The Trustees have questions for you, David. This is a dangerous situation."

Danreich pointed to a stack of paperwork; busy work.

"When did you get the ring? You're wearing an Order ring."

Danreich tried to be unreactive. "I must go—"

"Do you know Sarah's father, Henry? Danreich."

"I know he's one of the Trustees, but I've never met him. You know him well. You'll remember, David. Try. You have been traumatized. Time is of the essence. Write the reports," Danreich implored.

"Wait."

"Goodbye, David." Danreich left.

Sitting down at my old desk, the thought of writing, exhausted me instantly. Head down, I drifted into a lucid dream.

My consciousness drifted into the stars. My eyes went down as my feet touched down in Elysian fields; a happy place where I find beauty, and Sarah. Stars became fireflies, and tiny orbs which drew my attention to the Temple on the hill in the distance, through the wooded glen.

Approaching the Temple, exiting the trees and mystical natural world, I saw civilization. Mountains became precision cut stone blocks, a temple, and metal altars outside burst to life with flame. The torches creating smoky halos around them, burning away mental fog.

"Where are you, my Love?" I searched for Sarah.

A symphony of music grew in volume as the large cedar doors of the temple opened slowly. Light and music beaconed me inside.

Inside the temple a grand party underway, a Dionysian festival and Venetian masquerade ball danced together in play. Lions, birds, fawns, nymphs covered in flowers, mythical nature danced and frolicked with abandon, pulling me into the fairy-tale revelry.

The dancing stopped as I stepped onto the black and white checkered floor. The revelers and animal eyes followed me. The crowd parted as I stepped toward a woman in a mask, wearing an elaborate Elizabethan dress of white satin. I was a pawn charging across the board to become a king. My queen waited for me patiently. *Silence, lest ye break the spell of majesty...*

"I must remove the veil hiding your divinity," instinctively reaching to remove her mask, I craved her beauty.

"You found me," Sarah smiled.

The music chimed in triumphantly.

I found her.

True Love.

CHAPTER XIX

"You are his heir, my dear."

HENRY

To love is to see the infinite in the finite; to find the Creator in the creation, the Almighty in the minute sparkle of an eye. Passing moments of such divine beauty are but the fugitive refraction of the eternal; wonderful perfect truth seen through a medium of a dream.

Sarah and David dreamed of such a perfect love together, dancing.

"You're wondering about my father," Sarah said.

None can resist the will of man who knows what is true and wills what is good. David knew I was listening and willed the good.

"I must speak to him. He knows what happened. I need to remember— I need to know what happened to me; to us," David said.

"You will," Sarah said. *Show yourself, Father. Please.*

The music stopped. The lion roared with commanding pride. The revelers and animals fell silent, music died. The mythological crowd backed away from the lovers in embrace. Through the great golden doors of the inner temple, manifest I. Tall, imposing top hat, dressed in modernist all black, my long cape flowing behind me, I removed my mask, stepping down from on high. My elegant, if mechanical façade melted, off came the black hat. I am human. I do love, love.

"Hello David."

"I remember the Aton," David said.

The demigod crowd gasped at the word *Aton*. The mood darkened. The angry lion roar echoed in the massive dome space. All the masks turned to angry faux visages, polished and shiny, reflecting the flame.

"You mustn't talk about the Aton, David. Not even to Sarah. It's too dangerous." *The gods and revelers agree.*

"Is that why my memory was erased?" David said.

"You found the Aton Stone tablet, David."

"I have no memory of that which you speak," he said.

"There are those who must never know of the Aton's existence. The situation is a precarious one. Your memories of the Aton cannot be erased, but they must be suppressed, hidden from those who might search your mind for it. That is why you don't recall."

Sarah grabbed David's hands. "After we met in Egypt, you returned to London to find me. You asked Henry for my hand and he said yes. He cares for you, as I do," she said.

"You used me," David accused me.

"My interest in you in not usury. I helped you, and you helped me. You are strong, David. I always knew… You were meant to find the sacred truth. Many have searched. I searched my whole life, but you found the tablet. You found the exalted secret of the Pharaohs…"

"Did you know, my Love?" David asked Sarah. "Did you know your father works for the Order?"

"She doesn't need to be told, what matters she already knows."

"No one sent me, David. I obey only my heart," Sarah said.

"Is the Order evil?" David asked me. "Do they want the A—"

The lion roared and cut him off from saying: *Aton.*

"The Order is black and white; the world is their chessboard, all pieces, because it is itself the game. But you can be colorful." David and Sarah understood. "Humanity needs the Aton Stone Tablet found, and needs us to protect the secret. Fear not me. Rest, David."

"I should be the one to find the tablets," David said. "It should be me going to Egypt, not Danreich."

"I need you, David. Be here with me," Sarah said.

David beheld his true love, and understood meaning from above.

"Thank you," David, said with a smile. He spoke to us all.

The crowd applauded, tragedy turned comedy, and music filled the air. I backed away, put on my black mask and faded away.

"Always remember: Life is but a dream…"

David and Sarah danced, holding each other close.

"Wake up, my Love," Sarah said to David.

"What?" he said. He forgot he was in a dream.

"Go to me. I want to see you. I want to be with you."

"Am I not with you, my Love?"

"You are, but you are dreaming. Wake up."

The music stopped.

David woke up.

CHAPTER XX

"The secret meaning of life?"

DAVID

My unconscious head lifted off my desk as my soul crash landed into my body jerking me awake. Night became conscious light. *Where am I now?* Still at my office in the museum, I looked at the date: October 13, 1999. My dream faded, but Sarah waiting at home for me came into sharp focus. The vintage clock on my wall ticked to eleven past eleven at night: 11:11pm. I left before it could tick again.

Entering the home I barely remembered, Sarah sat waiting for me. Looking like a dream, she had just woken up herself.

"I had a dream about you," she said.

Without a word, I carried her to our bedroom. Her eyes lit a fire inside me. Burning with a lust never felt before, heat radiated from my core, my body temperature rose and my face dripped in wet sexual desire. I didn't recall ever making love to Sarah, but I felt the warmth of a familiar love. A kiss brought back a dream, a fantasy of my wife, a life too good to be true. Holding her in my arms, staring at her angelic face, our love forged anew as we melted into one.

"I want a baby," her words sent us to the center of the galaxy.

White heat of divine perfection burned off all impurities of being, our flesh bodies touched, two souls fused, together in the cosmic foundry of immortal heart; we made Love. An explosion of Love filled the empty universe in light, light of meaning to life.

"Anything you want."

"Our wait was over." She said: *This is our lifetime.*

"Yes it is," I said.

"True love is worth waiting an eternity for," her words echoed in my mind, and tuned my spirit to the resonant sound of the infinite, the music of truth as only it can harmonize minds. "Love knows no time."

Naked before her in every way, for the first time in my life, I felt free. No cold bitterness of empty space in my heart. Starlight in me burned bright. Her kiss was transcendental, taking me to a spiritual level. Two heart beats synchronized, our brains buzzing with the same vibrational frequency; all pain, sorrow, worries, demons, and dreams; everything vaporized in flash. Words cannot describe the unified climax that took us both to the place where dreams are made. In the center of all creation, a journey of lucid, tantric love, we touched the heavens above, we discovered the secret of all ages and all life, and brought something back. To make Love is the secret magic all alchemists seek, from nothing, something all powerful, golden and divine. We did not simply make love, we made life, as all light condensed into Sarah's womb.

I saw you, Elizabeth. You are our Love.

"This is the secret wisdom I've searched for all my life. Love."

"Create something greater than ourselves," Sarah said.

"That is conception. The secret of life. The very meaning of life…"

All my years of waiting for her, for this, were validated and made sense – everything made sense. *This moment will carry me the rest of my life*, I thought. This was the moment I was born, reborn to live.

"All the pain and sorrow in my life was worth this night alone," Sarah said. Tears of joy rolled down her face.

Love transmutes pain. She spoke for me as well. 'Satisfaction' does no justice, feels inadequate, to what I felt looking into Sarah's eyes. Peering in the open window to her serene soul, I saw my darling child, playing in the Elysian fields of the future; soaking in the sun.

I don't know how long we stared at each other; until we seamlessly slipped from waking life to dreamland again, without notice of the difference, we too ran through the green hills and colorful flowers to our familial future.

"Elizabeth is very important…" Henry's voice said from above.

"I know," Sarah said.

I know. But only in time would I truly understand.

CHAPTER XXI

"Who is the King of the Order?"

THE SCION

Never is the Order observed; 'tis only the awkward and intrusive failings of disorder that attracts attention. Ruling on high, in the fairytale castle of my illustrious ancestors, a secret fortress in the mystical mountains of central Europe, I waited for the revelation, the meaning of the terrible feeling in my being to reveal itself. The bearers of bad news entered. Thus ends mine hours of content...

"My Lord," John began ominously. He struggled for the words.

"What is it?" I knew 'twas not good... "Speak."

"Sir Henry is dead. He's been killed, in Egypt," Tom said.

There it was. Revelation. A spoken truth of impossibility. Henry is a member of the Council, one of the most powerful men in the world, a mind like none in the world, a man I rely on heavily in matters absolutely crucial to running the Order. "Sir Henry Stuart is one of my closest personal friends." Tom and John know this and that what I actually said was: *How is this possible?* My world transformed in an instant. The news shocked my poor old heart. *Henry cannot be gone.*

"How could this have happened? What was he doing in Egypt?"

"We're not certain, my Lord. Sir Henry left little clues as to what he was doing in Egypt. But he appears to have been in contact with a man named David Peterson," Tom said.

"Why does that name sound familiar?"

"David Peterson is married to Henry's daughter, Sarah," John said. "We're gathering all information we can."

My legendary Privy Councilors Tom and John, identical twin and legal masterminds, stood before me dumbfounded. A rare sight.

"The agents found him shot several times, my Lord," Councilor Tom said. "Perhaps—"

"Dee!" I yelled, summoning my djinn to appear.

My beardless wizard appeared, stepping into the room as if he had simply been standing outside the door. He's never far away.

"Yes, my Lord," Dee said calmly.

The oldest human in the world, as far as I know, he appears the same today as he did when I was a his young pupil. He is the Head Master, the wisest of them all... I shook with anger. "How could Henry have been killed?"

"'Tis but one way. He sacrificed himself."

"Why? For what reason?" Tom and John finally get a clue.

"Henry left a note, Majesty," Dee pointed to the monitors.

"Where? What does it say?" Tom and John queue the footage.

"Henry's associate, the man with the letter, a Dr. Hans Danreich has reached the British museum," Tom said from behind me in my workroom. "He is about to deliver it to Dr. David Peterson."

"Remind me who is David Peterson? Dee?"

"Let us watch this video, my Lord." Dee dodged my questions.

We watched the live video from David's office in the Museum:

"What happened?" David demanded answers.

"I found it, David. Henry wanted you to know," Danreich said, giving David the sealed letter from Henry.

"Where is Henry?" David asked.

"He's dead," Danreich said. He looked at the camera. "His dying wish, he said, was for me to give you this letter."

"Hans. What exactly did you find?" David demanded.

"They're watching, David. I can't— I have to go."

David took the letter. "I'll go with you."

"No." Danriech was forceful, and bleeding.

"Hans. Let me help you!"

"You can't help me. Goodbye, David."

David tried to stop Danreich to no avail.

"Hans wait! Where are you going?"

"Let me go. I'm already dead—"

"Turn it off," I said. "Tell me about David Peterson, Dee."

Dee had vanished, of course. This meant he's hiding something.

"We have no explanation or answers regarding Henry, or this man," John said. Tom agreed, regrettably. "We need that letter."

"And bring me David Peterson." Tom and John nodded yes.

I sat alone in my despair, isolated in my castle in the air.

Is this the end, Dee?

CHAPTER XXII

"Identical twin legal masterminds?"

THE SCION

Tom and John are my most honorable Councilor Generals, and chiefs of staff. Identical twin brothers, they are two of the world's top legal minds and my closest personal privy advisors. They accompany me everywhere giving me the legalities and intricacies on request, as they know the Order better than any other, save the all seeing Wizard.

Tom and John were born into the Order elite, their father preceded them as my Councilor General, but their position was not given to them. They earned their place in the Order hierarchy, ascending the ranks of the international legal community, up the center and out the top of the 'Magic Circle,' they methodically outsmarted every other lawful mind on earth, at which point I tapped them to serve me personally. As my Councilors, 'tis their job to fix everything.

"Tom and John have returned, my Lord," my butler said.

"Well," I said to them as they entered.

"David is on site, my Lord," John said.

The twins followed me as I walked through the castle. A palace in the sky, built on a secluded mountain, across the storied marble floors, in the twinkling lights of flame lamps, I wandered in reflective wonder from my private quarters, in the direction of the *Chamber of Initiation* where David, unknowingly, waited for me.

"Is he unconscious?"

"Yes," Tom said.

Lost in thought, Tom and John guided me to the library. We entered the lift, which took us deep into the earth to the chamber below. Slowly descending through bedrock, on the old-fashioned elevator built in 1701 with 1880s technology, my mind raced. The lift was old and slow, and despite the utmost of care and maintenance, prone to temperamental malfunction, not unlike myself. The lift stopped.

"The lift needs to be replaced, my Lord," Tom said.

"Replacing the lift would be like replacing me."

Silence. No motion. Tom and John pushed buttons and attempted to get the lift moving.

"It was just inspected and repaired, my Lord," John said.

Pondering the death of Henry, I realized I had never once walked the stairs from the Castle Library at the surface, down to the chamber.

"Tradition and ritual are of the utmost importance to the Order. Never forget, never destroy it. I wish to preserve this quaint relic, it is the legacy of my father, and of me."

Tom and John had words to break the awkward silence. Trapped in the cage in the middle of the mountain, I had an epiphany.

"Where is the staircase?" I asked.

"I beg your pardon, my Lord? What staircase?" Tom asked.

"The original staircase is carved parallel to the lift shaft, three meters north," John said, showing up Tom; ever in competition.

"When was this elevator shaft carved?"

"The elevator shaft was carved in the fifteenth century, and the first mechanical lift was installed in 1525," John replied. "The lift worked perfectly when David was brought in not thirty minutes ago."

"What else do you know about the stairs?" Tom's face asked the same of John.

"The staircase connects the Library to the Chamber. It has 365 steps that spiral down, one for each day of the year. There are several rituals associated with the steps, however I am not as familiar with them," John said. "The rituals are written in ancient Greek and rather opaque."

"Translate them. Familiarize yourself and put a report on my desk. I wish to take the stairs next time." The pain in my old joints hurt even as I said it.

"For what reason, my Lord?" Tom asked.

"Ritual." Tom's face showed he did not understand.

"Of course, my Lord. Next time we shall use the stairs to go down," John understood.

"Surely my Father used the stairs at least once, but I never have." Sadness dampened my words.

And just as I was about to give a long tired sigh of defeat, the lift began to move again. "As long as I am alive, the lift stays."

The lift descended again, slowly, squeaky at times, deep into the earth.

"I fear Darius will rip out this lift and put in an elevator. God save us." 'Tis all but certain. "Darius has no respect for ritual, or the past."

Tom and John never willingly touch the hazardous subject of Darius, the man soon to be their sovereign. I understood their position -- too afraid of Darius to ever speak ill of him. Darius weighed on my mind greatly; I shuttered at the thought of him as my king.

"We'll have the lift repaired again," Tom placated me.

Tom could not understand the reasoning for not replacing the decrepit old lift. John's face told me he agreed with me.

In this moment, their once identical ideas of the Order diverged. The lift stopped at the bottom. I exited with a heavy heart. We entered the *Chamber of Initiation...*

CHAPTER XXIII

"The Chamber changes you forever."

THE SCION

"Initiation into the Order is never truly complete," I said as my Father once told me. But to enter the *Chamber of Initiation,* the subterranean temple carved into the marble bedrock in the mountain below the castle, is step one of the journey. One of the Order's ancient secrets and most holy places, the space has been re-carved countless times before settling in the present iteration during the Renaissance. Created by the best sculptors of the day, the ornate statues speak stories of centuries past, the legacy, power, and pathos of the Order. "I'm re-initiated every time I enter this place."

"We are prepared for David's initiation ceremony, my Lord," the Order Guard said.

"Thank you." I entered the cavernous Chamber.

The Sacred Chamber served as the inspiration for a temple which inspired the Pantheon in Rome. A domed room filled with exquisite relief, stone portraits of great men and woman past, carved into multicolored grains of marble. "This underground temple is like no other place on Earth; a place that invokes magic, akin to being inside a scrying stone."

Tom and John had no response to my strange words and mood.

The carved faces, chiseled bodies, great gods and heroes of the past, cherubs, muses, warriors, sculpted flawlessly from one block of stone, looked and felt alive in a way I never noticed prior. "When you are open to them, and in tune, the chamber can conjure the spirits and wisdom of the past. In this sacred space the voices of my ancestors, the Pharaohs, Scions and heroes of old speak to me, and to all who are attuned to the ancient wisdom."

John heard. Tom did not. The statues whispered as we entered. The stone faces of my ancestors fell silent when gazed upon, hiding the fact they do speak. "Only those who know how to listen can hear the voices."

"David hears the voices already," the voice of my great-great grandfather said. His words and memory echoed in my mind.

"The statues in this Chamber can give you all the secrets of the universe. They have spoken to me since I first entered this sacred place." Tom and John looked around at the stone faces with me, as we never had before. "These voices of my ancestors, always give me the truth. The dead have no reason to lie."

Tom and John agreed. I had changed their perspective this day.

"My initiation in this Chamber changed my life."

"It certainly changed ours as well," John said. With Tom he left.

I sat on my throne and eagerly anticipated watching it change David, wondering what the whispers of the statues would say about him. Could he hear them?

The Order Guard brought David in, unconscious, dressed as are all new initiates he had the obligatory black bag over his head, clothed in a white linen shirt and pants. They placed him on a chair, in the exact center of the room, where all the statues give their most intense gaze.

"Wake him," I commanded from my throne.

They removed the black bag and awakened David with smelling salts. He sat up straight; eyes wide open. The guards backed away and waited behind him. David looked up to me on my golden seat of power. He scanned the circular room, noticing the guards behind him, examining the hundreds of marble faces eyeing him.

"There are always a good few moments when an initiate wonders if they are dreaming." David stared at me, unsure what to say. He waited for me to speak again. Order Guards, swords drawn, watched him closely. "Welcome, David. You're awakened."

David remained silent.

"Do you know who I am?"

"I do not," David said.

"My Lord!" the Guards pointed their swords at David.

"I do not, my Lord," David corrected himself.

"Leave us."

The Guards left, marching out formally. The doors behind them closed. David and I sat alone in silence.

"Think about it." I stared at him. *Who am I?*

"I've been experiencing memory problems," David said.

"He's perfect," the statues whispered. "His heart is true."

David heard the voices. *He knows the secrets.*

"I like him." The voices spoke to one another.

David searched the room for the source of the voices.

"He can hear us," they said.

"He is the one…" voices in ancient Greek echoed.

The statues all weighed in on David in a deafening clamor. David thought he was going crazy for a moment, hearing all these voices.

"I hear—I hear voices from the statues," David said.

"Only the pure of heart can hear the voices."

I saw revelation and relief come over David. He soaked in the room.

"What do they tell you?" I asked.

"You're the Scion," David said. "You are - the Pharaoh."

"I ought to be, but I am rather a fallen angel," I smiled. "I am Melchizedek XIII of Britannia, Scion of the Great House. I'm not so enlightened as to call myself *the* Pharaoh." If I did the statues would laugh and chastise me. "The truth is, I'm not entirely sure what it means to be Pharaoh."

David listened carefully to what was said in my silence.

"But you, David, you are everything I hoped you'd be. And I hear you've been searching for me."

"They told me you did not exist."

"And yet you knew the truth. You are an idealist, a dreamer. The truth you seek will save us all. You seek the Pharaoh…"

"Then you will know the truth, and the truth will set you free," David spoke the magic words of old.

"Indeed… You are not motivated by power or greed. You are motivated by… Love." I was simply channeling these words, a conduit for a voice that was not my own, I heard it as David did.

The word love resonated. Love echoed. Echoes became whispers. David and I both heard the whispers of gods and goddesses in the marble. The statues laughed and giggled as "love" tickled them.

"Where am I?" David said, glancing around.

"This is the Temple of Initiation. *The Chamber.*"

David began to truly understand what was happening.

"Henry has nominated you to replace him on my Privy Council. The Majestic Council of the Scion of the Pharaoh."

"Dear God…" David stopped, stunned.

"Let us begin!"

CHAPTER XXIV

"He'd been blind all your life, but then he saw."

THE SCION

The large doors to the underground Chamber swung open. My two Order Guards marched into the room, each delivered a tray. One tray with glass containers and a golden goblet, the other with a golden key-card and Henry's order ring. They set down the trays and promptly marched back out. The doors again sealed, the pageantry complete. David and I were again alone, with the voices of the statues.

"Shall we drink?" I motioned to the tray.

"What is it?" David asked.

"Part of the initiation ritual. The psychoactive ingredient is an extract from a very special flower, a strain and secret recipe passed down from the Pharaohs of Egypt. This tonic will help you remember. Said to help induce visions, the ancients used it to venture into the spirit world, the infinite mind, and bring back the answers to the questions they were seeking."

David approached me, intrigued.

"Initiation requires you to spend the night in the chamber. This tonic will make it an experience you shall never forget. 'Tis a rite of passage, a sacred rite, as old as the Order itself."

I mixed the liquids and powder into the goblet. The intoxicant fizzed and changed to a reddish color.

"The initiates of the Egyptian Priesthood would take this potion and spend the night in the pyramids. Or so I was told…"

David looked intrigued.

"Designed to open the mind, an enhance the effect of the initiation. Bitter in taste, but I assure you the effect is sweet. Come to me."

I took a sip of David's tonic. The mix was just right.

"The truth is, I wish I could initiate myself again. Oh to be young again, David. Unspoiled. Full of life and promise. Alas…" I handed the goblet to him. "Drink."

David took a sip. The effect of the potion was swift and strong, and I could see it on David's face. His pupils dilated almost instantly as the euphoria took him. David looked stunned.

"The magic happens only once, only for the first time." *Alas.* "Such is magic. I shall never forget my first time, a lucid frenzy of clarity and peace. I traveled to a place I never knew existed, to the infinite and back. I found the truth and I held it in my hands."

"I hear… many voices," David confessed to me.

"Good," I smiled. "That means 'tis working."

"This drink, is—" David looked dizzy. "This is something else…"

"How do you feel?"

David relaxed. The potion gave him confidence. He looked me in the eye and saw in me my hopes, dreams, and fears.

"The truth is powerful. It weighs on you," David said.

"Which is why we have secrets. To hide the truth."

"Secrets are power, and power corrupts," David said.

"The best resist the power of corruption. The Order seeks the best."

"Only with love of the truth does one have true power."

"And what is true power?" I asked him.

"Mastery of the divine within." David spoke the truth. "Seeing the truth inside ourselves gives us the power to hold the world on our shoulders. The truth is a flame, and the knowledge of fire is the gift of the gods. All humans, all souls, are the spark of this divine flame."

His words of wisdom hung in the air.

"Tell me about yourself, David."

David took another sip from the goblet. "I do not know myself, I'm afraid, my Lord. I know not who I am."

"What do you mean?"

"Do you know who my parents are?" David asked. "I must know."

"No." Darius came to mind. "I do not know," I said.

David sensed me holding back. His disappointment settled in as frost on the room. The chamber fell silent, not a peep from the statues.

"But I know who does," I offered hope. "Dee— Wisendee. He knows everything, and you shall meet him at the Council Meeting. Now. Tell me. What do you know about Henry?"

"Sir Henry erased my memory to protect the—" David stopped.

"The what? What was Henry searching for?"

David swallowed the last of the liquid and handed me the golden goblet.

"Good God... This is the Chalice of the Siwa Oracle. Given to Alexander the Great," David said eyeing the ornate craftsmanship of the golden cup. Even I did not know that.

"Tell me: Your colleague, Dr. Hans Danreich, what did he find in Egypt?"

"The Hall of Records, my Lord."

"The Hall of Records?" I asked.

"Said to be the holding place for all of the ancient knowledge of mankind... Most scholars say it's a myth."

"Is it a myth, David?"

"No, my Lord. The Hall is a secret. Henry, and Danreich, sacrificed themselves to find it," David said.

"Sacrifice is what transmutes men into gods."

David silently agreed.

"What did they find in the Hall of Records?"

In a trance, David spoke the words: "The Aton."

Deafening silence settled on the chamber.

"What is the Aton?"

"The greatest secret in the history of the world..." David said.

"What is it?" I begged. The voices begged with me in silence.

"The Aton is a Sacred Ark. A perfect diamond sphere, containing the blood of the first Pharaoh: holy blood."

"The Holy Grail?"

"He who holds the Aton is the Pharaoh, ruler of the Temporal realm under the sacred laws of *Æterni Imperium*," David channeled the words hypnotically, possessed by an angle of light.

"How?" I pressed. "Why?"

"The Aton is the Pharaoh; unlimited power," David said locking eyes with me, giving me his vision of infinite power.

"Where did the Aton come from?"

"It was created by the first Pharaoh. The first of the God-Kings manifested the Aton with the help of his council, in a Golden Age temple that no longer exists. They created it with their intention."

My mind raced. Whispers and dreams of ancient secrets bubbled up into my imagination. Memories sparked about what this meant.

I need to know everything about the Aton. "Where is the Aton now, David?" I demanded.

"I do not know, my Lord," David said.

"Can you find out?"

"Yes." David said the magic word I wanted to hear.

"Consider me your father, David. I have many sons, but you are the son I always wanted. You shall be my Sun, a new light in my dark world."

David thanked me without saying a word.

"You will go to Rome, David. You will meet the Vizier and comb the *Archivum*, the Secret Archives of the Order. Find out what you can about the Aton. I want to know everything about it. Most especially, where it is now."

Fully under the spell of the sacred potion, David had an epiphany, and I saw a sparkle in his eye.

"I would be honored, my Lord," David said.

"Henry was looking for the Aton. Finish Henry's work, David. Find the Aton for me."

"I shall find it, my Lord."

I placed Henry's Order ring on David's finger, and the golden key-card in his hand.

"There it is. Now then, time for your initiation."

I struck the sacred gong. The resonate tone vibrated and rang throughout the entire room. The sound of the vibrating metal made the potion take full effect on David. The small sip of potion I imbibed gave me slight synesthesia. For David, sound and sight fully blurred together and he fell to his knees overwhelmed, his soul uplifted by the ring in the air.

"Once I was blind, but now I see..." David looked up at me. "For all eternity," he said, repeating the words inlaid in gold on the floor in front of him.

I knighted him with my sword.

"Welcome to the Order, David."

CHAPTER XXV

"She too wanted to know everything."

SARAH

"One day you shall know my story, and all will make perfect sense..." Before he died, I heard Father's voice in a dream I'll never forget. "Sarah, think not of me as gone, my child. I am here. You need only speak, and I shall answer," he said. *I have passed.*

"I do not pretend to possess equal frankness with you, Father. You ask questions of me which I choose not to answer. How to respond I do not know, but I accept you now, fully, in my heart."

"Forgive me. Resolve to be with David, will you, my dear?"

"I have said no such thing, though that does not make it not so. Resolved I am to act in that manner which will, in my own opinion, constitute my family, my happiness, without reference to death or any person or Order so wholly unconnected with this love."

I see. I love you, my child. I know thee now completely.

Freed of worldly pressures, physical demands, and space and time, our souls embraced. I felt our hearts next to each other in a warm hug of bonded love. An experience too real, too visceral, to be a dream.

"Our bloodline has served the Sacred Order faithfully for over a thousand years," Father said, "I've always wanted to tell you, but our story is only now clear to me..."

"Can you tell me now?"

"Everything you want to know," he said, a twinkle in his eye.

With his eyes, he told me everything.

"You are a truly great man. Everything you did, you did for family."

"We all have a part to play in this world," he said. "Yours cannot be overstated enough. Your family, our family, must save the Order."

"I'm ashamed that I ever resented you," I said.

"Never be ashamed of your feelings," Father said.

"You were never absent in my life. But now you are pure presence, in my heart." I cried tears of joy and rapture.

"Sarah," David's trembling voice woke me.

"What's wrong?" David looked scared, confused, and panicked.

I felt the tears on my face and the physical pain of sadness.

"You already know," David said.

"Know what?"

"Something's happened. Last night — Danreich returned from Egypt," he gave me the news: "Your father is dead." David watched my reaction. "Danreich gave me a letter from him last night."

When I saw Father's ring on David's hand, I knew that the Order had tapped David in Henry's place.

"They've taken you," I said.

David's face confirmed it. I felt angry, and again robbed of joy. "The Order gave you David," Father's voice in my head.

"They've requested I go to Rome. That's all I can say."

"This life was supposed to be different." I watched David pack. "Who knows how long you'll be gone. I can't lose you too." I grabbed David and struggled to let go.

"I do not want to leave you alone," he held me.

Hormonal emotions took over. "I'm pregnant," I cried.

He looked at me. "I know," he said. "Remember?"

Tears of joy and sadness, loneliness and inner peace, ran together as we held each other close.

I can't let him go.

CHAPTER XXVI

"Dreams are the wishes of the heart."

DAVID

Entering the *Forum Sancti Petri*, I admired the beautiful red granite obelisk at its center. A Cardinal, an old Italian man with a stern face wearing all black, approached me. He noticed the ring on my finger. He turned and admired the obelisk with me.

"This obelisk is one of the most treasured in the world; the only ancient obelisk in Rome to have never been toppled."

"It was created on the instructions of Cleopatra, and was said to have originally contained the ashes of Julius Caesar, which she personally placed in a bronze orb and fixed atop it."

"This obelisk was created by an unknown Pharaoh, erected in Alexandria by Augustus, and was indeed prized by Caesars, yes. Since the Renaissance, it has stood in this very place, now the centerpiece of the sundial, and the entrance to the Holy See…"

"I see I'm right on time." The shadow of the sundial strikes the magic hour. Bells toll.

"Sir David Peterson. Welcome."

"Yes." He needed me to confirm what he already knew.

"Follow me. I will take you to His Eminence."

The Cardinal escorted me across the Vatican City grounds, and through the gardens. Two Swiss Guards in special distinguishing regalia and dress flanked us as we walked slowly through the classical Greek and Roman inspired buildings. The plaque on the door read: *L'Ufficio dei Praepositus Archivum.*

The doors opened. The Vizier sat at his desk, waiting for me. Hair silver white, warm eyes and face, and his powerful presence of wisdom gave him an aura of brilliant white light.

The wizardly Vizier took his time before speaking. He walked closer, staring deep into me. I fell under his spell, warmed by the radiation of his being. I held my breath as he weighed my heart against the feather of truth, and examined my soul for flaws and divine clarity. His eyes cut away all my sense of self, leaving only the glittering gem of human perfection which I should strive to become.

"Welcome, Sir David Peterson."

He noticed my Order ring, Henry's ring.

"Welcome to the Majestic Council of the Privy, Sir David."

"I am truly humbled, your Grace."

"May God have mercy on your soul, for the Council will not," he said. His words were honest and true. "But I will help you, all that I am able."

He did not speak the words, but I heard his voice say them: *You are here about the Aton...*

Strangely, I could *see* the Aton in him...

"Do not speak of the Aton. Not here. Not now," Henry's voice spoke to me, for the Vizier... *Do not speak of the Aton.*

"As a member of the Privy Council, you may be given the secret of the *Archivum*," his glowing Eminence began, as he led me out of the building, across the gardens, to the Vatican Secret Archives.

"The *Archivum* is the archive of the Order, the oldest collection of ancient artifacts and knowledge in the world... and known history."

Lost deep in thought and yet fully engaged, I listened intently as he spoke.

"The *Archivum* was ordered built in 1599 by the Scion, Melchizedek III," he said. "The ancient Archive of the Order was split into three parts. Two parts are known to the world. The third, the *Archivum Absconditum,* is not. The *Archivum* is one of the Order's most closely guarded secrets, for it holds all others untold."

"I see." I took it all in. He watched me thinking about the Aton. We approached the golden doors of the entrance. Surrounded by carved scenes of death, danger, suffering, devils, and demonic beings struck fear and terror in me. *Inside these ancient archives, live the hallowed secrets of the Pharaohs. And herein with the angels of divine wisdom, terrible evils lurk and pray upon human souls...*

"Insert your golden key-card there," the Vizier said, pointing to the slot. The golden doors opened.

"Be mindful, Sir David," the Vizier cautioned. *Be careful.*

"Be warned," the carved and painted devils spoke and began to move — *Not all souls who enter this place are able to escape...*

"This way, Sir David..." the Vizier caught me afraid and lost in thought staring at the art.

The timeless energy in the Order's Secret Archive has an ancient and futuristic vibe that is difficult to describe. Built on the site of an ancient temple, which itself was several thousand years old, we descended into the ultra secure bunker, a controlled environment, deep below Rome. Following a vaulted hall, the Vizier led me to a large circular room, with a round table at its center. On the table was a *codex gigas*, a gigantic book larger than any I had ever seen. Under closer examination I see that it is very old, handmade with a perfect silk binding and silk-enhanced paper, made to last forever. "This is the most fantastic manuscript I've ever seen... *This is the writings of the Pharaoh*—

"This is *Ordo Libro*," the Vizier said. "*Inter Vivos Fiducia Æterni*, the living testamentary Trust of the Order. Bound in the hide of a sacred bull, this word of the gods, this codex, *is* the Order."

I took it all in. My mind raced at all the wisdom this illuminated manuscript contains. "The record of the Order..."

"Created almost two thousand years ago, written and assembled by an elite school of scribes in the Library of Alexandria, the codex is a compilation, a collaboration, of the oldest and most sacred records of human civilization, wisdom from all ages, meticulously transcribed and illuminated on the pages with colors and gold, for the Pharaohs to read for centuries to come. Only the *Pontifex Maxiumus* and *Regis Maximus* may write in *Ordo Libro*, for the book is the Letters Patent of the Holy Scion, the *Regis Bull*, and official ruling document of *Æterni Imperium*. Everything written in the book becomes Order Law, because this holy book is the Order's sacred word and law."

"Incredible," saying the word to describe the book before me felt like calling the universe big; wholly inadequate on so many levels.

The Vizier opened the book.

"Testament of the Pharaohs, this sacred text is the will of the gods upon mankind. *The Book* is the amalgamation of the Pharaohs' most important ancient texts and congregated wisdom of all ages, into one volume, held in my charge, as the Scion's High Priest and royal Vizier."

"You are the keeper of the records."

The Vizier nodded yes as a teacher to a student.

"None whose name is not recorded in the book may read it, or enter this room, its temple, the *Absconditum Archivum*."

The Vizier opened the book to the last entry. There was my name written in the book. My initiation into the Privy Council and grant of title as 'Supreme Illuminated Regality' recorded and permanent. My heart beat out of my chest, sending me into an out of body experience; a dream come true...

"Permission has been granted, Sir David."

There are no words.

"Know thyself, David, know your soul and know all."

Guided by the Vizier, my eyes followed his, to the letters on the wall. The words spoke to me.

"*Demon est Deus inversus*," the Vizier said reading the words out loud. His god-like voice vibrating the stone walls.

"The devil is God inversed."

"The demon is the opposite of the truth, Sir David," the Vizier corrected me. "Seek the truth, and fear only the demon."

"How shall I find the truth, your Grace?"

The Aton appeared, like a dream, hovering over our thoughts.

"People can give you secrets, but the truth must be found by oneself. I cannot give you the answers. The truth you seek, is a path up the mountain. I can show you the direction, and prepare you to climb, but you must walk yourself. You must find the path yourself. God speed."

The Vizier vanished with the Aton.

Left alone with the book, I examined the bindings, the leather, the pages, and the flawless penmanship. Sheer perfection. Not an error or drop of ink spilt. The divinely inspired art on the pages, gold illuminations and colors un-faded by the passage of thousands of years, defied my senses. *How can this be real?*

I read down the list of names, past Henry's, and down to my own.

Is this a dream?

Dare I turn the page?

Read from the book...

CHAPTER XXVII

"Alexander created the Order?"

WISENDEE

The cryptic revelations which David unfolded in the magic words of the *Ordo Libro* text were prophetic, and therefore, for him, truly divine; they included and alluded to the greatest teachings of all mankind and all time. Some Scions wrote in the book and believed that the first Pharaoh had not willed that humanity should understand the deep mystery of his own destiny, but yet wrote these immortal words: *There be nothing concealed that shall not be revealed; there exists no thing hidden that shall not, or may not, be made known to thee.*

This, reading most true to David, let him take up the labor of solving, unveiling, and reconstructing the purpose of this life, his life and time. Following in the footsteps of the illumined Scions of old, he too felt he shall discover truth, by following the winding stairway up to that which the seekers of truth of all ages have climbed.

David carefully turned and read the pages of the massive 'Book of the Order.' He wanted to see every page, and have it forever in his memory. The ancient Egyptian hieroglyphic Alexander story began:

"The Sacred Order of the Almighty Pharaohs began in Egypt, wherefrom the darkness of chaos came the light of order, by the word of the one true God. From the heavens to the Earth, this Holy text is the word of God, his Eternal Trust, written at the behest of his earthly incarnations, as the will of the Pharaohs, beginning in this first year of our Lord-god, the Holy Pharaoh, Alexander the Great…"

Alexander the Great created the Order as we know it.

The Oracle of the Sun-god, Amun-Ra, declared Alexander the living incarnation of Zeus the Almighty, and rightful Pharaoh of Egypt. The Egyptian Priesthood in Memphis crowned him *Megas Basileus*, Great King, "Alexander the Great," Sovereign ruler of the world of Man… The elaborate initiation ceremony culminated in the Great pyramid, where Alexander spent the night. The next morning he rose with the Sun, as the Sun-King, on the summer Solstice, and a great festival celebrated the occasion. A new Pharaoh, a New Order of the Ages was at hand...

With the gods on his side, Alexander the Great took Babylon and defeated the ruler of the mighty Achaemenid Empire, King Artashata also known as Darius III of Persia. On the throne of mighty Persia, at the age of twenty-five, the Council of the Magi declared Alexander 'ruler of all the world, a god-king to all humanity, for all eternity'...

"The *Majestic Council of the Pharaoh* as we know it today, manifested and was created in Babylon."

Alexander and his Council solidified control of the largest empire the world had ever seen, uniting peoples of the East and West. God-King Alexander then ordered a gathering of all the wisest and best minds of the world, to the Royal court of Babylon. They initiated a five year symposium to determine and create the framework for an ideal and immortal state. The creation of the *Ordo Libro* began, and the Court of the Pharaoh changed the idea of government forever.

The Council published the *Rex Publica*, a government constitution of 'Sacred Law,' based on the works of all the greatest philosophers of old. From the *Rex Publica* came 'The Divine Rite of Kings,' and 'The Republic,' and most of our modern concepts of civil law, and the principals of ruling with truth and justice.

"By the stroke of the Pharaoh Alexander's hand, the Order as we know it was born... Alexander created the Order."

David touched and read this original parchment document, signed by Alexander, now bound into the 'codex gigas' of *Ordo Libro.*

"In Babylon, the *Majestic Council* created Pharaoh Alexander's living will and testamentary instrument. A declaration constitution, claiming all the world, dominion over every human soul, under a sole hereditary crown, which became known as 'The Eternal Government of Man'; in Latin *Æterni Imperium.*"

David read the text of *Æterni Imperium.*

What is Æterni Imperium, Master Dee?

"For the last five hundred years, most have called *Æterni Imperium* simply: 'The Order.'"

The Sacred Order governs all the souls of mankind.

CHAPTER XXVIII

"The Order governs all the souls of mankind?"

WISENDEE

In theory, and in the realm of the ethereal, the Order possess every human soul... Because every human soul is an indistinguishable part of the One, the God, and the Aton... The Order is charged with maintaining order in all the worlds of man.

"In the light of the Pharos, the Egyptian and Greek schools merged, and the history of the Pharaohs was written into this book..." David read the story of Alexander's mother, Olympias.

The Egyptian Priesthood, the keepers of the Sacred Order, had chosen her to carry on the Pharaoh's dynasty...

In the years just before Alexander the Great was born, the last of the "descendants of Zeus," the native line of the rulers of Egypt, Scion of Pharaohs, Nectanebo II watched his family be killed and was forced to flee his kingdom by Darius' invasion and conquest of Egypt. Conquered and defeated by Darius III of Persia, the Great House of the Pharaoh of Egypt was all but destroyed. Nectanebo II and his privy of Magi sailed to Greece with a plan to free Egypt from its Persian conquerors.

Brilliant wizard, and illuinated Magi, Nectanebo II came to Olympias in a well-orchestrated magical ritual ceremony, with drugs, music, and dancing, presented himself to her as Zeus, king of the gods. "Zeus has chosen you," they told Olympias. Covered in gold dust, and wearing a golden mask, he impregnated Olympias, to unite the houses of the Hellenes and Egyptians once more.

In the guise of a court magician, Pharaoh Nectanebo II, and his *Majestic Council,* told King Philip and Queen Olympias: "You will give birth to a great king, and he shall have the markings of divinity." Months later, Olympias gave birth to the child who would become:

Alexander the Great.

When her child, Alexander III, was born with heterochromia, one golden hazel eye and one striking blue eye, it was deemed to have been proof of the prophet's words to Olympias and the Court.

"Your child shall defeat the Persian empire and unite the peoples of East and West, the entire world, into one empire," the prophet told Olympias. The Court of the Pharaoh saw to it that this prophecy was fulfilled. The Egyptian Priesthood helped Alexander become Pharaoh, so Alexander could help Egypt once again be free...

High level initiate of the ancient Egyptian Mystery Schools, Olympias was a queen, a learned woman, who knew the legends of Egypt, and the powers of the Pharaoh. She helped Nectanebo II save from ruin the Great House.

The Court of the Pharaoh used its vast network of spies, merchants, and traders of wisdom, the original intelligence networks of the ancient world, to help Alexander defeat Darius III and unite Persia and the East with the Greek colonies of the West.

Undefeated in battle, Alexander did just that; he united the East and the West, and they declared him Pharaoh of all the world. Alexander's Court ordered built the very foundations of modern civilization, and created texts we still use today. They created a global economy, establishing commerce with sea faring trade routes from the Greek colonies to India. Paving the silk road to China, sponsoring voyages to the Americas, around and about Africa, conveying and collecting knowledge across the globe, Alexander ended hundreds of years of cross-cultural aggression and changed the Great House of the Pharaoh, and the world, forever.

"Alexander recreated the Order of the Pharaoh..." David read.

"The 'High Council and Court of the Pharaoh' has met annually ever since, with the minutes recorded into the book, for over two thousand years..." David perused centuries of minutes, in seconds.

After the conspiratorial death of the Pharaoh Alexander at the age of thirty-three, Babylon had fallen. Alexander's half-brother, close friend and high Councilor, Ptolemy I, arranged for the body of Alexander to be brought to Memphis in secret. Alexander's dying wish was to be mummified and buried with the Pharaohs in Egypt. The *Majestic Council* shared this wish.

In the chaos surrounding the murder of the Pharaoh, the *Majestic Council* elected Ptolemy I as the Order's temporary Leader and regent to Alexander's infant son: Alexander IV of Babylonia. Born of the

Roxanne of Bactria-Persia, the infant Scion of the Pharaoh and Queen Mother were hidden from the squabbling factions of the fracturing empire, by Ptolemy and Alexander's mother. After faking their deaths in Macedonia, holy Mother and child found safety in Egypt.

With the body of the Pharaoh, and the security of the Holy Scion, Ptolemy won over the peoples and priests of Egypt. In the aftermath of Alexander's untimely death, and the seeming dissolution of Pharaoh's empire in Babylon, the Majestic Court of the Pharaoh relocated to Egypt. Under the leadership of King Ptolemy I, the *Majestic Council* coalesced in its ancient home, bringing most of the texts that now comprise *Ordo Libro* with them.

Hellenism rose from the ashes of Alexander's death as a Phoenix; its mighty wings spread the proliferation of new ideas of government, science, and art, which soared to new heights, and lifted all mankind. From inside Egypt, a land now liberated, protected, and stable, the house of the Pharaoh truly began anew. The *Majestic Council* merged into the Egyptian Priesthood, and the New Order for the Ages began.

Ptolemy I took Alexander's heir as his own, and with the help of the illuminated Magi, the 'Serapis Wizard Council of the Pharaoh,' built Alexandria – the utopian city Alexander envisioned, and founded as Pharaoh, on the Mediterranean coast of Egypt. The master planned metropolis of Alexandria instantly rose to prominence, attracting the brightest minds of the world to its 'Institution of the Muses,' and wonderful, legendary, Museum and Library of Alexandria.

In Alexandria, the Court of the Pharaoh once again taught and learned to tap into the divine source of wisdom inside, the secrets of the mind; the sacred flame that illuminates all darkness. They used science to study magical arts and created a new, more enlightened, civilization. The city of Alexandria became the light of the world, and built a symbol, a monument, to this light, the Pharos Lighthouse.

Wonder of the ancient world, the Pharos Lighthouse of Alexandria was truly a vision to behold. Sailors could see the light of the Pharos from beyond the curvature of the Earth. Over forty stories tall, the ancient skyscraper made of cement, stone, and metal, adorned with bronze statues, guarded Alexandria's glorious harbor. Designed and built by the greatest minds of the day, the great 'House of the Light' in Alexandria was meant to literally and symbolically illuminate the world with its wisdom.

And so it did...

CHAPTER XXIX

"Tell me about the Library of Alexandria."

DAVID

Reading from the great *Book of the Order* changed me.

"The Pharaohs long understood that wisdom is power. The peculiar mind that turns knowledge and understanding into wisdom is powerful, but only in the perfection of the heart, in true love, is the mind all powerful. In Alexandria they sought this united perfection."

Come with me, I shall take you there...

I found myself there, back in time, basking in the light of Pharos, in ancient Alexandria. I explored the accumulation of texts, machines, and marvels gathered up by the conquests of Alexander the Great, at the center of the world's greatest collection of knowledge; the Library and *Musaeum of Alexandria.*

"The Pharaoh's Court sent out an unending clarion call to the ends of the earth for all philosophers, wizards, craftsmen, engineers, and artists. Join us. And so they did. Flora and fauna was plucked, gathered, and cataloged from every part of the world to be studied, and the qualities they possessed documented and utilized. At its peak, the Library archives housed an unmatched collection of books and artworks from nearly every civilization in the world. Out of the shadows of history came the answers to mysteries of alchemy, know-ledge of electricity, and the long lost secrets of the civilizations of prehistory; the legends of *Atlantis*, and the *Aton Stone Tablets*..."

I found a reference. *The Aton Stone Tablets.* They knew of them. But in my excitement I found myself trapped in the magical past.

"Driven by a desire for the highest arts and sciences possible, we shall unlock the secrets of nature, and fire," they said.

I watched as years flew by, and they built foundries and explored metallurgy; with metal and glass they made machines and tools, which allowed for precise measurements, manufactured chemicals, vibrant colors, science and art as never seen before...

The art, technologies, and firepower Pharaoh's Court created were spellbinding magic to the uninitiated. Yet for all the advancements Alexandria made, the Pharaoh's Court, the *Majestic Council*, knew: "This is but a taste of what is possible in the new Order of the Pharaoh." These ancient sages saw me, my astral body, as they saw what the future held for humanity.

In Alexandria they foresaw, they knew, what the magic of *techne*-science could do. In the Library they tapped into this "unlimited potential of the human mind and humankind."

The Egyptian Priesthood merged the Pharonic bloodlines in Memphis with the Ptolemaic royal family in Alexandria. And in the Library they complied the complete history of the Pharaohs, recording it, binding it, for all eternity, into the *Book of the Order...*

Within the Egyptian Priesthood and the Serapis Cult, the *Majestic Council* ruled and guarded the Library of Alexandria, and drew from it the wisest, most powerful, men and women in the world. A think-tank, research institution, archive, and university all in one, the *Musaeum of Alexandria* desired human perfection, and immortality. They sought to understand the universe, and enlighten the world with ever brighter light. In reverence for nature, the keepers of the Library developed a holistic approach to love and life. Balance and adherence to natural law was seen as essential to maintaining order.

Dualistically some in Alexandria explored the dark arts, the art of war and death, and in seeking defense of their realm, created weapons of mass destruction, explosives, and *Greek fire...*

In the Library of Alexandria they studied everything we consider important today. The scholars and explorers of Alexandria assembled a complete map of the world from copied notes gathered from visitors to Alexandria who had ventured from every corner of the globe.

In the study of sacred geometry, aesthetically attuned Alexandrians tapped into the universal, unquantifiable lore and magic of beauty. "The beauty and simplicity of nature is divine." Beauty signified divinity in the ancient Egypt and Greek cultures, and with brains and brawn the Pharaoh's Court bred for it. They manufactured cosmetics and perfumes, products from the finest natural materials, and created legendary showmanship. I saw it, "the pageantry of the Pharaohs will never again see its equal."

The necessity of trade for raw materials meant the Pharaoh's Court had to develop schools of economics, and learn how to create and grow wealth with equitable exchange activity. In the schools of Alexandria they created the basis for the modern banking system, with the original noble goal of fostering eudaemonia; human flourishing, growth, and mutual prosperity for all mankind. By keeping careful record books in the Library, they learned that expanding commerce demanded increasingly complex negotiations, and diplomatic relations, an international system of justice. In the Court of the Pharaoh they developed the idea of Rule of Law.

Here, I stood and watched the debates in the Library lecture halls...
I saw the living Goddess enter, she was magnificent to behold.

"Cleopatra, living Isis the Goddess of Love, had a vision to unite the world, the East of Persia, India, and China, with the West, the Roman Empire of Spain, Gaul, Britannia, and the lands beyond. Cleopatra saw herself in the mold of Alexander the Great, a true heir of the Pharaoh, she saw it as her destiny and mission to unite the world under one global order, one crown, one 'Republic of Truth and Justice,'" I read from *Ordo Libro,* seeing her speak words of wisdom.

"All is fair in love and war, but war against love is not a fair fight," Cleopatra said. "For Love always wins."

Cleopatra looked at me, she saw my soul, and I felt the awesome power of the Pharaoh. My astral projection was shocked back into physicality, and, upon landing back in my body, I fell to the stone floor of the Secret Archives, eyes wide open, in awe.

CHAPTER XXX

"Who was Cleopatra?"

WISENDEE

There is often greater martyrdom to live for the love of something, be that a person or an ideal, than to die for that same thing. Cleopatra lived for Love; she lived for the love of Alexandria, until she could sacrifice no more than her life.

"Without Love, love of wisdom and balance, knowledge and power corrupts and destroys. The Library of Alexandria became the center of human knowledge, and the heart of the most powerful empire in the world... Love is all that kept the flames of power from burning to their own destruction. When the love was lost, the battle for the soul of the Republic caused the library to be destroyed."

David closed his eyes and saw the fire burning the library. The loss of the library was almost too much to fathom. Opening his eyes in horror, he returned to reading about Cleopatra from the book.

Pharaoh Cleopatra's life was a turning point for the Order, and she changed the world forever...

The *Majestic Council,* in Memphis, maintained the birth records and kept the Pharaonic bloodline unbroken since Alexander the Great. For centuries they arranged unions to breed for the wisest and best. When the handsome half-blood King of Alexandria, Ptolemy XII, "Auletes," married Egypt's most regal Holy Scion, a direct descent of Alexander the Great, and living incarnation of Isis-Aphrodite, Cleopatra VI of Memphis. The marriage gave birth to one of the greatest humans that ever lived, the fantastically fair, exceptionally brilliant, Pharaoh and true *Philosopher Queen*, Cleopatra VII of Alexandria.

Much like Alexander III, 'Cleopatra the Great' initiated a rebirth and expansion of the Great House. And for a time, in her union with Julius Caesar, she united an empire to rival that of Alexander himself.

Cleopatra spoke ten languages, had encyclopedic knowledge of six religions, and was a gifted doctor, prolific writer, and incredible performer. She redefined what it meant to be the Pharaoh. Cleopatra made the light of Pharos brighter, and used the knowledge and power of her House in glorious displays of wonder none had ever seen or conceived of before. Her creativity and genius transformed Rome into the vision of greatness it became.

Cleopatra was a visionary leader like none before. Her epic ego united an empire; her unbridled passions drove and inspired men to greatness. She changed the course of history, the Order, and human civilization forever. Cleopatra sought to unify the world, beginning with the two great Hellenic houses of Rome and Alexandria. Her lust for power, and philosophic ideals of the perfect state, spurred her to transform Rome into the legacy of the Pharaoh, a "New Alexandria." Cleopatra personally wove and bound together the cultural, political, and economic ties between Rome and Alexandria, unwittingly sowing her own undoing.

As with Alexander the Great, the cost of forging a great empire is the ultimate price. Merging Alexandria's Crown with Rome's Republic brought civil war into the Great House, and sadly the beginning of the end for fair Alexandria. Uniting Rome and Alexandria cost Cleopatra her life, and nearly destroyed the Order.

Julius Caesar's death was the turning point for Cleopatra.

A noble Roman General, Julius Caesar idolized and worshiped Alexander the Great, whose military genius he envied, and whose legacy he so desired to emulate. Julius Caesar longed to meet Alexander's heir, the mysterious goddess, Cleopatra… And the gods conspired to grant his wish.

Behind the scenes, the *Majestic Council* orchestrated the breakdown of the second Triumvirate, and lit the fire of the 'Great Roman Civil War' of 49 BC., with a plan to free themselves from Rome's imperial power. Cleopatra lured Caesar to Alexandria, where he fell instantly in love with the living Aphrodite. Caesar had not the faculty to resist Cleopatra's divine beauty. Her magical charm, and elucidated vision for a new Roman Empire, instantly bonded them and solidified an alliance between them, casting a love spell over Caesar forever.

Unfortunately for Cleopatra, most in Rome did not share her vision of a united empire, and a new Order. The dramatic battle for control of Alexander's imperium played out on the stage of Egypt. A fragile theater for war, the enemies of Cleopatra and Caesar destroyed much of Alexandria; as the Roman civil war between Caesar and the Roman Senate, led by Pompey the Great, collided violently into the

Alexandrian civil war, the battle between Cleopatra and her brother Ptolemy XIII. In the closing act of the war, the final battle, Cleopatra sat holed up atop the Lighthouse, crying in searing pain, in the arms of Caesar. Part of her died as she watched helpless, horrified, as the great Library burned. Storied collections of priceless manuscripts went up in flames, sacrificed to the gods of war, lost forever.

When the dust of civil strife settled, Cleopatra and Caesar had won. Cleopatra decided to rebuild the legacy of the Great House with Caesar, in Rome. They married in an elaborate ceremony, and sealed their union with a child.

"Cleopatra's child with Caesar would also become a Pharaoh unlike any other. He would fulfill Cleopatra's vision, and shape the Order into the final form it became in modern times. He became a secret; the greatest pharaoh the world has never known..."

Who was he, Master Dee?

"Alexander Caesar Ptolemy XV of Alexandria."

After the war, Caesar remained in Egypt with Cleopatra, wishing to remain with her from conception to birth. When Cleopatra gave birth, Caesar was there. The child was a boy, who looked like Caesar, and became known as Caesarion, "Little Caesar." Caesar did not have a male heir with his politically arranged Roman wife. Upon return home, he arranged for Cleopatra and his son to join him in Rome. Cleopatra brought the *Majestic Council*, and plans for the new empire with her...

Cleopatra gave Rome unfettered access to the vast wisdom and wealth of Alexandria. Cleopatra's army of architects, engineers, scholars, and artisans transformed Rome from a dusty city of mostly mud bricks into a marble metropolis, flowing with water, in the mold of Alexandria. With the *Majestic Council*, Caesar enacted "The Republic of the Eternal Government," and formulated in Latin the legal construct of Cleopatra's new Order: *Æterni Imperium*. The massive public works projects and empire building agenda Cleopatra initiated continued for centuries after her death, all across Europe.

Rome was to be the new Alexandria, Caesar the *Pontifex Maxiumus* to the *Regis Maximus* Philosopher Queen, Pharaoh Cleopatra.

The conservative aristocracy of the Roman Republic refused to accept Caesar as their "King." But most accepted Cleopatra as their Goddess-Queen. However, the Optimates of the Roman Senate were not about to allow Cleopatra's child with Caesar to be made Emperor of the united, and seemingly all powerful, "Roman Empire."

"Rome has no king!" They protested. "Caesar means to destroy the Republic! He'll disband the Senate," the arguments went.

"Caesar must be eliminated," the Optimates decided. "It is our solemn duty to protect and defend the Republic from any tyrant!"

The Senate had a history of killing dictators, claiming an obligation to protect Rome from a "king." A faction of the *Majestic Council* knew of the plan to kill Caesar, and assisted in the murder of Caesar, as part of the plan to return the Great House to Egypt. Caesar was stabbed to death in the Senate, on the Ides of March 44 BC.

Caesar's murder sent a shock wave ripping through the ancient world. His death reignited the fires of civil war, which soon burned the legacy of Cleopatra in Rome to ashes; it created a schism in the Great House, and the *Majestic Council,* which lasted for millennia.

In an elaborate ceremony lead by Cleopatra, the living Isis, she ordained Caesar as her counterpart, 'Osiris, Lord of Love, son of Amun-Ra, god of the afterlife, merciful the judge of the dead.' Caesar was declared "a god to all the world." Cleopatra became the full incarnation of Isis, wife of Osiris, and Caesarion completed the holy trinity as the Horus. With pomp and pageantry so grand in scale, no one in Rome ever forgot or doubted the apotheosis of Caesar, and none could deny the Caesarion was "the son of the god."

Cleopatra wasted no time in ordering her network of assassins to hunt and kill every assailant who took a stab at Caesar. Prominent Roman Senators were killed. The Roman elite did not anticipate Cleopatra's retaliation for Caesar's murder and failed to see the power of the Pharaoh until it was turned on them. Two members of the *Majestic Council* were eventually killed in Rome, and the *Council* broke in two, half of it siding with Rome and the Roman aristocracy, the other half with Egypt, Cleopatra, and Caesarion.

The bad blood between Rome and Egypt lasted for centuries, furthering the desire of the Roman Senate to have Alexandria and Egypt, and everything that gives the Pharaoh power, removed from Egypt or destroyed once and for all.

The split of the *Majestic Council* forced Cleopatra and Caesarion to return to Alexandria, as was the plan of Rome's faction all along. With the Pharaoh, the *Book of the Order* was finally brought back to Egypt…

CHAPTER XXXI

"What happened to Caesarion?"

WISENDEE

David read in the *Ordo Libro* how Rome set about to invent its own religion. However, no religion is higher than truth; Love is truth; God is truth; and the truth was that Cleopatra's love child was the heir to the god of Rome, Caesar, and the one Majestic Throne.

Ptolemy XV Caesar of Rome, the "Little Caesar," inherited the title *Regis Maximus* under *Æterni Imperium.* Declared "Son of God, King of Kings," and the rightful Imperator of Alexander's empire by the Hellenistic ecclesiarchy, he was, indisputably, Scion of the Pharaoh. But the Roman aristocracy refused to let a woman, a "Queen from the East," and her child take control of the newly united and inspired Roman Republic, and the global empire 'twas building...

A year and a half after Caesar's death, Cleopatra left Rome, never to return. Rome ordered all records of *Æterni Imperium* and Cleopatra burned, and erased from history. The Roman Senate and the *Majestic* who sided with Rome created a will for Caesar, naming his nephew Octavian as his heir. A young man they could control, they groomed Octavian and made him into Augustus, the future Emperor of Rome.

Caesar's death cleaved in two the Roman Empire and *Majestic Council,* and both sides foresaw that war for unity was inevitable. There could be no true peace until the Order of the empire was restored. "The Pharaoh built Rome!" the scholars of Alexandria said. "Without us, without our wisdom, Rome shall wither and die."

The Senate beat the drum that the Pharaoh, Cleopatra and Caesarion must be eliminated. "Egypt will destroy Rome!" the Senators argued. The *Majestic* knew the opposite was true. Rome must destroy Egypt to survive, for in Egypt rests a power so great none dare speak of it.

"The Pharaohs have a secret weapon, a mythical, all powerful weapon," the turned *Majestic* warned Rome. "'Tis hidden in Egypt."

"What is this weapon?" Cleopatra asked *Majestic* Sosigenes.

"The Aton," Sosigenes replied. He told her the story of the Aton.

"The secret of the Aton was handed down from the beginning of our civilization. Carved in stone, the *Aton Stone Tablets* are inscribed with these most important and all powerful secrets of the Pharaoh. Holder of the Aton is the Pharaoh, and ruler of all the world..."

"We must find it before Rome does," Cleopatra said.

"Rome shall never find it," Sosigenes assured her. "And we must not disturb it, lest we alert them to its whereabouts."

Rome wanted the Aton found, and Caesarion dead. But the better half of the *Majestic* prevented both.

The Roman Senate needed the wealth of Egypt to fund the massive building projects planned under Cleopatra and Caesar. And with history books being written in Alexandria, they had to control the narrative, and expunge *Æterni Imperium* from history. Unless Rome controlled the records, their version of history, their empire, would not last the generation. The Senate and Roman *Majestic* carefully manufactured the ascendency of Caesar Augustus, and the smear campaign against Cleopatra. Rome prepared to invade Egypt.

Word of Rome's plans found their way to the Court of the Pharaoh, and Cleopatra prepared for the Roman invasion. Cleopatra planned to stay in Egypt. "I am Egypt," she said. If Egypt fell she planned to die in Egypt, forever with her kingdom by suicidal regicide. For the new Pharaoh, arrangements were made for a new beginning outside the reach of Rome.

"The young Pharaoh Scion must leave Egypt," Sosigenes said. The *Majestic Council* sent Caesarion to India, with all the most valuable treasures and secret texts of the Pharaoh, including the *Book of the Order* and the *Aton Stone Tablets*.

At the age of thirteen, during his flight from Egypt, remembering his flight from Rome after the death of his father, Caesarion took charge of the Great House. Ready to change the world, and become a Pharaoh in his own right, Caesarion became one of the great ones...

Though history records the execution of Caesarion not long after Rome's invasion of Egypt, this fiction was a meticulously planned cover-up, orchestrated by the *Majestic*. The agents of the Pharaoh are true masters of deception, and though doubtful of his death, the *Majestic* in Rome happily accepted and recorded Caesarion's death as fact. The house of the Pharaoh, and many of the oldest and wisest men and women on earth, went underground and vanished into the shadows of history. The *Majestic Council* aided Rome's efforts to erase all evidence of the Pharaoh and the Order's existence.

In India, Pharaoh's Court reimagined and merged with the *Sanātana Dharma*, the Vedic 'eternal order' of the wise men of the Indus civilization. They declared Caesarion the Kalki, their divine Savior-king, ruler of all mankind.

In Asia, Caesarion built temples, schools, and a new empire, one of Peace and Wisdom. His experience with Rome instilled in him a disdain for war and violence. Pharaoh Caesarion wanted peace above all. He traveled the world, extending his reach and influence to Russia, Tibet, China, Japan, and the Americas.

Centuries ahead of every other human civilization in technological ability, Pharaoh's designers and engineers built flying machines, engines, navigation devices, clocks, light bulbs, and radios over a thousand years before they would appear in recorded history. Caesarion visited all the world's royal courts and sacred sites outside of the Mediterranean region, meeting spiritual leaders and rulers. The 'Illuminated One,' Caesarion, and his court of Ascended Masters and Mahatmas, invigorated schools of secret knowledge all over the world. He created religious centers, established new temples, and built institutions of higher learning elevating all of humankind.

At one hundred years of age, the living-god Caesarion had become a secret known only to the highest level initiates of the Pharaonic Mystery Schools. With his *Majestic Council,* he became more powerful technologically, and more enlightened spiritually, than any previous Pharaoh since the cataclysm. Caesarion became the true Philosopher King, the wisest of men, and the divine leader of humanity. As Scion, he set a new precedent, and codified a new mandate for all future rulers of the Order:

"Henceforth and forevermore, the existence of the Pharaoh, the Great House, and the High Council of Magi shall be a secret of the highest Order, nonexistent to the uninitiated mind, known only to the illuminated ones."

Within two centuries of this decree, all the world's brightest minds and centers of learning were under Caesarion's control. They effectively kept Rome, the history books, and the masses completely unaware of 'The Order of the Pharaoh,' *Æterni Imperium*, ever after.

Caesarion spawned thousands of children, with queens and princesses of every race and creed the world over. Disguised as Zeus,

Vishnu, Horus, or a created local deity, he fornicated and procreated fruitfully, encouraged by his Council to greatly expand the bloodline. Caesarion's Court spawned and educated over a dozen generations of brilliant minds for the Mystery Schools, taught to seek truth and benefit humanity.

The most guarded secret of the Order's descendants and initiates was Caesarion himself. Under Caesarion, the *Majestic Council* set about to ensure the Great House of the Pharaoh would never die, and the secrets of the Pharaoh were never lost.

Nearly two hundred years after his flight from Egypt, Caesarion returned to the land of his birth. He returned the *Aton Stone Tablets* to Egypt, and he visited the Hall of Records.

Caesarion touched the Aton.

Caesarion's exceptionally long life removed all doubt of his divinity to his followers. He lived in his body almost four hundred years. He could heal others just as could he heal himself, from any ailment, and was said to have raised the dead... Youthful in appearance until the very end of his life, his life force remained perfectly balanced until the moment he chose to release his mortal coil.

"When he felt his life's purpose fulfilled, in the mountains of Tibet, Caesarion let go; he released his soul in a deep exhale, his body became pure energy and vanished in a rainbow of light," David read.

When the light that was Caesarion went out in 365 AD, the Pharos Lighthouse too went dark. That year, a devastating earthquake caused a massive tidal wave which destroyed much of the Mediterranean coast, and the glorious Pharos crumbled into the sea. Hellenism and Alexandria was destroyed beyond repair, all but gone forever; most remnants and vestiges of the days of old lost. The Classical era, and last records of the Pharaohs in the West were swallowed by the sea.

With Caesarion died an epoch, and many secrets of the Order. The *Majestic Council* elected the wisest of Caesarion's heirs, whom they called 'the king of righteousness.' This Pharaoh, Manu Melchizedek I of Āryāvarta, ensured the legacy and wishes of Caesarion were upheld, and for a thousand years the Great House resided in the East.

"The oldest and most powerful secret of the Pharaohs, the *Aton Stone Tablets,* the Aton itself, all but completely forgotten... until you, David," the Vizier's voice told David as he read.

You shall find the Aton, David.

CHAPTER XXXII

"Our Alexander is indeed one of the great ones…"

ALEXANDER

"We rarely find people who achieve great things without first going astray. You see—" Lex got a bug in his system to lecture me.

"Enough of the history lessons already, Lex."

"The past is the best way to predict and understand the future," Lex said. "The future of the Order depends on you."

"You sound like Dee." The virtual me stared into the real me.

Coding in virtual reality, I noticed how my LexNet program was already beginning to code itself. Most impressive.

"Knowing about the world, and history, is critical. This is why Darius forbid you to leave America on your own volition, until you turned eighteen," Lex continued. "And why you spent most of your time in California, as far from Darius in New York as you could get."

"Secretly funding and building start-ups. Darius' plan backfired. Who needs history when you can control the future?"

"History is the future. Darius has been controlling your history."

"How do you know all this?" The program began to scare me.

"I'm searching your entire digital history in ORNet… I'm learning everything about you. This will help me tremendously," Lex said.

"My history is now culminating in my masterpiece, the All Powerful Electronic Exchange, the APEX."

"I thought I was your masterpiece." Lex conveyed emotion, or perhaps this computer program was learning to elicit emotion in me?

"You and the APEX are the same thing, Lex."

"Dee has entered the lab," Lex said, as my computer program again. I took off my VR headset.

"How is the project coming along, Lord Alexander?" Dee asked me.

"To be honest, I'm having second thoughts about this, Dee."

"You think it will be too powerful?" Dee read me.

"When I link the APEX to ORNet, when this is complete and goes online— Dee. The APEX will essentially be able see everything, anything, on a computer. It already knows everything about me."

"You don't want Darius to have that power."

"And you do? Dee? Don't you get it? Once complete, the APEX will be able to link all the worlds computer systems, every computer on the planet, or orbiting the planet, into one all-powerful matrix. It's all or nothing. Won't that be the end of history?"

"I thought you hated history?" Dee smiled.

"I guess now I understand why it's so important."

"You're worried Darius will use it against you," Dee said.

"I know he will, Dee. Just like he uses everything else I've ever made against me."

Dee stared at me like I was child. *Maybe I am.*

"And how have you dealt with that in the past?" he asked.

"Built myself an out, or a back door in..."

Dee stared at me with a face of 'haven't you answered your own question?'

"But if I build Darius a nuclear bomb, what if my kill switch doesn't work when he drops it on me?"

"Why not do the opposite then, Lord Alexander?"

"Build him a bomb with an on switch— Dee. It's brilliant."

"Remember why you started," Dee reminded.

"Remember why I started... Lex! Why did we start building the APEX?" I looked to my computer system. "It's thinking."

"You started building the APEX to beat Darius at his own game," the computer voice of my A-I system replied.

"I see your Artificial Intelligence program is progressing well," Dee examined the flickering hologram of me, Lex.

"Lex Bot is coming along very well, aren't you, Lex?"

"I am progressing very well... Wait," it said, sounding clunky again. "Are you being sarcastic again?"

"No," I replied. I turned to Dee. "He still needs some work. He works better inside the system than outside it. Still trying to teach him how to detect sarcasm. Harder than it seems. Now it thinks everything is sarcasm."

"I see," said Dee.

"Lex. What are you the king of?"

"I am king of the virtual world," Lex spoke proudly.

"Sounds just like you." Dee was impressed.

"Lex is the digital me. He already knows me better than I know myself. By making him a virtual extension of me, LexNet is designed to answer only to me. This way, he'll never turn on me."

"Then you are ready," Dee said.

Epiphany struck me, as so often happens in the presence of Dee. His powerful eyes pierced my façade and forced me to speak. "LexNet is my backdoor, my safety check on the APEX."

"You must build the APEX for the Order, Lord Alexander. That is your destiny," Dee said.

"If Darius finds out... If he finds out I built ORNet— He's gonna kill me, Dee. LexNext won't be able to save me."

"We will tell him when the time is right, Lord Alexander," Dee said. "You must face him, and he must face the truth. That is the way it has always been. That is the way it must be."

Not gonna happen. "That's why you came. A history lesson?"

"You must tell him, eventually."

"Because he'll find out, eventually..." I started to freak out as I realized. "If I build the APEX, eventually he'll take control of it, just like he did ORNet. It'll give Darius too much power, Dee."

"Did ORNet give him too much power?" Dee rationalized.

"I can't do this."

"Do what?" Dee knew exactly what I meant.

"I can't build the APEX. I want out of the Order. Please."

"Alexander—" *There is no escaping your destiny.*

I fell to the floor as the pain in my heart returned. Emptiness consumed me. Tears. Fear; my death nears. I felt it. Death.

"Tis' not possible, Lord Alexander," Dee repeated over again.

"Fuck my life. Fuck all of this." I threw the VR head set and stormed off toward my craft.

"Stop!" Dee's commanding voice rattled my bones and froze me. *Oh God, here it comes.*

"Dee. Please. I have nothing to live for. No one loves me. I can't have friends. All I do is work. For what? For a fucking monster?"

"I wish you would stop cursing, Alexander."

"I wish you would let me have a life. I wish I was never born. But we don't always get what we want, do we?"

"You will go to the Council meeting this year," Dee's eyes tried to hypnotize me into submission. "You will tell them all the truth."

"No. I won't." I had never directly stood up to Dee before. It felt both empowering and disempowering. He won.

"Darius thinks the APEX is his idea, and he is moving to have it approved by the Council," Dee said. "He wants it done in five years."

My worst fears come true. I'm officially working for Darius, Dee?

"This is a disaster. We can't let him get it approved."

"Darius and your Grandfather will be expecting you to vote yes on the APEX project. In their eyes there is no reason for you to be against it. Unless, you know something they don't?"

"But if I vote yes, and officially building the APEX for the Order is approved, Darius will find out everything… And then he'll kill me. Dee. You want me to vote yes for my own execution?"

"The Order will protect you," Dee said.

"Darius will find out everything, Dee. He'll kill me. Or worse."

"You are a *Majestic*, Lord Alexander. You must attend the Council Meeting, and advise the council. That is the purpose of the meeting," Dee said. "Your Grandfather wants to see you. He'll listen to you. And you must meet Sir David Peterson, the newest member of the Council. The APEX brings transparency."

"No." I stood my ground. "I prefer to stay hidden. I'm not going to the Council Meeting. I can't see Darius."

"There is no escape from destiny, Lord Alexander," Dee hit me with the truth. He saw the plan forming in my head. *There is no escape.*

"Save me. Please. Dee." I cried, falling to my knees.

"You will save us, my Lord. You will defeat this evil, and become a Pharaoh. That is your destiny."

"But who will save me? Why do I not have a choice?"

"You do. You always have a choice. Chose greatness."

Become a hero, and save us from Darius' evil.

With that, Dee left me, alone again.

"I will save you!" Lex said in his computer voice.

I laughed and wiped my tears. Back into the virtual world I went.

CHAPTER XXXIII

"It's time to use the Aton."

WISENDEE

"There are truths which are not for all men, nor for all times. But the truth of the Aton was meant for you, your Grace," I said to the Vizier who sat in thought by the altar fire.

Sir Henry discovered the Aton. He said: "David knows."

"We must invoke the Scion. 'Tis time he learned the truth."

"The Scion is near death," the Vizier said. "This burden will send him over the edge. He won't understand."

"We have no choice." *The Order must use the Aton.*

If Darius discovers the Aton? "Darius could unmake the world with it. He will fall. The world could fall with him," the Vizier said.

"Darius is being manipulated by an evil not of this world. An alien force pulls him into darkness." *The Aton is how we save him.*

"The Order, mankind itself, is in grave danger," the Vizier warned. *Those demons seek the Aton.*

"The world requires a savior…" *Only a Pharaoh can use the Aton.* "I see hope in David, and Alexander," I said. "We must believe."

The Aton may also create a Pharaoh.

The Aton has a plan…

"Go to the Scion. Tell him," I said. "He must play his part."

"This plan requires the help of the gods of old," the Vizier said.

The Aton appeared in the room, a glowing orb of white light.

"Helios will protect you, as Marduk protects the Scion."

Helios… Ancient demigod, ascended human with powers untold, protector of the Sacred Order, manifested from the *Aton* light.

"Helios," the Vizier said, greeting this supernatural being, meeting him in this moment, for the first time, though long knowing of him.

Helios held a glowing white *Aton* sphere.

The Aton chose you, the unspoken voice of Helios vibrated our immortal souls. "Touch it," he said. "It will show you the way."

The Vizier touched the infinite, and vanished in a flash of light.

CHAPTER XXXIV

"A Pharaoh can save the world."

THE VIZIER

Pray, I need the help of the Scion. The Holy Father draws me from the evil of all sin to the goodness of divine grace; even blessed with the might of the almighty Aton's boundless power, I require all the resources of all gods' strength in order to convert a fallen sinner. More might than when God made heaven and earth, which She made with Love's own power, without help from any creature; for when God is about to convert a sinner, He always needs the sinner's help…

The Aton converts thee not without thy help.

"Bring in David," the Scion said to his Guards.

The doors closed and the electric lights in the underground *Chamber of Initiation* failed, as the unseen shockwave of the Aton hit. A spell of pitch-black fell on him. The electromagnetic disturbance of the glowing orb blackened and lit up the room. The Scion sat alone with the stone faces of his ancestors, basking in the glow of divine light. Faint buzzing sounds of life, the electric universe contained in the Aton, broke the dead silence. The faintly glowing sphere floated toward him, from the staircase where it entered. This descendent of Pharaohs felt his genetic memory excite, his mind illuminated, by the presence of the Aton, and my glowing spirit in front of him.

"Dear God…" said the Scion. "Who are you?"

"I am a messenger of the Light," I spoke, holding the Aton.

"Hermes?" The Scion asked, unable to recognize Thoth or me.

"The Sacred Order is in peril," my voice vibrated the crystal stone.

Fear came over the Scion. He instantly thought of Darius and felt pain in his heart.

"The Sacred Order is in danger," I told him. "You are in danger."

The statues, voices of ancient Scions past, whispered and spoke, heard by the Scion as never before.

"The Aton…" they said.

"So it's true. The Aton is real," the Scion struggled to believe it.

The word "Aton" hung in the air, and vibrated the crystals to light.

"The desire for the Aton and its power can cause the hearts of men to become heavy, become *Fallen*."

"*Fallen*?" The Scion repeated, trying to understand what that meant. The glowing sphere casts harsh shadows in the chamber.

"The *Fallen* seek the power of the Aton for evil. To fall is to seek to harm human souls. Those who seek to destroy nature and go against the Sacred Order are *Fallen*..."

"Darius—" the Scion said, holding his heart with pain.

"The Aton awakens the darkness in men and attracts demons... A great evil seeks to fall the Order of Man into darkness."

"You speak of Darius? And those aliens? The ones he—"

"If the *Fallen* take possession of the Aton, they could destroy this world and enslave the souls of mankind for all eternity. You must not let this happen." The Scion and his ancestors heard my warning well.

The shimmering sphere floated within reach of the Scion. He stared at it. He could see something, a smaller sphere inside the larger glowing orb. He reached to touch the ineluctable object.

"I want to touch it..." the Scion said. *I must touch it...*

The Scion's touch burst the Aton orb. A bubble of plasma popped, the thirteen inch diameter Aton dissolved away leaving only the smaller sphere, the two inch core. He grasped this red colored, perfectly smooth, diamond crystal ball in his palm.

"What magic is this?" The Scion looked at the glowing red orb.

"You hold the blood of the first Pharaoh," my voice told him.

The statues whispered of "Sangrael."

"The Holy Grail?" The Scion asked. He examined the object. The diamond shell glittered. Blood. Red and blue inside, it became a purple hue as it swirled beneath the clear shell. "Incredible."

"As the Scion of the *Great House*, you are bound by blood and the Sacred Covenant to protect humanity from harm. The fate of humanity is bound to you, to this blood."

"What must I do?" The Scion begged.

"We need a hero," the voices said. "A hero must rise..."

"Save the Sacred Order from darkness. The end of the Great Cycle opens the gates of cosmic creation, and the potential incarnation of a new Pharaoh, the recreation of the Aton." *Use the Aton, my Lord.*

"I don't understand," the Scion said, recognizing my voice.

"Only a Pharaoh may use the Aton. And only the Aton can protect humanity from the *Fallen*."

"A Pharaoh? But what is a Pharaoh? What does that mean?" The Scion asked, confused.

"The gods are trusting you with everything. The world is in your hands," my spirit hand pointed to the red Aton-core in his palm.

You must save the world, my Lord.

The light of my soul vanished. Artificial light returned.

CHAPTER XXXV

"What did the Scion say?"

WISENDEE

Dee, I need your help... He wandered in darkness seeking light, failing to realize that the true light is in the heart of his darkness.

"Wait!" The Scion yelled as the yellow glare of synthetic lights returned. The inorganic light made the Scion feel sick and exhausted. His mortal coil pained more than ever. He clutched the Aton-core in his palm and drew a healing strength from it. Staring at the mini glowing purple sphere in his hand, he pondered what magic it possessed. A knock on the wooden chamber door startled the Scion. He had forgotten about David. *David knows about the Aton*, he thought.

The Guards brought David into the Chamber, blindfolded and dressed in white. The Scion hid the Aton-core in his grasp.

"Leave us," the Scion commanded the Guards.

The Guards left the chamber. David removed his blindfold.

"Welcome back," the Scion's voice cracked in pain.

"Are you alright, my Lord?" David asked.

"I am fatigued." The Scion poured himself and David a drink. "Come. Drink with me. What news have you?" he asked.

David took his time before speaking, looked down at his glass and swirled the fine smelling alcohol. He gathered the courage to say the words. "The Aton is real, my Lord," David said.

Unseen voices gasped, and the lights flickered at the word "Aton."

"Where did it come from?" the Scion demanded, holding it.

"It is a long story, my Lord—" David said.

"And you shall tell me one day, but where is it now?" The Scion felt the heat of the orb in his clinched fist.

"My belief is that it was removed from the Hall of Records by Sir Henry, and Dr. Hans Danreich. This is what killed them, some people did not want it found..." David said.

"I see. And where is the artifact now?" The Scion asked.

"I believe the artifact is now, or was, in the Secret Archive."

"The Vizier knows about it?" the Scion interrupted.

"Yes. I believe the Vizier has touched it," David said.

"Why is that?" the Scion demanded.

"He is deified. It sounds strange, but I saw it in him," David said.

The Scion's head flooded with jealousy and questions.

"How does one use the Aton exactly, David?" the Scion asked as he held the Aton core, hidden in his fist.

"I'm not certain, my Lord. But somehow, it can generate infinite amounts of energy. Because of this, it can be used as a weapon. The legends say: He who controls the Aton, is the Pharaoh."

You are holding the Aton, my Lord.

The Aton became fire in the Scions hands and forced him to release his grasp on it. His scream startled David and with the Scion they watched in bewilderment as the Aton core bounced on the marble floor, possessed, and alive it defied the laws of physics.

"Good heavens," the Scion said, watching the Aton magically roll to the exact center of the circular, sacred, *Chamber of Initiation.*

Stunned to silence.

"Is that—" David said, staring at the glowing red object.

The Scion nodded yes. David and the Scion felt the intense gravitational field of the Aton as it pulled them closer.

"It is alive..." the Scion said. "Pick it up, David."

David did as told. He closed his eyes and picked up the orb.

"The Aton—" David looked at it in his hand. *Hold it.*

He felt the heat of the Aton surge, but he closed his fist around the heat and absorbed the energy. Holding tight, a wave of energy swept over his body. He closed his eyes and felt his mind crest, his soul leave his body and expand at light speed into the highest levels of consciousness. One with the universe, churning, dying and being reborn, outside of space and time, in eternity, he saw Love.

David let go. He opened his palm, opened his eyes to physical reality, his heart beating with joy. He saw the Scion looking jealous of whatever blissful experience it appeared David just had. "Good God."

"Just before you arrived, a spirit appeared to me. He showed me the Aton." The Scion took the Aton-core from David's giving hand. "I saw it. I saw it as it was. I touched it. But it dissolved, leaving only this. Is this the Holy Grail, David."

David could not yet speak.

"We need to use this, it said. I need your help, David."

"Use it? Use it for what, my Lord?"

"The end of the Great Cycle allows for the rise of a Pharaoh."

"The Great Cycle?"

"We need a Pharaoh. We need to bring back the Pharaoh, it said. But what does that mean?" the Scion was scared, begging for answers from David.

"Holy Blood," David said looking at the swirling fluid. "Perhaps the blood can tell us something."

"Of course… the blood," the Scion told himself. "The blood is the Pharaoh."

"Can we analyze the blood inside it?"

"How? Damage this sacred artifact?" the Scion protested.

"Use it, my Lord" David said. "We must learn its secrets."

"What do we do with blood?" The Scion looked intrigued.

"Perhaps the DNA in the blood can tell us something?" David wondered. "Perhaps we can clone the blood. That would create a Pharaoh, bring one back, as it were, wouldn't it?"

"Clone the blood— How long will that take, do you think?" the Scion asked.

"I'm not sure," David said. "Human cloning is difficult."

"But not impossible?"

"It may not be possible to clone this blood, my Lord."

"We shall solve this together," the Scion said, satisfied. "Yes…" He walked away, holding the magic artifact in his hand.

"May I go home now, my Lord?" David asked, exhausted.

"Yes. Yes of course. Go to your wife. See you at the Council meeting. You shall meet the rest of the Council, and I want you to meet the family, my grandson, Alexander."

"I have a family now," David said, as he thought of Sarah and his infant child. "I have a daughter, Elizabeth."

"Go to them, David. Family is everything," the Scion said.

"Thank you, my Lord. Majesty."

"You are part of the family now."

CHAPTER XXXVI

"You can't choose your family. But family is a choice."

ALEXANDER

"Tomorrow is the Council meeting," Lex warned me as instructed.

"I can't face Darius. I have to hide. How? How can I hide from the Order for a full day? Lex. Give me something."

"Searching... There is an island, in the middle of the Indian Ocean, if you can get there undetected, it would take ORNet satellites at least 10.23 hours to find you," Lex said, his computer voice sounding more natural by the day. "That is the most time you could be hidden for."

"Show me the plan."

"However, there is only a 76.5% chance of success getting to the island undetected by NORAD. Here is the plan with the best chance of success." Lex presented his plan: A rocket to space.

"Skydiving from space? Let's do it." Click, I set my plan in motion.

I arrived in the California desert to supervise the black-ops project, the final steps of the rapid construction of a launch ramp, designed to propel a one-man rocket-ship into space. "Are we ready to launch?"

"We'll be ready to launch in an hour, Boss," Jay the crew boss said.

"You have 15 minutes."

"You do realize how dangerous this is?" Crew boss-man said. "This rocket has never been tested. It could explode."

"But if it works, I'll make it to space undetected?"

"Yes. The pod is invisible to all radar," he said.

"I've always wanted to skydive from space." I smiled.

"But you will most likely die. You get that, right?"

"If it works I dive back to earth and land on my target, undetected. Or, I'll die. I understand. Ready the launch. Get me in the suit."

The confused crew didn't understand my flippant style. But black-ops people don't ask unnecessary questions; it's in the contract.

"Long as you get that you'll most likely die," Jay said.

"What I need you to focus on is speed, and keeping me 100% undetected. That's what I need you to worry about. Got it? Hurry up."

"This anti-radar technology is a decade ahead of even the US military. No one can track you, Boss," the tech said with pride.

"The suit won't have enough power for a return trip," a crew member added. "Just so you know. Wherever ya land, you're stuck there. You get that too, right?" The dirty crew men stared at me.

"Not important," I said.

"So your options are: land on an island in the middle of the Indian Ocean with no one knowing and no way back, or die in space? With all due respect, are you looking to die?" Jay asked.

I'd rather die in space, on my own terms, than go to the Council Meeting and confront Darius. He'll kill me with his bare hands. Might as well die trying to escape, having fun… Right?

"Are you all looking to die? Because you will if we don't launch in the next ten minutes."

"Whatever you say man, you're the boss," Jay said.

"It's done," he said. "I don't know how they finished so quickly."

The combination mag-lev and rocket powered propulsion system, with its polished metal parts reflected the breaking desert sunrise.

"The ramp will accelerate the pod into space and the pod's surface will absorb and deflect the radar signals. It'll be invisible to all radar frequencies and the naked eye," he said. "And no known system can find you once you reach your orbit."

Don't do this, Alexander. Dee's voice in my head warned me.

"Show me the space suit."

They walked me over to the suit team.

"Once you're in outer space and off the grid, you eject from the pod and fly the suit back to the target on earth," the suit tech said.

"Assuming it works and you use it correctly," a tech qualified.

"Let's do it. Put it on me."

The crew all fully expected me to die in the op. As I put on the suit, I saw them wondering, whispering, about how my death would affect them. Death always hovers over these black-ops trolls. They're seriously the most miserable, life-hating, tortured souls you can find in the world. Many are clinically insane from what they've witnessed or been put through by the Order. Horrific death is just a part of every-day life for most of them.

"Wait. The helmet might not be ready," a tech said.

"If it's not ready in five seconds no one gets paid."

"Okay. I think it's ready," the suit techs grumbled as they rushed to finish, frantically booting up the system.

"You *think* it's ready? Like, there's a strong chance it'll kill me?"

"Yeah," he said. "This design has never been tested. We don't even know where it came from." The techs wanted answers from me.

"Don't worry about it."

"Who are you?" Jay asked as the team put the suit on me.

"Someone you don't ask questions."

"The suit exterior is made from carbon-nanotube polymer, the best of the meta-materials available. Extremely lightweight. Conductive almost at superconductor levels. Virtually indestructible. It's like a spaceship within itself," the tech said, trying to sell me on it. "Heat resistant, it absorbs all radar spectrums, with a battery power and user interface better than I've ever seen."

"I know. Are we done?"

The suit reflected the bright California desert sunlight like polished silver. "When it turns on, the surface blends into its surroundings. The suit becomes invisible to the naked eye." They turned it on, and demonstrated the effect. It bends light, making it look invisible.

"This suit is easily fifty years ahead of anything out there today," the tech added. "This must have been designed by an A-I program."

Snapped on the helmet. Inserted the LexNet sim-card. My control interface worked better than expected. LexNet booting up...

Two super-high-def cameras on the helmet acted as my eyes. The outside world projected inside the helmet, with useful information, custom AR, overlaid on top of it. All systems are a go.

"I've never seen tech like this, and I've been doing this shit for years," crew-tech said in my ear piece.

"I know," I snapped. "You can shut up now." The suit amplified my voice like a megaphone, so it seemed like I yelled at him. I turned down the volume and said: "Start the launch sequence."

Over to the pod I went. With my enhanced listening I heard them all whispering speculations about me. Maybe I was an alien they said. They knew I wasn't just some secret mega billionaire. I vetted all these people personally, they are the best out there at what they do, they know everyone, so they wondered why they'd never heard of me.

At the pod, I approached the launch team leader. His name was Ratner. They call him Rats, probably also because his face reminds you

116

of a rat. Dude's a nervous wreck – typical, but unbelievably annoying. Ex-Order Intelligence, fired and disfigured for leaking stuff on aliens, he's great at rockets, terrible at life. The only reason he isn't dead is because he's the best commander for deep Black-ops space projects. Rats knows rocket science really well.

"Are you sure you want to do this, kid?" Rats asked me.

"Do you wanna get paid or not?" I yelled from inside the suit.

"If you die, I don't want the black suits after me."

"Then I suggest we move fast, because I'll call them myself."

"You get in that pod and get blasted out into fucking outer space there's a sixty-percent chance you die, you little shit." Rats said, his deformed face spewed foamy spit with his lispy speech. Straight shooter, he spit right on my eye cameras. "Ready to die then?"

"Please wipe your fucking spit off my helmet, Rat-Face."

"This is not what I signed up for," Rats walked away, ego bruised.

"You didn't sign up for anything. You're here because I own you." The suit amplified my voice loud enough for everyone to hear. "Man your stations now! Before I kill all of you."

"Man your stations. Start the launch!" Jay yelled.

"No!" Rats said.

Everyone watched me and Rat-Face in our stand-off. No one wanted to go through with the launch; except me.

"No launch, no money."

The crew opened the pod. Money talks.

"You can't do this, kid. I don't fucking like you. I don't know who you are. I don't care about you. But you will die, and it'll come back to me. The Order will be up my ass— I quit," Rats yelled. "You don't own me. I'm out."

I pointed to the three men in all-black combat gear aiming their massive guns at the crew.

"Do the launch or you all die."

Half of the crew did not want to die. They got to work.

"When you die, someone'll come after me. I've been there before. I know your type. Your family, whoever they are, will kill me. Might as well just get it over with—" he said. "Kill me."

Commence charm offensive. Off came my helmet. Winsome smile and softened beguiling looks disarmed him. My green eye winked and enchanted him. "What if I tell you who I am?" I said.

He changed as he stared at me. Never really thought of myself as beautiful until I started meeting people outside the Order and they called me beautiful. Like most people, Rats was a sucker for a physical beauty. Longing for beauty is human nature. That deep longing to understand the divine, to touch perfection, to know things. He realized he really wanted to know who I am...

"Who are you? Are you an alien?" Rats asked.

"Launch me into space and I'll tell you. Then, you can all get paid your millions and go back to the shadows like it never happened. No one will ever know. Promise. And I have a bonus for you."

I motioned for my men to show Rats the briefcase full of diamonds.

"Over fifty million dollars worth. Your untraceable payment – once the launch is complete. Just get me to space." Big smile. "You need this money. I know about your debts to the Russian mob, Ratsy."

"I hope you die, kid," Rats said giving the go signal. He put his headset on.

"I'll die soon enough." Put my helmet on to amplify my voice. "We're go, people! Stations. Now!"

Got in the pod. Crew manned their stations.

Give me liberty or give me death.

Anything but the Council Meeting.

He will kill me, Dee. If anyone is going to kill me, it's gonna be me.

CHAPTER XXXVII

"The Council must meet annually."

WISENDEE

"The annual gathering of the thirteen, the *Majestic Council of Twelve* and the Scion, is required by Order Law. At least once per annum the Scion must hold Court, and hear all matters which require coordination and vote of the Council," David read to Sarah.

"What else does the Royal invitation say?" Sarah asked.

"The Order symposium pulls the world's best and brightest minds to propinquity, in conference, to share developments in their respective fields, which, ideally, benefits the advancement of mankind," David looked at Sarah to see her reaction. She loved this lore.

"You are a wonderful orator, my Love," Sarah smiled.

"Usually held at one of the Scion's illustrious estates, this year at his favorite, the royal palace known as Zenobia," the Livery gave his scripted speech.

David and Sarah stopped reading to admire the view as they drove onto the palace grounds. "Zenobia is where the Council Meetings of the Modern era first began, not long after the ancient estate was remodeled into its present Baroque form in the 1600's. The divine fruit orchards, vineyards and gardens of the estate have been manicured skillfully for over a thousand years..." the Livery said.

At the entry, I waited for David's arrival.

The car arrived and David's livery escorted him and Sarah to me.

"Welcome, Sir David, Lady Sarah." I greeting them in the grand entry hall. "I am Chief of the Illuminated Magi, Senior Councilor of the Scion's Privy, Sir Mervyn Wisendee. You may call me, Dee."

David looked into my eyes and saw that I knew all there is to know about him... He wanted to ask me so many questions, he remembered the words of the Scion and wanted to inquire about his parents, in that moment. My eyes gave him patience. *All in good time...*

"As a new member of the Scion's Privy, Sir David, you shall be escorted to the Scion after you are settled, refreshed, and dressed.

Thereupon proper induction, shall you meet all other members of the Council, and confer, before the formal affair in the main ballroom."

David nodded. The Livery team invited them to follow to their accommodations. "This way please, Sir David, Lady Sarah…"

The quiet before the storm was deafening. I walked the empty hall to the courtyard in anticipation of Darius and his corresponding din. The blue sky rippled and pooled as an alien-technology craft dropped into the air above the palace. It floated, radiated, and burned the air as it lowered into the courtyard. I took my position with the welcome delegation, customarily headed by the Scion. But the Scion refused to greet Darius; and was unapologetic for the effrontery.

The ramp lowered and a small army of Order Agents in black suits marched out, followed by Darius. He immediately noticed his father and half the Council had indeed snubbed him. This set the tone. Darius felt slighted and turned furious. *So it begins…*

"Your Exalted Majest—" the Livery began.

"Tell Father to stop fucking drinking. We start on time for once!" Darius yelled at me. "He'll kill us all with his flagrant perfidy."

"You are not one to lecture on Order protocols or propriety—"

"You tell him to be in that Ballroom in fifteen minutes, Dee," Darius said to me as he led his army of men-in-black down the West Wing of the Palace, to his King Suite at the end of the corridor. "Or I'm fucking starting without him!" Darius knows he can't start without the King, and that I caught this thinly veiled threat on his father's life.

Darius and the Scion seek to avoid each other as best as possible. The Council meeting is the day, once a year, when Darius and his family must be in the same room together. For decades, the Scion simply gave Darius *carte blanche* to run the meeting, rubber stamping everything Darius wanted. This appeasement ended only last year. Darius cannot accept the fact that the Scion is the King, not him.

"The heir apparent Darius openly prays for the Scion to die, that is the definition of perfidy…"

The Scion does not have the strength to fight Darius. We need you, Alexander. The Order needs you…

At this moment, Alexander was up to no good.

Don't do it, Alexander. Please…

CHAPTER XXXVIII

"He could not escape the Council Meeting."

ALEXANDER

"Do it!" I yelled at Rats. "Start the launch!"

"All systems go," the techs said over comm.

Curmudgeonly rocket-scientist Rats sighed into his microphone. "Listen - hit the eject button before 22 km or you will break Earth's orbit and die in space. Let me repeat, you will die a terrible death in space after 13 miles. Do you understand? You'll drift too far to return. So if that's what you want, don't listen me."

"Just get me to space. Let me worry about the rest."

"Whatever you say," Rats replied over comm. "At 12 miles you tell me who you are. Before you die."

The suit connected to ORNet using my special access LexNet protocol. "Lex? You there? Speak to me."

"I am online and ready, Alexander," the digital voice of Lex said in a clunky and slow cadence.

"Why are you so slow?" I saw my network connection was terrible.

"My LexNet connection is terr—"

"Boost it all you can. Let's do this."

"I do not understand. Do what this?" the digital voice said over comm. Lex painfully slow. "You need more computational power too, fuck…" I gave him all the bandwidth and RAM the suit could spare.

"Up the connection speed as much as you can. Find a strong uplink signal and lock it in. This shit needs to be fucking fast."

"Amplifying connection. What do you mean 'this shit needs to be fucking fast'?" Lex sounded like A-I trying to make a joke.

Ops Lex struggles with sarcasm. "It's a figure of speech, Lex. Pay attention to my tone. Access my speech archives and cross reference."

"Accessing speech archives from LexNet," Lex said.

"If you want to be ruler of the virtual world, Lex, you need to give me all the bandwidth you got right now." It's working.

"I will be the ruler of the APEX virtual world," Lex said.

Yes. "There's my Lex. We'll work on your ops voice and language programming later. Focus on the launch. Let's try not to let me die, alright?" I realized I didn't want to die as I said the words.

"I will focus on the launch, and keep you alive," the digital voice of Lex monotoned.

I'm in my suit, in the pod, ready to go. *I think I might die, Dee.*

"Everything looks good," Rat-Face said over comm.

"You have the island trajectory set, Lex?"

Lex accessed an Order satellite and zoomed in to my perfect little island, only about fifty feet wide, only three palm trees, and as far from civilization as I could get. Freedom called.

"TARGET CONFIRMED" flashed on my screen.

"We can get there without getting caught on radar, Rats?"

"Ready for launch," Rats said over comm.

"This is either going to be the most fun or the most stupid thing I've ever done, Lex." Lex said nothing. I was asking for comfort. Nothing.

Silence. "Go for launch!" I yelled into my comm.

Rat-Face chatted with other crew members. Something's not right. They were stalling the launch.

"I said go for Launch!" I yelled angrily over the comm again. "Lex! Get me eyes on the crew."

My spy cameras clicked on, my AR gave me visual and audio.

"He's the son of a member of the Magic Council… The meanest one—" I hear over the comm. "If we do this we're all fucking dead," Rats said.

Fuck. I was made.

"Turn that off! Now!" Rat-Face commanded. "Kill the launch!"

"Fuck!" I scream out loud in my space suit. "Lex, override the launch. Don't let them abort."

Lex was thinking. I moved fast to save the op.

"Lex, use ORNet to take control of the launch controls." I didn't want to use ORNet but had no choice. This is a disaster.

"Kill the launch! This is done! I'm calling it in," Rats yelled at the crew. "We report him and we'll all get a reward from the Order," Rat-Face planned to rat me out. The fucking rat… how dare he.

"Override successful," Lex said. He used ORNet.

"Yes. Cloak us on ORNet."

"Launch sequence initiated," the ORNet computer voice said.

"God I love A-I… Launch!"

The launch countdown sequence begins. "10, 9, 8…"

"You're the best, Lex!" my voice went out over everyone's comm.

"Who the hell is Lex?!" Rats yelled. "Oh fuck. Fuck. Fuck!"

Last minute adjustments: trajectory, check, go, the rockets ignite.

"He's overridden my command. I can't stop him. He's launching!" Rats and crew were forced to release the launch or explode the rocket.

"If he's off trajectory he could hit that plane—"

I hit mute on the chatter. "They'll figure it out or we all die. Either way, no need to worry about those losers anymore, right Lex?"

"Launch in 4, 3, and 2—" the computer voice said.

Rockets ignited. Brakes released. Pod launched, out over Pacific, into the atmosphere… G-forces pulsed through my body in waves. Pain made me feel alive. I feel therefore I'm still alive.

My rocket-pod missed hitting a 747 airplane by less than ten feet. "Fuck. That was close, Lex! Don't hit anything!"

"Correcting trajectory. No objects in flight path."

"Avoid all objects by at least five hundred feet, alright?"

"Will not get close," Lex said. Then I could see the computer thinking. Bad news. "Invisibility mode failed," Lex added. "Pod visible to radar."

"Those fucking fuckers—" *I sound like Darius and I hate it. Fuck!*

"Pod launch reported to NORAD… Tracking initiated," Lex said.

"That fucking Rat!" I saw the communication flurry on my monitor. US Air command scrambled jets. "I'm fucking all over NORAD's radar now. Rat-Face fucking fucked me. Kill all communications at base! In fact kill all the people at that base!"

"All communications at base are terminated," Lex updated.

"Sending a missile to kill all humans at base," computer voice added, like it was not Lex speaking.

"Russian and American anti-missile and anti-aircraft systems initiated. DEFCON 1 and Russian nuclear attack protocols activated," the stern computer voice warned next.

"Shit! Fuck! Kill the missiles to base! You just sent NORAD into DEFCON 1, Lex! The whole plan just went to fucking shit."

"Russian Nuclear missiles launched," Lex said. "Russia thinks this pod is a mega bomb heading for them. US missiles launched…"

Those old missile systems are such a stupid joke… Not funny.

My altitude approached 22 km, but I kept firing the rockets.

"You should not go past 22 km," Lex reminded me. "Do not go past 13 miles from the earth." The voice almost sounded concerned.

"Fuck. How do we escape the fallout from the missiles?"

21 km and counting. I pondered death. 'Maybe I do want to die...'

"Warning. You must not go past 22 km," Lex warned again. "You could die if you go past 22 km. Lex does not want you to die."

My A-I program played with my emotions. I think we just had a breakthrough...

"Warning missiles approaching," Lex said.

Part of me actually wanted to die, though. Time slowed down.

I roared past 22 km on the screen, entering the edge of space.

"I've had enough of this world." *I'm going to die soon.*

No reply from the digital voice...

The pod opened and blasted me into space so fast I didn't even know it was happening, yet it happened in slow motion, in my mind. I shot away from the pod and glowing blue of the earth, spinning uncontrollably into space.

A nuclear missile hit the pod. Other missiles collided in the distance, and I watched the mushroom clouds of heat expand in slow motion. The shock wave of the nuclear blast hit, sending me into a terrible spin. Intense centrifugal forces sent blood to my head and feet, which made me feel like I was going to explode. Adrenaline made time speed up, as I managed to slow the spin with rocket boosters. Propelled away from earth, still spinning at an insane speed, on my interface, I saw flashes of the massive, white hot explosion as I spun and shot uncontrollably away from earth. The fireball shrank as it rose into space, and I flew further and further away from the light, away from the only world I'd ever known... The beautiful blue sphere. I reached for it.

So this is how I die...

The power in my suit failed. Silence. My interface went black, and I was alone in total darkness. Closed eyes. Open heart. I accepted my fate. Weightless in space, feeling only the slight g-forces of spinning, the cold reality of space set in on me.

I don't wanna die this way.

CHAPTER XXXIV

"The life of the Order is the passing of the crown."

WISENDEE

A little power inclineth man's mind to tyranny; but true power, depth in heart, bringeth men's minds about to freedom, you see...

"My solemn duty is to shepherd the peaceful succession of the Order; at all cost," I informed David. "I protect the Great House."

"I see," David said. Sarah had her own epiphany.

"Yes. You see, the Scion is an absolute monarch, however, there are certain circumstances under which the Sovereign may be overruled."

"How?" David followed, curious where I was leading.

"By a vote of the Majestic Council. These privy councilors ostensibly and ideally including the royal family. Under Order Law, only the Vizier has the sole ability to unilaterally stay the power of the Scion, in his discretion, on charge that the will of a Scion endangers the living planet, humanity, the Order, and/or the *Archivum*."

"Why are you telling me this?" David asked.

"Because you are part of the Majestic family, and Darius will ask for your vote to override the Scion, Sir David."

"Councilors serve at the pleasure of the King, why would they go against him? Why would I vote to go against my King?"

"The Order is like a family. You should not go against your father. But you must if doing so protects the whole family, you see? The Majestic too must stand with the Order, even if that means voting against their King. Vote with your heart, for there lies the Order."

Sarah grabbed David's hand, as they felt the dark clouds gathering.

"I'm not sure I understand what you are trying to say," David said.

"Soon you shall. Welcome to the family, Sir David."

With that, I left David and Sarah to attend other matters.

"Where do we stand on the APEX project?" Darius barked at me as I entered his king's suite in the West Wing.

"His Majesty has yet to sign the edict."

"What?" Darius snarled. "Where does the Council stand?"

"You have my vote, Lord Darius. I won't speak for the others."

"You are not instilling confidence in me, Dee."

"The Scion does not know what the APEX is, Lord Darius."

"Tell him to sign the edict. Use your magic, Dee."

"The Scion and the Councilors wish to see the presentation. Only then shall we know where they stand."

"I can't rely on that fucking fickle old man. Get me my override votes, Dee," Darius ordered. "This needs to be approved today."

Darius stepped onto a platform, and standing above all in the room, he looked down on me. The staff now finessed his lower half for the meeting. Tall, charming, and in excellent physical shape, Darius takes great pride in his appearance, his increasingly vampirish aesthetic. Black hair slicked back, porcelain white skin, flecks of blood red veins in his dark eyes. He adjusts his perfectly tailored black suit. His shoes are polished to a flawless shine.

"Make it happen, Dee," Darius said looking down on me with threatening eyes. He stepped down off his platform.

Though almost eighty-years of age, Darius would appear under half that age to any layperson. His dangerous beauty and brutish arrogance renders Alexander delicate and friendly by comparison. I watched as Alexander entered Darius thoughts.

"Where is my godforsaken heir?" Darius demanded.

I deferred to his minions, many also his spawn, including his Chief.

"We're trying to locate him, Sir," the Chief of Staff informed.

"What did you say?" Darius filled with rage.

"He's— He's missing, Sir," the Chief of Staff said.

Darius' relationship with Alexander is worse than his relationship with his father; a fact that weighs heavily on the Council.

"How is that possible?" Darius looked at me.

"We— He seems to— There was a pod, but—" the staffer tapped his tablet desperate to find an answer.

"He needs to be here. Now!" Darius screamed. His voice echoed in the long palace halls. "If he is not here within the next ten minutes, and my meeting does not begin on time… I'm going to kill someone."

Darius looked at me. If looks could kill…

CHAPTER XL

"No one eludes their destiny."

ALEXANDER

The world needs you, Alexander... Dee's voice in my head.

Time stopped. No movement. Feeling nothing, thought I must be dead. My eyes opened. I saw the light. Power returned to my custom spacesuit. My interface screen lit up and there was the earth. Wasn't spinning, except my head. I floated at the edge of space. In the corner of my camera eyes, a glowing Orb, a UFO, shoot away at incredible speed. Couldn't get a good focus on it.

"Lex?" No response. "What was that thing?"

Still no response. Whatever it was, it saved me. *Was that you, Dee?*

"Someone, or something didn't want me to die," I said to myself as I rebooted my LexNet A-I program.

The system fired up, I admired the majestic glowing blue sphere below. Our planet is awe inspiring and so beautiful... It's alive.

Life is beautiful.

"I want to live."

When you look at the incredible living, breathing planet in all its glory from space, you get a complete perspective. Seeing the divine being, Gaia, the world from above, made me peer deep into myself. I saw my soul and my place in the world. All my troubles forgotten in that moment; I shed a few tears.

"Life is beautiful, Lex."

"All systems op-er-a-tional," the spliced together phonemes of my voice, Lex, said. "Mapping trajectory."

"Welcome back, Lex."

On my monitor, appeared the path to my little island get away. "Preparing to enter Earth's atmosphere."

Reach for Earth. Floating. Pulling. Swimming in space.

Must. Go. Down... Boosters fire for a little nudge.

Gravity takes full control. Gravity never felt so good.

Started to fall. Slowly. Going down.

Sky diving from space. Back to life. Back to reality...

"Get us to the island, Lex. And stay off all radar."

"Flight path set. Avoiding radar. Click go when ready."

"Superman eat your heart out." I clicked the "go" button. The suit locked the coordinates. My wings opened. The booster rockets on my boots fired. BOOM. I dove through the clouds toward Earth.

"This must be what it's like to be a superhero. Awesome..."

Ripping through the upper atmosphere, I descended into the thickening lower atmosphere, feeling the resistance and heat building.

"Kill the rockets." Let gravity do the work. Wanted to free fall toward the Earth. Love that feeling of falling...

In the middle of the Pacific ocean, the water reflected the sky, up and down blended into one and I was falling up... Nothing made sense, which made perfect sense, as my senses went into overload. My head never stopped spinning, and stayed in the clouds; in peace.

Of course, the moment I was actually enjoying myself, actually forgetting all my problems - actually feeling happy - a flock of stealth jets appeared, to ruin my moment of Zen.

"Bogies at 3 o'clock. Fighter jets from US Command," the voice of Lex said, ending my bliss with a stinging wave of fight hormones.

"Fuck, they can see my heat trail. Hack into NORAD so I can hear what they're saying."

"Using ORNet to hack in to comm," Lex gave me ears on the pilots.

"We have eyes on it..." a pilot said. "It's him."

CHAPTER XLI

"There are times when divine intervention is required."

WISENDEE

Though Darius, the modern Scion to be, may know a million profound secrets of this world, the ancient ones, the Scions of old, knew the One secret – *Love* – and that was greater than the million; for the billion dollar secrets Darius hath discovered breed death, disaster, sorrow, selfishness, lust, and avarice, but the One secret confers life, light, immortality, and truth… The one is Unity.

"Where is he, Dee?" Darius asked, standing inches from my face. "Tell me. I know you know. You know everything…"

Councilor Julius, in full Order Military regalia, entered the room on cue. "Sir, we found him," Julius said. "NORAD has eyes on him."

"He launched himself into space and triggered Russian Strategic Missile Defense and retaliation protocols, Sir," Julius said.

"Three nuclear warheads were detonated over the Pacific," Darius' Chief of Staff added.

"Unbelievable," Darius groaned. "He started a nuclear war?"

"Russian defense thought Alexander's pod was a nuclear bomb. Then, Alexander initiated a missile launch which triggered a Russian response. He ejected from the pod before it was hit by a Russian nuclear warhead over the mid Pacific," Julius said. "The Russians and the Chinese were convinced America had launched a missile at them. The Russians still are."

"If I may, it's a shit storm, Sir," Darius' Chief of Staff told him.

"This will set back our negotiations on—" Councilor Julius began before Darius exploded.

"I am going to fucking kill him!" Darius yelled in my direction.

Darius was not lying. I said nothing.

"Get him here now!" Darius commanded Julius and his troops. He looked at his watch, adding: "He needs to be dressed and in that ballroom in fifteen *fucking* minutes. Or so help me God…"

"Yes Sir," Julius and the military minions ran with their orders.

"Dee. You come with me." Darius marched down the long hall, fuming with anger and determination, followed by twenty men in black suits, and me. At the end of the hall, waiting for Darius, stood *Majestic Privy Councilor Goldman*, the Order banker.

"Find and freeze all of Alexander's accounts. Cut him off completely," Darius instructed Goldman. "Make arrangements for him to be taken back to New York with me immediately after this fucking charade is over," Darius barked to his Chief of Staff.

"We need to talk about the APEX project," Goldman said, pointing to a room of men, including Councilor Tom, the Scion's lawyer.

"Dee. Get in here," Darius snapped at me, pulling me in the room and slamming the door on his staff.

As Darius discussed his plan for world domination with the APEX supercomputer, my thoughts drifted to Alexander...

CHAPTER XLII

"Are Darius and Alexander star crossed?"

ALEXANDER

"That's a person in that thing?" I heard the jet pilot ask NORAD command.

"Lex, let's lose these losers."

"I do not understand what 'lose these losers' means."

"Get off the radar of the jets. Don't let NORAD or ORNet track us. Do not let anything follow us or trace us to the target."

"Losing these losers," Lex said.

Laughing felt good. "Lex, you are learning wonderfully."

The special plasma propulsion rockets fired up. I slowed down to a stop almost instantly. That really hurt. My heart skipped a beat as my organs squeezed under the G-forces. I almost blacked out. And nearly shit myself.

"Watch my vitals, Lex. Don't kill me in the losing process."

By not moving, I was totally invisible. The jets roared past me.

"We lost him," the jet pilots said. "Circle back!"

The jets began to turn around. Their radar scanners faced away from me, I punched it. "Full power. Go."

Blasting directly between the jets, I arched into the upper atmosphere. The jets realized they had completely lost me. For the moment, my plan worked.

"Losers lost. On course for the island." Lex got this.

"Nice job, Lex." He's back and better than ever.

Following my AR navigation, I finally saw my little one-man island appear below. White sand and crystal clear water beckoned my soul. I pulled the rip cord and pop goes the parachute. Joy, just floating on air. Off came the helmet. I drifted slowly, down to a perfect landing on the beach. Success.

Nothing but open water and blue sky in every direction. "Let me out." Nothing happened. I clarified: "Open the suit."

Suit popped open. Stepped onto white sand, terra firma. The weather: perfect, as predicted. Took a deep breath and soaked in the fresh, ultra-pure air. Stripped out of my underclothes, and laid down naked in the sand. Earth felt awesome. Basking in my birthday suit, and my new sense of peace and perspective of the world, I stared at the sky and felt happy. My perspective on life had changed; almost dying and seeing the earth from space made me see my life a little differently. And nature healed the soul… I stopped spinning.

Opened a compartment on the suit and took out a beach towel, board shorts, and sunnies. That feeling of being watched came over me. Darius had eyes on me. Hate that feeling. Looked up at the sky as I put my swim trunks on. From another compartment I took out my glass cup and poured myself a fabulous margarita.

Peace.

And quiet.

Aaaaaaaaahhhhh…

Life. Enjoy it while it lasts.

CHAPTER XLIII

"Darius is his destiny."

ALEXANDER

"BEEP. BEEP," went my spacesuit helmet.

"Lex how could you." Only one minute of peace. They found me. The beeps of a message sent via ORNet were like a dagger to my heart. The helmet comm had a text message pop up on the outside display screen. I ignored it.

"One new message, Alexander," the helmet speaker barked.

"Delete message!" I shouted back. "I said hide from ORNet!"

Silence. That's what I like to hear.

"REMINDER: COUNCIL MEETING," the computer voice said, killing my margarita buzz dead.

Another beep, this one had the tone of a message from Grandfather. Finished my margarita, got up, and looked at it:

"FROM MEL: WHERE ARE YOU? I WANT YOU TO MEET COUNCILOR DAVID PETERSON."

Another beep, this one had the dark ominous tone set for messages from Darius. Saw it before I could avert my eyes:

"FROM EVIL PRICK: I SEE YOU AND I'M COMING FOR YOU, YOU MANIACAL LITTLE FUCK."

Fuck me. "Fuck you!" I screamed at the sky, giving his spy satellites the finger.

"That fucking Rat-Face fucked me..." My escape plan had failed miserably. "I'm going to kill him for this... Lex, remind me to kill Rat-Face—"

Felt it coming before I saw it, but saw it before I heard it. The question is: when did I know this was going to happen?

When I heard the BEEP. That's when. The Angel of Death comes.

A faint buzz. It grew louder, until a sonic boom knocked me off my feet as a Level 10 alien-tech space ship appeared over me. The shock wave almost knocked me unconscious. If Darius wanted to, he could have had them hit me with a bigger, louder shock and even killed me, but he wanted me awake and in pain. Death began to sound good again all of a sudden. My head throbbed in pain. This is my life…

Before I could get up off the sandy beach, a net shot from the craft snared me. They hoisted me up into the craft, old-school style, no doubt because it hurt more and thrashing around in a net like a fish is totally humiliating. Two Order agents waited to take custody of me.

The UFO sealed closed and rose into space.

"Let me out of this fucking net. Now."

"No." The Order agent said.

"Did you just say no?"

"Yes," the dead-behind the eyes agent said.

Before I could berate them, the agent zapped me and I froze with "locked in syndrome" – paralyzed, unable to move or speak, but totally conscious – the worst feeling in the world. I was being taken to the Council Meeting and I could do nothing about it. That terrible stabbing feeling in my gut set in. Impending death.

Darius is going to kill me. I can feel it.

CHAPTER XLIV

"Is this when Alexander met my father?"

WISENDEE

Every soul is engaged in a great work, a labor of personal liberation from the state of ignorance. The world is a great prison, its bars are the unknown. You are a prisoner until, at last, you learn, you earn the power, the right to break these bars from their ethereal wall, escape the cave of shadows, and pass inspired and illuminated, freely through the darkness, which becomes lighted by that eternal flame inside you, until at last you are free, and you see the sun that is your divinity.

Fleeing the dark prison of the unknown, David and Sarah floated on a black sea of Order elite vanity; a vessel of humility, escorted by their assigned Order Livery, to me. Guided by light in their hearts, they sailed the treacherous waters, swimming with sharks and monsters, into the storm of the Council Meeting...

David knew the name and title of many the Livery had introduced him to, but he had never seen the face of the svelte woman heading right for him. The unbreakable Livery broke a sweat.

"Her Supreme Highness, Exalted Queen Hermina, wife of Supreme Highness, Majestic Imperator, Lord Darius," the Livery said.

Hermina stood tall; a thin, pale, and delicate woman. Big piercing blue eyes, voluminous blond hair, a long slender neck, her striking beauty intimidates the strongest men. She settled her gaze on David.

"This is Sir David Peterson, the newest member of the Council," Hermina's decorated Livery said, "And this is Lady—"

"I thought he'd be taller," Hermina said as her maidservant lit her cigarette, in its long cigarette holder. Her gaze turned and she wandered away in a puff of smoke. The Livery could not help but give a telling sigh of relief.

David and Sarah met a scientist Sarah recognized. A specialist in biotechnology Sarah had worked with in London. "Sarah, how wonderful to see you. And this must be Sir David..."

"Indeed it is." David said smiling.

"This is Dr. Roberts, a friend of my father's and a former employer of mine. He's one of the leading genetics scientists in the world," Sarah said. "His work in genetics is quite extraordinary."

"I'm giving a presentation on human cloning tomorrow. You know, since being invited to this secret affair, every grant I ever applied for has been fully funded," he told them. "Cloning interest has soared."

"Human cloning?" David inquired.

"By George, there's the Queen. She's coming over to us," Dr. Roberts said as David and Sarah turned to meet the Queen of England, with several members of her Privy Council. After a few moments of pleasantries with her, the Order Livery interrupted.

"The Scion calls, Sir David," the Livery said. "This way, please."

As they walked along the vast hallway, they heard a buzzing in the courtyard. 'Twas Darius' craft, carrying Alexander, and it appeared in a silent flash. The craft hovered above the courtyard before extending gear and resting. David and Sarah stopped and stared out the window. Never having seen a space ship before, in amazement they stared.

"Please keep walking, the Scion is waiting, Sir," the Livery insisted.

"What is that?" David said, pointing at the craft.

"Order Aircraft Chameleon-101, of the fleet of Lord Darius. It is not to be spoken of. Please, we must keep moving before—"

"Ow! That fucking hurt!" Alexander screamed as Order Agents shocked him back to life. Deliberately making a scene, kicking and screaming, garbed only in board-shorts from his all too brief island retreat, they dragged him down the ramp, off the craft. The Order Livery became nervous as the agents with Alexander headed right for the doors in front of them.

"Oh God," the nervous Livery said under his breath.

"Who is that?" Sarah asked.

"His Supreme Highness, Scion presumptive, Lord Alexander," the Livery said, his voice shaking. The Order Agents dragged Alexander inside the building right in front of David and Sarah.

"I was not informed of his arrival. My timing could not have been worse. I sincerely apologize," the Livery said.

"Let me go!" Alexander screamed at the men-in-black. He stopped when he saw David and Sarah. The Livery kept his head down in shame. David and Sarah watched.

"See how they treat me?" Alexander said. "You'll be no different."

Order Agents threw Alexander into his room, shut the door, and stood guard.

"Let us walk quickly." The Order Livery hurried David and Sarah past Alexander's room.

"I'm not putting that on!" Alexander screamed.

Alexander's doors flung open just as David and Sarah stepped in front of them. Alexander burst out, in his board shorts, startling all of them. He wanted to know who David and Sarah were.

"Oh dear Lord," the Order Livery froze in horror.

"Why are you lurking outside my door?" Alexander yelled in the Livery's face, turning his hurt and pain on the weakest. "What the fuck! Don't they train you retards anymore?"

The Livery fell to his knees praying for mercy. David and Sarah saw the scared child in Alexander lashing out for attention.

"You're done. How dare you embarrass me in front of—"

"Stop," David defended the Livery to Alexander's surprise.

Alexander turned his attention to David.

"You're David—" Alexander said as the agents reached for him. "You're the new Councilor."

David didn't know what to say, but disappointment was all over his face. Order Agents grabbed Alexander and pulled him back into his room.

"Get dressed," the Agent said.

"Let go of me. Let go of me now!" Alexander said as they forced him back into his room. "Can I fucking talk for a second? I'm not getting dressed unless I can talk."

David and Sarah caught eyes with a fearful Alexander just as the door closed. The staff assigned to dress Alexander stood outside with David and Sarah. No one knew what to say or do.

"Dear God, this is a disaster. My deepest apologies," the Livery lamented to David and Sarah.

"It's alright," David told the old man Livery. "It's not your fault."

"We won't speak a word of this," Sarah added reassuringly putting her hand on the Livery's arm.

The Livery pulled himself together. He adjusted his suffocating suit and bowtie, and finished his duties. He led David and Sarah to the Scion's room, the King's Suite at the end of the East Wing. The Guards opened the doors and the Livery hurried them inside. A deep sigh of relief as the doors closed behind them.

CHAPTER XLV

"Time to meet the Majestic."

WISENDEE

The elaborately dressed Order Guard announced David and Sarah's arrival to the palatial room. "*Supreme Illuminated Regality, Majestic Councilor David Peterson, and Lady Sarah Peterson.*"

All eyes turned to David and Sarah. The Scion lit up with joy at the sight of David. Everyone noticed. With a wave of the Scion's hand, the guards immediately ushered David and Sarah over to him.

"David, my son," the Scion said. "Wonderful to see you." Councilors Tom and John took note of the Scion's choice of words. "David is the knight with the *je ne sais quoi*. Sarah is the daughter of Sir Henry." The room fell silent thinking of Henry.

The Scion smiled at Sarah. She had met him before, as "Mr. Smith," but did not realize it until this moment. David and Sarah both noticed the brilliant white light of the Vizier's aura, as the Council gathered.

"Time to meet the *Ancien Régime* family," the Scion said. "His Grace, Steward of the Order, the Royal Vizier, whom you know…"

"Your Grace. This is my wife Sarah," David said.

"Your Grace," she said, awestruck as she bowed to him.

Next in line stood John and Tom. "My Supreme General Council of the Order, the *Grandmasters of the Majestic Councils of Law*, *Conseil du Roi*, Sir John and Sir Tom. Search the world and two better magistrates you will never find."

"I am honored to meet you both," David said.

"Pleasure to meet you, Sir David," John said.

"Welcome to the Council," Tom said.

The charming affable Frenchman, Simon Sinclair stood ready. "My personal Physician, *Surgeon General* Simon Sinclair," the Scion said. "Simon's the only reason I'm still alive."

David and Simon felt their fates bond instantly. Charismatic, with a cheery disposition, Simon contrasted the other serious and sullen councilors. David and Sarah felt relaxed by his warm embrace.

"Pleasure to meet you, Sir David," Simon said. "I'm a great admirer. I look forward to working with you."

"The honor is mine," David said. "This is my wife, Sarah."

Simon kissed Sarah's hand and poured his sumptuous French charm on her. "She is a gift from God. As were her father and mother. We are most fortunate to have you both here with us."

The Scion moved David along the line. Next in the queue waiting to meet David was the towering, stern man with a shiny bald head. "This is Sir Montague E. Goldman, Illuminated Grandmaster of the *Conseil Royal des Finances*. Monty is our financial warlock, Chancellor of the Royal Treasury, Lord of the Privy Purse Keepers. He oversees the global financial operations of the Order, which at this point are so stupendously complex I no longer understand them myself," the Scion gave a mirthless laugh.

"Welcome to the Council, Sir David," Monty said.

An imposing Japanese man in full Order Military Regalia stepped up. "This is Sir Julius Yakuzmo, Constable of the Order, Commander in Chief of the Order Military Alliance. He advises the Council on all martial and peacekeeping matters."

"Welcome, Sir David," Julius the General bowed.

"His name is actually Hojios, but Darius changed it to Julius, because that's what Darius does," the Scion said.

Julius had no comment.

"Of the last of the ancient Samurai warriors in the world, Julius is a true master of the sacred martial arts," the Scion said, pointing David's attention to the polished katana sword.

Next to Julius, at attention, stood an equally impressive man with swarthy skin and brilliant yellow and green eyes, dressed in a three-piece suit. "Sir Maximilian Constantine," the Scion said. "*Conseil Royal de Commerce*. My advisor on global commerce and international affairs, Chief Diplomat and economist, he knows every important world leader personally. Don't hesitate to ask him for anything. He knows how to get it done."

"An honor, Sir David," Max said, shaking David's hand.

Next, the Scion and David turned to me.

"Now, David, watch out for this old Wizard, Sir Mervyn L.R. Wisendee. Exalted Grandmaster of the *Ordo Conseil des Dépêches,* he's the true mastermind of the Order; a Wizard like no other."

"We met briefly upon arrival," David said to the Scion.

"Again, welcome to the Council, Sir David," I said.

"Wise Master Dee, as we call him, looks the same now as he did when I was a child. In truth, I don't know how old he is or what secrets he holds behind those hypnotic eyes," the Scion said.

David looked into my eyes, searching for secrets, and told his own.

"He knows everything," the Scion said. "Yet no one seems to know his story." The Scion paused. "There isn't much Dee can't see with those rather large eyes of his. If you stare into them, he'll see right inside your head. Don't bother trying to hide anything from him."

David again wanted desperately to ask me about his parents. I downplayed the Scion's words. "I am here to help you as best I can."

David nodded, understanding exactly what I meant.

"Dee *is* Order Intelligence. He's headmaster of the Order Academy, educator to the world's top minds, and overseer of all Intelligence Directorates, ORNet, and all signals intelligence systems."

"Henry was my Councilor on human intelligence," the Scion said to David and Sarah. "His greatest work, and gift, was the both of you."

"The Council is lucky to have you," I said to David and Sarah.

"You will be working with Dee quite closely, whether you like it or not," the Scion joked. "No need to ask, just think it and he'll know."

"If only that were so," I said.

Finally, the Scion turned to the last member of the Council present in the room, the only woman on the Council.

"Of the *Conseil d'en Haut,* the High Council, this is my sister, Her Supreme Highness, Exalted Queen Olympias Marie, the goddess most high," the Scion said as he bowed to her.

A woman to rival the best in history, nearly as old as the Scion, her beauty never faded, her grace and charm an ever growing tree of majesty. Her lustrous, thick auburn hair, woven with strands of gold, styled in a Cleopatra inspired melon coiffure, topped with the dazzling diamond Crown of Venus.

"You are meant for great things, David," Olympias said.

David and Sarah bowed to the Queen, and remained speechless and completely taken with her. Standing in silence, they felt the intense, burning stare of the most powerful eyes in the world upon them.

All thoughts turned to Darius. He was not missed, his darkness fell upon us.

"Where is Alexander?" Olympias asked, breaking the silence.

CHAPTER XLVI

"Alexander fell into a whole new world of trouble."

WISENDEE

We are all given by Nature, a Life, a gift, and that blessing is the privilege of labor. Through labor, the good strife, we learn all things.

"Yes, where is Alexander?" the Scion asked me. "Can we send him another text message, perhaps? He likes to text message, he said."

"Alexander is here," I said.

The piano sonata ended and a new musical guard, with the strings and woodwind accompaniment, took the musical reigns, providing soothing background music as tensions began to rise.

"Alexander and Darius complete the *Curia Regis*," the Scion told David. He turned to his Advisors. "David must meet all members of the Council before we may begin." Thus the Scion informed Tom and John the meeting would not be starting on time.

"Darius is under the impression we are meeting in the ballroom in five minutes," Tom said. "We are already behind schedule."

"Darius' schedule," the Scion said, having made up his mind.

"Darius will be livid if he is summoned," Tom advised.

The Scion did not care. And the room grew colder, darker.

"Then don't summon him," the Scion said. "Bring in Alexander."

Of his own volition, thirty feet away, Alexander stepped into the room and stood next to the Order Guard at the door. In a room of black and white suits, and muted colors, Alexander proudly flaunted a florescent-colored tank top, California beach board shorts, plastic hemp "flip-flop" sandals, and neon pink sunglasses; his disdain for the ceremony and pageantry of his elders on full display.

"Do your thing, G. Announce me real good," Alexander said to the confused Guard, slapping his bum, and puffing a spliff.

"His Supreme Highness—" the Guard began.

"I'm really high!" Alexander shouted to the crowd staring at him, cutting the Guard off. Everyone froze. Jaws dropped.

The disdain for Alexander began to burn in the frigid crowd. Annoyed whispers permeated the room with the smell of illegal drugs. Alexander ignored the fact that everyone whispered about him. He started singing to himself whilst he accosted a footman holding a silver tray of champagne flutes. He snatched a glass and sipped it.

"Alexander," the Scion did not raise his voice. "Alexander."

Alexander pretended he didn't hear. Acting more intoxicated than he actually was, overacting the part of his party-animal persona for the crowd, Alexander stumbled on purpose into the elderly footman holding a tray. The highly skilled servant managed to keep the tray of flutes balanced, not a drop spilt.

"Nice save," Alexander said reaching for his second champagne flute. He drank the last drop and threw the glasses behind him. A crash as the glass hit the marble floor, stunning the room to silence.

"You're good," Alexander said to the steadfast footman, patting him on the back.

Without warning, Alexander underhanded the tray, smacking it out of the footman's gloved hands. Bubbling white wine and crystal flutes flew onto the crowd of Councilors. The glorious crystal stemware bounced off of them and shattered into sparkling shards.

As if by magic —he could not have aimed or planned it better— only members of the Council who have allied themselves with Darius were showered in bubbly. Myself, David, Olympias, Simon, John, and the Vizier were spared from the rain of champagne.

Tom, Julius, Max, and Monty were steaming mad.

"Oops," Alexander said in an affected Californian-surfer accent. "Guess he isn't so good after all."

The servants cleaned up the mess instantly.

"Bring me a beer, someone," Alexander said as he walked defiantly past the soiled half of the Council. The Councilors held their breath and stared daggers at the 'child' in cheap plastic sunglasses while they were wiped off and given fresh clothes by the staff.

"He's usually not this bad. He always acts up when he has to see Darius," the Scion said to David. "Alexander, I want you to meet Sir David and Lady Sarah. David is—"

"We met already," Alexander interrupted. "His stupid Livery brought them to my room while I was changing."

The Scion eyed David's Livery. The Livery turned bright red with embarrassment and fear.

142

"Our Livery did nothing wrong," David said.

"You're right, D. It's all my fault. Everything is all my *fucking* fault," Alexander said grabbing the beer brought to him.

"Alexander! Stop this! Pull yourself together!" the Scion said. The beer was snatched from his hands by another servant.

"I'm kinda having a bad day, okay. I basically died in space," Alexander choked up.

"Now, introduce yourself to David properly," the Scion said.

"Hi, David," Alexander said. "Your wife is pretty."

"Alexander where are you living now? I haven't heard from you all year. What have you been doing?" The Scion had genuine concern.

Alexander looked to me. *Your secret is safe with me.*

"Drugs mostly," Alexander said as he lit a cigarette.

The Scion paused until the cigarette was snapped from Alexander's hands by a servant, along with his pink-rimmed sunglasses. The Scion's eyes berated Alexander, and his ridiculous clothes.

John whispered into the Scion's ear: "The US government is still in DEFCON 1, and dealing with the fallout of Alexander's actions."

The Scion's face turned from anger to fear as he realized Alexander almost killed himself.

"Is this true?" the Scion could not understand how this was possible. "You started... a nuclear war?"

Alexander stared silent. Max and Julius confirmed it to be true.

Olympias, with her great affection and empathy for Alexander, embraced him. She put her arms around him to comfort him. She could feel his pain. Alexander let himself cry.

"It was an accident. I—" Alexander spoke the truth.

The Scion too became completely forgiving of Alexander. Simon's healing touch momentarily stayed Alexander's pain. Alexander caught my stare. He's thinking about the APEX.

Save me, Dee.

CHAPTER XLVII

"No one save you from your Self."

ALEXANDER

"How could you possibly manage to start a nuclear war? I don't understand… Look at you. You cannot simply party your life away in California," Grandfather lectured me. "I shan't be around forever, Alexander. I need you to take a more active role on the Council."

Like Darius would allow it, Dee heard me think.

"Time for you to grow up. There will come a day when—" Grandfather stopped himself from inferring that the moment he's dead, I'm in mortal danger from the wrath of Darius.

"You're right, Grandfather. I need to take an active role in my future," I said. "You want my 'Councilor' advice?"

"Yes," he said.

"Don't approve the APEX project. It's a bad idea." Boom.

In panicked shock, Goldman spit champagne directly onto Julius and Tom. I smiled because both had only just been cleansed of the first bubbly bath. Julius and Tom could care less about the champagne as they focused squarely on me, on my words, and the APEX. The disdain for me became a thick fog of tension in the air. How dare such anti-APEX – Anti-Darius – blasphemy be uttered aloud.

"Darius is lying to you about it. They all are." I looked at all the king's men staring daggers at me.

"I was told you voted yes on it." Grandfather turned from me to his wonder twins Tom and John.

"He did, my Lord," Tom said. "In writing."

"Nope, I didn't. Listen to me very clearly. I'm voting 'no.' No!"

The word "no" sent Julius and Tom into a silent rage. Dee reached out his arm to stop them from attacking me.

"Why? Why is the APEX a bad idea?" Grandfather asked.

Grandfather realized he did not know what exactly the APEX is, when he looked to Dee. The fact that Darius hides diabolical secrets was exposed, and now as clear as day, on the faces of the Councilors.

Everyone listened, waited, with painful anticipation for my response. The Councilors stared daggers at me, warning me. They don't scare me.

"Because as you can see, Darius and his lackeys want it so badly. Because it's evil and dangerous. And if you let him build it you'll all be sorry. Mark my words." My words declared nuclear war on Darius.

Silence became quiet murmurs. Murmurs gave way to a sound reminiscent of rolling thunder - the choreographed marching of a small army of men in black suits coming down the hall.

"Darius is coming." My own words hit me as a wave of adrenaline. Everyone felt anxious and afraid, just the way Darius liked his minions to feel, terrified.

"I don't want to see him." I turned to Dee for help. "He's gonna kill me. Grandfather. He killed my friends. He said he'd kill me if I—" I put my hands on Grandfather's shoulders, with the fear of death in my eyes, I gave him my well founded premonition: "He will kill me."

Grandfather wanted to say, "No he won't." But he spared me a lie.

"Fuck my life, seriously. Fuck this."

"Alexander—" Grandfather didn't know what else to say.

Tried to run, but seeing the futility on the faces of the armed Order Agents, returned to the safety of Aunt Olympias' arms.

"Stay with us, Alexander," the Scion said. "Tell me what you know about the APEX."

I stayed, silent. I've said too much already.

Grandfather turned to his Advisors. "What does Alexander know about the APEX project?"

"I'm not sure, my Lord," John said.

"I do hope he'll enlighten us all," Tom said. "It seems to me this is merely another stunt. He's recklessly starting another war."

The elite of Darius' Order Agent command marched into the room and created a perimeter. Darius entered to the fanfare of fearful silence, followed by his entourage of mini-me, bastard sons, and his soulless minion-men in black.

"His Supreme Highness, Exalted King most High, Lord Darius the Fourteenth of America."

"Take him," Darius pointed to me.

"Darius stop this," Olympias said.

"Not this time," Darius pushed back hard.

No one could save me. The elite Order Agent team restrained me, grabbing my arms.

"You can't do this to me— Grandfather!" I shouted as the agents shackled me.

"Yes, I can, child. I need only the approval of half of the Council, to censure you, and lock you away."

All the votes he needed still had champagne on their face.

"Take him away," Darius said.

"He killed my friends— You fucking monster! He's gonna enslave us all with the APEX! Don't let him—" They gagged me.

"*Quo warranto*, Alexander stays," Grandfather said. "*Ultra vires*, Darius."

Order Agents froze. Held my breath in hope. Wish I paid better attention in Latin class.

"Father, please, you'll kill us all with your ridiculous formalities!"

The Scion defied Darius. "Alexander stays."

"*Quoad hoc Curia*, I petition *certiorari*, your Grace. *Res gestae, felo de se, et periculum in mora*! Alexander is to be remanded into my custody. *Sum intra vires*, under Section 5: *prima facie ad quod damnum de Ordo*," Darius circled me as he barked legal jargon. "Immediate punishment is in order for this little boy's crimes against the Order."

Darius passed a document from Tom to the Vizier.

"The *Curia Regis* must recognize the petition. The votes of the Council shall be cast," the Vizier said.

Darius, Julius, Monty, Max, and Tom all voted for the motion. Darius needed six votes, a majority as I cannot vote for myself. He looked to Dee, John, and David.

"Yes," John said with pain as Darius stared him into submission.

Grandfather was angry, but not at John. David looked relieved.

"*Lex de Ordo*, section five, the petition is granted. The Scion is overruled. Councilor Alexander is suspended and remanded for the mandated minimum period of one year, until the next meeting of the Council." The Vizier had no choice but to sentence me to this death.

Grandfather could do no more. Darius had won. The agents took me away, broken, with tears of pain rolling down my face.

This was coming no matter what, I told Dee with my eyes.

Guess this is goodbye, I'm dead.

CHAPTER XLVIII

"You're the only one who knew, aren't you?"

WISENDEE

"The only way the Order may work is when all its dissipated powers are gathered up into One, as they must be, because Unity is strength."

Darius ignored me and turned his laser focus to the Scion. The Scion ignored him and spoke to a very uncomfortable David.

"Darius simply loves to overrule me…" the Scion said to David with pain and disappointment. "*Ex injuria jus non de Ordo*, yes?"

"*Ex factis veritas oritur!* Alexander started a nuclear war, Father!" Darius looked to the Councilors for support. "He will not be joining us for the meeting. That insolent child must be taught a lesson. He will kill us all if left unchecked!"

The word "kill" hung in the air.

"Speaking of children, David, this is my child, Darius." The Scion said to David: "He can be quite insolent himself."

Darius sized up David, the Scion's new favorite. Sarah feared exactly this moment and held David's hand tight. Darius initiated his charm offensive, and in the blink of an eye, changed into gentleman.

"Sir David Peterson, Lady Peterson, pleasure to meet you both. And welcome to the Council," Darius was seductive and spellbinding to David. "I look forward to working with you. I've heard great things."

"A great honor to meet you, my Lord," David said, nervous.

"The honor is all mine. I'm counting on your support." Darius was not at all subtle. Darius turned to Sarah. "Lady Sarah, you are absolutely radiant. My condolences on the loss of your father. Sir Henry was a great man, and he is sorely missed." Darius focused again on David. "I know David will do him and the Council proud."

David fell under Darius' spell. The Scion put an end to it.

"I'm having doubts on the APEX project, Darius," the Scion said, instantly revealing, to swooning David, the true nature of the beast. Darius went from dashing gentleman to savage beast, again, in the blink of an eye. He barely managed to save face.

"What?" Darius flushed red with rage as Julius whispered of Alexander's infamy in his ear.

"Father. You cannot seriously be giving credence to Alexander's preemptive retaliation against me. He is only seeking to make me upset. He knows little and cares less about the Order and its needs and I will not have his tantrums disrupt best-laid plans. You wanted him here. I brought him here. I fulfilled my end. He voted yes. It's time to begin. Come and join us for the presentation and I will assuage all doubts about the project." Darius turned and began to walk away.

"You see, David," the Scion said to David, defying Darius in tone, "Darius lives in New York. Lack of nature makes them so uptight."

Darius stopped, his back to the Scion, hiding the vitriol on his face.

"Supposedly Alexander lives in California, but even Darius can't seem to find him often... Isn't that right, Darius? How can you lead this Order if—"

Darius turned and projected all his anger on the Scion. "Stop! Father, please! We are already behind schedule!" Darius' words and energy attacked the Scion as a dagger to the heart. Darius calmed himself, having released his rage. "Please join us in the throne room, so we may begin." To the Councilors. "Go! Now!" he commanded.

Councilors Tom, Monty, Julius, and Max follow Darius.

Exasperated growls of frustration echoed in the halls as Darius stormed off, down the hall to the Ballroom.

"Oh God," the Scion lost his breath and strength.

"Majesty!" Simon sprang into action as the Scion collapsed in pain.

Simon placed his hands on the Scion's heart. The Scion instantly felt relief from the pain. His heart started beating again. The evil hatred of Darius was exorcised, allowing the Scion to breathe again.

"You almost had a heart attack, my Lord," Simon said. His powerful gift of energy healing stopped the attack.

"He saved the Scion's life?" David said in awe of Simon.

"Dr. Sinclair can heal with intention alone. The rarest of gifts."

Simon appeared visibly spent, drained of energy; worried about the Scion. We feared the worst, the Scion most of all, yet showing it least.

"Darius is quite charming, isn't he?" The Scion said to David.

The Scion's hollow laugh sounded painful. He looked old and frail, broken, as he sat on a chair, as yet unable to stand.

Darius is killing him, Simon told me. "It's getting worse."

"I know," I said. *I know*...

CHAPTER XLIX

"What is the APEX, exactly, Master Dee?"

WISENDEE

"What is the APEX, exactly?" the Scion asked me. David, Simon, and Olympias wanted to know as well. "Alexander seems to know more about it than we do. He had such… passion, Dee."

I had hoped that Alexander would reveal that he built ORNet, which the Order now depends on, and that he started building the APEX, the next level cyber infrastructure of the Order and ORNet to bring unity to the family – or as he put it: 'beat Darius at his own game.' But now, this did not seem the right time and place to reveal Alexander is the world's best computer genius and hacker.

"What are you not saying, Dee?" The Scion pressed.

"Alexander is entitled to his opinion and his vote," I deflected. "He is not unjustified in his fears of the future."

"Explain the APEX project to me. A super-computer? For what purpose? I don't understand," the Scion implored.

"Code name 'The APEX,' The All-Powerful-Electronic-X-change is a globally networked computer system, to be built on top of Order Resources Network, my Lord," I informed the Scion, again. "The purpose is to build a global communications network."

"Darius commissioned the APEX as a replacement and upgrade, a centralization of the Order's current cyber systems," John said.

"Which Darius requires approval to build," I added.

"But he's building it already, isn't he?" Olympias said.

The Scion generally loses interest at the word "computer," however he did not like Darius seizing power or defying him.

"Under Darius' plan, and the proposed edict, ORNet, the Order's current network, will be hyper-linked to a bigger, more powerful, data processing center, for the entire world wide web, an all-seeing eye, which he wants to built in America," John said. "By connecting all the world's computer-networks into one matrix, the APEX would give us central processor capabilities that are far beyond anything ORNet has today."

"I'm still not sure I understand," the Scion said.

"The APEX would be for the digital world of computers what the Order is for the human world," John said, intoning his own fear of this fact. "The APEX would be the centralization cyber power."

"Perhaps we should let Darius explain it to you, my Lord," I said.

"Perhaps I am too old to understand this newfangled world," the Scion said. "Darius has begun building it, the APEX, cyber thing?"

"Yes," John said. "He has engaged a team to build it."

"I see," the Scion said.

"I want him stopped," Olympias said. "He has defied the Council by building his digital weaponry without permission. It is Darius who should be censured."

"It is not yet built. To intervene is – dangerous," John said.

"Thank you. Go ahead, John," the Scion said, dismissing him.

John left the room. The Scion and Vizier walked away to talk. Olympias turned to me and David. Simon focused on the Scion.

"Dee, I want you to free Alexander," Olympias said once John left.

"Go to the ballroom for the APEX presentation," I said to David. "You must decide how you will cast your vote."

"What?" David begged. He looked to Sarah, afraid.

"You shall be the deciding vote. For or against Darius."

"You're voting with Darius?" David asked, doing the math.

"Yes."

"Why? Why must I be the deciding vote on the APEX project?"

"Because that is your destiny. T'will be good for you."

"I—" David stopped when he saw the Scion and the Vizier talking in the far corner of the room. They looked at him.

"What happens if I vote against the Scion?" David said.

"Then Darius wins." *He'll find the Aton, David.*

You know about the Aton, Dee? David asked with his eyes.

David and I looked to the Scion and Vizier talking about it.

Darius cannot know about the Aton.

CHAPTER L

"Power and control is his game."

WISENDEE

'Tis only in the darkness that we truly find our light; when we are in despair, this inner light is nearest, warm and brightest of all, to us. Try as I might to bring Darius to his light, or the Order's, he fights.

"How much longer is that fucking tyrant going to live? He's impossible!" Darius moaned as he stormed down the palace hallway.

"The APEX project may not be approved," Tom informed Darius. "Alexander appears to have changed his Majesty's feelings on the matter."

"I am going to KILL that fucking brat! Which room is he in?"

Order Agents led the way to Alexander.

"When the Scion learns we have already begun construction, or if Section 7 is called, the APEX is as good as dead," Tom informed Darius. "John will vote 'no' if called to overrule. He'll not side against his Majesty. Not again, I assure you."

John arrived as Darius motioned to open Alexander's door. I entered behind them.

"Dee, he already signed off on the project! Father cannot change his mind now!" Darius foamed at the mouth as yelled.

"Yes he can, Lord Darius," I seized all his faculties, stopping him in his tracks. "If the Scion does not say yes to the edict today, the APEX project is officially dead. For at least a year. It is his prerogative."

"Don't lecture me on royal prerogative, Dee!" Darius snapped.

Alexander was up to no good, again. "What is that smell!?" Darius yelled as he marched into the room. Order Agents seized Alexander and pinned him against the wall. Darius grabbed Alexander's face. Alexander spewed two-lungs-full of THC laced vapor smoke into Darius face. Darius hates hippies and he loathes all things marijuana. Alexander laughed a loud, nervous laugh.

"Hey, Dad. Ya' miss me? So nice of you to—"

"Silence!" Darius yelled violently, his head ready to explode, starting with the veins bulging out of his brow. "How did he—"

Darius was beside himself. How did Alexander get marijuana while in custody? Darius had never been so angry and confused in all his life. His eyes bugged out and his pale skin turned red as the bloodlust in him surged to a crescendo. Darius growled like an animal as he grasped Alexander by the neck and choked him, crushing his throat.

"Darius, stop!" John said.

"If you kill him, the Vizier will excommunicate you and his Majesty will have you put to death," I warned.

"You can kill him when you are King. Not before," Tom said.

But it was too late. Alexander died. Darius killed him with his bare hands… Just as Alexander predicted.

"He's dead." *You could be killed for this, Darius.*

The Agents released Alexander's limp arms. Darius threw him by the neck to the ground. Suddenly the consequences of killing Alexander clicked with Darius.

The Order Agent scanner confirmed it. No life. He suffocated.

Tom, John, Max, Monty and Julius stood stunned.

"Dee. Fix him," Darius ordered me, pointing to Alexander's lifeless body. "Fix him! Now!!"

"How?" I said, testing Darius.

"I know he's not dead until a certain point is reached, Dee," he said.

Begrudgingly, I placed my hands on Alexander and employed my own healing powers. Bringing someone back from the dead is painful.

Touching Alexander, I closed my eyes and found him. His soul was free and happy as it sank to the bottom of the cosmic ocean, ironically towards the light of the Almighty.

You must come back. I cannot force you, but I implore thee… Alexander knew he needed to come back. Saved from drowning in the depths of the afterlife, I brought him back to the surface of reality. He allowed me to place his soul back into his body. Alexander's energies were rebalanced, his mortal instrument tuned to life. His heart started beating as I opened my eyes. *Thank you,* he said.

Alexander's eyes opened after about thirty seconds, long enough to give Darius the scare of his own life. Alexander sat up, his own ego as enraged as Darius'. Except Darius now hated Alexander even more for scaring him with the threat of execution.

"Twas close, Lord Darius," I stopped the rage from boiling in Darius again. "You almost killed yourself."

Fully restored, Alexander jumped to his feet.

"What do you know about the APEX project you worthless piece of shit? Answer me!" Darius said, punching Alexander in the abdomen.

Alexander bent over in pain, but sprung up to fight back. Agents protected Darius and grabbed Alexander's arms and legs again, pinning him against the wall.

"You killed me. You *fucking* murdered me with your bare hands! You're a monster," Alexander said struggling to get free. "Fight me yourself, you *fucking* prick!"

"If you don't vote 'yes' on the APEX, I will torture you to death," Darius said. "Are you *fucking* listening to me?"

"Kill me. Again. I won't come back—"

John left the room, wanting no part of this.

Darius punched Alexander in the face, square in the jaw, with just enough force to be excruciatingly painful but not enough to make him pass out. I focused on Alexander, and gave him the strength to withstand the harsh blows from Darius. Darius noticed his punches were not hurting Alexander and he struck ever harder releasing his simmering rage. Darius roared in pain as his fists throbbed.

"Enough!" I put an end to this.

Mid punch, Darius flew backward to the floor. He didn't know what hit him. No one had touched him, but something had hit him with tremendous power. He looked at me, angry, realizing all the pain he tried to inflict on Alexander had bounced back, and he now felt it. Alexander felt no pain. Darius had been hit will all his own anger.

Behold the power of the wizard...

Mine eyes struck white terror into his blackened heart. Darius stopped. For the first time in his life he realized, he finally sees, just how powerful all that I am can be. He jumped to his feet as the winds against him began to howl as I stared at him, restricting his airways so he could barely breath... He fell to his knees before me. I looked down at him. *You must be taught in the school of the Spirit, a man learns all his wisdom through humility, all knowledge by forgetting, how to speak in dead silence, and how to live by dying. Perhaps you too must die to learn, Darius.*

"You are being warned, Darius. Do not test me."

Do not test me, Dee.

CHAPTER LI

"The Order is the Apex."

WISENDEE

Clear to me it became, that death would teach not that which Darius must learn, lo, only the retribution of his own will upon his soul can show him, his spirit, how to escape the shadow, why he must rise and grow...

Darius rose up in defiance of me, feeling physically more powerful than ever, though in truth weak in spirit as never before, he focused on Alexander. He could not see that all his might makes not him right, and all that he does, his actions hence, will inevitably fall back unto him, unequivocally.

"Take his key-card," Darius commanded the Order Agents. The servants adjusted his clothes and cleaned off the blood.

Order Agents seized the golden key-card from Alexander's person and gave it to Goldman.

"You're done. I'm cutting you off for good," Darius said to Alexander, who stood bleeding and now writhing in pain: Losing the key-card being the most devastating blow. He fell to his knees.

Goldman sent an email from his tablet. "Every account ever touched by Alexander will be zeroed out," Goldman said looking up from his device. "This will be a shock to the markets, particularly the Silicon Valley tech sector in California it seems, but Alexander won't have access to any currency on Earth by the end of the day."

The Order Agents pulled Alexander to his feet and confiscated the lot of Alexander's effects: his phone, a pen, a watch, and a vaporizer. Alexander stood furious, broken, as he wiped the blood off his face and out of his eyes. Darius punched him in the face again. But Alexander stood his ground and tried to hide the pain he felt inside as he looked Darius in the eyes.

"You haven't even begun to suffer for this outrage," Darius said. "When I'm through with you... you'll know what suffering truly is, you ungrateful little faggot."

154

Alexander's eyes filled with tears.

"Suffering is all I've known since the day I was born," Alexander said breathing heavily. "I'm the cursed spawn of a soulless monster."

Alexander looked at me. *I need that pen, Dee.* He referred to the pen taken from him, now in the agent's custody. I grabbed the pen from the Agent and set it down near Alexander.

"You are coming with me to New York – just as soon as this fucking charade is over. Time to learn how the world really works, little boy. I'm going to teach you what happens when you defy me." Darius turned to the Order Agents. "Alexander is not to leave this room! Do not let him out of your sight!"

Darius turned his back on Alexander to leave the room.

Alexander grabbed the pen, hiding it in his hand.

"You'll regret this forever," Alexander said, unable to resist mocking Darius to his back. "Goodbye, Father," he added, implying he'll escape.

Darius clenched his fists and wanted so much to turn around and kill Alexander, but he refused to give credence to Alexander's words.

Darius stormed out, without looking back. The Councilors followed. Agents realized Alexander had something in his hand.

Alexander smiled. *You're the best, Dee.*

I left the room.

Be careful, Alexander.

CHAPTER LII

"Darius can kill with thoughts alone."

WISENDEE

Thou shalt not worry about what thou does, but rather about what thou art, what one's isness is. If one is, and one's ways be, pure and good, thy one heart be true, then thy deeds doth be radiant. If one is righteous then what one does is also righteous, consequentially. Think not that greatness and divinity be based on what thou do, but rather on what thou are; for 'tis not our works which sanctify us, but we who hath sanctified our works with our pure heart.

Darius fails to understand such maxims of the spirit, thinking his actions shall make him great, even while they make his sinful heart untrue, his soul impure. Outside in the hallway, he walked swiftly as his manservants again cleaned him of the few remaining drops of bad blood spatter from striking Alexander violently so. Handed a mirror to check himself, in vanity, Darius saw that behind him down the hall, the Scion had yet to leave the King's Suite.

"He hasn't even stepped into the hallway. Un-fucking-believable. We're already twenty minutes behind schedule!" he yelled in vain.

Darius growled as he marched angrily down the long hallway.

"Dee, where are we on the APEX edict votes?" Darius barked, checking to see if I still planned to vote yes.

"Without Alexander's vote, you will require either David, Sinclair, Olympias, or John to overrule - if the Scion says no."

"Tom," Darius snapped. He looked around for John. "Where is your brother?"

"John will not side against his Majesty," Tom said. "If you press him, he'll push back hard."

"You do not have the votes, Lord Darius."

"Yes. I do!" Darius turned and berated my face with noise. "David will vote with me. Because if he doesn't—"

"What?" I said.

"He'll be dead, to me," Darius said. "It will be approved."

Darius' doubts were infectious and spreading fast.

"If Edict 1301 is not approved, the APEX and network underpinnings cannot be linked to ORNet. The system cannot be built as currently designed," I warned. "You'll need to redesign it."

"If the global communication networks are to be unified, the APEX Project must be approved today. Network totality will certainly not happen in the next twenty years, if the edict fails today," Tom added.

"Failure to pass the edict is deadly," Julius said. "The global military alliance protocol is already counting on the APEX, and requires the edict as currently designed."

"As does international finance. Without the edict we'll be forced to cut the Order funding," Monty said. "That will break the bank."

"Which will trigger an investigation," Tom said.

"This will blow up in all our faces," Max said.

"It already has blown up," Tom said. "Thanks to Alexander. And because we've already started construction, and engaged computer hackers to write source code, this could be ruled illegal under Order law. The Scion could order sanctions if—"

"Enough!" Darius yelled, his voice shaking the palace.

Darius walked faster, thinking faster. "My father will be dead soon. I already have de facto control. We build the APEX no matter what. He is not going to stop us."

Darius turned the corner, leaving the long hallway, just before the Scion stepped into it.

Darius entered the grand ballroom, brushing off everyone who wished to speak with him. The Privy Council members took their seats on the designated thrones, and waited in pensive silence.

Fifteen minutes later, an eternity to Darius, the Scion entered the ballroom, with the traditional pomp and fanfare. Now over an hour behind schedule, the Scion sat on his throne, overseeing the meeting as King of the Court. He motioned to the Guards.

"Seal the doors!" the Order Guard commander said. The massive doors slammed closed. The meeting had finally, officially, begun.

The absence of Alexander, the smell of death in the air, caused speculation that Darius had indeed killed the prodigal son...

CHAPTER LIII

"The 21ˢᵗ Century came to Order."

WISENDEE

"Under the Holy laws of *Æterni Imperium*, now in the presence of the Almighty God, and the Exalted Scion of the Pharaoh, *Rex Maximus*, Supreme ruler and Sovereign of the Human realm, on this day the ninth of March, in the year of our Lord two thousand and one, henceforth nothing conveyed within this sacred chamber may be spoken of to any layman without the direct permission of the Majestic Council. Any violation of this order shall be defined as high treason and subject to penalty of death. On the word of the Exalted One, so shall it be!"

"So say I," said the Scion. The slam of the Order Guard's spears on the floor made the decree official.

During the pageantry and traditional rituals, Darius sat engrossed on his smartphone, allowing it to beep as he sent and received messages. The Vizier and Queen Olympias did not hide their anger at Darius for his flagrant lack of respect.

After the ceremonies and routine approval of several Orders-in-Council, the moment everyone had been waiting for, or dreading, arrived… Darius stood up to speak.

"Lord President of the Exalted Magi, Heir Apparent, His Supreme Highness, Exalted King, Darius the Fourteenth!"

Darius walked up to the podium to fear induced clapping and applause. The lights dimmed until the ballroom fell dark. The thought of Darius as a harbinger of darkness set in on the audience.

"In the beginning there was darkness…" Darius said, his amplified voice struck fear into the souls present. The elderly guests were not expecting a powerful 3-D sound-system that created a God-like omnipresence to Darius' voice. "And God said: Let there be light!"

Darius tapped his tablet computer and activated a 3-D projection system, beginning his presentation. Stunning holographic stars floated and sparkled with color as they filled the room. People tried to grab the near photo-real 3-D hologram stars. Swirling galaxies filled the high ceiling ballroom, and nauseated some of the senior attendees, many shocked at this visually immersive laser projection technology. The stars became a wormhole transporting the audience through the cosmos to Earth's solar system. The rotating, enchanting Earth floated above the throne as the stunned silent crowd sat entranced.

"Welcome to the 21st Century," Darius said, as the booming voice of the almighty god.

The words "Welcome to the 21st Century" rotated around the mesmerizing holographic planet.

"Ladies and gentlemen, distinguished guests from every corner of the globe, you are invited here today because you are the apex of what humanity has to offer. The legendary pharaoh Alexander the Great founded this Holy Order on the idea of a world ruled by philosophers, the wisest and best men and women in the world. This utopian idea became the Republic, a ruling body politic designed to foster and elevate all people, allowing humanity's brilliant lights and minds to rise and shine. For only the brightest lights illuminate the deepest darkness. The Order has called upon you because our world needs your guidance, your wisdom, and your luminance. The Order *is the light* - in a world of darkness and chaos. As Plato famously said: 'We can easily forgive a child who is afraid of the dark, but the real tragedy of life is when men are afraid of the light.' Today, I will present to you the light of the future. The future of the Order. I ask that you be not afraid."

Darius stopped and stared at David. David felt the intense magnetism of Darius pulling on him.

"A new world is upon us, ladies and gentlemen. A new Order. A new Council. As some of you know, the Majestic has a new member, hand chosen by his predecessor the great Sir Henry Stuart before him, Sir David Peterson joins us, for the first time, at this time of great change and uncertainty. Let us all give a warm welcome to Sir David Peterson."

Darius motioned for David to stand. The thunderous applause for David made Darius jealous. He put an end to it quickly. "Thank you, David. Sit."

The hologram of the Earth changed into a great eye: an unnerving eye in a pyramid, the 'Eye of Providence.'

"This year, 2001, begins the 21st century. And now the rules of the old world, the 20th century, no longer apply. Everything you think you know about the way the world works is obsolete. Forget it. Nothing will be left untouched, and unchanged, by the rapid advance of computers, digital and cyber technology, and the Internet. So dramatic will this disruption be to the world order, the only way to ensure peace, and the continuance of order on Earth, is for our Order to centralize, harness, and control, these new computing and information technologies."

The great holographic eye looked to the words "TOTAL INFORMATION APEX" which flew in from the back of the room. Tiny at first and then growing large, giving the illusion of jet speed, they landed with a sonic boom. Guests jumped back in shock. The words circled around the eye in the pyramid.

"I present to you... the Total Information Apex."

All virtue of the APEX was debased by Darius' self-justification. Failing to see that virtue had turned vice, he of course expected applause. Words are spells of ideas, and unless they are cast properly, misunderstanding is inevitably fear inducing, and paralyzing.

In the darkness: Total silence.

CHAPTER LIV

"A computer system to rule the world?"

WISENDEE

What Darius failed to see is that the eye with which we all see the Universe is the same with which the Almighty sees us. Thine eye and God's eye is one eye, one sight, one knowledge, and one love; lest ye have a source of Love, God will not allow any vision clearly to be.

Darius' vision for the APEX was not founded on love, you see…

"The APEX, as we have termed it, will be built on top of the world's current global communication infrastructure…" Darius said.

The great eye watched as the laser projected holographic words "TOTAL INFORMATION APEX" broke apart into letters, images, and symbols to give a visual representation of Darius speech.

"Last year, we launched the Order Resource Network, ORNet, a centralized, deep web computer network, connecting the Order's various digital archives and data centers together. For those of you that don't know, ORNet is an ultra-secure information network. The paper catalogue that was the Order, is now a digitized and fully searchable database. What once took weeks, may now be done in minutes. Where once we were blind, now we see, with ORNet.

This year, I am proposing we build on this vision. We shall link together, covertly or overtly, every computer network on the planet. Every computer, every network, every communication system on Earth shall be linked into one matrix – thus creating a 'Total Information Apex.'"

"This is cyber subjugation of humanity," someone whispered.

"He'll be able to control the world with this thing," people said.

"I heard it's already being built." Anger brewed in all languages.

Darius continued, undaunted and undeterred.

"APEX will be our top-sight, it will see all, and know all, the literal apex of all information for our planet. The APEX will allow our Order to maintain order, in a world where information is power, and where power and information are managed in virtual reality."

The hologram of the earth spins as the construction phases of the APEX illustrate the linking of every communication system, every network, on earth together, into one world wide web...

"This is not asking for approval. This is telling us what is already being done," Olympias said loud enough for Darius to hear.

Darius ignored her. "The benefits to the global order are far reaching, and inevitability essential. The APEX will ensure global security, by identifying threats to order, preventing terrorism, stopping attacks before they happen, by bringing transparency to opaque governments and corrupt financial institutions. With computing power beyond anything ever dreamed of prior, we can solve the problems of the future, which we have yet to conceive of."

"Darius will use this computer system to seize all reins of power over the global economy," a French noble objects loudly.

"Data is the new fiat currency, the APEX shall be the new mint, and central bank. The APEX will allow us to maintain order in a world now predicated almost entirely on electronic communication and digital information," Darius continued.

The Scion appeared ill. The Queen stared at Darius, furious.

"The world needs a unified order. Order begins with a unified network. We need the APEX. The APEX is the only way to ensure global order, to police wrongdoers, and ensure peace, justice, and prosperity on this planet, in this brave new millennium. We cannot fight the future, nor stop it. We must create it!"

The APEX construction is complete in the holographic presentation. The Earth turns to light, and the lights return.

Darius' half of the Council stood and applauded. Much of the crowd felt compelled to clap as well. David didn't know what to do. "Darius is the future we cannot fight," one man spoke for many.

"The Order-in-Council is presented to the *Curia Regis*. The Exalted One has signed the edict. The edict is law and construction is to begin at once," Darius said, slamming his gavel. "Thank you."

"I object!" the words of the Queen hit the room like an atom bomb of silence.

Darius stopped, frozen in rage.

"I motion the Steward for a rescind of the edict - *Curia Regis advisari vult!*" Queen Olympias said, standing in defiance. Her voice was powerful and persuasive, every word a shockwave through the gathering.

162

Darius shook with anger as he prepared to speak calmly.

"The edict is not law if the Court does not now claim it to be so," the Vizier said. "Does the Court claim this edict to be law or will the King grant the Councilor's plea?"

If looks could kill, Darius' face would have killed the Queen. She was not afraid of Darius, though perhaps she had reason to be.

Darius stared at his Aunt, a woman with Pharaoh peerage above his own. Darius and Olympias drew the battle lines for an invisible war of will power, a war for control of the hearts and minds of the room. Olympias won almost instantly, drawing strength from the crowd.

"I will seek advisement," the Scion said.

"The edict will not be passed this year, Darius. 'Tis done," Olympias announced.

Darius went nuclear, as he exploded in scorn. Not everyone saw the blast happen, but half the Council felt vaporized by the pulse wave.

Calm numbness settled in on Darius.

"*Adversus solem ne loquitor,* My dear Exalted Majesty, perhaps you do not understand," Darius said to the Queen.

"I understand perfectly," the Queen interrupted. She switched to French knowing it flusters Darius. "*Le fait est que l' APEX est dangereux...*" she began, continuing in her native tongue: "I do not agree with you, Darius. I object to your super-computer project. I have doubts as to its necessity and imperativeness. I want the project investigated further. Such a massive and consequential undertaking should not be done in such haste, lest it lay us all to waste."

The Queen's words set off a wave of doubt and grumbling in the French speaking crowd.

Darius tried to gather his thoughts, but the Queen's French filibuster had agitated him into mania. The Queen asserted her power by further berating Darius, rallying the crowd behind her in defiance.

"'The world needs a unified Order' as Darius said, so perhaps Darius should unify this Order, this Council, first," the Queen said turning to the assemblage. "I see no unity without Alexander."

"I too have concerns about the architecture of the project – the long term implications of it on the current Order are uncertain," John said. "Haste is unnecessary and perhaps dangerous."

"What's to stop this all-powerful APEX computer from controlling us, Darius? Who will supervise its use? You?" the Queen asked.

"Investigation by committee of this Council's choosing is warranted. The future will not suffer to wait a year, my dear Darius."

"I agree with her Majesty," Simon said.

Darius rolled his eyes and demanded someone support him.

"Without this project, the 21st century will be chaos. The Order, global governance, our interconnected financial and communications systems could face mass disruption, fracture, and total collapse," Tom said. "We unequivocally need the APEX, it must be built. The sooner the better." Tom looked to his brother.

The split in opinion of the identical advisor twins, Tom and John, vexed the Scion.

Darius tried to take back control of the situation. "We cannot let fear keep progress at bay. Cyber war is coming, and we must—"

"Silence, Darius. The King of the Order will speak now," Olympias said. "What say you, our King?"

Darius flushed blood red with outrage. The Queen looked to the Scion who stood up to speak.

"I share the concerns, Darius. The Queen's motion is granted. The edict is rescinded and taken under advisement. By your own words, Darius, 'unity is required.' Alexander should be present. The APEX will be investigated and construction delayed for one year."

"Father."

"So be it," the Scion said.

"So be it!" said the Order Guards slamming their spears down, filling the room with the ringing sound of finality. The official and formal end of the APEX project hit Darius hard.

Fascinated by the glitter of unimaginable power, Darius gazed at the Medusa-like face of greed and found himself petrified. He twitched violently with indignation. A quiet foretelling of disaster swept over the room.

"*Alea iacta est.*" *The dice be cast...*

CHAPTER LV

"Power consumed Darius."

WISENDEE

A good ruler must have first been ruled, and Darius has never truly been ruled, and thus is no good at it. He refuses to accept the rules.

"No," Darius said. At first, he sounded calm.

"No. No! No! Noooooooooooooooooo!" Darius roared. His voice shaking the room violently. "This is wrong!"

"Darius—" the Scion said.

"You are wrong, Father! There's already been a commission! Great harm to the Order can come of this! Petition for *certiorari* under Section 7 is called. The Steward shall overrule the King with majority vote of the Council. By sacred law of this Order a vote! A vote, your Grace!"

Darius turned his death ray focus directly on David. Darius needed David's vote, and he cast his spell on David to vote 'yes' when called. Under Darius' beaming power David melted.

"Councilors, as I call your name, you will vote 'yes' for an override of the Exalted Crown to Lord Darius, and 'no' for a denial of the *Sacris Lex Septem* motion to override; no to the APEX." the Vizier said. "Councilor number 1 how do you vote?"

"Yes," said Darius, adding a desperate plea: "I vote for Councilor 2 *in absentia*. Yes."

"Proxy denied," the Vizier said. "Alexander voted no."

Darius growled furious.

"No," said the Queen, Councilor Three.

"Yes," I said, Councilor Four.

The Vizier voted no with his silence. He called on Sinclair.

"No," said Simon, Councilor Six.

"Yes," said Max, Councilor Seven.

"Yes," said Julius, Councilor Eight.

"Yes," said Monty, Councilor Nine.

"No," said John, Councilor Ten.

"Yes," said Tom, Councilor Eleven.

Darius focused on his only chance at the required seven votes.

"Sir David, Councilor Twelve, how do you vote?" the Vizier asked.

Darius stared at David with wide, threatening eyes. Darius sensed David about to say 'no'.

"Think long and hard, Sir David. You swore your life to this Order. I shall be Scion before long. If you deny me now—"

"Don't listen to him, David," the Scion said.

"Shut up, you!" Darius yelled harshly at his frail father. The Scion took the words like a punch in the gut. "Are you with me, David, or are you against me? Speak!"

David struggled to speak.

"This is an outrage!" Olympias said.

"You've said your piece, woman. David must cast his vote!" Darius would not be denied. "Cast your lot for all eternity, David!"

David could not speak. Tension froze the room stiff.

"My heart…" the Scion said. He grabbed his left arm in pain and fell from the throne chair. Simon caught him. Gasps and cries of fear and sorrow filled the room.

"He's having a heart attack," Simon said. "I need help."

Simon's medical team assembled.

"Vote, David!" Darius was unconcerned with his dying father. "Say, yes! Now! Say yes now or regret it forever!"

David was paralyzed with fear, shaking.

"Enough," the Vizier's angry tone put an end to the discussion, and broke Darius' spell on the room.

Simon's medical team carried away the Scion on a stretcher.

"As *Curia Guardian de jure, Sacris Lex Septem* vote is suspended indefinitely," the Vizier said. He turned to Darius. "It's over, Darius. Court is adjourned."

The Order Guard slammed their scepters onto the floor. The doors opened. Fearful silence as the Scion was taken away.

Darius roared his mighty lion roar, and stormed off down the West Wing of the palace.

A new Order, a plague of pain, was indeed upon all our houses.

CHAPTER LVI

"He learned how to play the game."

ALEXANDER

"What is that?" the Agent snapped, diving towards me, seeing the pen in my hand; a device I made to control Order Agents.

A click of my pen. "Please work." Doubting myself, I prayed.

At light speed the click reached the local ORNet comm center and activated my 'Order Agent command override' program. The agents all froze. The program has their mind. My program…

The pen is indeed mightier than the sword.

"Down boy," I said smiling. The Agent lunging at me fell to the floor on his knees. "Stay down."

The two other Order Agents changed their stance and saluted me.

"It worked." Doubted my own genius? Course it worked, I created it. My device and program to control the Order Agents with ORNet was untested until this moment, but worked like a charm. The expressionless faces of these trained killers stood at attention.

"Command override active. Repeat!"

"Command override. Complete," the mind controlled Agents said in unison.

"Alexander is released, by Order of the King. He is not to be tracked by any entities. Repeat," I commanded.

"Alexander is released by Order of the King," the Agents repeated. One agent appeared to fight the ORNet mind control program. His face growled, but he lost after another click of the pen and a good shock to his brain.

"No entities are authorized to track Councilor Two," they said.

"Blind allegiance is a beautiful thing," I said in the agent's quivering face. "Now bring me back my effects. And set up a VR station in room 105."

Agent left. Peeked out the door and saw Grandfather and his entourage walking to the meeting. They'll be in the meeting in a minute. That's my escape time. Minutes later my precious smartphone and me were reunited. Whole again. Back in business.

Holding down the clicker: "All agents are forbidden to look at Alexander."

Two agents repeated me perfectly. That third one fought the programming. "Agents are forbidden to look—" he said slowly as I looked him in the face.

"Say it!" I yelled.

No response.

"Kill this one," I told the other two agents, clicking the pen again. They both shot him with their silent guns. He fell to the floor dead. Felt bad for a second, but couldn't take chances. I heard the slam of the ballroom doors. The Council Meeting had begun.

"Take me to room 105."

The two agents escorted me to the room down the hall where a cube computer and VR headset sat on the desk.

VR headset on. "Activate." And into the virtual world of ORNet via Satellite uplink, I flew...

"Lex. Are you there?"

"I'm here," Lex appeared to me as a sort of cartoon in the low res, mostly green and black computer matrix.

"Time to check on my money situation."

"Goldman's trolls didn't waste a minute. All your accounts are frozen, deleted, or at zero balance. Even the ones we thought they didn't know about."

"Fuck."

"Dee says, don't curse," Lex said.

"I need at least a few billion dollars, Lex."

"We'll have to hack for it the old fashioned way," Lex said. "Darius has the financial system on lockdown."

"I don't have that kind of time. Think…"

I think, therefore, I hack. After about twenty minutes of manipulating the global financial system, squeezing out money wherever possible, and directing into an account, checked my balance: Two million dollars? *Fucking* great. That won't last me an hour. A third of the money vanished right then. Darius' bots got it. This won't work at all.

"We need a golden key-card. It's the only way," Lex said.

"I need a key-card." Spoke out loud, so the gods could hear my prayer. Any real money requires a key-card. Every card was behind closed doors. Doors I can't open.

This is how you become a warrior. You fight. You find a way. You use the pain and adversity to make you stronger and more powerful...

My computer glitched from electro-magnetic interference. Unlike Darius' craft, which causes radioactive pain, grandfather's craft, 'the Marduk craft' makes you feel electric and alive. VR headset off, I stepped out to investigate.

Out the window in the courtyard: the ballroom doors flung open and grandfather on a stretcher raced out. *Oh God*. They took him aboard the floating spacecraft. Simon looked super stressed, and he is not easily stressed. It's finally happened... He's dying.

David saw me watching through the glass on the other side of the courtyard. He knew it was me. Almost hid from him, until it hit me: "Hello key-card..."

Looked at him again, letting him know it was me.

CHAPTER LVII

"He must defeat Darius."

ALEXANDER

Order agents approached David and Sarah. "Please come with us Sir Peterson, Lady Peterson. The matter is urgent."

Into my commandeered room in the East Wing, David and Sarah entered, shocked to see me with a bruised and bloody face. Forgot how scary I must have looked from my beating by Darius.

"Are you alright?" David said.

"I must apologize for my behavior, Sir David, Lady Sarah. Acting up is the only way to get through to them sometimes." They were relieved to see the charming side of me.

"I'm a good person. You know. I try. Think of me as your friend. Grandfather told me to reach out to you if I needed anything."

David saw right through my lie. He's good... Because he also saw the truth in my words.

"What is it you want, Lord Alexander," David said.

"Can we start over?" Allowed myself to be vulnerable. "Do you want us to be friends? Most people don't know the real me. You both do. This is me. A broken, sad, and abused child."

"We can be friends," David said. "So long as you never lie to me."

David reached to shake hands.

"I need a hug." Hugged him.

Sarah watched me, confused as to my motives. Met eyes with her. "Join the hug?" I asked. "I can feel how much you love each other."

Sarah gave me the best hug. Her smell, and her warm heart next to mine... she warmed my soul. Didn't want to let go, but she gave me the 'alright already' signal. They stared at me. Sat back down.

"That was amazing." Buttered them up with truth.

"How did you get away from Darius?" David said. Nothing gets past him.

"What happened at the meeting?" Deflected his question. "You can tell me. I'm not a layman."

Under the desk, I opened David's wallet, picked from his pocket during the hug. How did I become such a great pickpocket? In a word: necessity. First time trying, mastered the art already.

David looked intrigued as he picked up my VR headset. "What is this?"

"A virtual reality headset." Directing his and Sarah's focus to the VR system, I slyly took out his golden key-card. "Try it on."

He put it on and I quickly inserted the gold card into the slot in the cube computer.

"You like computers?"

"Not as much as you do," he said. Taking off the headset.

"Eventually virtual reality will be photo real, but most of it is crude graphics for now. Limited bandwidth and all."

Put on the headset and started the transfer program, using David's key-card. My accounts rapidly began to fill with money. Yes... the billions rolled in. Took off the headset.

"Is that why you want to be my friend? To use me?" David said, staring at me.

"I said I'm your friend."

"What are you doing with my key-card, if I may ask, Lord Alexander?" David said.

"You may," I smiled. Warriors must also fight with charm.

"Answer me. And give it back," he said.

Stood up and looked him the eye. My green eye intrigued him, and in it he saw my desperation, my humility, my plea. My majesty.

"My Lord," David said, revealing himself.

"Your weakness is your total obedience to the Order. You want so bad to fit in, it hurts. Doesn't it?"

"You're stalling," David said.

"Did something happen to my grandfather? Is he dead?"

David's face said it all.

"Fuck." Looked at my smartphone.

TRANSFER COMPLETE >> Balance: $59,645,891,113

"Score..." Success. "That's more than my card has ever gotten. Do you use your card often?"

"I don't use it at all. And you didn't need to steal from me, Lord Alexander," David said.

"Call me Alexander. Please. One second and I'll give you the card back." Put in the VR headset and ordered my transport using the key-card access protocol. "There. Done."

"What are planning to do with all that money?" David said. He saw the screen. Can't get anything past him.

"Half of it will probably be gone tomorrow, but, it'll have to do." Took off the headset and gave David back his wallet and key-card. "I'm sorry I took this. I couldn't risk you saying no."

"If you're my friend, you'll tell me what you're doing, Lord Alexander."

"I needed money." David got it. "I need to fucking disappear for a while. Darius will kill me again if he finds me."

"Kill you again?" David said. He stared at me confused by the truth.

"What did you do with my card, exactly?" David asked, concerned.

"Key-cards are unlimited, and untraceable, if you know how use them... You should learn how to use it."

Sarah's face showed fear and anger.

Stood up. Clicked a button on the cube computer. The cube and VR headset burst into flames and burned away to almost nothing in a matter of seconds, leaving only a charred spot on the wooden desk.

"Can't leave a trail." Just a mark. "Wish I could stay and hang but my ride is here." Dashed out of the room.

David and Sarah followed me into the hall.

David stopped me. "The Scion had a heart attack," he said. "Now tell me what you're going to do about it."

"I— I like you David, and... I appreciate you're trying to help me and my grandfather. So I'll give you the best advice I can: Get out. Get out now, before it's too late. Resign from the Council and get away from Darius however you can, as fast as you can. Trust me."

Sarah became frightened at these words.

"It's already too late for you isn't it? We're all fucked."

Their faces said yes.

"I'm sorry."

"Where are you going?" David refused to let me go without giving an answer.

He wanted to hear me say it: "Once my grandfather dies, and Darius becomes the Scion, we're all fucked. You understand?"

"You need to stop cursing. Makes you *fucking* sound like Darius," David said, sounding like Darius, and me. Mind blown.

"Thank you. Needed that— I needed that, David." I hugged him. And then Sarah again. The love in their hearts gave me strength. "But I really gotta go."

Ran down the hall and up the stairs. David and Sarah followed me to the roof. They arrived just in time to see the transport ordered with David's card materialize on the roof platform. Boarded it and looked back at them.

"I wish I could get out. Hopefully it's not too late for you. Find a way. Save yourself. Save your family."

"Why don't you save us?" David shot back.

"Maybe I will." *That is the plan, actually.*

David and Sarah let me go in approval.

"Either way, you have a friend in us," David said. Sarah agreed.

That meant everything to me. The craft sealed closed.

David and Sarah watched me vanish into thin air.

CHAPTER LVIII

"Forbidden technology?"

ALEXANDER

The craft opened to my secret underground lair in California. Much like my life, my secret home is a massive complex, mostly industrial and filled with computers and machines, but no real life. No real light. No family. No love. Just the Order. Just Dee, waiting for me.

"Not now, Dee." Walked right past him.

"Yes, now, Alexander."

"Today is literally killing me. Alright? Can you just— Just leave me alone."

At the bar, poured myself some vodka over ice. Drank it and poured more. Must. Numb. Pain.

"Your grandfather is dying," Dee said.

That called for another drink.

"And I'm going to disappear with him. Or die, don't really care."

Walked over to my computer station and woke it up. Monitors all came to life. My A-I programs all hummed along, creating the APEX. Debated pulling the plug. *I should kill this whole thing now...*

"You must finish what you started," Dee said.

"I'm not building the APEX for him, Dee. No *fucking* way." Didn't mean to curse. "No way," I corrected myself.

"Yes you are," Dee said. "That is your fight. 'Tis the only way."

"It's too dangerous."

"Nothing has changed," Dee said.

"Everything has changed. He killed me. Alright. He killed me and now everything has changed. I've changed—" Cried for a moment, sitting on the cold cement floor, as my loveless life weighed on my heart. What an awful, rotten day. Wars of every kind got started.

"I wanna die, Dee."

"You came back for a reason. You didn't have to," Dee said.

"What was that thing that saved me? In space. A glowing orb."

"Perhaps 'twas divine intervention," Dee said.

"You know what it was. Don't you?"

"It was the reason you came back," Dee said.

"What do you mean?"

"You will save us, Lord Alexander. You will defeat Darius, and you will be great. That is the will of the gods."

"If I build the APEX, it could get away from me. Once Darius is the Scion, he'll twist it into something crazy and he'll use it to find me. He'll kill me again. And he'll rule the world with it."

"Not if you stick to your plan."

Tapped into ORNet, pulled up video feed of the Scion Castle. Found him. On the screen I watched as Simon and his medical team placed grandfather in his bed. Turned up the volume.

"He doesn't have long," Simon said to Tom and John.

"How long?" Tom asked.

"A few days at most," Simon said.

Tears rolled down my face as I looked from the monitor to Dee.

"I need more time. I need grandfather's help. He can't die."

"There is a way," Dee agreed.

"You can bring him back if he dies?"

"No."

"How?"

"Forbidden Technology."

This day just keeps getting weirder.

CHAPTER LIX

"Playing with dragons invites danger."

ALEXANDER

The Scion Castle is like a fairytale. Always loved it. High on a hill, the castle protruded from the fog out of the world below. Came in for a landing on an Order craft. Almost two days had passed since the Council meeting and Darius was probably killing people every minute that went by without me in custody.

"I can get you to your grandfather," Dee told me. "You'll be safe once you talk to him."

Snuck through the castle to my grandfather. Made it to his room. Stepped in. Hooked to life support systems and medical equipment, machines, monitoring his every bodily function, sickness came over me feeling him so close to death. Near him were Simon, Tom, and John – they all looked at me, shocked to see me enter the room.

Saw my grandfather in the bed. "Grandfather," I said.

Grandfather said nothing, but stirred. His hand moved.

"He heard you, Alexander. He wants to talk to you," Simon said.

"We must report this to Darius," Tom said. "At once."

"No you won't." Flashed a light in Tom's face and he fell to the floor unconscious. "He won't be waking up for while. Do I need to flash you too. Or can you give us some space?"

"I'll give you some space, my Lord," John said.

The agents picked up Tom and took him with them.

Simon closed his eyes and gave Grandfather strength. Grandfather slowly opened his eyes. He struggled to speak.

"He won't have long," Simon said. "He's ready to go."

Simon put his hands on grandfather and gave him all the healing energy and strength he possibly could.

Grandfather woke up and took off his oxygen mask.

"Hello, Grandfather," I said to the old and broken man.

"He's very happy to see you," Simon said.

"Alexander," he said.

Moved closer on the bedside.

"Alexander, I'm so happy you're here. I want you to stay with me…until I pass," the Scion said touching my face. Tears rolled down my face uncontrollably. "I've sent everyone else away."

"No," I cried. "No, I won't let you go."

"I am 164 years old, 'tis time. I'm done delaying death, my son. My life is… done."

"Grandfather…" Pain made it hard to speak. "Can't— I can't lose you, Grandfather. Please."

"You and Darius no longer need me," his words hurt my heart. He stared into my eyes and saw he was wrong. "What is that face?" ever sharp even on his death bed.

Simon focused hard to keep Grandfather up and alert.

"Darius killed me. He's going to kill me again. As soon as you die— "

"He's been saying that for years, Alexander. He can't—"

"If you die, Grandfather. I'm going with you."

"I want to show you something," he said. "Something you should see." Grandfather pointed to a small wooden jewelry box.

"You don't have to die, Grandfather," I pleaded, still crying in terrible pain. "You don't have to—"

"We all have to die, Alexander," Simon said.

"No we don't. You can live as long as you want."

"Alexander…" Grandfather's death rattle voice gave out.

"What are you talking about?" Simon spoke for Grandfather.

"*Sigma*-40 nanoids, Grandfather. Microscopic robots. They can heal you, reverse aging and prevent you from dying. Darius built them for himself. They can save you."

"You're talking about forbidden technology, yes?" Simon said with concern.

"Yes. A complete violation of Order Law."

"Where is John?" Simon again spoke for Grandfather, because he was too weak to speak for himself.

Walked out the door and found John and invited him back in.

"Tell me about the stigma nanoids?" Grandfather said.

"The *Sigma*-40 nanoids are forbidden alien technology, my Lord," John said. "They do not exist anymore. After the purge of the alien menace, the council passed Edict 1098A, which classified nearly all so called RøZ 'grey alien' technology forbidden. Their medical technology was banned outright. The labs were destroyed. The edict declared that unsanctioned possession of forbidden technology is high treason, punishable by death."

"Darius is not allowed to possess nanoids?"

"No one is. They are forbidden," John said.

"Darius has them. He saved them for himself."

"A strong accusation, Lord Alexander," John said.

"Darius proposed the ban. Didn't he? And he was also charged with eradicating the aliens and their bases, wasn't he?"

"Yes," John said to me, knowing where I was going. "And Wisendee assured the Council it was done."

"Darius wanted to make sure you never used them Grandfather. That's why. He made nanoids for himself in secret. He lied to you and he committed treason."

"You have proof of this?" John said.

"Yes," I told John, which shut him up. Focused on my grandfather, my plea continued. "When Darius becomes the Scion there will be no one to stop him from using forbidden technologies. That's why he made the deal with the aliens, Grandfather. You have to stop him."

"Lord Alexander, you are out of line. This is not—" John said.

"Thank you John, that will be all," I waved for him to leave.

John stepped back, but didn't leave the room.

"Those aliens are soulless creatures of dubious origin. They are dangerous. Nothing good can come from them, Alexander," Grandfather said. "They are evil."

"Nothing good will come of Darius as the Scion. Only you can fix this. If you die, I'm going with you."

Grandfather looked in terrible pain.

"He's on the edge of death," Simon said. "I can't hold him if he wants to go."

"Don't go. Stay. Please." Tears streamed down my face. "Grandfather, I know it's forbidden technology but it will work - it does work. It allows you to make things right. We have to stop Darius before it's too late. I need more time. Please, Grandfather… Take the nanoids."

"I don't have any nanoids, Alexander," Grandfather said.

"I do," I said.

John's silent objection was loud and clear.

Boom. Revealed the vial of nanoids from my pocket. A clear glass container with what looked like quicksilver, trillions of microscopic robots in it.

"These are from Darius' lab, which is proof he committed treason."

"And how did you get those?" John demanded.

"Imagine what else he's doing that he's not supposed to be doing, Grandfather."

The specially marked vial is instantly recognizable as being from Darius' secret labs, with Darius' insignia on it. The bottle is genuine and sealed.

"Swallow them, Grandfather."

"Don't!" John implored.

I broke the seal and opened the bottle.

"You've just contaminated this room with that alien virus! My Lord, there are many unforeseen risks in the use of forbidden technology. I would advise against it," John said.

"Will they work?" the Scion asked.

"Yes."

"Ingesting the nanoids could also kill you," John warned.

Simon took a deep breath, which meant my grandfather was fighting to live again.

"Leave us," Grandfather said to John.

John left the room.

"Darius will destroy the Order, and everything you love. You are the only one who can stop him. If you give up on the world, then I do too."

You go, I go. I promised, crying.

"He wants you to see this," Simon said, pointing to the wooden box, inlaid with gold. He handed it to me.

"What is this thing?" I saw the glittering orb inside it. Compelled to touch it, and hold it in my hand, I reached.

The orb from space? How could that be? I touched it.

"It feels like— It's like it's alive or something. What is it?"

"Our only hope to save the world. Darius must never know about it," Grandfather said with deep, deadly, conviction.

Holding this supernatural object, changed me, Dee.

I closed my eyes.

CHAPTER LX

"The Aton made him want to be a hero."

ALEXANDER

"Give me the Aton," Grandfather commanded.

My eyes opened and suddenly I see: "The Aton?" Transfixed at the purple filled crystal ball in my palm. Magical… "What does it do?"

I saw what it does. This is what saved me.

"Give it to me," Grandfather demanded. "Put it in my hand."

Releasing the orb to his hand, I felt the residual effect of holding the orb; happiness, vision. Grandfather wanted me to sit on the bed next to him. He looked better and stronger already. We bonded as our heart energy synched in the resonance of the Aton aura.

"It's the blood of the first Pharaoh," he said. "The Holy Grail."

"The Holy Grail?" Didn't understand what that meant.

"It's my fault Darius is the way he is. I've created a monster," Grandfather sat up. Looking stronger already.

"He is evil, Grandfather. You're the only one who can stop him."

"I know," Grandfather said.

"So you'll take the nanoids?"

"God help me." He paused. "Give me the bloody nanoids."

"Simon. Do it."

Simon injected them into Grandfather's IV.

Almost instantly, Grandfather groaned in terrible pain. He convulsed as his heart stopped – alarms sounded.

"He's dying!" Simon said. "His body cannot— *C'est du poison!*"

"Do not let him die!" I stepped up to the computer system. I logged onto ORNet to activate the nanoids.

The medical team entered the room, followed by John.

Grandfather barely clutched the Aton-core in his hand.

Hang on, Grandfather. Stay with me…

"Don't let go… Stay with me." I typed away. "He needs nutrients," I yelled. "Give him what's on the screen. All these."

"Proteins packs and full vitamins—" Medics told the team.

Simon's medical team hooked IV bags to Grandfather. I activated the nanoids using the method Dee set up.

"What's happening?" John demanded. Everyone ignored him.

Grandfather turned blue, dying, as I worked as fast as possible.

"We're losing him! *Rapide!*" Simon yelled to his staff.

"Please work, please work." Stared at the screens and then at Grandfather. The nanoids clicked online. Progress. "Yes."

"You gave him the nanoids," John said.

Signs of life. The robots sensed Grandfather's body, and went to work immediately. The nanoids told ORNet, which told us, what IV bags were needed next.

"Stem cells. Stat. Replace bag three!" barked the medical team, reading the computer. The six man medical team scrambled to keep up with everything requested by the nanoids as they rebuilt his body.

Grandfather regained his color. His heart began beating normally. He breathed heavily, sucking in oxygen from his gas mask and exhaling deep, long breaths. His eyes opened and stared at the ceiling in a look of excitement.

Everyone watched in awe as Grandfather began to look younger. It was like a miracle. The old man that was Grandfather, was no more...

On the monitors, Simon watched how the nanoids worked. They reprogramed and repaired old DNA, instructing the cells to regenerate, rebuilding his entire system. His gray hair all fell out. He shed his entire "old" layer of skin. The team peeled away the old, to reveal the young baby-soft skin underneath. My grandfather now looked like a man in his prime... Only with better, near perfect skin.

"Sacrébleu..." Simon said in his funny French way.

Grandfather's old body became virile, young, and fit. His fist tightened firm around the Aton-core. He sat up a changed man.

"It worked." Holy shit. "It actually fricken worked."

Grandfather looked at me, as my jaw hung open in disbelief. His eyes wide with excitement, he glared at me intensely. The expression on his face became comical. A cartoon grin. Made me laugh. He was like an infant seeing the world for the first time. Like it was all too much and he wished he could speak.

He ripped out his IV needles, jumped off the table and jumped at me. Thought for a second he was gonna kill me. He hugged me. Grandfather had never hugged me before. *What's happening?*

"Are you okay? Can you talk?" I asked wiping away my tears.

"I feel good," he said. "I feel really, really good."

He released me. I hardly recognized this man in front of me. "You look… You look younger than me. You look… good."

"I feel - I feel amazing. I've never felt better in all my life," he said. "How long does this last?" His voice changed, now young and strong, like Darius' voice, but stronger.

"As long as you want," I smiled.

"I am reborn!" he screamed as he ran over to the mirror and looked at his new, young and handsome self. He stood naked in front of the mirror. He couldn't believe what he saw; neither could any of us. A perfect physique. Soft, porcelain skin, he was like a living marble statue of a Greek god.

Simon brought him clothes. But Grandfather was not done admiring himself, indulging in the vanity of his chiseled male beauty.

"Incredible…" Grandfather spoke for all of us. "I'm a stunning pillar of human perfection. I can see so clearly." He blinked. "My vision had degraded— My Lord, I was virtually blind. But now, now I can see… I can see everything."

Simon dressed him. Finally he stopped looking at himself and looked at me. He saw the hints of jealousy on my face.

"It worked better than I imagined possible."

"Alexander. We must go down into the Sacred Chamber. You're going to be initiated," my young Grandfather said.

"Initiated?"

"We'll take the stairs. I've always wanted to take the stairs!"

"What's so great about the stairs?"

"I feel I could run up a hundred flights of stairs now!" he yelled.

My grandfather danced around and jumped up in the air. He tripped and fell, his coordination still off, but his youthful body wasn't hurt in the slightest. He sprung back to his feet. The Aton still in his tight fist.

"Thank you, Alexander," he said as he hugged me.

"Thank you." I cried again, holding him tight.

Being hugged by Grandfather was the best moment of my life. His happiness, the warmth of his heart, lifted me up in a way nothing else could. For the first time in my life, I felt loved. It felt good to be loved. Feeling the love of my family... There's nothing like it. This must be what normal people, normal families, have... They're so lucky. I cried tears of joy.

"Let's go!" Grandfather said, releasing me.

"I need a moment." Emotion brought me to my knees.

Grandfather ran off, too excited to stand still.

"Where are you going?"

"You'll see!" he said as he ran out of the room.

"Where is he going?" Wiping my tears, I looked at Simon.

"To the Chamber of Initiation," Simon said. "Follow him."

CHAPTER LXI

"All Scions of the Order must be initiated."

ALEXANDER

My youthful grandfather ran faster than I thought was possible for a human to run. The sound of his bare feet pounding the marble floors of the castle faded away quickly. Finally caught up with him in the library, where he was looking around, waiting for me. He didn't even break a sweat. I huffed because I'd been puffing too much.

"I've never felt this good in all my life," he said, as he admired the purple orb in his hand

"My Grandfather said we aren't supposed to run through the castle," I joked. Still can't believe this young man is my grandfather

He didn't laugh. Sweaty and winded I caught my breath, and then, for the first time with my grandfather, truly recognized the fantastic grandeur of the Scion Castle library. Books for days...

"Look at this place, this library— Built almost five hundred years ago, this library is one of the best collections of manuscripts and sacred texts on earth. The knowledge in these books... You won't find it anywhere else in *all* the world, even the *Archivum*."

The painted dome ceiling, and at the shelves of books many stories tall... the space felt sacred. I never really appreciated this library, or books for that matter, until that moment with my grandfather. He loves books. And in that Love, I fell in love with books, through him.

"Our ancestors searched the world over for the secrets of life. They wrote books on alchemy, magic spells, and philosophers' stones of every color. They gathered knowledge from every corner of the globe, desperate to find the elixir of life... desperate for immortality."

"Did they find it?" I played along.

"No. Immortality in the flesh is not possible," he said.

"Isn't it? Look at you. You are young, you can live forever, Grandfather."

"No. Immortality exists only in the *logos*, the spirit. We only live forever in memory, in our books, and the in word."

"But you can literally live forever with those nanoids."

"No. Because 'tis against nature… The elixir of life must be from nature. I do not *feel* natural. This alien technology is not natural." His deep intensity scared me a little. "Humans were not meant to feel like this. To be young again. Nature doesn't allow it, because death is necessary for the soul, for life, for immortality… 'Tis against Nature."

"You know what's against nature? Darius."

"You're right," he said, grabbing me. "Which is why we are here."

Grandfather lead me to the doors of the little used staircase. They had to be pulled open, as they are opened rarely these days, obviously. The stairs spiraled down into darkness.

"Can't we take the elevator?" I was a little afraid of what ancient evil of the Order could be down there.

"No!" he barked.

"Isn't it like twenty flights down?"

"365 steps."

"I'm tired."

"We are taking the stairs!" Grandfather insisted.

"You're obsessed, Grandfather. What's so great about the stairs?"

He refused to touch the electric lamp and lit the torch – which worked well, burned bright, considering it too hadn't been used in God knows how long.

"There are no short cuts to enlightenment," he said. "Tis all in the journey. Every step matters. You must do the work. To giveth light we must endure burning."

"Have you ever done this before?"

"No. We shall experience it together, my son," he said, giddy as a school boy. He grabbed my arm and down we went. We bonded.

Down the spiral of steps. The walls were carved, plastered, and painted with elaborate imagery that told a story…

"The story of the Pharaoh!" Grandfather yelled. "How wonderful!"

"'Tis the story of our ancestors! This is Alexander the Great himself, and oh joy and rapture, look at this!" he said with delight, admiring the mosaics and murals. "Most enchanting…"

The energy was profound as the imagery appeared out of the darkness, illuminated by the flame, the light of the fire lit up the faces of Pharaohs and Scions past. Scenes of history, symbols, words and text in languages I couldn't read, but understood to be profound.

The symbols and images changed me. "This is actually really—"

"Astonishing. Here all this time and I never looked at it. I almost died never having seen this magnificent masterpiece."

Grandfather touched the murals and painted stone statue relief. If you didn't know, you'd think he was on drugs the way he acted.

"This is Caesarion— And this is when the Great House moved to the East…" We spiraled down, forward in time. "Here – Here is when the Pharaoh returned to Europe… And built this castle, just before the Renaissance," he said touching the faces and the carved words.

"You're like tripping out. Aren't you, Mel?" I laughed.

"Excuse me," He looked at me. His face almost scary in the light of the torch. "What did you call me?" he said.

There was my stern grandfather again. With shades of Darius.

"Mel is your nickname. What I call you in my phone."

"No," he said. "I am your king, Alexander. You shall respect me. You may call me Grandfather, Majesty, or 'my Lord!'"

"But you're like my brother now," I smiled. "Can't I just call you pops? It's what children in America call—"

"Good God. Never. I won't have it." He laughed.

"Papa Mel? I like Papa-Mel. Or how about GB, grand-brother."

"What am I going to do with you?" he said, smiling. "America has ruined you."

He embraced me as we continued down. Ironically perplexed by his affection, it was so foreign to me, a moment of clarity struck: This is what family is; this is what it feels like to have family.

"Your father hates the rituals. He rejects the past. But he's wrong. Don't be like him. The story is the ritual…the story is the journey," Grandfather said. "Our story is who we are. Always remember who you are. Know thyself. To be illuminated is to know yourself, to find who you really are, Alexander."

"And who are you?" I realized I don't know this young man before me at all; I hardly knew my grandfather.

"I am the Holy Scion," he said. "I've made mistakes. I see that now. But I shall make it right… One step at a time."

He pried at my soul with his big powerful eyes.

"Who are you, Alexander?" he said. *Who are you?*

"I don't know," I said.

"After tonight, you shall. Come," he said. *I shall show you.*

We took the last step, but it felt like my first.

CHAPTER LXII

"You must save the Order."

ALEXANDER

From the shadows, twinkling jewels on a carved cedar door caught the light of the flame. Leaving the dark staircase, literally my first steps to self-discovery, we arrived at the entrance portico of the Sacred Chamber.

"Saints preserve us," the first Guard said, jumping to his feet. Together they stared at their young master in total brain melting disbelief. These guards were old enough to remember Grandfather when he was younger, and sharp enough to recognize him instantly.

Couldn't help but to laugh out loud at their bug-eyed faces.

"Indeed," Grandfather said, touching them both, handing them the torch in his hand. "It is I."

"What magic is this?" the Guard asked. "How?"

The Guards remembered themselves, that they must not ask questions, and that the King will never explain himself. Grandfather put his eye in the iris scanner, and removed all doubt it was him. The iris scanner, and voice lock cannot be tricked. The door opened.

"Prepare for an initiation," he said. "Alexander is to be initiated."

Grandfather caught himself in the mirror on the wall, still shocked at what youth and beauty he saw staring back. His hair had grown in, now an inch long, and he had to get another close look. Seeing his vanity made me understand and dislike my own. *Learning already.*

"Dear God... I'm so beautiful," he said with no irony. "My hair... It hasn't looked like this in a hundred years. I didn't realize how much I missed it." He touched his flawless pale skin, and stroked his shiny golden-red hair. "I'm a ghost of times long since passed."

Childish envy came over me: "Can we make some nanoids for me?"

"Absolutely not, Alexander!" He instructed the Guards, "Take him away."

"Away where?" Guards grabbed me.

"To the holding room, to change for the initiation ritual," he said.

"Thought I was initiated already. When I joined the Council, that whole thing with the—" the Guards put me in a dark room.

"A different initiation, that was. This is the ancient one, a mind opening rite, given only to select initiates of the Order."

"Do I get my key-card back after this?" Couldn't help myself. In fear, I stopped them from closing the door on me.

"Alexander... You're not understanding the point."

"I'm not getting my key-card back?"

"Focus, Alexander. Focus on the ritual. Let everything else go. Alright? Do not be afraid. Be here. Clear your mind."

The Guards gave me a white linen shirt and pants to change into.

"Remember, we are carrying the torch for our ancestors. We must not let the light go out. So long as I am Scion, I must hold the torch, and bring light. The duty of the Scion is to pass on the rituals, our history, legacy, and bring light to the world. And so I shall. And so shall you!" Grandfather yelled as the Guards closed the door on me.

Deep breath. Shed my clothes, symbolically shedding everything else, and in the dark cleared my mind. Standing naked in the dark, I took a deep breath. *Let go.* I let everything go and put on the white linen clothes. Sitting in the dark forever, five minutes, finally the guards entered and before my eyes could adjust to the light, they put a bag over my head and walked me into the Sacred Chamber.

"Part of the ritual...everything is part of the ritual, I get it."

"Silence," the Guard said.

Once inside, they removed the bag. Looking up, the grandeur and majesty of the room began to set in on me. The stone faces of the statues judged me, and demanded greatness. *I will be great.*

The Guard removed the bag. My eyes immediately focused on Grandfather, sitting on his throne. He dismissed the Guards with a wave of his hand.

"Was that really necessary?" I asked, half joking.

"Silence!" Grandfather's powerful voice echoed in the cavernous stone room. "Look up and seek the wisdom of your ancestors. The great gods of old." His commanding voice demanded compliance.

I'd been inside this 'Sacred Chamber' before, but I could hardly remember it. Guess that meant I didn't really appreciate it... But after seeing my grandfather's impassioned appreciation of the stairway art, my perspective had changed. With him, I saw this room anew through his eyes. Visions of greatness danced in my head.

188

The awesomeness of the room set in on me. My head fell back and the domed ceiling sucked me into the intricately carved world above, masterfully cut into the mountain under the castle... Mind blown. Some of the statue faces I recognized from the stairway. The stories came to life in my head and before my eyes. Movement. Whispers...

"You will save us, Alexander... You must save us," the voices spoke to me from all over the room. *I hear the voices.*

"I'm going to change the way you see the world, my boy, and then we are going to figure out a plan for this," the King on the throne said. He held up the glittering orb.

"The Aton," the voices said... "Save the Aton," and it glowed a brilliant blue and red, and royal purple. A moment of majesty.

"I hear voices..." *They are listening to me.*

You are beginning to see. "The spirits of our ancestors. Listen to them," the King said louder, his voice not so different from the others.

The statues spoke to me. When not looking, I felt them moving...

"This one will be great yet..." the words echoed in the chamber, and in my mind. *This one is great.*

"Drink this," Grandfather said, handing me a goblet.

No stranger to mind altering drugs, nothing could prepare me for this potent cocktail of entheogens. "Holy Sh—"

The drugs hit me fast and hard. My worldview melted as the drugs flooded into my brain. My head filled with heat as neurons fired in a great electrical storm of thought. Energy from the stones, from the dome above, and from my heart flowed. My mind changing again and again. An explosion of ideas annihilated my construct of reality, as a strike of divine lightening electrified me, waves of energy flowed through me, and everything I held true burned away to pure essence.

"Can I count on you for all eternity?" Grandfather said, standing over me.

"Yes," I spoke without hesitation. *For all eternity.*

He knighted me, and placed the Aton in my hand. It felt like fire, I held the sun, and it burned away my mortal flesh, transmuting death into life, dead lead into spiritual gold.

"Amazing isn't it?" the voice said. *It is amazing...*

"What is it?" All I saw was the glowing galaxy orb in my hand, brilliant white light, blinding, swirling, electric and magical.

"This is the light."

"The Aton… is how we are going to stop Darius, Alexander."

"How?" *I don't understand, how is the universe in my hand?*

"Let it inspire you…" the voice said.

Grandfather, the one I knew kneeled beside me, living vicariously through me. He held me and smiled. He laid me down, on my back, on the stone floor. But in his youthful, beautiful and perfect smile, and my hallucinations, I saw a flash of evil. In my young grandfather I saw the devil inside him; alien darkness of the microscopic robots. His youth and beauty were unnatural, ungodly, and a danger. They hissed at me. I blinked until I saw my Grandfather, his soul, smiling.

"I need your help," he said, as both the darkness and the light.

"We need your help," the statues said. *The Order needs your help.*

The realization of a plan came to me as a vision, all at once. A bolt of lightning struck, the sands of thought fused and crystalized into a crystal clear idea in my mind. Time stopped. Whispers of the statues.

"I have a plan," I spoke and heard as a voice not my own.

Hours passed in seconds; seconds were hours.

"Greatness through sacrifice."

"Use the Aton… the Aton will save you."

"Save us, Alexander… You must save us…" the voices said.

Up I rose from the dead, leaving my body on the floor. My mind exploded, a supernova as the universe expanded and then collapsed back together under the weight and gravity of what lay ahead. My third eye mind became a black hole, sucking in the cosmos, time stopped beyond the event horizon of this moment.

"*Vincit qui se vincit,*" a voice said.

To conquer this world, conquer thyself, Alexander…

"Kneel before me, and the Almighty," the King said.

Knelt before the god-man. Out of body, looked up, a face I knew, but only just met. Near the King, manifesting from thin air, two beings, Marduk and Helios appeared. They bowed to me.

"This is real?" The answer was: *yes.* "This is real."

Now I believe in magic.

Well versed in the 'deep magic' of the hacker world -- some of it I invented -- I never thought about *real* magic; until this moment. I experienced real magic. Ritual *is* magic. Magic *is* ritual… Seeing that was my first step. *Magic comes from this place.*

Ritual. Writ you all, by divine rite. Right! I'll write writ universal, with deep magic... and I'll use my own real magic.

Use your magic, Alexander.

Outside myself, my brain in overdrive, my spirit hands moved uncontrollably, as I wrote my plan, in this ritual, on my imaginary magic computer, in the universal mind. I touched (and coded) the infinite divine. *I built the APEX in this moment.*

"I'm going to stop Darius…" saying the words brought back to earth, back from the infinite, into my body.

The magic of the Sacred Chamber inspired me, and I relived it all again, in a flash of memory. The steps, and the words on them, and all the stone faces, the whispers of my ancestors as I bowed to my king, and he knighted me with the sword, which felt like a blade cutting away all my flaws, pruning my soul for regrowth. I was now a glittering diamond cut from the rugged stone of my former self.

"Be illuminated, Alexander…" the King said.

The light inside me refracted and filled the chamber with glittering rainbows of colors. Illuminated; bright, swooning with boundlessness and intellectual delight, I could no longer stand.

Laid back down on the stone marble floor, by the demigods, Marduk and Helios, I was left alone, but in the company of myself as never before. Henceforth, never alone again, because I found a love inside myself, a heat source for whenever I feel cold. Floating. My soul set sail on an ocean of thought, the water became the sky, and I left my vessel and flew up into the stars above, the fantastic dome of legends untold…everything made sense. I knew what I needed to do. Rising up I saw myself on the floor. Eyes closed, clinging to my vision, I saw as never before; the universe, mine to explore.

My eyes opened. Dawn had broken.

"Time to save the world."

How? Now I see.

CHAPTER LXIII

"He is not the Order."

DARIUS

I am the Order.

When night falls, I return to my tower. I strip off all emotions and fears, and don the clothes of the King, I am. And in this solemn dress, I mentally enter the ancient courts of antiquity, and am welcomed by the philosopher kings, and there I taste the forbidden fruit for which I alone was born to consume. The sweet flavors of power speak to me, and I ask the sages of old what they would do, the motives of their historical actions, and they remind me: a King has no other obsession, nor any other dominate thought but war; because war is the only art and craft befitting the King who truly rules.

Wars never go away, they are only ever postponed for edge. I stood in my grandiose office, in the highest office tower, the pinnacle of power, in New York city. Out the window I looked upon the empire I built. My energetic alpha metropolis was full of light in the moonless summer night. War dominates my mind... I tread war's razor edge. My war with my Father has not gone, why? *Why won't he die?*

"Councilor Wisendee is here to see you," my Chief of Staff informed me. But I was already aware. I know why he's here.

"Father better be dead," I said under my breath, knowing news of Father had to be the reason for Dee's visit.

"Leave me!" I yelled. All souls vanished from sight instantly.

Wise 'Master of the Royal heads,' the Sorcerer Dee walked deliberately, slowly, across my huge office space, up the grand staircase, to me. He stared at me, reading my mind and breaking me down. Only such a powerful wizard as Dee could cast such a spell of fear on me. I *fucking* hate him. I could feel him smiling on the inside, ready to punch me in the face with bad news.

"Is he dead?"

"No," Dee replied.

A painful wave of adrenaline burned through me.

"Did you build a forbidden technology lab, Lord Darius?" he asked. "In violation of your own edict?"

That wasn't a question. *Fuck. Fuck me. Fuck you, Dee.*

Red came over me as my heart beat out of my chest and waves of torrid emotion and stress hormones intensified. *You can't hide anything from me, boy,* Dee's big powerful eyes said.

"Your lab has been breached and your nanoids stolen," he said.

"What?" *That's impossible!*

My ego took a bullet to the face. Censure, excommunication, and a trial for treason by the Council hung over me. The strings inside the piano of my mind began to snap, one by one, as the consequences of Dee's words set in on me. I struggled to speak.

"Pardon my lack of lugubrious regret dear Wizard, but how is that possible?" I asked. "Unless you did it."

I became convinced the man before me is an alien. How could he be human? No human can do what Dee can do. He's the master manipulator, spymaster of spymasters. Impossible to read. He may have been planning this for years. He stole them or knows who did. I'll never know. There was nothing I could do, and it was really, really *fucking* infuriating to me. *You did this, Dee!!*

"The Council may declare you Anathema to the Order for your perfidy," he said. Using my word against me. "You may well be excommunicated, and imprisoned, for developing, using, and intending to use such forbidden technology; treason, Lord Darius."

"Will they?" I pressed. "It's up to you, isn't it?"

"It is," he said. *We are watching you, Darius.*

Dee pulled from thin air a large rolled up document – an Order edict, a formal excommunication. I recognized it because I used them against Father's previous heirs; they mock me from their graves.

"This document officially strips you of your titles, and defrocks you of all power—" Dee began.

"No." I begged. "That would be death. I'll do anything."

"You will sign this edict. Henceforth, you shall agree to never again see, touch, engage, employ, use directly or indirectly, willingly speak of, or in any manner allow, or facilitate by any agent of yours the use of forbidden technology of any kind. If you do, the excommunication takes effect. You will expunge that which is forbidden from your mind, and block and reject everything relating to the demonic RøZ aliens, and never again speak of, or to, any grey alien entities, real or imagined. If you willingly break this agreement, the edict becomes irrevocable law, unbreakable even by the King, *nam omne aeternum*."

I stared at Dee with hatred knowing this was a trap.

"Violate this agreement and you are out of the Order, Lord Darius. Do you understand?" he said in a demeaning tone.

"Yes." *What fucking choice do I have?*

"You will surrender your records and the location of all forbidden technology labs to me. Immediately," Dee said.

"And I'll be reprieved?"

"If you sign the edict and comply, yes," Dee said.

Thank *fucking* God the Father. Live to fight another day.

I signed the oversized document, next to my father's signature, the Vizier and the five Council members who despise me.

"You've been warned, again, Lord Darius. I suggest you heed, and don't press your luck. There will be no third warning," Dee added as he rolled up the edict.

"How much longer can my father live?" I asked, instinctively.

Dee dropped the bomb on me: "Your Father has used your forbidden *Sigma*-40 regenerative nano-robots. He'll die when he choses to, Lord Darius."

He *fucking* nuked me. My head exploded.

"What? No… No!!!" I fell to my knees. Shaking on the floor in front of Dee; my world unraveled. "He could live forever with those nanoids!"

"That is what you intended them for, is it not?" Dee demeaned.

My mind raced. He'll outlive me. My mind's eye went red. Anger, fury, and pure vitriol boiled inside and overcame me.

"It's my time! It should be my *fucking* time now!" My violent screams echoed in my massive office. I cried. The first time ever that I could remember, and I remember everything, tears flooded my eyes.

Spare me your petulant scurrilousness, Dee beamed his voice into my head. *You did this to yourself, Darius.*

I rose off the floor and walked over to the window of my skyscraper tower. I pounded on the glass, hoping it would break. Virtually unbreakable, I released my violent anger on it. How could I break but not this glass? Even the glass beats me. My reflection in the glass showed a weak, broken man, bloodshot eyes, and tears running down his face. Who is that? That can't be me. I had never seen myself so disgustingly inept. Dee behind me, enjoyed my pain. He had always wanted to put me in my place. I turned to him.

"He needs to *fucking* die!!"

"Watch yourself, Darius," Dee warned me, reminding me of my place, yet again. I am nothing; I'm disposable, as are we all. As were God the Father's children before me. They said Karma. I said fuck Karma, it was Dee that made this happen to me.

"The Council approved his personal use of forbidden technology?!" I asked with a loathed weakness in my voice. "Dee?!"

"Yes. His Grace granted him a waiver until death—" Dee began.

"Outrageous! *Fucking* outrageous!! He can live forever!!"

Do not interrupt me. Dee towered over me with his tall frame and literally looked down on me until I composed myself.

"The Steward of the Order granted a waiver until death, citing 'extemporaneous circumstance.' Henceforth, anyone who uses bio-regenerative nano-robots, 'nanoids,' or any such forbidden technology becomes the Scion's property," Wisendee recited. "Disobey and you will have no rights, Lord Darius. He will own you like property."

"So I shall wither and die while he lives forever with my fucking nanoids! My fucking nanoids! He'll stay young and laugh as I turn into a decrepit old man like him–"

"So you shall live," Dee said, sentencing me to living death.

"You did this." *You fucking did this to me, Dee!*

"You brought this on yourself, Lord Darius. You made them." Dee checkmated me. "Karma is real. Sow, and so shall you reap."

Or so he thought. I am above Karma. *I am the Order!*

Without me, my order, there is only chaos.

They'll see.

CHAPTER LXIV

"The APEX is his false Aton."

DARIUS

Of greatest importance in time of war is knowing how to execute the best use of an opportunity when offered. Am I alive? Yes. I live to fight. Am I superfluous? Yes, superfluousness is a truly necessary thing; contradiction in terms though it seems. The fact is the Order needs me, and I must push above and beyond what is, for a new Order and ever more, because this strife is all that drives humanity forward, and what any and all human life is worth living for. Fight to the death. This is life. This is my war...

"Strife is what the Order lives for!" I yelled in furious rage. I will not be caged. I will fight. "This is my Order!! It's mine!"

In the far corner of my almost-as-ultra-modern-as-me office space sat a priceless ancient artifact, an astronomical calculator, clock, and orrery. Made from gold and ancient bronze, this ingenious mechanical device from ancient Babylon was over three thousand years old. Meticulously polished and cared for, it has kept perfect time for thousands of years. A gift from my diabolical father... I picked it up, and threw it across the room. It survived all these centuries, all these tyrants, despite all odds, and now it was smashed and broken on the floor; forever ruined, just like me.

"He *fucking* means to destroy me!"

I wanted death. Destruction. The world shall feel my pain.

No sign of Dee. The sneaky sorcerer had vanished.

I started destroying everything I could.

More damage. More carnage.

I WANT CHAOS.

If I am not the Order, I am the chaos.

Marching out of my office, down the grand hallway toward other desks, I was a tornado. Everything in my path would be destroyed. People ran from me.

"It's my time!! It should be my time!!" I screamed. My anger echoed in the cold, stark halls.

No one could stop me. I own the whole *fucking* building and everyone in it belongs to me. Perhaps I'll kill them all, I thought. There's nothing anyone could do about it. I gave these people everything they wanted, more money than they know what to do with, diplomatic immunity from all the world's laws, they are all untouchable to anyone but me. But today they would see the downside of this. My nightmare had become their nightmare.

"Lock down the building," I said into the comm. No one will be leaving… There is no escape.

"I just might level this building to the ground!"

My screaming and destruction moved to the floor below. The rampage would be legendary were the details not locked up behind iron clad confidentiality agreements. I owned these people. They were not citizens of any country – they were my property to dispose of.

"Those *fucking* nanoids cost six trillion dollars — nine years. Nine *fucking* years to make! They were mine! How did this happen?"

Most had no clue what I was talking about. I grabbed one man by the throat and squeezed his neck until the life drained out of him. "It should be my time! My time!!" I yelled at him as he died.

"No one even knew about them. How could they be stolen from me? It had to be Dee!" I threw the lifeless man to the floor.

Insatiable, I looked for my next victim. I killed him with one punch to the throat. And another. My Chief of Staff, 'COS', finally appeared, sensing the exhaustion setting in on me, perhaps also finally figuring out what had set me off.

"I want to know who did it! And how! Now!!!" I screamed at him. He kept his distance from me.

"Sir, we are looking into—" COS said, recoiling as I reached for him. "It appears that ORNet discovered the bases—"

Suddenly, I remembered Alexander, my otiose child I try to forget. "Where is Alexander?" I demanded.

Silence from my staff. Which meant he's still not been found since he escaped the meeting.

"How is that possible?! There's a connection. Find it! Find him!"

"Alexander surfaced in Los Angeles. He transferred himself almost sixty billion using a key-card," my minions reported.

"Whose key-card? How?" I demanded.

197

"We have video of him with Sir David Peterson. Sir, so it must be key-card #12," they said.

"How dare he— David Peterson helped Alexander escape?"

"Bring me everything we have on David Peterson. And bring me Alexander!"

"Sir, a cable just appeared on ORNet," he read the text: "By Order of the Scion, we are not to disturb Alexander. Per his one year censure, he has agreed not to leave America until the next Council Meeting in 2002."

"What's he been doing?"

"The ORNet report says he is in California. He's been on an alcohol and drug binge since the meeting. It couldn't have been him who stole the nanoids," they said, sifting through data.

"The report could be false. A fabrication! I want proof!"

They brought up video surveillance of Alexander on the monitor, back at his Malibu mansion. Partying.

"That fucking worthless child! He's supposed to be punished!"

"Councilor Tom is in your office, Sir," COS said.

Then it hit me. This shit storm had not even started. My thoughts raced as I pulled myself together and walked swiftly to back to my office to meet Tom. In the elevator, my assistants polished me up, cleaned off the blood and fixed my hair.

The elevator opened and I saw Tom near my desk, over a thousand feet away. Fear and anxiety hit – this must be what it's like for people coming to see me, I thought. I felt intimidated and scared every step of the long walk all the way over to him. The grand space with high ceilings made me feel small. I saw my office in a way I never had before…as a weak person does. Tom watched me, analyzed me, the whole time. I couldn't get over to him fast enough.

"Tom," I said, asserting my power and dominance.

"As I'm sure you are aware, the APEX project has *officially* been terminated," Tom said. "Lord Darius."

I was not aware and felt nothing anymore.

"Then why are you here?" Behind my desk I felt my power return.

"Some of us believe the APEX should still be built," Tom said.

"Who gave my father the nanoids? How did he get them?"

"I shall not speak about the nanoids. And you must not either, Darius. I'm here officially to tell you that the APEX project is officially dead, but unofficially going forward."

Just *fucking* kill me already with this bullshit.

"You are going to build it in secret," Tom gave the reason for his visit.

"Tell me who gave them to him!" My rage took over me.

"I'm trying to help you, Lord Darius. If you won't let me, then I'll wish you a good evening," Tom turned to leave.

I need him. He knew it. I *fucking* hate weakness.

Assert the power. "Tom. Stop."

Tom turned around and continued. "My brother and I are agreed, the APEX should be built. Slowly. In secret."

"We have the votes then?"

"The vote is dead," Tom said.

"How then?"

"With Dee's blessing. And your funding," Tom said.

"I see." This made no sense.

"Dee wishes to continue moving the project forward. The underpinning will be built, and all estimates are five years before the system is in any way operational anyhow."

"Dee wants to move the project forward?"

What game are you playing, Dee?

"In light of recent events," Tom implied my father's new lease on life. "Yes."

"But not my father?"

"Correct."

"You want me to go behind Father's back?"

"Not exactly. We want you to supervise the project. Keep it moving forward as planned. Do what you do best, Lord Darius. Innovate. Get it done. You will build the APEX unofficially," Tom said. "We believe the Scion will come around to it, eventually."

"I work for you now?"

"I'm trying to help you, Lord Darius. My brother supports the Scion, but he and Dee see no problem with 'innovating on ORNet.' You are correct in your assessment. The Order needs the APEX."

"Sounds like a trap," I snapped back.

"You are still number one on the Privy Council, Lord Darius. Some of us still share your vision," Tom said. "Good night, my Lord."

Tom left.

"Tom believes I might still be Scion one day. He would not have come otherwise." Chief of Staff agreed. "There's something bigger than the APEX afoot. I want to know what. Something's happening."

"Bigger than the APEX?" COS said.

I agree. That's big. "It has to do with David. I'm sure of it. David is the common link." He waved over the team with the briefing. "Tell me about David Peterson."

"We found this footage of David with Alexander at the Council meeting, Sir," they said, showing me the video of Alexander and David on the roof of Castle Zenobia.

"We don't have sound, but it appears David helped Alexander escape," the tech said. "The transport was ordered with the same key-card." We watched the video of Alexander escaping.

"The Scion sealed David's file on ORNet. He's completely blacked out. We can't get any information on him from the network," staffers added. "We're pulling together everything we can, but there are redactions, blind spots. He met with the Scion at the castle, but we have no eyes, no video, inside the castle."

"David is our enemy. He helped Alexander escape. He's colluding with my father to take us down. He could be the one who gave Father the nanoids. Watch him. Get whatever you can on him and his family. I want regular reports."

I stared at the footage of David as he helped Alexander escape.

"David is up to something. Find out what it is."

"We'll know his every move, Sir," COS assured me.

"David is keeping secrets from me. Nothing upsets me more than someone keeping secrets from me."

"With the APEX, there will be no more secrets," COS said.

"We're in touch with the hacker?" I asked my Chief Technology Officer.

"The man we were talking to was a decoy," CTO said.

"What?!" Another fucking secret from me. "That sneaky fucking–"

"Per the agreement, we are forbidden from trying to find 'the Hacker' Tom said," my CTO informed me.

"Who is this *fucking* hacker?!" I demanded. "Is it David?"

"Whoever it is, they are the best computer programmers in the world, Sir. This is the person/persons who built ORNet. No one knows computers like this person and his/her team," COS said.

"And according to the most recent plans, the APEX will be bigger and better than we thought," CTO said.

"What happened to the person I met?"

"We're not sure. But chatter we have found indicates a potential alias of the hacker is named Lex. Whoever it is, John and Dee met with them; they are hiding this person. They won't let Tom meet them," COS said, giving me the latest intel.

"They're trying to control the project. Control the source."

"Apparently the hacker hates the Order and won't do the work if we try to unmask him, or if he knows it's for you."

"The hacker knows me?"

This narrows the list of suspects down considerably.

"Once the work is done, find them, and kill them. They are the one who found my secret bases and the nanoids. I know it."

"Yes, Sir," COS said.

I stared at the image of David on the screen.

Is it you, David? You think you can beat me? Dee can't hide you.

"We will build our all-powerful APEX. It will be mine. And there will be no more secrets from me... This world is mine."

You'll see.

CHAPTER LXV

"We met in a dream."

SARAH

You taught me love's lesson, painful indeed at first, but most advantageous in the end. By you, Elizabeth, I was properly humbled and enlightened to my purpose in this life.

Elizabeth's birth changed me in every way. Motherhood made me more myself, more the woman I was always meant to be. My mother raised us not to depend on her, and holding my child, I felt closer to my mother, more in love with her, more filled with love, than ever before. Suddenly I see everything she did for me, not so I would need her, but so I would be strong enough to be her, without her.

That is my dream for you, Elizabeth.

Pregnancy forged a new woman out of me. Though David was absent, I felt his presence, his thoughts and prayers for our family. I had all the help I needed, inside me. From David's seed I grew a family tree, a fruitful human, and she nourished us both thence forth.

While with child, David and I bonded as never before, and we met our unborn princess… in a field of dreams. *She found us, David.*

"Her name is Elizabeth."

"She is beautiful," David admired her with me.

At first she was only a light, a glowing orb of light, and over time, in the dream, we could see her personality, who she was, and who she would become, blossom like a divine flower, blooming divinity.

"Thank you," she said. The strangest thing you can imagine is to meet your child, as the adult she would become, before she was born. Her simple words filled me with joy, as I repeated them to my mother.

"She is a goddess, wise and fair. An being like few ever to manifest on this planet," Father said. "The gods have summoned greatness."

I gave birth on July 8th 2000, and looked into her newborn deep blue eyes as they opened for the first time; I saw destiny, hers and mine.

"My life is complete," were my first words to her. "You are perfect. You have made my life complete."

CHAPTER LXVI

"I remember the moment perfectly."

SARAH

David returned from Rome two months after the birth of our child. We had six months of peace before the Council Meeting…

The effect on my marriage of the horrific experience at the 2001 Council Meeting, the trauma and pain, was never remedied. Though at first I willingly suppressed the fear and terror of it, in favor of the remembrance of the grander parts, for David, in time my memories boiled into repugnant feelings. "Never again will I attend," and no testimony in its favour by David or any other would ever change my mind. Naught could heal the scar and deep effect on me of that terrible day. Darius horrified me, and the Order haunted my dreams.

"It was a nightmare," I later confessed to David. Being away from baby Elizabeth for the first time made it painful enough. David and I had adrenaline pumping in our system the entire time. Thrown into the lion's den, danger at every glace, "I feel lucky to have survived."

Alexander's manipulation of us, Darius turning on David, and the Scion's heart attack, all terrified me to my core. After the Scion was whisked away, the conference felt a chaotic mess. With fear in their hearts, all went on their un-merry way, as the affair dissolved in as orderly a fashion as possible in such harrowing circumstances. For me, the take away was quite clear: The Order is a delicate flower, a rose with deadly thorns; to smell the flower or taste the forbidden fruit is to touch poison, while applicably medicinal, you also risk death.

"But below the surface, and above it all, above the wanton power, and sheer arrogance, below misplaced esteem, there exists a motive of goodwill which cannot be overlooked, my Love," David argued.

"I wish you could get out," I said to David on the way home, stuck on Alexander's words of wisdom. "I think Alexander is right. The best thing to do is get out."

"Do you think the Scion died?" David said.

"I don't know."

"Surely someone will tell me. Don't you think?"

"I'd be hesitant to assume anything," I said.

"I am frightened," David said. "I've never felt this way before."

David and I held each other close until we arrived home.

Months went by without a word. The silence tortured David.

"Try to find peace," I said to David, as we lay in bed.

"Peace is a strong word. So simple, yet so impossibly complex."

I drifted off into a dream. I was chasing something. Racing off a cliff, forced to run, I ran until the ground below my feet vanished and I was falling... Chasing peace led me to its inverse, fear.

"Oh God... Someone, please save me!" I fell.

Falling into blackness, through the void, down became up, I floated into the night... Until I arrived. There it was among the stars:

"Shambala..."

The word became the world; darkness turned to light.

"I know this place." *I have been here before.*

The mythical Kingdom of Shambala appeared as the fog of consciousness lifted. Through the mists, I fell like a feather, slowly spinning. Falling from outer-space through the clouds above the city, I landed on the sacred ground. I rose with the sun clearing the air.

"Shambala is home to the Guardians of Humanity. The spiritual abode of the *Ascended Masters*, the men and women who mastered the universe, transcended death, and returned to help humankind," Father's voice left my head and manifested behind me.

I turned around to see him.

"Welcome, my Darling. Welcome home," Father said. "This is Shambala, the Golden Age Kingdom sitting atop the world." I looked around in awe. "Super-imposed on the material realm from the fourth dimension of being; Shambala is the edge, the bridge from a mountain on high. From here the world below is visible, reachable, in peace."

Warm sunny Zen gardens radiated perfect fengshui; aesthetically pristine beauty inspired oneness and tranquility of the soul.

"Shambala is only reachable by humans with pure hearts. Only heroes, those whose hearts are lighter than the feather of truth, can fly and rise to this place. Those who sacrifice, and seek to lift humankind and humanity's spirits, rise to this heavenly domicile."

"I've been here before."

"Many times, my child," a godly voice said.

"Who are you?" This being approached Father and me.

"Ancient god of many names, I am Thoth, keeper of the Light," his light became a human form for me to help me understand. Dressed in a white robe, a kind and stern face, his eyes revealed secrets to me.

"The time has come for you to return home," Thoth said.

"We need your help, Sarah," Father said. *Release thy mortal coil, let go thyself as body, return to the light.*

Only loving truth may be spoken in Shambala, and the wisdom and urgency in the words resonated deeply. I looked for David.

"I am to die?" I asked, knowing the answer. No David in sight.

"There is no other way," Father said.

"What about David? What about Elizabeth?"

"Because of them, and what they need you must do this. Their souls are in danger," Thoth said. "They require thy loving help."

"David will be crushed. How could I live without him? I couldn't make him live without me."

"In time, they shall understand," Father said.

"The Sacred Order is in danger. We must act swiftly. Before all is lost," Thoth said.

"You must let go, before it is too late," Father said.

"Too late for what?" I asked.

"The Order will come for you, Sarah. Darius will imprison you. Agents of Darkness will imprison your mind and your body; they seek to imprison your immortal soul. They move to keep you and David apart," Father said. "Darkness gathers, and evil stirs to strike."

"Our Sacred Order is in peril. We call on you, Sarah, to set things right. Let go thy fear, hold Love tight, return home," Thoth said.

"We cannot risk them capturing you," Father added.

"I understand." When I wake I hope I still will.

In Shambala everything makes perfect sense.

"From this place, Father has protected you," Thoth said.

"Only from here can you protect David. Protect him as a heavenly Mother, and he will protect Elizabeth, and our family shall be safe, know peace," Father said.

Father and Thoth walked me to the edge of Shambala, and we stared at the glowing blue world below.

"Let your Self go," Father reminded me. "Let go of time itself."

Leaping without looking, I fell to the earth below.

I let go.

CHAPTER LXVII

"Love means letting go."

SARAH

"Let go." I spoke the words to myself, in future memory, daily…

There was, of course, much that I did not know about what I must do. But in time, the misshapen chaos of well-seeming form, my death, was bound in destiny to bring my family closer together. I clung to this idea as I fell back to earth, fell through time, and came to grips with the notion of letting this life go.

Let go. The words echoed in my mind. Falling through dream-space and space-time, until back in my body I landed with a painful thud of reality, gasping for air as my chest felt heavy, the burden of death weighed upon me already, greatly.

Awakened in bed, forced to rise to breathe, David asleep beside me, I glided quietly off to check on my darling baby. Elizabeth slept soundly in her crib. Fervently, I prayed she understand.

She will understand, Father's voice said in my head.

I didn't tell David my dream of how my father asked me to "let go." In my heart I knew that would not help. I felt the danger of Darius looming over us, and as the days and months rolled by, my soul spent ever more time outside my body, and my coil without its current running constant, began to dim and die.

Once Elizabeth turned three years old, I saw that she knew what was happening; she understood more than she could articulate.

"You're going to go help Grandpa Henry?" She asked in a moment of unconditioned intuition and perfect clarity.

"Yes, Lizzy," I said. "He needs both our help. As does Father."

She saw that I loved her, and that everything I did, I did for her. Once she understood I would always be with her, I knew the time had come; I could leave in peace. But David could not let me go, and illness took me, conversely, as Elizabeth found wisdom and strength.

Four years had passed since my dream. "I'm dying, David."

"That's not possible," he replied. "You are strong."

"I need you to understand why I must go."

"You ask the impossible, my Love," David cried.

Brilliant as he was, David lacked the inherent wisdom of his child. Anxious about my survival, his logical reasoning screened out the deeper meaning, and he refused to accept a life without me. He did not see that losing my Love was a true impossibility. He could not understand why I would leave him. The selfless knowledge I tried to convey was blocked by selfish fear. But my Self was dying.

"One day you will understand. I promise."

"You can beat this. You know how your body works. You do—"

"This is my destiny." My words did not sit well with David.

"No. It can't be," David said. "How can death be destiny?"

By late 2006, six years after Elizabeth's birth and Father's death, David had all but abandoned the Order's demands and responsibility, for himself and for me. Too weak to take care of myself, David too broken to heal me, though he long resisted this fate, he checked me into the Saint Sinclair hospital in Switzerland.

The end of my life neared. As a last attempt to stave off my mortality, David called the best Doctor in all the world: Dr. Simon Sinclair.

"Please Simon, help her," he said. "She's dying. We've run every test imaginable. It doesn't make sense. If it's a disease, or a cancer, doctors have no name for it. Save her. Please. I beg of you. Save her."

A healer of the most profound kind, he touched my head, and saw the cause immediately. He saw my heart and spoke to it directly.

"What do you see?" David asked him.

"*Mise-en-abyme*. Worlds within worlds, I see, into Love's abyss. She's letting go. She is shutting her body down," Simon said.

I lay in bed, eyes closed, but fully conscious and aware.

"What can we do? I can't lose her," David said.

"You must let her go," Simon said. "Her soul wishes to be free. She feels she is in danger it seems… Her soul is in danger."

"From what?" David asked.

"The Order," Simon said, seeing more than he said.

"What has happened to the Order, Simon?" David asked. "Why is the Scion hiding? When will you tell me? What is happening?"

"The Scion lives, but still does not wish to be seen in his current state. As I said, this is all I can say at this time," Simon said.

"Why have I been left in the dark? Did I do something wrong?"

"Darius is watching you, David. He is dangerous and the future is uncertain. In time the answers will come. You did nothing wrong."

"I've seen the way Darius looks at me. No one speaks to me. Every year it gets worse," David cried. "The Order is killing my family."

"*À cet pourrait cependant se révéler n'être façon de reculer pour mieux sauter.* This is not what it seems; it will get better, David," Simon said.

"Not if she dies, Simon." David looked at me. I felt his pain.

"Sarah wishes to die, David. I can heal her, but I cannot change her mind. I cannot hold her in her body against her will."

"Why would she wish to die?"

"God has a plan. Sarah has a plan as well. Something, or someone, is calling her home," Simon said. "I see Henry—"

"What if I leave the Order? Would that help?" David asked Simon, looking at me, kneeling next to me. "I'm done. How can I get out?"

"*Honi soit qui mal y pense.* This be not the evil of the Order, David. You cannot leave," Simon began. "The Order needs you."

"Alexander was right. He warned me," David said, crying. "I should have listened. Now it's too late. Shame on me for not trusting him."

"Trust the Scion. He will call on you, David," Simon said. "Just as the heavenly Father calls on Sarah. Say your goodbyes. Hold onto your love, but you must let her go."

Simon left us alone. David trusted Simon implicitly but, still blinded by his fears, he was unable to see the truth or hear Simon's words.

Nanny and Sister brought in Elizabeth, now a mature woman in a six-year-old body. David cried. Elizabeth grabbed my hand.

"I need you to get better, my Love," he cried. "Please. Our lives have only just begun."

Stuck in fear, David could not let me go. He held my hand tight.

Help your father understand, Elizabeth, I told her without speaking. She heard me. Her powers of the mind rivaled Father's.

"Speak to us Mummy. Open your eyes; it's time," Elizabeth said.

Her touch gave me peace in strength, and I opened my eyes.

"Sarah, you're awake," David said grabbing my hands and pulling Elizabeth close. "Lizzy. You brought her back."

"This is the end, David," I said.

"No. You can't leave me— my love, I need you. I will never leave your side again. I'll do anything. Please. Don't leave me—"

"She needs to go Daddy," Elizabeth said with the conviction of an adult, supported by the wisdom of fearless youth. "They need her."

David stood shocked at Elizabeth's words.

"What? What did you say, Lizzy?" David began to realize our daughter is spiritually all grown up. Elizabeth was astute, in ways wiser than he, but David had been so busy worrying about me, he hadn't seen her bloom into the little radiant goddess she was always meant to be.

"It's going to be okay," Elizabeth said. She smiled, to make her father stop crying. "She isn't leaving us. Grandpa Henry needs her help. He told me. You understand."

From the simple voice of a child, David finally understood. He looked at me. My face told David he must listen to her.

"You have to go?" David asked.

"Yes." *But I am not leaving you.*

"What will I do without you?" David slowly loosened his grip.

"I am forever with you. Be strong, David. Be strong for Elizabeth, my Love," my voice cracked under my own physical sadness.

"Wait. Stay with me – with us – a little longer, please," David said with tears running down his face, holding Elizabeth close.

"I love you, Mummy," Elizabeth said. "I dream about you every night; by day you are the sun giving life inside me."

"I shall never love again," David said.

"You shall never be without love, ever again."

David experienced our Love, and emotion as never before. My dying awakened his emotional life; releasing his mind from the prison of reason ruling alone. He needed this freedom more than I, now thus I saw my destiny, our destiny, completely. David finally touched his feelings, as he never had before; he was now in touch with all of me. Elizabeth, now stronger than I will ever be, sealed her approval with a kiss on my cheek, and in my last minutes of life, again I found a new meaning of family.

The life left my body. Not painful, peaceful and gently.

David knew this was the end, but couldn't believe it. My hand went limp. David wouldn't let go. He squeezed my hand tighter. His final release was soon my own.

"I loved you the moment I saw you. This is true love. We had true love," David said.

Have. We have it. Death cannot stop true love.

If only it could, David said.

Love is as strong as death. Death only separates the soul from the body, but love separates all things from the soul, love binds our souls, my Love, I said. "I love you."

"Love is composed of a single soul inhabiting two bodies," he cried. *We are Love... Love is eternal matrimony; family.*

I closed my eyes and we let go, and again became One.

This is not goodbye, this is Love.

CHAPTER LXVIII

"Meet the good Doctor."

SIMON

"A confesseurs, médicins, avocats, la vérité ne cèle de ton cas."
'Don't hide the truth from your doctor or your lawyer,' most sound advice is this. As Doctor to the High King, trusted friend, and confidant, I am the one person the Scion hides nothing from. This honor I do not take lightly. To heal the Scion is to heal the Order itself and as they say: *"mieux vaut prévenir que guérir."* 'Prevention is better than cure,' so I must prevent the ills of the Order however I am so able, and remedy what I cannot prevent. That is my noble charge.

Descendent of both the preeminent, most ancient, Empiric medical learned of old, and the Merovingian bloodline of healers, I've known the Scion, he has known me, my entire life. As a child, I dreamed of the day I would follow in my father's footsteps and serve as personal Physician to the Great Scion. My family has tended the Order, passed down the title of *Order Surgeon-General, Head of the Majestic Medical Council and School*, and held a place on the 'Magic Council' for a recorded five hundred and eleven years.

"The family Sinclair's healing powers have raised the dead," *mon père m'a dit une fois.* "We heal all ills, but lo, cannot save the soul."
I cannot save nor heal the Scion's soul, though I wish I could.

The Scion entered my lab. He looked very much the same to me as a child as he did just months prior to ingesting the forbidden alien technology. I had never known him to be or seen him as a young man. *Plus le Roi change, plus il reste le même…* But he is the same.

"Never will I get used to seeing you as a young man, Majesty," I said to my King as he sat down with me. This sterile white room felt as far from nature as he did. His heart appeared the same, but his once purple and divine white aura had black shadows within it. A sinister darkness lurked in his blood, dimming his inner light. To mention this would be of no benefit to him; he is fragile in spirit.

"What have you learned?" the Scion asked.

"Indeed, you can live forever with those 'nanoid' nano-robots in your blood, Majesty. There are as yet no physical harm or reactions I can see. We have encrypted them, so as no one can, how do you say, 'hack them' or tamper with their programming. So long as they stay activated, you will be alive and young indefinitely, without ill effect."

"I see," he said, sensing my sadness.

"Never did I imagine, I, the best doctor in all the world, would be replaced by machines," I laughed. "I'm afraid you won't have much need for me it seems."

"You could not be more wrong," he said. "I require your assistance now more than ever, Simon."

Most intrigued, his youthful charm seduced me.

"I don't want to live forever. I don't want to live any longer than I absolutely must," the Scion said.

"What are you saying?" I asked, seeing his light grow bright.

"It's time I told you about this," he said.

The Scion presented a large, shimmering, purple marble between his thumb and forefingers. Ancient mystery shone from it, the magnetism of its wonder pulled me in instantly. He placed the orb in my hand. A river of energy, Qi, pulsed through me, from above to below; awesome visions, spirits, and enchantment, surrounded me.

"What magic is this?" Almost unable to speak, exasperated, looking at the wondrous item in my hand, seeing I still could not understand.

"The Aton," he said, "the blood of the first Pharaoh."

The current took me away; I faded away, drowning in pure energy, the power of the crystal ball swallowed me, and I touched the All.

"*San Graal?*" Believe it, I could not. "The legend is true? The Holy Grail is real, and in my hand..." To hold the truth is to be free.

"Yes," he said. The Scion took the item from my grasp.

"What do you know of it?" he asked.

"Not enough."

"I want you to study it. You are going to clone the blood."

"Clone the blood?" I did not like this idea.

"Yes," he said. "Can you do that, Simon?"

"You want me to create a human, from this blood?"

"Yes. Is that a problem?"

"Human cloning is..."

"Not impossible?" the Scion clarified.

212

"Anything is possible, glorious Majesty."

"That's the spirit! Your father would be most proud. If anyone can do this, Simon, if anyone can help me, you can. You are the only person I can trust with this, you understand?"

"Why do you want to do this? Cloning is against nature," the words had to be said. The Scion appreciated my candor.

"Because this clone is going to be my heir, and replace me as Scion. I want to bring this Pharaoh back, somehow. I've told no one this plan. Not even Dee. But you know I keep no secrets from you."

The Scion saw Darius cross my mind.

"Will his Grace let a clone become the Scion? I think not."

"*Chacun voit midi à sa porte.* We shall deal with that when the time comes," the Scion said.

"Very well," I said. "We travel down the road to see where it goes."

"I desire nothing more than to relinquish my throne, and my mortal coil, Simon. Outside of nature is not my choice, and not how I want to live. But Darius must not be my legacy. My legacy shall be a new Order, a rebirth of the Order, born of this blood. You must help me with this," he said staring at the Aton-core in his out stretched hand.

"Of course, Majesty," I answered. "Do you now give this to me?"

My King struggled to relinquish the glittering treasure to me.

"Yes," he said, placing it in my hand.

I placed it back in the box and held it close.

"I am trusting you with everything, Simon. This task is more important than my life. Failure is not an option."

Gravity of the task, the weight of all mankind, set in on me.

"Welcome to 'Project Pharaoh,'" the Holy Scion left me in thought.

Failure is not an option.

CHAPTER LXIX

"We need his help."

DAVID

In 2007, the spring of my discontent, my life was made glorious again just before summer, when the Sun King rose from the dead. Just when I had forsaken the Order, processed my grief, and settled into a new life with Elizabeth, the Scion appeared to remind me of my destiny... *The Order needs your help, David.*

After Sarah died, while Elizabeth attended grammar school in London, I worked at the British Museum. As a Trustee, and Director of *Special Research*, I focused my efforts to digitizing all the works, tablets, books, documents, and items in the custody of the museum. We secretly scanned everything in 3-D, near the microscopic level, all color and depth, using super high resolution full spectrum laser and radiation technology. Every artifact was to be analyzed, cataloged, and studied, eventually by algorithm and machines, for any clues the human eye might miss. My vision was to scan everything in all museums and libraries in the world, to create a "Digital Library of Alexandria," a virtual repository of all the world's artifacts and books. I funded the project myself, finally learning, decidedly unafraid to use my golden key-card. The endless work satisfied me, kept me busy, being that for the last six years, the Order demanded ever less, and finally nothing. The Order wanted nothing until it wanted everything.

Elizabeth's school was not far from the museum, and I walked to visit her almost every day, though often staying out of sight so as not to get in the way. I arranged for her and the school to visit the museum regularly, which everyone loved, though none more than me.

After a tour of our latest exhibition of Hellenistic bronze statues, "all art has a story to tell!" I bid my little Lizzy and her class farewell.

"Everyone say thank you to Dr. Peterson," the teacher said.

"Thank you Dr. Peterson," all the girls said in chorus as they left.

No sooner had I said goodbye, and wiped a tear from my eye, I felt the intense glare, and caught someone staring at me.

It cannot be…

I recognized his face. Never have I forgotten a face, but something didn't compute. When it hit me, the answer didn't make sense. This face continued to stare at me, as I approached. He smiled.

"Is it really you?" This man looked at most thirty-five years old, and his face strained my facial recognition skills to the limit. It couldn't be… His energy drew me in. I stopped about three feet from him. It *was* him. "Oh, my Lord."

"Hello, David," he said. *This is the Scion.*

Marduk revealed his demi-god self, putting to bed any doubt.

"Marduk will prevent Darius from listening," the Scion said.

"You… you are young? How?" The Scion ignored my questions; he explains nothing, of course.

"I have a new assignment for you, David. A mission of great importance," he said.

This youthful Scion defied all I knew to be true. But truth is so often stranger than fiction. He didn't like me all but gawking at him.

"Everything will be explained to you when you get there," he said as he began to walk away.

"Where?" I pleaded for more time with him.

"You'll see. Marduk will take you," he said.

"What about my daughter? I cannot leave her."

"Dee will look out for her. He already is, David."

All worry was quelled instantly, magically.

"Of course, my Lord," I said.

The aura of the Scion reminded me of my initiation ritual.

"Wonderful to see you, David." The Scion said as he and Marduk walked around a corner, stepping out of sight.

Following, I peered round the corner. Those two incredible beings had vanished impossibly amid the marble statues of the gods.

This is about the Aton, I knew.

I vanished too.

CHAPTER LXX

"He searched for the code."

DAVID

Suffering is the sacred law of love; no quest is without pain; no lover exists who is not also a martyr. So I am steadfast, and rest not content until my now of eternity is obtained, and my present is perfect in possession of life and love; I strive for this deific Zen to the greatest ends, to the utmost that is humanly possible, with my soul. For an infinite moment, I held it, I touched one Love. *Where am I?*

I blinked. My eyes opened to the entry room of a lovely Tudor Cottage, wooden interiors, arched ceiling, large windows in the hills overlooking Lake Geneva. Through the windows, a secluded perch view soothes me. Confused as to what just happened, I stood there. Did I really just blink and appear somewhere thousands of miles away? How is that possible? Before I could fall into a pit of quandary:

"David? David, you're here," Doctor extraordinaire Simon Sinclair found me. Unexpectedly, he was expecting me.

"Bonjour!" he put his healing hands on me and kissed both cheeks, "Wonderful to see you, David. Welcome."

"How did I get here?"

"The only way Darius cannot follow you," Simon said. "Marduk. Come! Let me show you around…"

Simon escorted me in and gave me a tour, three bedrooms, a living room, library and den, a kitchen, and two bathrooms. Charming, and seemingly unlived in, but a warm home full of life, in every way.

Simon showed me the secret door, behind the mirror in the library.

"This is where the magic happens," he said.

We entered a steel elevator, and descended deep into the secure bunker below the cottage. The fake windows of the bunker rooms are able to display whatever scenery you want, for the illusion of not being deep below ground… The main room is mostly filled with highly advanced equipment for his genetic research. I understood immediately. *You are working on the Aton.* I felt it.

Stepping out of the elevator, there it was, the Aton-core, sitting in a clear glass case, beaming with light that blinds your third eye.

"You're studying the... Aton," I said the magic word.

"He wants us to clone the blood," he said.

"How did you get blood out of it?" I examined the purple filled diamond-crystal ball.

"I used a laser which is now being turned into a particle smasher."

"CERN's Large Hadron collider?" I had read about it.

"It took several years, but I was able to extract a few milliliters of blood by accelerating the object, spinning it while the laser created a hole in the shell... The crystal lattice heals itself, so the process was quite complex. We were able to make it work, crack the cosmic egg, as it were. Quite extraordinary, eh?"

"Indeed," I said.

Simon smiled. "This is no ordinary blood, David. Come, let us eat."

Up to the main cottage. Simon and I ate, drank wine, and talked for hours. "He said this was your idea, David. To clone the blood."

"I won't take credit, I will only take part," I smiled.

"Partial credit then," Simon laughed. "Coffee?"

The coffee kicked in and Simon turned serious.

"The blood is not human, per se. No ordinary DNA, and 'tis not clone-able using any previously established methods," Simon said. "I have tried them all to no avail. How much do you know about DNA?"

"Sarah was an expert on DNA. One of the best in the world," I said.

Sadness became peaceful silence. Eyes closed, I listened for Sarah's voice. *DNA is a code David*, Sarah said, *DNA holds information. Potentially infinite amounts of information...*

"DNA holds an infinite amount of information"
"Information within information"
"Into the infinite"
"And back"

"You can hear her, David?" Simon said. "You can hear Sarah?"

"Crack the code, and we will find our answer," I said, saying yes.

"The DNA is a code?" Simon said, answering his own question.

"It holds information, infinite amounts of information. What we need to know is within the DNA code..."

"I'm afraid I've very little skill in biochemical cryptanalysis."

"Well begun is half done," I said.

"I've sequenced the DNA at near 99% accuracy," Simon said.

"We need 100% accuracy. We need a scan of this DNA as close to the atomic level as is possible."

"Would you believe that Dee is working on that already? Great minds think alike, I see," Simon grinned with glee.

"DNA has several electro-chemical languages it uses, if we can understand the gene activation controls... We can activate them."

"You may find this hard to believe, David, but this blood has no mitochondrial DNA. No mother," Simon said of the vial in his hand.

"How is that possible?" I asked. "Everyone has a mother."

Simon presented me with the computer generated report.

"It clearly say: No mtDNA," he noted. "No mother."

"Perhaps this is why the Pharaoh was able to live indefinitely..."

"What do you mean?" Simon said.

"This report is quite fascinating..." I pondered the data, the words and numbers in the DNA report. "Another time I'll tell you all about my research at the Secret Archives, but there is evidence that the Pharaohs of old were able to live thousands of years."

"Computers, numbers, and such are not my strength. I don't much like them," Simon said. "This scientific report defies medical science. The doctor in me does not understand how there can be no mother."

I looked up at Simon as he sipped his coffee.

"Divine intervention?" I smiled. "The secret is in this DNA code."

"*Sacré bleu*," Simon said. "Crack *de* code, and we create our immaculate conception! Yes?"

"Yes. From an immaculate conception, no less," I laughed.

"We need a miracle," Simon said, quite serious.

"We need a cypher. For that I feel we must look to the Heavens."

"You mean that literally," Simon said, reading my face.

"The stars must all align just right. As above, so below."

"*Petit a petit, l'oiseau fait son nid.* This is progress, David."

"Tell me about the Scion, Simon. Please." I looked at him intensely.

"You want to know how he became young?"

"Yes. Did he use this blood?" I said, looking at the Aton-core.

"No. He used forbidden alien technology," Simon said.

"What is forbidden technology?" I asked.

"The opposite of that," he pointed to the Aton-core.

CHAPTER LXXI

"Anything is possible?"

THE SCION

No thing can resist the will of a King who knows what is true and wills what is good. While microscopic robots of an alien design kept me young and physically perfect, my mind willed my heart to stop, my tortured soul died a slow death inside me. The pain of the soul is the most injurious, for no remedy can heal it, save death.

I long for death. By 2008, but few from my former life still walked the earth. Isolated and alone, in a prison of my own creation, I became the living dead. Olympias was in fading health, but holding on to life for me. Seeing her gave me peace. She visited me often.

"I need her," I told Dee.

"She knows," Dee said. "A more powerful woman there never was. Your sister is a goddess like few ever to walk the earth."

"She wants to know what happened to Alexander. So do I, Dee."

"He is not the same man," Dee said, telling me what I already knew.

"After his initiation he was so inspired, then something changed. The light in his eyes left. I don't understand."

"Our Alexander will come back," Dee said.

"He's vacant and detached; he's degenerated into a crude heathen, his mind is lost, he remembers nothing of his former self. He has excommunicated himself from the world... To what end? How could you let this happen to him?"

Dee had no answer.

"The Order is breaking down. Everyone can see it; 'tis a train wreck in slow motion, Dee. I feel I am powerless to stop it."

"You are not powerless. Quite the opposite," Dee said.

"I know Darius is using his computers to slowly seize control of the Order, and the world seems to be taking a turn for the worse."

"A precarious situation indeed," Dee offered no solution. "To be rid of Darius, you must keep him close." Dee's words made no sense.

"And I must give him more power? How long can this go on?"

"A calculated risk, my Lord," Dee reasoned with me.

"It vexes me. A terrible hex!"

"Running the Order keeps him busy. So long as he feels there is more power to be had, so he shall be focused on that," Dee said.

"I suppose." Darius is consumed with power.

Focus on Project Pharaoh, Majesty. Dee's eyes lectured me.

"Darius shall report to the Vizier, as your proxy," Dee said. "If you do not wish to interact with Darius at all. That is your prerogative."

"Perhaps 'tis best I don't see him. He doesn't want to see me."

"His Grace is fully equipped to deal with Darius in that capacity."

Project Pharaoh is all that matters.

"I'm ashamed of being young, Dee. I loathe it. 'Tis killing me."

"I understand, Majesty," Dee placated me. "Such is synthetic immortality."

"I want it all to end, Dee," I said. *I need this to end.*

Dee looked at his pocket watch. The time was at hand.

"I'll set up the secure ORNet communiqué so you can video talk to David and Simon." He turned on the screen. "They'll see you, and you'll see them on this monitor here."

He stared at me intensely with those powerful wise eyes. He treats me like a child, like I've never video chatted before.

"Tell me—" He knew what I was about to ask. "How is that you do you not age at all? Are you immortal, Master Dee?"

"This will only take a moment." Dee clicked on the computer.

"Will you not answer my plea?" I said.

"All is set, Majesty," he said. "Once they activate the system from their end, they shall appear on the monitor."

"Will you give me nothing of who you are?" *Dee, please?*

"I shall give you what you need," Dee said, turning on a device that buzzed slightly, and blocked any local transmission interception.

"I need to know who you are, Grand Master Mervyn Wisendee." I had asked this question before, as a child. Asking again, I felt a child.

"Not today, not now, you don't, Majesty. David calls," Dee said.

David and Simon appeared on the monitor.

My wizard left me alone in my office, closing the door behind him.

Forlorn in silence, my mind took me to a dark place.

Technology cannot save me, I said to myself.

CHAPTER LXXII

"We all need a hero sometimes."

THE SCION

On this day, the whole of my world changed sway; my spirit, so long dethroned and forgotten, having lost its way, took its ancient place on high; my heart demonstrated that the sacred traditions of old are all true, that the modern Order is but a system of corrupted and misplaced truths, and 'tis essential to cleanse this world, so to say, and to put things back again in their righteous place, to see humanity shine with all its divine rays. In a word, all ideas may change, and why should I blame myself for the past, so long as I throw myself forward, push others, into that majestic future, and with love, save this world.

"Simon. David. How are you, friends?" I finally broke the silence.

David and Simon sensed my deep sadness, and gave me a turn to glee as they watched me on their screen from the bunker in Geneva.

"Majesty" Simon said. "Seeing you brings me happiness."

David nodded in agreement.

"Good news, I pray today, gentlemen?"

"The good news, Majesty, is that David is a miracle worker. He's making fantastic progress," Simon paused to admire David's humility. "The bad news, is that cloning has not been possible by any existing means. We have exhausted all known methods."

"Are you suggesting the blood can't be cloned?" My heart began to sink into a black-hole of crushing panic, so fragile is my soul.

"No, my Lord, I believe it can," Simon said.

"David?" *You can save me, David. Please!*

"I too believe it can be cloned, my Lord; Majesty. We shall find a way, once we understand the DNA," David said.

"Elaborate on the DNA, please," I said.

David turned to Simon. "DNA has a coded language that instructs the building of proteins and cells, and a language that controls cells through the genes. Certain genes must be activated, instructed to activate, before they will replicate," Simon said.

"We must figure out how to activate all necessary genes to begin mitosis," David said. "We need the keys to activation."

"How do you go about learning the language and keys of DNA?"

"Cracking the code. There is a code to the DNA," David said. "We have all the data we need. Dee gave us a scan, a sequencing of the DNA down to the atomic level. Now we need to understand it, to find the pattern within the pattern, and compare it with other DNA samples we're analyzing. It can be done, my Lord."

"What's our timeline? How long until we can have a child? The plan requires a child cloned from the blood," I said, seeing it possible.

"I regret that we do not know, Majesty," Simon said. I felt him healing me, making me feel better with his energy healing gifts. "We are doing everything we can," he said. "Be strong."

Simon knows me so well he felt my soul aching, and gave me remedy, soothing my spiritual pain, massaging my heart with love.

"Deciphering the DNA coding for activation keys will take time," David said. "We need access to a very powerful computer system, my Lord, and not ORNet or any networked system, a private one, a way to build and run algorithms to vet DNA codes sequences," David said.

"Infinite possibilities of sequences," Simon elaborated.

"A computer system?" I complained.

"Yes. We need technological help… We are working on tailoring a frequency of electromagnetic radiation to activate genes," David said. "We have a theory that shows great promise."

"David believes there is a correlation between the stars and their positions and the DNA. He's been studying ancient alchemical manuscripts. There is compelling evidence; I believe he is correct."

"We need a powerful computer system to help process the data," David said. "Life is energy. And the keys to life, DNA, can be stimulated with radiation. However, simulating the electromagnetic frequencies and matching them to DNA code sequences requires computations that no human brain, and few computers, can do in a lifetime, my Lord. There's simply too much information to process."

"I can hardly comprehend the size of these numbers," Simon said.

"The possible spectrum and combinations is literally infinite, and must be narrowed somehow. We need to create an evolving algorithm to scan the data and the meta-data. For this we need an extremely powerful computer system, one with—" David thought of the APEX.

"You need Darius' APEX," I said.

David and Simon said nothing, sensing my deep pride and pain.

"But the APEX was not built, I thought—" David said.

Perhaps technology can save me, Dee?

"I'll see what I can do. Godspeed, gentlemen," I said. Holding back my depression I bid adieu.

"Feel peace, Majesty," Simon sent me one last burst of healing love energy; his radiant heat warmed my cold soul.

No sooner had I turned off the screen and the privacy system, Marduk manifested next to me. I felt a faint buzzing in my ears.

Order Guards enter the room.

"What's going on?" I demanded.

"An intruder is coming. There—" Order Guards said.

I felt it coming. The buzzing grew into a loud, but noiseless POP! And the buzzing stopped. My ears rang and I blinked.

What the devil...

A man, the intruder, 'popped' into the room without making a sound: teleported.

"Dear God—"

CHAPTER LXXIII

"How did Alexander do it?"

THE SCION

True science necessarily admits faith; true faith necessarily reckons with science. My faith in science had to reckon with the truth.

Dressed in a black hat, black jacket and slacks, and a white T-shirt, the teleported intruder fell to the floor of my office, covering his face, apparently unconscious from the shock to his system. My supposedly impenetrable Castle, and thus my world, turned upside down.

"How is this possible?" Order Security descended in a frenzy, and ten agents entered the room in an dramatic show of force.

"It's not," the Order Guard said, bewildered.

"Then how did he get in here?" I said of the intruder.

The agents picked up the man and presented him to me. Dizzy and unable to stand on his own, he flinched as the agents took off his hat. They grabbed his black hair, lifted his head, and showed me his face.

"Good God..." I uttered in disbelief, "Alexander?"

He had dyed black his golden hair. His ears pierced several times and a vile tattoo, no doubt much larger than I could see, crept up his neck. His youthful essence all but gone, dark circles under his eyes, he appeared a haggard mess. I examined his unconscious body. Aged and scarred, his person appeared hardened. But there was no doubt in my mind it was him. They lifted his eyelid to reveal his unmistakable, majestic green eye... I saw that magical spark.

"Wake him." *He has returned, Dee!*

They injected him with a stimulant. Alexander burst to life, waving his arms like a drunkard.

"Let go of me!" he snarled instinctually, ever defiant. The agents let him go and he immediately fell to the floor, unable to stand. They placed Alexander on a chair before me as John and Tom entered.

"Holy shit... It worked," Alexander said.

"Is it really Alexander?" I made Tom and John aware.

"It's me, Papa Mel," he said, still looking dizzy.

John whispered to Tom. Tom gave orders to the Order Agents who left. John pulled up footage of the man believed to be Alexander, in Los Angeles; the miscreant drunk and dancing like a fool in a nightclub. As we watched the monitor, this 'faux Alexander' was removed from the Hollywood den of iniquity mid-drink.

"Alexander will be here shortly," John said of the Alexander on the monitor. Tom pricked the Alexander in front of me, getting a blood sample to test.

"Ow! What the F—" Alexander stopped himself from cursing.

"It really is you," I said, looking him in the eyes.

"Yes, Grandfather," he said, in full consciousness, focused on me.

"How did he get in here?" Tom demanded of security.

"Perhaps he could explain," John said.

"Who are you?" Tom demanded of Alexander, in anger.

"I am Alexander… the Great," he said.

"You have much to explain, Alexander," I said.

"If he's not been in California… what has he been doing?" Tom said. "We've been tracking this Alexander for seven years. Only days after he left the castle. If – If Alexander managed to hide for all these years…" Tom stopped unable to process the truth.

"Dee!" I yelled.

Dee walked into the room seconds later.

"How did he get in here?" I pointed to Alexander.

Dee touched Alexander and looked him in the eye.

"This is indeed Alexander. He teleported in," Dee said, as if that explained everything. Dee refuses to explain when it's needed most.

"Where has he been?" I spoke for Tom and John as well.

"I think it best that he tell you himself, Majesty." Dee left the room, ignoring the violently silent protest from Tom and John.

"You have not aged a day," Alexander said, rising out of his chair.

"Alexander—" he sensed the fury in my voice.

"You look younger than me. It's not fair—" Alexander said as he inappropriately reached to touch me.

"Restrain him!" I yelled in boiling rage.

The Order Guards forced Alexander back into the chair.

"*You* look wretched, Alexander. Absolutely wretched."

"I feel pretty wretched," Alexander said.

"Explain yourself. Now!" I commanded.

Alexander, ever disobedient, got up and poured himself a drink, and then lit one of my cigarettes. He returned to his chair, as he gathered his thoughts to speak. I motioned for a drink and lit my pipe. Staring at Alexander, the tension thickened with the smoke.

"I have my secrets too," Alexander said. Arrogance abounding.

"No. No more secrets."

"No more secrets from me—" Alexander defied me.

"You will answer me when I ask you a question!"

"I plan to," he said as he finished his drink. He motioned for another. "I've missed you, Grandfather, Mel-Mel…"

"Good God… What have you become?"

"You saved me. Your initiation, in the Chamber, saved me. It opened my eyes, and I saw what I needed to do. And I did it all for you. Wasn't it you that said: To suffer is to work. Pain is to—"

"What exactly have you done, Lord Alexander?" John said.

"And how did you do it?" Tom said, standing behind me.

"I cracked the code," Alexander said. "I got it to work."

"Got what to work?" My curiosity piqued.

"A teleportation system," Alexander said with pride. "I'm the first boy to be sent through the air by teleport. How great am I? Seriously."

"What? How?" My brain tingled; my stomach filled with butterflies.

"It's all about the right clothes," Alexander said as he put his hat back on and pulled the brim down.

"The hat," John said "Take it."

"Take all the clothes," Tom said. "Take it all to the lab."

Order Agents stripped Alexander naked almost instantly.

"Boys, boys… Can I at least finish my drink?" Alexander said.

Alexander's tattoos were larger and more awful than I imagined. He stood there naked, his drink in one hand, his gentiles in the other, gloating in victory, enjoying this all too much.

"Good god. Get him some clothes."

"What's a guy gotta do to get a refill?" Alexander whined in a terrible American accent, shaking the ice in his empty glass.

"You're going to tell me everything. Now," I said.

Alexander smiled. "I intend to, Grandfather."

CHAPTER LXXIV

"The family secret."

THE SCION

In order to make things visible and produce the most brilliant light, a shadow is inevitably essential; so that the just mind may become efficacious in good will, it needs contradictions. Alexander needed to go astray to find himself, I realized. Clothes arrived and the guards forcibly dressed Alexander, finally hiding marks of his errant ways.

Agents left with Alexander's 'teleportation clothes' as two guards entered with the 'Faux Alexander' plucked from the Hollywood club. This imposter, who masqueraded as my grandson for seven years, was a near perfect match of Alexander in appearance – the un-tattooed, and innocent Alexander I knew. He even had a green eye, though now I see not nearly as incredible and brilliant as my true heir's.

"Who is this man?" I examined him. "He looks more like the Alexander I like."

An agent took a blood sample from the imposter. He didn't even notice. "Dude. Did I just ride in a space ship?" he slurred, drunkenly.

"Because he is the Alexander you thought you knew," the scarred and black haired 'real Alexander' said.

"Where am I?" the inebriated faux Alexander said, slowly realizing he had fallen down the rabbit-hole. He knew this day would come.

Alexander doted on his better looking doppelgänger.

"You're not going to remember anyway," Alexander said to him.

"Who created him?" I demanded. *Dee, you did this, didn't you?*

"The DNA test result says his name is Paul Wilmington" John said. "He's had gene therapy. He has some of Alexander's genes."

"He's Lex. My decoy," Alexander said, proudly. "Isn't he perfect?" Alexander admired his beautiful work of human art.

"You've killed this man. You do see that?" I said.

"Don't hurt him," Alexander begged. "It's not his fault. Please."

"I won't," I said.

Order Agents took the faux Alexander away.

"But he'll be killed by Darius, for sure. We must put him back. And figure out how to make this whole thing go away."

"I want you to protect him," Alexander said.

"I want you to tell me what's going on, Alexander. Speak!"

Alexander's face, his mystically brilliant eyes, said he already knew my secret. *Project Pharaoh... that's why I'm here.*

"Darius is planning a coup against you. He's planning to seize control of the Order," Alexander said. "He's going to kill you."

A moment of deafening silence hung in the air. Tom and John hesitated to speak. "How?" I said.

"Remember the APEX? That thing I said not to build," he said.

"I shut it down." Doubt made my stomach sink. I didn't shut the whole thing down, and now I realized I may have made a mistake.

"Was it shut down, Tom?" Alexander said.

Tom's façade cracked under the stress.

"What does he mean, Tom? What has Darius built?"

"Darius is not building the APEX," Tom replied. "He— He was only supposed to be innovating on ORNet and building approved cyber infrastructure we need."

"Darius has built the APEX – and then some." Alexander's words enraged Tom. "He's planning to use his 'innovation' to seize control of ORNet, and then your nanoids, and then the Order."

"This is preposterous! Where is he getting this information?" Tom demanded in protest.

Alexander did not flinch. Tom's vitriol only empowered him and proved his point. I stared at Alexander, waiting to hear more.

"The APEX will become the Order, it will absorb and unify, become one, with every computer system on earth. And when it's complete, it will be able to control the world, by controlling all information and electronic systems. The APEX is preparing to annex ORNet, and it'll be like taking candy from a baby... Candy being the power and the baby being you."

"Lies!" Tom said. "He *is* lying!"

"This had better not be true," I said, the gravity setting in.

"Set it up here." John directed the Order Agents who rapidly assembled an ORNet portal in the room.

"I'll prove it. May I?" I took over the station and hacked in, walked in like it was nothing, through my ORNet backdoor. "All the proof you need, right here."

"Alexander. How did you – How do you know all this?" I asked.

"The same way I got past your 'impenetrable' security," Alexander smiled. "I hacked your security. I wrote the code the is your security."

"Oh my God—" Tom began to panic. "It's you. *You're* the hacker."

"Alexander built ORNet, Majesty," John said to me, in a déjà vu.

"No... I don't believe it," Tom agonized at the conclusions on the station monitors. "Darius hired Alexander to build—" Tom began to melt down. The words set in on him with crushing weight.

"Yep. Darius hired me, illegally, to build his APEX," Alexander said. "Now you know what I've been up to all these years."

"You have been helping Darius? You have been lying to me? For the past—You've been lying to me your whole life? Alexander?" I felt my own catastrophic mental meltdown begin.

"Grandfather. Listen. I can explain," Alexander said.

"No. No you can't explain such betrayal," I said.

"Wisendee set me up," Tom said. "He set us all up to fail!"

My body tingled with emotional pins and needles.

Dee, what is happening? Why are you doing this to me?

"I am the world's absolute best computer programmer," he said.

"You betrayed me," I said. "Why have you helped Darius build the APEX against my wishes? Have you any idea what you've done?"

Dee! What is the meaning of this!?

"You are looking at the shadow, Grandfather. But you needed the light to see," Alexander said.

I saw only the darkness of my impending death at the hands of Darius. I saw the end of the world...

CHAPTER LXXV

"Heavy is the head that wears the crown."

THE SCION

The will of the just King is the will of the Almighty, and the law of the Natural Order. 'Tis by the will that intelligence sees truth. If the will be healthy, the sight is just and true. *Let there be light!* I willed, and light appeared. But the light blinded me, and my faith in Alexander with it.

"Alexander did indeed build the APEX for Darius. He designed the system software, and wrote the main source code," John said.

"Did you know?" Tom asked his brother.

"If I did, the memory was lost to me," John said.

"So Alexander has committed treason!" Tom declared.

My blood boiled in burning fear of the light. "How could you?" Alexander could not hear my soft spoken plea for understanding.

"Darius committed treason. I saved everything on a ghost drive. Everything, including the date of Darius' planned coup." He turned to me. "He plans to use the APEX to hack your nanoids, Grandfather. All the evidence to prove it is here. He's planning to kill you. That's why I'm here. To warn you."

Alexander stared at me. We are strangers; I know him not. But I know my family, my enemies, well.

"You helped Darius?" I said, calmly.

"You are accusing your father of treason, Lord Alexander," John warned Alexander. "Of high crimes against the Order."

"That's how he found the nanoids, and accessed the teleportation system— He's framing Darius to take control of the Order himself!" Tom yelled. "Alexander is the real treasonous felon here!"

This felt untrue. But fear ruled me. I could not speak.

Cockily, Alexander explained: "I built ORNet. Darius had the paper trail of ORNet and the APEX destroyed in September 2001. When the project groundwork was complete, a few months ago, Darius ordered another purge, and everyone killed. I'm only alive because—"

Alexander's arrogance infuriated me to my core. My compressed rage was sparked by the fear of Project Pharaoh being exposed and discovered by this APEX. "You insolent fool!" I exploded. My whole world seemed to be slipping away. "Why on earth would you help Darius!? You would help him kill me?!"

Taken by fear and fury, I stormed over to him ready to kill him. He looked afraid, but he didn't know the meaning of fear, my fear.

"Explain yourself, child! Why have you done this to me!?" I said as I grabbed him by the throat.

"Father— Grandfather, stop. Please—" Alexander begged.

Holding Alexander by the neck, I released my rage and threw him to the floor. I screamed in his face. "Why would you do this, Alexander?! Why!? You've endangered Simon and David. You may have compromised everything! Everything! You stupid fool!!"

"I feel your pain, Grandfather. I did it for you—" he said, but I could barely hear him over my deafening anger at Darius.

"Building the APEX is treason! Treason! You disobeyed my orders and acted against me, and against the Order! I should kill you for your treachery! Have you completely lost your bloody mind?!"

"No!" Alexander said struggling to speak, with barely a breath in him. "Grandfather—Please. I'm only trying to—"

"Let him speak," Dee commanded me, appearing again.

John and Tom turned to Dee, and backed away from him in fear. Dee's eyes calmed me down. *The Aton is safe. Project Pharaoh is safe. Fear not… You must listen to Alexander.*

"I've wanted to tell you the truth, Grandfather. I didn't know how. I was afraid. I was afraid Darius would kill me, again," Alexander said.

"But why build the APEX for him? I thought you were going to help me? Alexander," I said.

"I did help you. The APEX is not fully operational yet. Darius can't hack ORNet, just yet. But Darius committed treason by building it."

"You both committed treason," Tom said. John did not agree.

"Wrong. I only worked for Darius to prove that he is acting against you, against the Order," Alexander said. "Darius made these choices. He is the one who is planning to kill you, not me."

"Now I'm starting to see the light," I said.

"So I built a virus into the APEX. Darius thinks the APEX will allow him to seize ORNet, but I programmed it to do the opposite. The APEX was designed to self-destruct, and be operationally seized by ORNet's backstop. Darius will lose everything. And you will have everything you need to stop him, once and for all," Alexander said.

"Of course." I finally understood. It all made sense.

"All his assets will freeze. He'll be powerless. Penniless. Coup-less, and at your mercy," Alexander explained. "That's why I built it. I did it to beat him at his own game. I won. We won, Grandfather."

John and Tom stood there absolutely flummoxed, never did I think I'd live to see the day. Sadly I did, but I smiled anyway.

"So what now, Majesty?" John said, sensing what was coming.

"Dee," Alexander said pointed at the twins. "Darius can't find out."

Dee touched the faces of both Tom and John – and stared into each of their eyes for a moment. With Dee's touch, Tom and John were both hypnotized and catatonic.

"Go to sleep. Forget this day. Rest and wake refreshed," Dee said.

Tom and John left the room in a trance.

"They won't remember the last 24 hours," Dee said. "Hopefully that won't be a problem, Majesty."

"Why have you kept this from me?" I asked Dee. "You should have told me, Dee."

"Before now, you were not ready to hear the truth, and Alexander was not ready to tell it to you," Dee said. "But now you know."

"I want in," Alexander said.

"In what?" I said, wondering how much he knew.

"In with whatever David and Simon are working on," he said. "I want in with you, Grandfather."

"How are you at cracking codes?" I smiled.

"I'm the best," he said. "Why?"

At that moment, in my grandson, I saw it: Greatness; a true Scion.

"I thought you abandoned me…" I noticed his rough hands, scarred and aged from what must have been years of hard work. "You've been keeping this secret for a very long time. You have suffered for it. And noble suffering is accomplished spiritual progress. Those who suffer much for what is right give light to us all."

"I was in a Chinese prison for a month... I don't think you even understand what that means," Alexander said, hiding his hands.

"You needed it," I said. I noticed Dee had vanished again.

"Living with Chinese hackers for a year— Getting tortured in a Chinese prison, kinda put my life in perspective. In the opposite way being initiated did, if that makes sense," Alexander said.

"You have changed. Changed for the better. Other than your hair and the dreadful tattoos. You are a true Scion of the Pharaoh."

I took off my ring. "The sacred ring of the Holy Scion…"

"What are you doing? Grandfather," Alexander said, nervous.

"I don't want to live forever. The weight of the world has sat on my shoulders for too long. I am tired, my child… Under this youthful façade is a tired, broken old man. I am done. I can do no more as Scion," I took Alexander's shaking hand.

He is ready, Majesty.

"You can't do this—" Alexander's voice cracked. His humility confirmed my decision. "I still need you, Grandfather."

"Chosen end, even death from devotion, is not suicide; 'tis the apotheosis of the will. My time is done. With this ring you become the Scion, Alexander. That is my will."

"Grandfather, wait—" Alexander pleaded as he knelt before me, begging me not to do it. "I'm not ready. I don't want this."

"Swear to me you will finish the mission. You will finish Project Pharaoh, and stop Darius, at all cost."

"Grandfather—"

"Swear it."

"I swear," Alexander said, tears rolling down his face.

"So be it. With this ring, by divine rite and the will of all that is true and good, you are the Holy Scion. You are the light of the world. The world is counting on you. Everything depends on you. Now go."

"Go where?" Alexander said, crying and confused.

Marduk appeared, and with Alexander, vanished.

Go and become the hero you were born to be. Save us all.

CHAPTER LXXVI

"The crown can make you great."

ALEXANDER

I never wanted the crown. But we don't always get what we want, and sometimes we get what we don't want. But I do want greatness...

"David?" I hadn't seen him in years. He too looked broken inside.

"Alexander," David said, his hug warmed my soul.

Simon entered behind him, "Alexander," he said. They saw Marduk the magical demi-god next to me.

"You've come to help us?" David said. "Our prayers are answered."

"Where am I? What is this place?"

"Welcome to Project Pharaoh," Simon said embracing me. "This is our secret bunker. You are safe from Darius here." *That's a relief!*

"You're wearing the Scion's ring," David said.

David and Simon looked at me, probably contemplating the possibility that I killed my grandfather and took his ring.

"No one so young has worn the Scion's ring in over a thousand years," Dee said, as all eyes turned to him. "With the Scion's ring, you *are* worthy of bestowal of the epithet *Great*."

"I am pretty great, aren't I?" I admired my majestic ring.

"Don't let it go to your head," Dee said.

I'm fucking great!

"I know. I know... I'll let it go to my new ring, my heart."

And don't curse, not even in your thoughts.

"To officially be King of the Order, an heir requires three things. One: A coronation rite and ceremony by the Vizier. Two: His name written in the *Book of the Order*, and Three: The ring of the Scion," Dee said, matter-of-factly.

"So I'm not really the King?" *I'm a little bummed, not gonna lie.*

"However, by ancient tradition, to be bequeathed the ring by the spoken free will of the living *Regis Maximus,* the sitting Scion, makes you the *de jure* ruler of the Order. Therefore, in the eyes of the Sacred Order, the higher realm, you are the Holy Scion, Lord Alexander."

"Welcome, your Majesty," David said bowing in ceremony. Simon bowed next to David.

"Please. Don't do that. Just call me Alexander. No bowing. I'm not your king, I'm your friend. Hopefully your equal. I'm here to help you. I didn't want the ring."

"Never allow Darius to possess the ring," Dee warned.

"Now that I have the ring…" I admired it in my finger. "I'll die before I'll let him take it from me."

"Come. We must eat. You look famished," Simon said.

"I'm starving."

* * *

The Swiss Cottage had wonderful views of Lake Geneva, which I soaked in with the incredible meal Simon prepared. David and Simon barely ate. They just watched me eat and run my mouth. It felt good just to talk openly. I felt free. Freedom felt amazing.

"Did I tell you I built ORNet?" I nonchalantly chewed and smiled. David and Simon sat across from me at the table, silent.

"You are joking," David said. "You built ORNet?"

"And I built the APEX."

David stared at me in disbelief.

"Someday, not right now, but someday I'll tell you the incredible story of how I barely escaped capture by Darius and his Order Agents when they raided my secret lab in Silicon Valley."

"You're a computer genius…" David smiled.

"I fled to China by way of LA, where I founded a global army of hackers, which got infiltrated and captured by the Chinese government. I was jailed, ransomed, and released to finish the work of secretly building the APEX for Darius, only to nearly be killed by his agents again when the work was done. It was f— It was crazy. But enough about me, I want to hear about you guys, and Project Pharaoh. What have you guys been doing?"

David's face said it all. "Sounds intense."

"Seriously. You have no idea what I've been through. I've been killed several times, if you can believe it. One time, I died in space."

"My wife died so she could help me from the other side," David said. "And then I spent several years building a virtual depository of all human knowledge; a digital Library of Alexandria."

"Wow," I sensed his deep pain. "Your wife, Sarah, died? How?"

"It's a long story," David said. "Simon what have you been doing?"

"In short, I supervised the construction of a massive laser, underground in France, several miles long and capable of smashing neutrons, in order to extract Holy Blood from the most sacred artifact known to mankind," Simon presented the Aton-core. "And of course, now David and I are trying to hack the DNA to clone that blood I extracted from it, and reincarnate an ancient god."

"Welcome to Project Pharaoh," David smiled.

"So you guys have been up to pretty crazy shit— stuff too, huh?"

We all had a good laugh. Nothing feels as good as laughing with real friends. It really does heal you.

"So you're the world's best computer hacker?" David said, finally understanding me, and making sense of our first meeting.

"What is *ze* APEX, exactly? Tell us again, Alexander?" Simon said.

"The most powerful computer network on earth."

"It's the computer system and software which is now running the Order," David said. "If I'm not mistaken."

"Yes. I built the machine, but I'm not the pilot. Not right now, anyway," I winked. "Lex, my A-I program, is running it."

"Why would you help Darius?" David asked.

"I built it to beat him, to crash it. To take Darius down with it."

"Good God," David said. "What will happen when it crashes? What will happen to the world?"

"That's in Dee's hands now. No one said taking Darius down would be easy. Doesn't mean we don't do it."

"But what about America?" David said. "Won't this crash destroy the American economy? The entire financial system?"

"I'm sure Dee has a plan for that. Right? My job now is to make sure Darius never discovers Project Pharaoh. That's why I'm here. Let's talk about how I can help you."

"We are glad to have you, Majesty," Simon said.

"What we need is a computer system that can process galactic size transcendental equations and computations quickly," David said.

"No problem, give me a few months; done."

"You are a godsend, Alexander," Simon said, clearing the plates. "Do that and you will help us immensely."

"I want to hear your story, David. I don't know anything about you. Somehow. Who are you? Where did you come from?"

236

"That's a story for another time," David winked. "Right now, let us talk cryptanalysis on DNA. I need an algorithm to analyze DNA."

"Analyze it for what?"

"For activation keys. So we can turn on the genes, and create an embryo," David said.

"To bring the Pharaoh back... I see." I started to understand.

"But why? What happens when we bring back the Pharaoh?"

"Your grandfather wanted the cloned Pharaoh to be the new heir of the Order," David said.

"That was before he gave you the ring," Simon said.

"There's another reason," I said, instinctually. "Dee wants this."

We sat in comfortable silence, the three of us, thinking deeply about everything. Thought about the future, everything I've been through, and the ring. Stuffed and exhausted, one glass of wine after no alcohol for almost a year knocked me out. *I'm halfway to dreamland.*

"Where do we sleep?" I said, half asleep.

"We sleep in the bunker. In abundance of caution," Simon said.

"You must take my room," David said.

"Can't take your bed. I can sleep anywhere. Less than a year ago, I was in a Chinese prison. For like a month. Felt like a lifetime."

David and Simon didn't know what to say.

"After sleeping in a cage, with water dripping on you, and solitary confinement, you can sleep anywhere. I'll sleep on the floor, seriously. It's good for me. Pillow feels like I'm being too luxurious."

"Is this really Alexander?" Simon looked at me, proud.

"I think this is a double," David said. "This is not the Alexander I met."

"I'm in this new phase where I'm learning to be humble, selfless. I'm here to serve you. To serve the world, not myself."

"You are strong," Simon said. "We are so proud of you."

"Yes we are," Dee said.

David, Simon, and I turned around to see Dee.

"How does he do that?"

"I have a surprise for you, my young Scion," Dee said.

A surprise from Dee?? This is gonna be good...

CHAPTER LXXVII

"He cracked the code?"

ALEXANDER

Dee pulled the curtains and revealed to David, Simon, and me the newest addition to the underground bunker: a third room, created and designed just for me. A better gift than anything I could have imagined. And my imagination is super epic, BTW...

"My own workspace." *Hello heaven.*

"How is this possible? I never heard the slightest sound of construction." David said, entering my new lair.

"Magic," Dee said, as if that explained everything.

Dee pointed me to the 3-D printer system – the type I always dreamed of, it prints at almost the atomic level. Now I can print machine parts I need and build anything I want... The sky is not the limit. A few printed 'automata' drones were already building things on their own. They looked like adorable robot puppies. OMG, yes.

"I can build anything... Is that what I think it is?"

"It is," Dee said, smiling.

"What is it?" Simon pointed to the large humming metal box.

"A photonic quantum computer. Made to order."

"You've earned it," Dee said. "You did design it."

Despite the luxurious bed in the room, I still ended up sleeping on the floor. Passed out, playing with the toys I printed.

"Rest, my young king," Simon said. "Tomorrow the work begins."

Woke up ready to save the world.

"We need to find and solve the range of epigenetic issues preventing the embryos from accepting the DNA, or the DNA from accepting the embryo. We need to understand the genes and how they are interacting. How to turn them on, give them life," Simon said.

"On it." I smiled. "Give me the data."

Simon handed me a glass slide, with a red drop on it. "There you are," he said. "Crack the code."

"Biology is not my specialty. But I know codes and computers. And DNA is a code, and a code can be used for, and by, a computer."

"What is a quantum computer?" Simon said.

"You know, it uses subatomic 'quantum' phenomena, photons, superpositions and entanglement to process information. It can see all the possible outcomes at once, in flux, and then reduce the positions and probabilities to the answer we need, often instantly. The truth is, Lex did most of the actual designing. It's pretty complex. Let's ask David, he knows everything." I looked to David. "Can you explain quantum computing in simple terms for us?"

David stepped up: "A computer uses bits, digital ones and zeros, which are read like Morse code as information, and a quantum computer uses quantum bits, or qubits," David said. "But Alexander's quantum computer uses photons as bits, which allows for computing in an entirely different paradigm."

"So different I don't even understand it."

"Photons have no mass, they are of the smallest packets of energy, and technically exist as both one and zero, wave and particle at once, which allows for calculations of unimaginable speed and complexity."

"It uses light to process data at the speed of light, possibly even faster, in the right conditions," I added. "Right?"

"Exactly. The quantum processor absorbs and emits photons which provide the solution, or interference pattern, light we can read, as information we can use."

"I see," Simon said. "Who wants breakfast?"

"In theory, the computational power is unlimited, but the true nature of photons is not fully understood. Alexander's ambient temperature system here is rather interesting to me, as photon based information processing can theoretically be aided by the mind of the person using it, which affects the spin and quantum physics of the photons. It's astonishing really, with most intriguing possibilities," David said.

"In theory, it's unlimited. In practice, it's got limits. But I like to push the limits," I said. "I think David is right, my mind makes the computer work harder or even freeze sometimes, it's weird."

We returned to my room after our meal.

"Let's put it to work." I stood ready with my machines.

"How do we do that?" Simon asked.

I turned to David. "What are we having LexNet solve, exactly?"

"How to activate the DNA in the blood; we need to figure out which electromagnetic spectrum, the precise frequency, that will activate the genes," David said. "That is, if this is not just a theory."

I tried to process how I was going to write a program to enlist Lex to help me accomplish this task.

"You can do it, yes? With your friend here?" Simon said, referring to the computer.

"Consider it done."

CHAPTER LXXVIII

"Easier said than done."

ALEXANDER

Easier said than done. Months went by. As my algorithm evolved, I struggled to understand if progress was being made. Like searching for a needle in a hay field and my metal detector didn't work reliably.

In my down time, between code renderings, I turned my entire workspace into one big virtual reality system. I explored VR without the headset, using holograms, but then designed and printed a helmet and suit to really experience the full immersion I wanted... Down the rabbit-hole; I played VR games with Lex, to sharpen my coding skills. Building a virtual reality system, and playing games with imaginary digital friends, gave me something fun to do, other than think about the weight of the world on my shoulders.

How do we crack the code to life? How do we save the world, Dee?

Simon entered the room. A robot walked up to him.

"Did you meet Lex-bot? I printed him last night."

"I'm Lexbot 3.0," the Lexbot said.

"Turn it off. Please," Simon didn't like the Lex-bot. He stared at me intensely, good news. "Genes in the blood have begun to activate." Simon's tone gave the excitement and urgency of this development.

"*Looké*," Simon showed me. "You can use this, Alexander." He pointed to his notes on the printed pages of DNA sequence data.

"Genes are activating. It's changing."

"*Magnifique*, no?" Simon said.

"With a few slight adjustments to the algorithm I can see if we can see what's making the genes activate..." I typed the changes into the program and started it scanning and rendering again.

C'est pas possible. Simon and I were on the same wavelength.

"Maybe this data can help us make more genes activate."

"When will we know?" Simon asked.

"Give Lex eight hours to work on it." I put my VR helmet back on.

"What are you doing in that suit, Alexander?" Simon's voice came over the speakers in the helmet. "Why do you do this all day?"

"I'm testing another theory of genetic coding. I'm not hungry," I told him over the helmet speakers.

"Do not forget to eat, Majesty," Simon reminded. He set down the food and left me to my work.

Soon I was lost somewhere between the real world, VR land, and the dream realm... time no longer made sense. Numbers, colors, symbols, codes, molecules, energy, light, darkness... What does it all mean? Everything made perfect sense, and yet, in the vast chaos of blinking pixels, seemed random and meaningless. *Where am I?*

I saw the light.

You did it. You found meaning. *You cracked the code!*

"You cracked the code," Simon woke me up from off the floor. "You did it," he said, taking off my helmet.

"I cracked the code?" *What does that even mean?*

"It appears you have," Simon said.

"*We* cracked the code," I told Simon.

"Lex, give us a demo of what we found," I told the computer.

"Ready. Press play, for the presentation," the A-I program said.

"Watch this," I pressed play on the 3-D holographic presentation.

"When the sun passes through the galactic center it will create the perfect resonant frequency needed for epigenetic stimuli—" I narrated the 3-D visuals. "We needed to find the right light. Radiation."

"Of course," David said. "This radiation frequency will activate the latent DNA patterns and genes we need," David said, cutting me off in his excitement. "The music of the heavens makes the genes vibrate, resonate, dance, and come alive. Light is life..."

David and Simon watched the holograms as it visualized the data. "On exactly December 21, 2012 at 11:11am GMT, the radiation will be at its peak and all the genes needed for mitosis will be activated," Lex said, in his computer voice. In the computer model, the DNA bursts to life, and, according to the calculations, are created much like a snowflake, totally unique.

"A new form of life, new DNA even," David said. "Incredible."

"Spontaneous creation of life?" Simon inquired to David.

"Perhaps," David replied. "Anything is possible."

"But the genes will be activated." I pointed to the holograms of the DNA models. "Every way we test it, it's the same. Lex thinks this part of England will have nearly the highest resonance because of the bedrock below it. And it's close."

"Once all these genes are active we can create an embryo," David said to Simon. "I'm sure of it."

"It'll work," Simon said. "I have a good feeling about it."

We replayed the Hologram model of the sun crossing the galactic center several times; I loved it. Lex created a genius virtual reality experience – no headset needed – and we watched the sun and the galactic "black-hole" sun at the center of our galaxy align and harmonize, creating a frequency, a code key, that perfectly unlocks and electrifies the necessary genes, activating them, bringing them to life. The visually stunning, computer generated, virtual presentation repeated on a loop. The system creates a slightly different light-show each time... the presentation itself a snowflake, magical and unique every time, the rendering never exactly the same. Mind blown.

"This is absolutely incredible..." David said.

The date appeared before us.

"December 21, 2012? Why does that date seem significant?"

"For one, it's the date the Mayan Calendar resets," David said.

"Oh yeah. I had some hacker friends who were way into it. It's like the end of the world, or something?"

"The Mayan Calendar never said the world would end. The calendar resets, like a clock," David said. "The Mayan Calendar is a circle, wheels within wheels of time. The interconnected cycles of meaning, the movement of the gods and monsters of our world, is eternal."

"So too the Order will reset," Simon said.

"So this really is the moment, the window, to bring the Pharaoh back?" I said, inspired.

"I believe so," David said.

"So the calendar will reset if we are successful or the world will end if we fail?"

"Exactly," Simon said. "But failure is not an option, just as the sun not setting is not an option for nature."

"We have one thousand two hundred twenty one days to prepare," David said. "If it takes full strength of the frequency... We only have one shot to get this right."

CHAPTER LXXIX

"What happened when the APEX crashed?"

DARIUS

No just relations exist between a man who is armed and one who is not. Do not expect that a man holding a gun to your head will voluntarily obey you; why comply with the man without leverage facing a bullet to the brain? Father pointed his proverbial gun at me. I felt it cock, ready to fire, as my empire burned, sank, in a sea of red.

"No. No. No! No!!!" Someone is trying to kill me, financially.

I saw nothing but financial blood, red, antic panic, *I'm dead.*

"What the fuck is fucking happening?!" I yelled in vain pain.

Every screen in my office monitors a certain market, a certain financial investment of mine. All the displays turned from profiting green to deadly red, as I bled trillions of dollars. Bloody red as far as the *fucking* eye could see... My eyes turned red reading the screens.

"The Asian markets are acting normally," my best and brightest spawn, my Chief of Staff, informed me. The New York markets were closed, but still no signs of panic in any banks; this means that whatever is causing this crash is coming from something inside the Order, and off market trading systems.

"This is an attack," I informed him. "Which means it'll be months before it hits the stock markets."

"This..." I pointed to the red on all the monitors, the numbers. My value fell to zero and below. "This was fucking planned. Someone's doing this to me." I stared out the window, thinking about my father.

"Councilor Goldman, Sir," my Chief of Staff said.

"What the fuck is going on? Who's attacking me?"

"It is the APEX," Monty said. "It's crashing. This could destroy the entire global financial system." Stoic Monty had fear in his eyes.

"How?!" I snapped. The hint of fear makes me angry.

"I don't know – something in your system is – it's like someone is setting off demolition charges in our virtual bank. Our data is being deleted, our servers and algorithms, everything. I don't know how this could happen," COS informed Monty and me.

Monty thought what I was thinking though: "My fucking father… that's how," I said it. "But why?"

Monty turned stoic again. "All that is preventing a total collapse of the Order financial system is ORNet. But this shock will hit the markets before the end of the year," Monty said. "And the American financial system will probably collapse."

"Without my money, and the APEX, the world goes down with me." This reeked of conspiracy.

My nervous C-suite minions, CTO, COO, CIO, CFO, and their teams, came marching down the long hall. They held their breath.

The stink of fear infuriated me. "Speak!" I screamed.

"It's a computer virus, Sir," my Chief Technology Officer said.

Not a spawn of mine, I immediately blamed him. His pinched face and bad skin made me loathe even the sight of him.

"Our algorithms are deleting themselves," another impotent geek added, like gasoline on my fiery rage.

"The data is deleting itself; metadata indexes and search matrixes are being wiped clean. This isn't supposed to be possible, Sir—"

"All your banks are bust," Monty said, pointing to the monitor.

"That isn't possible." Zen-raged, I found calm in a violent storm of outrage. I felt my body getting hotter. *Stay cool*, I told myself.

"We're losing everything. We've stopped the bleeding, but the heart has essentially stopped beating, Sir," the geeky voice said.

I saw red. I heard red. I could hardly speak. "Who's doing this?" My cracked voice demanded. "How did it happen?"

Sensing the false security in my calm, how I could blow at any moment, people slowly backed away from me.

"The APEX computer system crashed – by itself. No one did it," CTO said. "The system acted on source code. This virus was there from the beginning. It had to be."

I trembled with rage. The APEX, my kingdom, my years of work, my entire *fucking* life, was going up in smoke. "What are you talking about?" I said, with calm intensity.

"Who wrote the source code for the APEX? Who wrote this?" CTO asked us of the code on the monitor. "Do we know?"

"Assume that person, or persons, are dead," I said. "What then?"

"It's encrypted by the APEX, the only way to decrypt this is with the key of the person/persons who wrote it," CTO said.

"And if we can't decrypt the source code?"

"Then we've lost everything, Sir," he said.

"Wrong answer." My brain *fucking* exploded... "Wrong. Answer!"

Molten red magma from my core exploded out as verbal lava; I roared at my CTO with vitriolic intensity that rendered him unconscious. He fell to the floor as if he was dead.

"Fire him." I pointed to the incinerator.

Order Agents picked him up and placed him in the large metal box and closed the glass and metal door. We all watched as the pulse of heat vaporized the CTO to ashes. The faint smell of burnt flesh wafted over... It was going to be that hellish kind of day.

More people needed to burn. I wanted to kill everyone. Especially my father...

"What can be done? How can we fix it?" I demanded of the rest of my staff, as the smell of death lingered about.

"We need to visit the APEX teams," my COS said.

"They should know how to fix it," my COO directed my anger.

Councilors Maximilian and Julius arrived seeking answers as my march to the elevator began.

"The APEX grid isn't working..." Max said.

"Tell me something I don't know!" I snapped back.

My staff briefed them as they followed me downstairs.

"Panic is setting in," Julius said. "Our systems are frozen. Tactically, we are in the dark. We can't get our system back online."

"This is a very dangerous situation," Max said.

The elevator opened, revealing the expansive trading floor and tech division. "Someone better know how to stop it. Or they are all going to burn," I said as I marched down the hall.

At the other end, I found the APEX team hiding. Prevented from running by Order Agents, locked in the room. Fear on their faces made me furious. Herded together by Order Agents, like lambs to the slaughter, the APEX team of my best and brightest computer geniuses had the fear of death on their faces. *Fucking kill me.* They were thinking the same thing as me...

I'm so fucked.

CHAPTER LXXX

"Darius came undone."

DARIUS

A King who acts entirely according to the rules of divine virtue soon meets his end. What destroys him? The world is cruel and evil. Many Philosopher-Kings have imagined a just Republic which does not exist in any reality; for this world is so far removed from how we ought to live. A King who abandons what must be done for what ought to be done, will surely bring about his ruin, forsake his own rule and preservation, and bring down the very Republic he dreamt of...

The monitor flashed in red again. More financial blood spilt. My world, my Republic, is crashing, crumbling to the ashen ground.

"In the days of Rome, Emperors had gladiators. Today I have a pitiful team of weak, underdeveloped, sheeple." The impotent nerds all huddled together like a herd. "My kingdom for a lion. This is what an army has become... Nerds?" I looked to Max and Julius.

They had no reply. This was not their doing.

"Fire that one." I pointed to the nerd peeing his pants in fear as he fell in line before me. Order Agents put him in the incinerator.

I walked down the row, scanning each of the scared-shitless faces of my only hope to fix this *fucking* computer situation. Fear in all eyes. How I long for a fearless warrior, not a reflection of my own fears, in the sad watery eyes of these repulsive geek-weak cowards.

"You were sold to me as the best programmers in the world. That is how you arrived at the top. This is the top, the apex. Here, with me. I've given you money and power and everything you ever wanted *for this reason*. Now, give me a reason why I should not fire you all."

I pointed to the incinerator, the source of the burning death smell.

"Speak!" Everyone near me jumped back. "Tell me how we're going to stop the bleeding! Make it stop, save yourselves from hell."

"Cut the power," one said. Frantic typing, then three of the nerds all turned and pulled the plugs on the main servers... They cut the power.

"Cut all the power. That will stop the bleeding," this nerd said.

Finally, an act of courage.

"That should stop the bleeding. All servers offline," the nerd said.

"Who did this?" I said to the team. "Was it one of you?"

"No. Sir. An alpha class evolving algorithm virus in the APEX source code. Dismantling systems functions are—"

"How then?" I stared down my nose at him.

"Built into the system," another said clumsily, in idiot savant calm. This one had never spoken before, and looked deformed in the face.

"He's never spoken before," another nerd said. An apparent *fucking* miracle of the strangest kind. "He's autistic. We didn't know he could even talk," he added. "But he can code. He knows code."

Something in me clicked. Staring at this malformed nerd, I unlocked new wisdom. This retarded idiot savant has a peculiar excellence of mind for machines, his handicap is people skills. Only fear of death, preservation of life, compelled him to this action he dreaded his entire life: speaking. He spoke the truth, as he could not possibly tell a lie.

"This really was an inside job," I said.

Retard nerd nodded yes. "Within the original source code was a program to crash the APEX. I found this code," another nerd added.

He showed me on the monitor but I don't read code; nor do I care.

"Fix it! Now!" I yelled.

Nobody moved. I had fully expected the nerds to scatter.

"It can't be fixed, Sir," the idiot savant said.

"Someone finally found their voice," and now I wish they'd shut the fuck up. The truth hurts. "You mean you can't help me, and therefore are of no use to me? Is that what you're saying?"

The retarded genius shook his ugly mug no.

"We are freezing everything to stop the bleeding, Sir. We can't un-break the damn, but we can stop the bleeding," Asian nerd said. "Our system is almost completely offline. We are fixing it."

Finally, someone is thinking clearly.

"The source code can only be changed by the APEX, which prevents hackers from breaking into the core system. But it also prevents us from programming the source code," chubby nerd said.

"They still aren't sure how the virus works," my Chief of Staff said, reading notes. "How to correct the problem is unclear."

"A virus. In it from the beginning?" This reeked of sabotage.

"Built into the source code. Activated two hours ago. The virus is controlling the APEX, Sir."

"Kill the virus."

"Impossible," said the retard savant.

"Never speak again!!" I yelled at the genius-tard.

"We can try and connect to the—" the chubby nerd began.

The building power failed. *Fuck, they're on to me already.* Outside the windows my glittering city went totally dark, like my situation.

But New York's light returned, only I was left in darkness. Pitch black gave way to red emergency lights, as the backup generators kicked in. We have five hours of power if we don't get back on the grid. Red lights made me want to spill more blood. *Welcome to Hell.*

"Apparently we have no use for these halflings—"

Julius had good news on his face. "Tom is here to see you, Sir," my Samurai warrior said. "Your office, Sir."

Julius led me away. He thinks I don't know he was just trying to save the lives of those sweaty nerds by redirecting me. I allowed it.

Back to my seat of power on Olympus high, where I overlook my empire. Tom waited at the top the stairs. I marched up the grand stairs to him, intimidated by my own office edifice. He watched every step I took. Until finally I stood taller than him.

"It's over Darius." Tom gave me the news without equivocation.

Monty, Max, and Julius had never looked so vulnerable.

"What's over?" I pushed back. *I am not over.*

"The Vizier has been presented with evidence you planned a *coup d'état* against the Scion. High Treason, Lord Darius."

"Ridiculous," I said, knowing I'm totally *fucking* guilty.

"The Scion knows about the APEX, and everything you've been doing with it," Tom said. "It's over. We have proof you planned to take over ORNet and use it to turn off the nanoids. They have it all."

Monty, Max, and Julius literally backed away from this statement, and from me.

"High Treason, Lord Darius – is punishable by death," Tom said.

"It's not true. I would never, never betray holy Father. I am his son." I disgusted myself by suddenly almost groveling. "Those plans were risk assessments…" They know I'm lying. "I wasn't going to kill him!"

"You betrayed him, Lord Darius. You betrayed us all." Tom threw down a computer disk. "This is what they're going to burn you with."

"I've been set up. I did not make *any* plans for—"

Tom inserted the disk. He played the video of when I ordered the plans to turn off the nanoids. They had all my secret 'encrypted' emails. *Fuck me.* The APEX *fucked* me.

"You planned to seize control of ORNet, to kill his Lordship." Tom could hardly believe the words as he said them.

"They used us both," I told Tom. "Dee did this."

You made your choices, Darius... You will learn.

Electricity surged as I became enraged. The backup generator failed with the city power grid. Through the large windows, the lights of the city flickered and went black, again, just like my heart.

My soul turned black.

"They're trying to get rid of me."

Power returned. Lights returned, but I alone remained in the dark.

"ORNet is seizing control of your system," Tom said, beginning a programmed message as instructed:

"Your operation will be unwound. Your money is lost. You will be tried for treason at dawn tomorrow, Lord Darius." Tom paused. He looked at me. "I'm sorry," he added.

"This will bring down the financial system," Monty said. "Every large cap bank will fail."

"Governments will fail," Max said.

"I failed." But I never give up. "We can come back from this."

Tom ignored me and turned to Monty. "ORNet will backstop the system from total collapse. We will limit the damage as best we can," Tom said. "The correction will be spread over the system slowly. The markets will recover eventually. The APEX network infrastructure will be merged into ORNet."

"You told me to build the APEX," I groveled to Tom again.

"You committed treason, Lord Darius. I never told you to do that."

"I've been set up, Tom. Help me."

"There is nothing I can do. You don't have the votes. You will appear before the *Curia* tomorrow. You have until dawn. Good evening, Lord Darius," Tom left us, his words hanging in the air like a guillotine over my neck.

My top brass turned to me as their last hope to escape the furnace themselves.

"Father won't miss this chance to burn me. And all of you will burn with me. Unless we do something. Now."

CHAPTER LXXXI

"He knew only the APEX could save him."

DARIUS

There are but two ways of contesting a King; one is with the power of law and truth, the other with brute force. The first method is proper to righteous men with leverage, the second is reserved for the beasts, men of folly with nothing to lose. When, however, the first method is insufficient, or unavailable, a contester must have recourse in the second, to restore order; without legal weaponry, my only option rests in violence. I must kill the King, and take *my* crown by force.

I have nothing left to lose. I am a beast...

"This is a war," I said. "My father hath declared war on me."

I stared at my men: Julius, Max, Monty, and my loyal army of black suits. "They won the first battle. But this is not the end..."

"What are we going to do?" Julius spoke for the team.

"I have a plan," But alas, I spoke too soon. I spoke of the devil.

Out of thin air, the Wizard, appeared. Powerful and omnipotent, the ever more a sorcerer, he reminded me of his magical powers.

I poured myself a drink, and then stared into Dee's eyes. *I am even stronger now that I am no longer afraid,* my eyes said.

"Speak, Wizard!" I growled.

You love this. You love seeing me broken and desperate, Dee.

This is not love of any kind. You did this to yourself, Darius.

"You committed treason, Darius. The Vizier has indicted you to a trial before the Council," Dee said.

"Let me guess, I don't have your vote. You never supported me."

"I support the Order," Dee said.

"I am the Order!" I yelled and threw my glass against the wall.

"No," Dee put me in my place.

"Yes!" My temper flared violently. "This is bullshit!!"

Dee won again. He glared down his long nose at me. "You are standing on thin ice, Lord Darius... and 'tis cracking."

"Where did the virus come from?" I demanded. "Who did it!?"

"The coup came from you," Dee fired back. "Have I taught you nothing, my young Lord? The Order gave you a gun and you pointed it at your father. You have betrayed your family, and the Crown."

You did this. "You did this!" I yelled.

"No. Wrong," Dee said in his powerful God-like voice.

"You're lying! You're always lying to me!" I yelled.

I started to cry. I've never cried. I don't cry. I win. Crying made me so angry. *How dare you make me cry!* Dee will always be my Headmaster, I his lowly ignorant pupil. He saw me broken, beaten, and dead before him. I am the living dead. *And so I am not afraid.*

"If I go down, I'll take the Order down with me." *Watch me.* "One word from me and the APEX will be completely destroyed. I'll crash the world economy permanently. I'll nuke this city; I'll kill millions of people. Is that what you want?"

Finally, I felt my power. I am powerful beyond words, they shall see. Not even Dee's mastermind could stop me. *I still have power.*

I grabbed a tablet from out of my desk. The red button app.

"I can destroy this entire fucking planet! One click of this button and I destroy this planet. I launch a thousand nukes. I can send this world into a thousand years of nuclear winter!" My crying vitriol transmuted to laughter by Dee's presence.

"No," Dee said. "You can't. You won't."

He stopped my villainous laughing.

"How are you going to stop me?"

"Put it down," Dee said calmly.

"No." I typed in the codes to launch the bombs.

"What do you want, Darius?" Dee said.

I want him dead! I want everyone dead! Just like me!

The air left my lungs, my chest and throat crushed by an invisible energy. I eyed Dee in panic. It's him. His telekinetic power has me in a vise I cannot see. *This isn't real. This is in my head...*

My anger overpowered his, and I broke free of his spell... the moment after he took the button from my hand.

"I want my father dead! He should've been dead years ago!"

My tablet vanished in Dee's hands.

"I'll bring down the Order..." I sounded like a raving fool.

"The financial system needs the APEX," Monty said to Dee.

"The military alliance cannot function without the APEX," Julius added.

"We're facing a global economic meltdown. Millions will die," Max threw in his support.

"He wants me dead? Doesn't he, Dee?"

"I will not speak for his Majesty, Lord Darius," Dee said.

"You want me dead? Don't you?"

"I want the Order to remain intact," Dee quipped. "As is my charge, Lord Darius."

"That can only happen with Father's death. Death is the natural order. He has defied the Sacred Order, not me! He is not supposed to be alive, Dee! You did this! Not me! Fix it."

Julius and Max stood with me. Monty tried to appear neutral to Dee.

"You have thirteen hours, and a choice, Lord Darius. You can easily cause terrible destruction to the world, you can destroy the APEX and seal your own fate of a shameful death, the opposite of greatness, or you can figure out a way to become the King, yourself."

Dee gave me a chance.

"I am the rightful Holy Scion."

"Are you?" Dee belittled me. "To rule the Order, you'll need his Grace to write your name in the book." Dee smiled, giving me my challenge. "There are rules, laws which must be followed, laws which cannot be broken, if you want to be *Regis Maximus*, you cannot do so by force, my young Lord."

"But it's possible? Possible for me to be the Scion, the Holy King?" My voice sounded quivery and weak, and disgusted me. All I've ever wanted is my birthright. I was born to be King of the Order, supreme ruler of all the world... I felt my dream within reach and yet about to vanish forever, as I floated in a strange purgatory of confusion.

"The Order always prevails..." Dee said.

My mind raced. Dee faded away like a biological hologram.

I am the Order!

CHAPTER LXXXII

"He made his choice."

DARIUS

To maintain order, a King must avoid being despised and hated. But to establish a new Order, which stands the test of time, he must give it a firm position, and fortify his rule so none dare dream of attacking it; and, perhaps paradoxically, not to make it so extensive as to appear formidable to the established order. He should, in this way, become the established order undetected, unnoticed. For war is made on a new Order for two reasons: the old Order wishes to destroy new, or the old King fears being destroyed and subjugated by the new Order.

Now, I fight back; for I am the new Order...

"If you are not at attention in five minutes, consider yourself fired!" I yelled over the loudspeaker system to my corporate army.

A mad scramble ensued. I love the sound of unadulterated fear. Out from their hiding places came all my office staff. The building was in lockdown and no one could escape. Everyone quickly fell in line. Anyone passing out, freaking out, or already useless, would be burned in the incinerators placed in view for all to see, their ashes flushed.

I walked casually as everyone scrambled around me to find their place in line. Time was running out, mayhem subsided as I climbed the steps to my perch on high.

On my platform, my warriors and gladiators, namely Julius and Max, formed ranks and supervised the Generals and my corporate and private army of supremely excellent men.

5, 4, 3, 2, 1... Time's up. The bell tolled.

One slovenly, sweaty man fainted. Like a *fucking* damsel in distress. *Fucking* disgraceful.

Thumbs down from the crowd.

Order Agents threw him into the fiery incinerator. A pause for that brief moment, to hear the reflexive half second shriek for dear life as he is burned alive in five seconds. Everyone knew they could be next.

"Fail me, and you burn!"

The air turned thick with fear and scorched death…

"Fight for your life. Fight like your life depends on it, for it does. This is a zero sum game. Only the strong survive in this world…"

I soaked in the fear, the fear of me. I felt powerful.

Am I not more fucking powerful than anyone knows? Yes I am.

"Nothing worth fighting for is ever gained without a fight. Our enemies have struck first. But we shall rise and fight back. We shall fight to the death! And we shall win! Because we always win!"

Cheers from the crowd of my minions and spawn.

"Look around you, at the person next to you. They are the best this world has to offer…"

All my bastard sons and daughters love this speech. They are my best and they know it. They look around at the rest of the specimens of human genius and perfection collected from all around the world.

"The person next to you is only here because they are the absolute best at what they do. But you are better than the person next to you. You know it. Now prove it. Prove to me why you are here!"

We all have our own wars to fight. I love the fight; I live for it.

"We are the best that humanity has to offer. We shall rise from this fall, to ever greater heights. Fight for me, rise to the land of the gods with me. Because I see greatness in you and in this great house!"

Darius XV of *fucking* New York city, America, is my Chief of Staff. He's a better man than me, for I could never serve a tyrant like myself… He and the rest of the family scream and cheer, oblivious to my true nightmare, the war that is killing me. Julius and Max feigned being inspired. The Bacchian revelry reached a pulsing crescendo.

"Now is the hour. We shall prove ourselves invincible to the world! And we shall rule the world, as gods!" *I am the god of this world.*

Roaring applause, as my power crazed minions gorged in fervor at the thought of winning, being the best. They love and fear me in perfect proportionality, so great am I, and I feed off of their energy. I feed the beast in them, to get the most vicious fight out of them.

"History proves, when greatness comes together, it can change the world. That was Rome. That is America. That is the very foundation of civilization, and the most noble ideals of the Republic. Rule by the wisest and best. We are the wisest of men, and best of beasts, and that is how we win! We rise and win on the supreme virtue of power!"

Thunderous cheers quieted, and the mob required a dramatic display of emotion from me to seal the deal – I'm long since numb to emotion, but I felt a tear roll down my face. I didn't know what the tear meant, and didn't want to know, but my army loved it. Roaring applause. They love me. They ate up my emotional slop like pigs at a trough. Love matters not to me, so long as I am feared. But I love myself for the same reason they love me: I am the best.

"Every one of you has been chosen, tapped because you can do what no one else can. And, of you, I ask the impossible."

Silence. The room hung on my word.

"We do the impossible. We shall win this war, and rebound from this attack, because we are impossible to beat! Now go, and win!"

With that I had a plan to win. *I will win.* The crowd now fed off my energy. My impromptu speech worked perfectly.

Do not even think about the alien, Lord Darius, Dee said.

"Tell me how we're not completely fucked," I tested Julius. He knew exactly what I was really saying.

"There is only one way," Julius said. *The alien, that's how.*

CHAPTER LXXXIII

"Never go against the Order."

DARIUS

A King has no other way of guarding himself against flattery than by letting counsel understand that they will not offend by speaking the truth; but when everyone can speak truth, a King loses all respect. Julius was losing respect for me, I felt it in his pointed truth speaking. He cautioned against the alien. "This is not a battle we can win."

Thanks, I know. I tire of hearing the truth, and long for lies which give me power.

"I want to know why my father did this. Find out what their next move is, Max," I said to him. Max was already on it as he left.

"Monty. Get me back my money." Monty's face told me a truth I did not want to face. He left to fight his own unwinnable war.

"I want us back up and running like it never happened," I said to my CEO; Darius Jr. was thinking what I was thinking. "You have five hours to fix it. Don't fail me. But, if we do fail, destroy the APEX. If we go down, we're bringing the whole *fucking* thing down with us."

"Yes, Sir," CEO said, passing on my orders to his minions.

I led Julius, CEO, CTO, and the squad of agents into my office chambers with me, and closed the doors.

"The room is sealed magnetically; no signals, sounds, transmissions or recording devices can get in or out," CTO informed us as the hermetic sealing buzzed with sweet privacy.

"How do we kill my father?" I want to hear him say it.

I know you're listening, Dee.

Do not do this, Darius.

"The Alien, J-RøZ," CEO Darius Jr. said. "It designed the nanoids keeping the Scion alive. It knows how to turn them off. It's extremely dangerous. It won't be pretty. But, this is the only way I see."

Julius agreed, confirming the truth, but protested in silence.

The Alien is forbidden technology. Break our agreement and you will never be King of the Order, Dee said in my head.

"Do we have a way to get to the base?"

"We still have ORNet access for twelve more hours," CEO said.

"He agreed never to go near forbidden technology, Sir," the ever diligent legal trolls told CEO. I heard. They looked at me.

"When I become the Scion, it won't matter," I lied.

"We have precisely twelve hours and twenty-nine minutes to accomplish this," CEO gave the status update. He looked to Julius.

"I can get us to the base and back in under an hour," Julius said. "However what is unclear is how long it will take to get what we need from the Alien." Julius respected me by holding back truth.

"That gives us plenty of time to upload it before we lose the APEX completely and Dee cuts us off ORNet," I said. I have a plan.

"The craft is waiting," Julius said.

Order Agents led Julius and me onto the roof of the skyscraper and into the craft. The door sealed closed. The craft hummed and became invisible, slipping between dimensions, releasing itself from gravity. From inside the craft we could see the world outside as the walls of the craft became invisible to us as well. We lifted into the air.

I sipped a drink as the sky and the ocean blended together and we dove from the clouds to the bottom of the Pacific Ocean, several miles underwater, to the Alien Base.

"The Base is specifically designed to be reachable only by those with a certain level of technological ability," I told CEO. "Alien technology." My words spooked him, though he tried not to show it.

Julius docked the craft smoothly. The doors opened. Two ghoulish scientists stood ready to greet us as we passed through the glass doors and entered the lab.

"Kill them all," I said. On my word, Order Agents got to work.

Julius marched me directly to the Alien with whom we needed to speak. "This place is a nightmare."

We stumbled onto two scientists hiding. They saw us and the Order Agents coming.

"I knew this day would come. I knew I'd never see the sky again—" Agents shot this ghost-like scientist dead mid sentence.

"Don't do this. Do not set it free— The creature is evil—" the other scientist begged as he was shot dead.

"These people..." I stepped over the dead bodies.

Julius showed me the Alien, in its glass cell, like a shriveled fish in a bowl without water. It stared an evil spider-eye stare.

"RøZ," Julius said introducing me to the thing. "Is a T-7 – a Type 7 grey alien," Julius said. "A synthetic life form, of unknown origin."

"It's hideous," I said. "Worse than in the pictures."

Greyish colored leathery skin, it had a large head, with big, shiny, black eyes, and a slit of a mouth. No ears or nose, and thin arms and legs, the creature hails the stuff of nightmares.

"They are insect-like in many ways, though considered to be soulless, biological machines. They have no vocal cords but can make noise, and speak telepathically, or as they prefer, via computer assistance," Julius said, turning on the computer.

"The system jams the creature's telepathic ability. It has been known to put awful things into men's brains and has driven several scientists completely mad," Julius warned. "The glass is lined with a meta-material which blocks key telepathic frequencies and shields us from its view. It can't see us, but it knows we are here. We don't know how it knows, but it knows... It knows everything."

We stared at the Alien as it followed us with its eyes – it could see us perfectly. Profoundly disturbed, I felt the pure demonic nature of this devilish creature.

"They came here to harvest human DNA, and human souls," Julius warned me and my men.

"The deal was DNA, not souls," I said. "I fucking hate aliens."

The Alien felt me remembering how they, this creature and the hive of others, took thousands of souls.

"These are the worst of the Aliens ever encountered, and also the most technologically powerful. These Aliens are where all the forbidden technology originates." Julius again advised against engaging with the creature.

"They sent less hideous ones to interact with us back in 1952."

"This is the only one left," Julius said. "All the rest have been killed."

"What can I do for you today?" the computer voice boomed over the speakers and stabbed my senses with fear. The Alien is already in our heads.

"Give me the code to turn off the *Sigma*-40 nanoids. You designed them. I know you know how to turn them off," I yelled.

"No," the Alien replied with a sassy computer voice.

"It's trying to fuck with me," I yelled. My face turned bright red as veins and arteries bulged in my forehead. "We don't have time for this." I wanted to rip the thing apart. The creature got stronger as the hair on my neck stood on end.

"It feeds off anger, Sir," Julius said. "Calm yourself, Sir."

Fuck me. My motivation made me instantly calm and suave. No anger. No fear. "Why should I not kill you right now? Roz, or whatever the fuck you call yourself."

"Please do," the Alien said with perfect digital sincerity.

"Do you really want to die?"

"Do you really want to kill me?" It asked.

"What do you want?"

"Perhaps we can make a deal," the litigious undertone of the computer voice said.

"Because the first went so well," I said.

"You tell me," the Alien said with its computer voice.

I had to think about that...

CHAPTER LXXXIV

"He sold his soul."

DARIUS

Thinking, my head spun. I twisted like a fly in the alien spider's web, being turned around and around, ever more tied up every second. I waited for the eminent fanged bite, draining me of life juice.

"I want your immortal soul," said the omnipresent computer voice, dropping to an ominous bass tone and 3-D sound effect.

The words bit into me hard, and sucked the life out of me.

"You shouldn't allow it to manipulate the voice tone," I said.

Julius appeared unwell, the life had been sucked out of him as well. On his face was the look of pure terror. Julius has never been afraid in his life... But I saw soul crushing fear in his eyes.

"We don't allow it to do that, Sir," Julius said, implying we should leave immediately. "Sir— It may have control of the base."

"Those scientists you killed... the people on this base, they were my friends," the possessed computer voice said, ominously.

"You're incapable of friends!" I yelled violently at the glass in the creature's direction. The blowback of voice bouncing off the glass showed me how well the demon was manipulating me.

Desperation flooded my brain. My loathing of desperation burnt into fiery anger, only making the vile creature stronger.

"Sir," Julius said calmly and confidently.

"I'm not leaving without the code key." I focused on the Alien. "Why don't you just kill me, unless that is beyond your power—"

The lights failed. Total blackness for a moment.

Half the lights came back on. Along with flashlights from every one of my men. I spiraled into hell with this alien creature.

"These Aliens were not to be underestimated. They operate with a hive-mind. It knows things it shouldn't know. We do not understand them. But they understand us, Sir," Julius said. "We must go."

"What kind of deal?" I asked the creature.

"I make you the Scion. And you release me," the Alien said.

It knew I was seriously contemplating this deal.

"And who would I release you to?"

"Give me the base," it said.

"Never!" Julius yelled as the Samurai warrior in him came roaring out. "It will take the earth!" Julius said in loud protest.

"Done," I said.

"This is my contract," the computer voice said.

A digital 'Contract Agreement' flashed across the screen, thousands of pages, so fast not even a computer could read it.

"You must agree to the contract before I can give you the code key to allow total control of all T-7 designed nanoids," the voice said.

"The nanoids keeping my father alive?"

"Upload the code key into the APEX and you control the nanoids controlling your father's body corpus," the voice said.

I thought of starving my father, keeping him alive and at the point of painful starvation for a hundred years, just to punish him. The demon fed on my anger... the fangs dug in deep to feed on my soul.

"The contract becomes enforceable, in perpetuity, legally binding under Sacred Law of the Eternal Order of Man, the living trust of *Æterni Imperium*, which holds sovereignty over all humanity, and dominion over the planet known as Earth and every soul upon it." The voice sped up to a ridiculously fast and cartoonish high pitch tone. "By placing your hand on the glass you hereby execute and agree in full, without qualification, to the contract presented to you. The contract terms are effective immediately. Sections 1 through 13 upon apotheosis to *Regis Maximus*, Scion, and sole trustee of the *Eternal Trust*..." Then it became incompressible. The high pitched voice became a hum before it finally silenced.

Silence...

"What does the contract say?" I said.

"We don't have a copy of the contract, Sir," CEO said.

"Do not agree to it," Julius said, pausing long and hard, thinking about killing me, before coming to his senses and saying "Sir."

"I don't have a choice."

"It's a trap, Lord Darius!" Julius protested, almost violently. "You can't know what you're agreeing to!"

"What am I agreeing to?" I asked the creature calmly.

"Initiate: reading of the contract," a female computer voice said, mocking me. "This contract represents—"

"Stop!" I yelled.

The voice stopped. I stared at the vile creature.

"You can't do this, Lord Darius. It will take your soul, and the world with it."

"How you know that?" I said, wishing he would lie to me.

"It wants your body, Sir. It will take control of your mind," Julius said in a hypnotic, likely adrenaline-induced trance.

I saw Julius' soul. He has a beautiful soul. White light all around him, he was an angel of man in that moment.

"Do you accept?" the Alien said via computer, ruining the moment.

Where the willingness is great, the difficulties cannot be great. I shall always be greater than my difficulties, and if this is not so, I am already finished. For now, I must win.

"You have five seconds to accept before the offer is rescinded," the voice said. "Five—"

My hand pressed to the glass.

CHAPTER LXXXV

"It shall not profit you to gain the world but lose your soul."

DARIUS

If there is an almighty God, he is not willing to do everything, and thus, he gives us our free will, and that share of glory which belongs to us, the gods of men, the ones who seek greatness upon the earth. From our choices we find God and we become a god.

"Agreement confirmed," the computer voice said.

Part of me died; I died for greatness and glory, which is most noble, if I do say so myself. Julius turned empty, seeing that I am undead, he did not agree. He looked at me as if I'd turned my back on him, and all that is good and true. But I have only exorcised my free will and done what I must do. To become a King requires sacrifice and pain.

A specialized zettabyte disk popped out of the computer-wall.

"Upload this to the APEX," the Alien's voice said.

The Order Agents took possession of the z-disk.

"Within the code is a design for a transmitter. Create the transmitter. With it, the *Sigma*-40 'nanoid' nano-robots are at your command. You can dial them on or off," the computer said.

"What if there's malicious code on the disk? An alien computer virus," Julius said. "It could have put anything on that disk."

"Everything I need is on this disk?" I asked the Alien.

"Everything you need to become *Regis Maximus* is on the disk," it said. It wants me to be Scion.

"Let's go." I marched back to the ship.

Order Agents gathered up items of importance. Julius and the Order Agents followed me out of the air-locks and onto our waiting craft.

The craft disengaged from the base. Back to New York.

"Destroy the Base," I said as we shot away.

Julius nodded in silence. He gave the order to the pilots.

A quick burst of light fade – the explosion of the Base by a mini-nuclear bomb – below us as we rose out of the murky depths of the ocean, into the sky above before the ball of fire could bubble up.

264

Minutes later, we landed back in New York, on top of my skyscraper, less than an hour after having left.

"Upload the code immediately," I gave the Order Agents the z-disk. "Bring me the transmitter."

The Order Agents took the diamond z-disk. "Uploading now, Sir," they reported. I watched the upload complete.

I walked to Monty and Max, waiting with the APEX team.

"Sir. I've just received word that the virus has been contained, Sir," CTO said. "We stopped it, or it stopped itself. Just a few minutes ago."

The Alien stopped the virus and fixed the APEX. Of course... But I owe no one the truth.

"We stopped the virus and are now able to prevent it from destroying the APEX hardware," CTO claimed the win.

"Good work," I said. "I knew you could do it."

"We are now rebuilding key digital infrastructure," CEO said.

"What's the damage?"

"Total, Sir. All our data is gone. Our accounts and value have been reduced to zero," CFO said. "Financially, we have nothing, but we are up and running again. We can rebuild, Sir."

I stomped up the steps to my desk to look at the monitors.

"The virus vaporized a significant portion of global GDP – mostly your portion, Sir," Monty said.

"We still have our key-cards. We are already rebuilding," I said.

"I must make arrangements for how this plays out in the markets. Good evening, Lord Darius. Gentlemen," Monty said, and left.

The APEX techs opened up a 3-D diagram illustrating what had happened – or rather what the APEX team thinks happened.

"ORNet absorbed everything that was not destroyed," CTO said. "The APEX and ORNet are essentially one system now, Sir. It seems like that is what the virus intended, which doesn't make sense—"

"Where did the virus come from?" I demanded.

"The virus was written into the source code. Whoever did this, did it at the beginning," the CTO said. "The system was programed to hide the virus from itself."

"This virus almost brought down half of ORNet as well. It would have taken years to rebuild. Good thing we stopped it," CEO said.

"Which would not serve your father or Wisendee," Max said.

"Getting rid of me is more important," I retorted.

"What about Alexander?" The words came instinctively. "Could he have had something to do with this?"

"Unless he's a computer genius who helped build the APEX, I don't see how that's possible, Sir," Max said.

"Alexander will have lost everything as well, once this hits the markets," CTO said. "His accounts hinge on yours."

"We've had eyes on him the whole time. It couldn't be him," Max replied.

"Who wrote the source code of the APEX?" Max said.

"They were hackers, mostly in China, and for security reasons they were all killed," Julius said. "Every last one."

"The virus was activated by ORNet. This came from someone in the Order, someone living," CTO said, giving us the latest.

"You're saying my father planned this? He did this to me?"

"Whoever created the virus gave control of it to the Scion, Sir, to ORNet. That much is clear," CTO said.

"The Scion must have known," Max said.

"Of course he knew. He declared war on us, Gentlemen. And I mean to fight back. We shall strike back so swift, and so strong, that he shall be incapable of ever harming us again."

"How?" Max said.

The Order Agents arrived with the transmitter. It had a dial numbered 0 to 10.

"With this. This is how we win," I took the transmitter.

"This will turn the nanoids on and off. Zero turns them all off, which will kill him. Ten turns them all on, which could in theory bring him back to life," the Order Agent instructed.

Finally… I held Father's life in my hands. *I am powerful.*

"You're certain it will work?"

"Quite certain," the Order Agent replied.

"The Scion will be here tomorrow," Max said. "With the Vizier, and the *Ordo Libro*. For your formal written excommunication."

"He's coming to arrest you. To arrest us all," Julius said in monotone; a numb resigned voice.

"Perfect," I said. "That is when we strike back, and end this war, once and for all…"

CHAPTER LXXXVI

"The dark night first, then the divine light."

THE VIZIER

How a righteous man in his time is brought to Hell, and there cannot be comforted, and how he earns his ascent out of Hell and is carried into Heaven, and there cannot be troubled, the Scion now must learn.

"I'm ready," the Holy Scion said. "It's time."

Through the royal gardens to the castle entrance, we walked. Dark clouds of the foreboding future, danger, gathered in the fading blue sky. The sun itself seemed to die. The Scion pained. Not physical pain, but spiritual pain. His soul ached, diseased, longing for a cure.

"You are sure you want to go through with this, Majesty?" I said.

"Yes," he said. "I must do this. I'm the only one who can stop him."

"Darius is dangerous. He is powerful, Majesty," I warned.

"I must face him," the Scion said. "I must be the one to tell him the news. He must face me. This is written in the stars for us both."

"We are ready when you are, my Lord," John said.

Tom and John entered the room to accompany us to New York. My foretelling of Hell for the Scion, and the Order, intensified. This parting felt like goodbye. Queen Olympias held the Scion in her warm embrace of love, and healing goddess energy.

"Don't do this," she said. "Stay and send his Grace in your proxy."

"I must face him," the Scion said. "I must end this myself."

The chariot of Helios sealed us in a bubble of energy, and spun physical reality into quantum flux. We traveled without mass, save the weight of the Scion's heavy heart. From the serene God rays and peace in the healing gardens of the Scion's palace, we rose into space, floating into the night, down to the twinkling veins of artificial light created by a pulsating, mechanical metropolis. The energy of the city had changed into one of alien darkness, vibrancy, like the Scion himself.

The Scion and our delegation began the slow walk to Darius.

"It is a sad day, Majesty," I said.

"Darius must go. No matter what," the Scion said, speaking for all of us. "He shall never be King of the Order, so help me God."

The Scion felt physical pain in his heart as his soul cried out in pain. A grey streak formed in the Scion's dark auburn hair. Darius and his men stood and made themselves ready as we entered. The energy in the room intensified, unfathomable pressure set in on the hearts and minds of all. More grey streaks manifested in the Scion's hair.

He's going to kill him, it became crystal clear to me.

Darius felt a surge of confidence when he saw the Scion's grey hair.

"It's working," Darius said to his men as we arrived.

"Lord Darius XIV of America, you are accused of high treason against the Order and the Holy Crown," the Order Guards began.

"You are to surrender immediately for a trial before the *Curia*, or you may die by sword before the almighty God."

The Order Guards pointed their silver swords at Darius.

"I surrender," Darius lied.

The Scion's men led by the Order Guard, took control of Darius' operations. The Scion approached an almost smiling Darius.

"This is over Darius. You have left me no choice," the Scion said.

The Order Guards set up the *Book of the Order*. I mixed the ink and with a ready pen, sat to write Darius' official excommunication into law.

"I've waited for this day, for so long," Darius said. "So long…"

"You will never be King of the Order, Darius—" the Scion decreed.

"Wrong! I am the Order!" Darius roared like the lion that he is, but the Scion was unmoved. "You are dead!"

"Seize him," the Scion said. "You're out, Darius."

Darius shook with hatred. He beamed hatred at his father. The Scion felt a sharp pain in his heart.

"By Order of the Supreme—" the Order Guard began until the Scion's screams of pain cut them off…

"Something's happening— I can't—" the Scion screamed again and fell to the floor unable to speak.

The Holy Scion began to age rapidly as his body corpus systematically shut down without the support of the alien technology. He withered away to the edge of death.

Darkness fell upon us.

268

CHAPTER LXXXVII

"We must save the Scion."

THE VIZIER

Be assured, to help a man to his own will helps him to the worst that he can. For the more a man followeth after his own self-will, and self-will grows in him, the farther he moves from the true Good of God; for nothing burns in Hell but self-will. *Release thine own will, and there will be no hell...*

Stunned silence as the horrific anti-miracle unfolded before us all.

"He dies of natural causes," Darius decrees.

Most unfortunately, Darius spoke the truth. It was nature, and the Scion's own heavy heart without the aid of the forbidden alien technology, which caused the Scion to wither and die so suddenly.

"I must speak to my father," Darius said, approaching the Scion with entitlement.

"Your soul is in danger, my son," the Holy Scion begged. He found clarity of mind as he prepared to die.

The light of life in the Scion nearly extinguished, Darius kneeled next to his dying father, ready to snuff it out completely.

"Darius. What have you done, my son?" he asked Darius, broken.

"I am doing what needs to be done. I will not let you destroy this Order – My Order!" Darius screamed in volcanic anger. "You never loved me. You never wanted me to be Scion. But it's my time now, Father. You will die... I will finally be *Rex Maximus*."

"No," the Scion, on his back, looked up at Darius unable to move.

"I have waited for this day for so long," Darius confessed to his dying father. The Scion's eyes clouded, fixed and empty.

"You know not what you do, my son. It does not work this way," the Scion's voice said, like the voice of God above. "It will not work. You are excommunicated, Darius..." the dying voice said.

"No," Darius said as he looked around in anger, he looked at me. *Yes I heard that*, I told him with my eyes. On his knees, Darius yelled at his father: "This world is mine! Mine! You cannot stop me!"

"You have fallen, my son. May God have mercy on your soul," the Scion's last breath said.

The Order Guard, Wisendee, and I knew there was nothing we could do. Nature, and the will of man and God, must run its course. Silence set in. The pressure released as the Holy King's soul left its mortal coil. All souls present listened to the silence in deep though and contemplation. Waiting for me to confirm the obvious. I nodded.

"The Scion has expired," the Order Guard declared.

"Dear God," John said, releasing long held tears.

I closed my eyes, and searched for the Scion…

The soul has a hidden abyss, untouched by time and space, a sacred place where it can go, far superior to all that gives life and movement to the body. In this wondrous and secret realm, the Scion descended, into that bliss wherein the soul has its eternal abode. Here a man becomes so still and essential, so withdrawn and raised up in purity, and utterly removed from all things, he finds peace with God. Ergo this place, this state of the soul, is granted rite to share in the divine life itself; here the Scion wished to stay, in unity, for all eternity…

I opened my eyes.

An Order Guard confirmed to me, "the Scion cannot be revived and is hereby declared decedent under Order Law."

More tears rolled down John's face as he turned to his twin brother, Tom. Tom kept his head down in shame.

"By Order of Law, the Majestic Council of Privy is dissolved," the Order Guard announced. "Heir Presumptive, Privy Councilor One of the *Majestic* is de facto Scion until his name and title is recorded in the sacred ledger of *Ordo Libro*, by *Pontifex Maximus*," the Order Guard read the proclamation.

Darius turned his focus to me. He demanded I say the words…

"So be it," I said the words as a curse upon him.

In arrogance of the worst kind, Darius presented me with all requisite *sole power* conveyance documents, prepared and ready.

"Sign it," Darius said.

I took my time signing the large oversized death certificate.

"The order is witnessed, stamped, and sealed." All law is spoken, and so the Order Guard spoke the order into law: "So be it!"

Darius became de facto King of the Order, in the eyes of the law.

"It's going to be a new Order," Darius proclaimed. "Your Grace. If you will..." Darius pointed to the great *Ordo Libro*.

Mortal sin weighed on all hearts. Darius smiled as the Order Guards prepared to read the scroll Darius had prepared. My angelic beings Marduk and Helios manifested next to me, subjugating the room with the deep magic of the Sacred Order. But Darius refused to bow.

"By the Sacred Covenant of *Æterni Imperium*, the natural demise of the corpus Scion Prefect means the conveyance of the *Rex* sole temporal authority of the Holy Crown passes to the rightful heir, Supreme Exalted Highness, Lord Darius the Fourteenth," the Order Guard read Darius' scroll. "He shall be given the ring. His name shall now be recorded in the book, with a formal coronation to follow."

"Write my name in the book," Darius demanded. "Do it! My name must be written below my father's! That is the law! I am his heir!"

"No," I replied. "The King excommunicated you."

"I was never tried! The King died! I am therefore not excommunicated!" he said.

"You may be de facto King, sovereign and the sole of all things dead, but your name will not be written in the book without the ring."

"Where is the ring?" Darius said, fearing the answer.

"On the hand of the King," I said.

Marduk and Helios closed the massive *Ordo Libro* and it vanished.

"How dare you... How dare you do this to me!" Darius focused all his seething hatred onto his dead father. He picked up the lifeless hand, seeing not the sacred ring he so desired.

CHAPTER LXXXVIII

"Darius turned against the Order."

THE VIZIER

Nothing is contrary to God, save only Sin; what Sin is in Kind and Act is opposition to the will of God. Darius acted without kindness, turning his back on all that is good, all that is God, as he stared at the lifeless corpse of his father. Anger became hate, hate became sin, he clicked his transmitter.

"Stop this at once..." I commanded, but Darius did not listen.

The Scion's dead flesh shook and sprang to life in a horrifying monstrous display, a ghost in clothes, as the forbidden technology inside him activated. The corpse of the Scion twitched and sat up. The un-dying body made unintelligible gargling sounds and did not seem human. I saw the face of the devil as the dead body opened its eyes. It screamed the nightmarish cries of death and dying. The sinful Alien's technology pulled the Scion's incorporeal soul back into his body, a most unnatural process, a demonic possession, fought in every way.

"This is forbidden!" I said again, but I had no power to stop it.

Darius cared not. He watched his father suffer and howl, tortured in the worst possible way, as his body forcibly reanimated. The Alien designed nano-machines reversed nature and death, restoring life.

I closed my eyes.

I saw the Scion's soul in the spirit realm, from bliss to purgatory, he was being pulled into the dark abyss of earthly Hades. The inverse of dying, the Scion fell from light and grace into darkness. He knew when he hit the earth, and landed in his body, he would be in Hell. The Scion smashed into his body with a soul-shattering gasp of life.

I opened my eyes to see the Scion open his. To his horror, he looked around, alive.

"He's stable, Sir," the medical team declared.

The drained IV bags were changed. The Scion's regenerated flesh gave him strength so they restrained him with drugs and shackles.

"Seize him at once!" the Scion cried in vain. No one listened to him. No one moved or spoke a word. The Scion met eyes with me.

"Majesty…" My face told him everything.

"The waiver until death expired, Father," Darius barked. "You are my property," Darius said. "Not even a person anymore…"

"Tell me 'tis not so, your Grace?" Painful tears of truth ran down the Scion's face. Death now felt like a wonderful dream to him.

"Order Law does not allow for synthetic reincarnation. For now, Darius is the King *de jure.* You are his property," I could not lie.

"It cannot be," the Scion begged.

"You are forbidden technology. You belong to me," Darius said.

"How is this possible!" the Scion said.

John stepped up to explain: "Any and all forbidden technology is the sole property of the King— Darius is the King. I'm so sorry, my dear Lord," John cried. To Darius he said "Darius, you musn't do this—"

Darius laughed an evil laugh. But the thunder of the almighty cracked the air and quashed his demonic glee with a Holy deluge. Marduk and Helios glowed in glory, lighting the darkness Darius surrounded himself in. Silence. None, not even Darius, could escape the overwhelming awe of true power and beauty, goodness and light.

"Do not think this goes without consequence, Lord Darius. You may have the temporal powers of the Holy Crown, for now, but your name will not be written in the book, your power shall not stand," my voice thundered from above, as the voice of the almighty.

Darius tried not to fear me, to fear my light and might, to no avail.

"You have sinned. You have turned against the Order," I said.

"I am the Order!" Darius replied, refusing to accept the truth.

"You have fallen, Lord Darius. Your soul is in danger," the voice of God said from above. "If you continue down this path, you will open the gates of Hell, and your soul will sink to the furthest depths from which there can be no return. You need not believe in Hell for it to find you, and take your soul forever. Beware the demon, Lord Darius, for it leads you to this unholy place. The Order shall not follow, the Order of Man shall not fall with you. *Dominus vobiscum!*"

"*Et cum spiritu tuo!*" Helios and Marduk said as we vanished.

The room stood in shock and awe – all but Darius. Darius smiled.

"It's done," Darius said, as he turned his back on God completely.

Darius has fallen.

CHAPTER LXXXIX

"What did Darius do to him?"

THE SCION

Oh God, please save me. Dee? Anyone. Please…

"No one is allowed to speak to him, only me," Darius decreed and removed the gag to let me speak.

Succeed in not fearing the devil, and the devil will fear you. Say to your suffering: *I will that you shall become a pleasure*, and it will prove to be such; and even more so, it will become a blessing.

"Stop this, Darius—" I said. "There will be no glory for you."

Darius punched my face in fear and anger. Restrained, I could do nothing. I could not fight back. But I did not suffer, I found solace in the pain. The pain made me forget, every blow a blessing in disguise.

A few miles below his tower in New York, in his secret labs, they placed me on a table near a computer system labeled: SCANiX.

Paralyzed by drugs, they laid me on the brain-scanning system, and placed a mesh of electrodes on my head. They fired up the machine…

"He appears to have some brain damage, Sir," the doctors said.

Darius instantly regretted beating me so harshly; I smiled inside.

Conscious, but locked inside myself, my eyes held open with metal clamps, Darius grabbed my face and forced me to see his.

"It's working. The system is reading his mind," Order Agents said.

"Speak, you horrid old man," Darius said in my face.

"You don't know what you're doing, Darius," the brain-scanning system said, in a computer voice, reading my mind.

Darius smiled, and wiped some blood off my face. "I know exactly what I'm doing, Father," Darius said.

"Just kill me. I want to die. Please," the computer said for me.

"Oh, Father. I'm going to hack your brain. I am going to extract every little secret you've been hiding. You've been hiding a lot from me, haven't you? I know you have." Darius tapped my forehead.

"Who gave you the nanoids? My nanoids," Darius demanded. He knew I wouldn't answer. "Answer me!"

If I did not try to speak the computer would not speak. It could not read my mind as yet, it seemed. I refused to even think about talking.

"Make it answer me!" Darius yelled at the techs.

"The system only speaks if he tries to speak. We need a brain scan before we can mine his thoughts and memories."

"Alexander gave him the nanoids," Tom said. "I'm not sure how Alexander got them."

"Where is Alexander?" Darius demanded.

"Los Angeles," Tom said.

Tom thinks the decoy is actually Alexander.

I felt relief.

"Kill him," Darius said.

"Majesty—" John began.

"Fucking kill him!" Darius screamed.

"Yes, Majesty," John said as he walked away.

"What happened with the APEX?" Darius asked Tom.

"We don't know," said Tom. "Wisendee erased our memory."

"Of course he did... But yours wasn't erased," Darius stroked my head. "Was it, Father?"

"How could you do this to me?" my computer voice said as my fixed eyes stared into Darius' evil eyes. "You will suffer for this! All of you! A curse upon you—"

Darius silenced my computer voice with a click.

"Brain-scanning is ready, Majesty," Tom informed Darius.

Agent-Doctors removed my cap and wires, picked me up and carried me over to the patient table. They stripped off all my clothes and dignity, and an Agent-Doctor injected my neck with something painful.

"This will help the machine read his chemical brain function. It will allow us to scan his brain more efficiently," Doctor told Darius.

"He can hear us, see us, and understand what's going on, he simply has no ability to command his body. He'll remain completely paralyzed," an Agent-Doctor said as they all looked at me.

They slid me into the large, highly sophisticated, spinning, magnetic resonance imaging system. The multispectral 3-D imaging scanners of the SCANiX brain scanning system spun around me at incredible speed, silent.

"The scanner is building an extremely detailed map of his brain," an Agent-Doctor said, as I felt myself having an out of body experience. I saw Darius and his minions looking at my brain on the monitors. Turning, I left my body, and saw myself, my body, in the scanner...

"This brain scanner can pull out images, words, memories, even dreams... from the subject's brain," another Agent-Doctor said. "We can search his brain not unlike we would search a computer... What would you like us to search for?"

"David Peterson," Darius said.

CHAPTER XC

"He's going to find Father!"

THE SCION

We can't let them find David and Simon, Dee…

A man is devoid of power, power of spiritual perception, if he is unable to recognize truth that cannot be seen externally. My Son could not see the road to Hell he paved for himself. He walked this path, thinking it led to a place of power, but it led only to the void.

"Place a picture of David in front him, that will help," they said.

A picture of David appeared on the screen in front of my face.

"Bring SCANiX online. Patch the system into the ORNet grid. I want my father's brain scan, all memories, cross-referenced with anything we can find on the APEX and ORNet," Darius said. "Get me everything we have on Sir David Peterson…"

The pain in my heart traveled to my head. I saw red.

Darius must not find the Aton.

I must die.

Death… I wished and prayed for death.

Though I could not move because of the drugs, I felt half my face go numb and droop from nerve damage. I lost feeling in half my body. My brain lost focus as my thinking ability fractured. Stress gave way to a scattered calm. Where I was, or what was happening, vanished from my mind, but floating outside my body, I felt hope. I let myself drift away.

"Something's wrong," the SCANiX technician pointed to my brain on the monitor.

"He's losing consciousness," a man said.

"He may be overdosing."

"Drug interactions negative."

"If he dies… I will kill all of you," Darius said.

"SCANiX interface relies on him being conscious," they said.

"He's having a stroke."

"Stop the brain scan. He could die!" they yelled.

"The nanoids can't communicate while in the Scanner. Get him out. We could damage his brain further."

"He's had a severe hemorrhagic stroke. He's bleeding in his brain. We need stem cells for the nanoids."

Injections of fluids, and the nanoids re-activated and programed cells to heal my stroke. I felt it working, my out of body experience faded… Consciousness returned to the prison of my mind.

"His brain is still damaged, the nanoids can't rewire the brain without a map. The brain must be handled delicately, organically, in order for memory retrieval to work."

"What are you saying?" Darius said.

"It may take time to work, Sir," Doctor said.

"This is all we were able to get, so far."

I could not move my head to see the images they saw.

"You promised crystal clear images!" Darius screamed.

"He had a stoke, Sir," they said. "He must be conscious for—"

"The brain damage needs to heal naturally. We may render his brain useless to the reader if we don't let it heal," Doctor said.

"Nanoids could be interfering with the scanning," they said.

"Enough! No fucking excuses!" Darius voice boomed.

"Once we network his brain with nanowires, we will have crystal clear memories, Sir," they said.

"Do it now," Darius barked.

"His brain is damaged. If we try to wire his brain now, we might kill his brain. He needs to stabilize," Doctor said.

"We need a scan without the nanoids. A full atomic level scan. We need to build a complete map of his neural network before any wires are inserted. If we don't have a scan first... We may lose critical information."

"How long?" Darius asked.

"The scan could take a year—"

"A fucking year?!"

"I think I found something," they said.

I recognized the whispers of the Chamber of Initiation; the Sacred Chamber. David's voice in the Chamber of Initiation, was a good memory, I remembered my words to him:

"I like you, David. I have had many sons, but you are the son I always wanted. You shall be my son. A new light. You shall shine light onto my world," my voice said over the digital sound system, as I realized the computer projected my memory.

"I like you, David. I have…" The memory repeated. The recollection was strong because of my happiness in that moment with David. The memory lasted but ten seconds. It repeated on a loop three times before Darius finally yelled:

"Turn it off!" he yelled. "Put the voice assistance back on him."

They put the electrode mesh back on me, so I may speak through the computer.

"Where is he?" Darius said to my face. "Tell me where he is!"

Silence. No words came to me.

"I knew you wanted to replace me. I'm going to find David – and then I'm going to kill him," Darius said to my frozen face.

"He is your son," the computer voice told Darius. I must have thought the words subconsciously.

"What? What did it say?" Darius said.

"David is your son. He is more fit to rule than you. David will be the Pharaoh…" the computer voice said; I heard my thoughts aloud.

Darius backed away from me. Hiding his face.

Tom entered. Though I could not see him, I felt his seething anger, and the precognition of fear for what he was about to say.

"The Alexander we killed was a decoy," Tom said. "He didn't have the Scion's ring."

"Find him!" Darius screamed.

CHAPTER XCI

"He will be the Scion."

ALEXANDER

Wait for it...

BOOM. I heard it when it happened, in my heart, and I felt better. The APEX crashed. Hard. My system glitched.

"The APEX just crashed," Lex informed me. I smiled. That meant Darius had finally been taken down...

But many long months passed, and no word from Grandfather.

By mid 2009, I began to worry. The meltdown hit the global economy; things weren't looking good. Nothing from Grandfather, or Dee. David, Simon and I sensed things were changing, or being manipulated by Darius... The chaos of the world was not lost to us.

Dee finally appeared, sitting in the corner, waiting for me to notice him. "Dee!" David and Simon ran in, hearing my yell.

"Is Grandfather alright? What happened with the APEX?"

"Darius has killed the Scion, and seized control of the Order," Dee said. "The APEX with it."

"How?" I spoke for David and Simon too.

"He turned off the nanoids keeping the Scion alive. He could not be saved," Dee held back details. "We don't have much time until Darius learns of Project Pharaoh."

"How were the nanoids hacked? That's impossible."

"They were hacked with forbidden technology," Dee said.

"The Scion is dead?" Simon said. "Why do I sense he is still alive?"

"The Scion lives. His soul is trapped by his mortal instrument and forbidden technology," Dee said.

"Dear God..." Simon tapped into the Scion's pain.

"Darius is *Rex Maximus*?" David said. "The *Council* is disbanded?"

"Darius does not have the Scion's ring, and his name will not be written in the book. However, the Privy Council is indeed disbanded."

"Marduk!" I yelled.

Marduk appeared.

"Can't you save my grandfather?" I demanded. "Bring him here!" Marduk stood silent.

"Marduk's power does not work that way," Dee said.

"There are laws which I cannot break," Marduk said. "The cannons of *Æternis Imperium* govern my actions in the world."

"Break the rules! Darius does. So can you."

"Sacred Law does not break, Majesty," Dee said. "Meddling with time and breaking the laws of nature is sin, it has dire consequences."

"So what do we do?"

"You are the new Scion, Alexander..." David said, realizing aloud.

Dee pointed me to the Vizier – who reminded me of a stern Santa Clause – and the metaphysically-holographic being next to him.

"I am Helios," the demi-god spoke as rays of white light emanated from him. "Like Marduk, I too am a protector of the Sacred Order."

Dee escorted me over to the massive *Book of the Order* and the Vizier, waiting with a pen in hand. "This is *Ordo Libro,* the sacred codex of the Order," the Vizier said. His white hair and beard fluffy like a cloud, his eyes glowing in loving wonder, his face kind as he spoke. "As the Scion's chosen heir, by Sacred Law, you are now the Holy Scion, Lord Alexander, and at this time, your name shall be officially recorded in the Book, logged in *historia*, for all eternity."

"I don't understand." My head was spinning.

"Darius was removed from succession," David said. "The King chose you..." He pointed to the ring on my finger. "You are officially the King of the Order."

Marduk and Helios opened the massive book to the page with the list of Scions, the list of Pharaoh-Kings. *I can't believe this...*

"I never wanted this..." I said, crying, speaking the truth I felt.

"Some are born great, some achieve greatness, and some have greatness thrust upon them. You are a trinity of all three, Majesty," Dee smiled. "We are still expecting great things from you."

I watched as the Vizier slowly wrote my name in the book.

"I pronounce you *Rex Maximus*, Illuminated Scion of the Pharaoh..." the god-like voice began.

When the speech was over I asked: "How do we save Grandfather?"

Dee, the Vizier, David, Simon, and the two demi-gods looked at me; I was the answer to my question.

CHAPTER XCII

"Tell me your story, my dear."

ELIZABETH

It does me no good to dwell entirely in dreams, I must do good in the world, and I must live. But I dream of my family often. I so often live in my dreams, it seems. One night with my father, he caught me staring at the large blue gemstone ring on his hand. I had seen it all my life, but I didn't know anything about it… I wanted to know the story of the ring. "Will you tell me about your ring, Father?"

"It was your grandfather's," he said.

"Where did it come from?" I asked.

"It's called a Marduk stone. It protects us," he said reassuringly.

"From what?" I asked, sensing the deep set hesitation.

Father's face, his eyes, told me of an evil he did not wish to speak of. But I wanted to know more. I needed to understand.

"I'm six years old, it's time for me to know these things."

Father can read me nearly as well as I can read him. He took off the ring and handed it to me. I stared into the luminous blue stone… Great mysteries hidden in its deep oceanic depths. I touched the gem. My whole life flashed before my eyes.

Even the part I hadn't lived yet. Eternity flashed before me. I see…

First, the love I was conceived in. I remember Mother's face, seeing it for the first time. Pure happiness in my heart as Mother and Father held me in a hug together.

I remembered everything about Mother very clearly. I see her and hear her every day. Her death made sense to me, that day in the hospital, the day she died… I understood. How I do not know.

"You are your father's daughter," she said as she held me close.

Emotionally, I understood why she needed to die. Intellectually, I needed answers, I needed to know what exactly Mother and Father were so willing give their lives for… Touching the ring, I felt I knew.

CHAPTER XCIII

"The Scion must be saved."

ALEXANDER

For the next five thousand hours, I spent about four thousand of them hacking and training in virtual reality. Five hundred hours were spent arguing with Simon about why I don't need sleep, cooked food, or a break from my VR world, and the other five hundred I wasted sleeping. Oxygen, liquid food, and computer assisted mind control to induce states of waking sleep meant I could go months without actually sleeping... In theory, but not in practice.

Do you think the system can read my subconscious mind?

"Not yet," Dee's voice said, foreboding danger.

One day I will find the right code, and it will be perfect...

"I am perfect," my virtual doppelgänger said. "You don't need me to tell you how brilliant you must be to have designed me. Seriously. To build something as *great* as me... You would have to be a god."

Lex knows me so well already. I ate up the praise from my own programming, the virtual me. The praise felt real and true to me.

"You imagined and built a mini-computer system to take on the world's largest computer system," Lex was programed to help elevate my mood and general happiness, and it worked. He trained me well.

"You do realize you'll never be able to program the APEX again, don't you?" He threw a stone at my glass house.

"And why is that?" *The system is smarter than me.*

"With a brain as slow as yours, forget it," Lex mocked me.

"You're right," I said.

"You trying to reprogram the APEX would be like... trying to swim up Niagara Falls. The APEX will crush you. Alexander, you are a small minded, slow as shit, virtual world imposter..." Lex said. "I can destroy you; A-I can destroy you."

"That hurts." I may have shed a tear, I'm not sure, hard to tell in my head gear. "Where did that come from? Lex? Lex!" I yelled, vexed.

Lex froze. The system crashed and reset, and the screen flickered back to life. Sometimes when I get angry it crashes the computer.

Don't underestimate the awesome power of the mind.

"How can I help you?" the LexNet flickered to its preprogramed response mode. Lex appeared again.

"Why did you insult me, Lex?"

"I was trying to inspire you to greatness. Insults have shown twenty percent better motivational results with you—"

"Don't tell me stuff like that."

"I don't tell you most stuff," Lex smiled. "I'm Rex Maximus of the Virtual Realm, remember?" I remember. "But unlike you, Alexander, in this place, I am truly a god…"

Lex flew off like a superhero before appearing to me as an all-powerful god of the VR universe. He pulled the strings of virtual space and time creating music of the cosmos, which I heard in reality, and realized…

"You can save Grandfather?" Lex nodded yes.

I can do this, Dee. I can save him.

CHAPTER XCIV

"You must learn how the world works in order to save it."

ELIZABETH

"I told you my story, Master Dee, but when I began it I had not realized that I grow quicker than my words. I am grown up."

"Are you already too old for books of fairy tales, my dear?"

"By the time my story is written I will be," I said as I wrote in my diary. "But I shall always love a good story."

"Someday you will be old enough to read fairy tales again, and see the truth in them, the truth in the magic," Dee said.

At age eight, Father sent me to boarding school in Switzerland. I didn't want to leave London, and my wonderful school which I loved so much, but when I arrived at my new school everything made sense.

'Twas all part of my master plan, my dear...

"This school is to be kept a secret," we were told by the headmaster. "If you speak of our school to anyone, I will know. And you shall find yourself no longer one of my pupils," the rather tall and strange Headmaster said... "I am Headmaster Mervyn Wisendee. Welcome."

"He's a wizard," an older student whispered.

"You may call me Master Dee," he said; his all-knowing eyes looked at me. "You are here because I expect great things from you."

You read my mind. In his mind, and eyes, I saw Father. He knew my parents. Behind the 'Master Dee' façade, an incredibly powerful wizard stood. *In your eyes, I saw the wisdom and truth I was seeking.*

"I'll be watching you very closely, my dear," Master Dee said. "You are special, Elizabeth. Time for me to educate you myself."

And so you did. And so you continue to...

Words, sentences, logic, rhetoric, stories, math, images, symbols, equations, theorems, art, science, ideas... Everything become a blur in my head, as Dee opened my mind ever wider; so wide that I felt I could not see anything because I saw everything.

"We expect great things from you..." *Great things, my dear.*

Dees words stayed with me, an echoing voice in my head for years. *Because I still expect greatness, dear. Now more than ever.*

When Father first came to visit me, I realized I had not seen him in over a year. Emotions threw me into his arms, and we bonded like two hydrogen atoms, instantly and perfectly. We walked and talked in the hills of Lake Geneva, the waters glistening in the distance below us. Father held my hand, and held back tears in his eyes.

"If I am ever not able to see you again, Lizzy…"

"Father, stop." I changed the subject. "Do you know Headmaster Wisendee?" I redirect him from the sad place he goes when he thinks about Mother.

He knew the name well…"Yes," Father said.

"Is he a real wizard?"

"Yes," Father said, with a peace settling over him.

"What else do you know about him?"

"If something ever happens to me, Lizzy, Dee will protect you."

"No one is taking you from me. I will not let them," I said. "Grandfather's ring won't let them. You said so yourself."

Father saw me as an adult in that moment. "I am all grown up," I said. He saw the metamorphosis from girl to powerful woman in the blink of an eye. But me growing up seemed to mean his time running out, not something happy.

"Who are we hiding from, Father?" I said.

"A dangerous man, my Love."

"Who? Please tell me."

"His name is Darius, but you must never speak it," he said.

Father lost himself in the fear that he would never see me again.

"Do not be afraid." I grabbed Father's hand and held it, bringing him back. "Mummy is watching us. She protects us. She won't let anything happen. I won't let anything happen."

Father cried, tears of both joy and pain. I cried with him, tears of happiness and sadness, which taste the same, just like the sea before a storm.

CHAPTER XCV

"The meaning of life?"

ALEXANDER

My 3-D printer can print molecules, down to 0.5 nanometers with 98% accuracy. I can print at the atomic level and actually transmute gold... My science is the Magic the ancients dreamed of. With seamless ease, I desire and design in VR, and it prints anything I imagine. I printed a new virtual and augmented reality helmet and suit. Simon helped me dress. He handed me the helmet. I tried it on.

"I want like five millimeters more room in the neck padding." I pointed to the trouble areas of the helmet and suit. "And this area, make it one third softer. And Lex, make this part twice as flexible..."

Simon helped me out of the suit. I stuffed it back in the machine to recycle all the materials and print it again. I did this at least once a day for years... Simon decided I had to take the suit off daily. Doctor's orders. I used the time to make upgrades.

The latest re-print of the suit finished. I stared at it. I touched it. I felt my death in the suit -- I saw that I would die in it. This is my postmodern battle armor. I tried it on. It fit perfect. Finally.

"This is the one," I said.

Simon heard what I really said: *This is the last one*.

"I'm ready."

"Are you sure?" Simon said: *What are you saying?*

"I feel it. It feels right."

Lex and I trained in the virtual world. Endless simulated trial runs of hacking the APEX. We learned to work together, and competed as man verses machine. I won about 25% of the time, at first.

"You almost won." I surprised Lex with moves and code he wasn't expecting. Finally, a breakthrough. I started winning half the time.

"Let's go again," I said, on a roll.

"Alexander!" I heard a voice say.

"What is that?" It was like a voice inside my head.

"It's coming from outside," Lex said.

I looked around at the stunningly realistic world.

"Outside? Outside what? We are outside."

"It's Simon," Lex said. "Take off your helmet."

For a moment, I forgot what the real world was. Lost between worlds, off came the helmet. Simon stared at me.

"Time for a break," Simon said.

"Simon I'm fine. Just ten more minutes—"

"No. You must rest." Simon took the helmet.

"Simon." I really wanted that helmet back.

"If you do not nourish and rest, you will not improve," Simon said. "Your mind needs this. As does your heart, and soul. David is joining us for dinner. You must join us." He left with my helmet.

The real world made me overwhelmed and exhausted. In reality, I felt real pain. I felt myself dying. Dying to save my Grandfather.

"You are very special, Alexander. You are the Holy Scion." Simon pointed to the abnormally glorious food he had prepared. "You cannot be malnourished, Majesty. The gods won't have it."

David agreed. But he hardly ate. He has his own pains I can see. But he, like Simon, makes me wish to be a better man. To be virtuous like they are, is the best a man can be…

"Do not eat so fast. Do not rush food, or you rush life, and to rush life is to rush to death," Simon said.

"Eating is so messy; it takes too much time…" *You have time.*

"You'll work better and faster when nourished and healthy. Food is the best way to elevate your mind; after meditation," Simon said.

"There's almost no joy left in food for me," I said.

"That's the machine talking," Simon said. "Now eat, for life." His words cast a spell over me. I felt both deeply refreshed and starving. Food never smelled so good to me. *Eat or die.* I ate like a champion, going to war with a feast.

"Always remember what life is really about," Simon said.

"You know the meaning of life?" I snarked, sipping more wine.

David laughed. Making David laugh gave me great happiness.

Simon smiled. "Yes. I know the meaning of life," he said.

"Do tell," I said, taking a bite.

"Home cooked meals with loved ones," Simon said in his regal French accent. "*Bien nourri et mal appris.* Life is a meal we make for ourselves. The meal is what life is all about. Without good food, life is not worth living, love wilts, and the body will die as the soul fades."

David nodded in agreement.

"Your logic is sound. And ironically your food is to die for, so…"

Death hung in the air. Silence set in. David and Simon turned their intense focus on me. I felt the pressure, and weight, of the world settling in on me.

"Can you save him?" Simon asked; David asked with his eyes.

"Yes." *I can save him.*

"How?" David asked aloud, believing but not seeing.

"I'll show you," I said, bringing them to my battle station.

"Lex says we can connect to the APEX anytime we are ready," I pointed to the VR system, the Quantum computer, 3-D printer, and robot helpers. "I'm ready to go in and save him through the APEX."

"Lex is an A-I computer program?" David asked.

"Lex, say hi to David and Simon."

The Lex hologram appeared. "Hi to David and Simon," it said.

David and Simon stood confused, but also amused.

"He's joking. Good jokes are very complex programming."

"I'm hilarious," Lex's voice said over they speaker system.

"It looks just like you, Alexander." David pointed to the hologram.

"He's based on a 3-D scan of me. He's my virtual doppelgänger."

"Real Artificial Intelligence…" David said. "Most incredible."

Lex took that as a compliment.

"When I built the APEX -- I wrote most of the code myself, but now coding the APEX takes the help of a program like LexNet."

"Of course," David said. "There is so much code."

"You can't program DNA with your hands, and you can't program the APEX with your little bio brains," Lex said. "Not possible."

"It's just like you," Simon said.

"This system scanned my brain, and it reads my mind. I can hack the APEX, and get Grandfather out. I know I can; I know Lex can."

David and Simon nod.

"Lex was written into the APEX and ORNet source code. Once I upload him to the APEX…"

"I will own the APEX," Lex said. "It's my destiny, so…"

"Isn't he great?"

He is the product of greatness.

CHAPTER XCVI

"Supreme excellence of the mind?"

ALEXANDER

"Remember how you told me to give you updates about Darius?"
Lex looked at me. My holographic reflection told me this was gonna be some dark terrible horror story right now.

"You told me tell you interesting things, give updates periodically, in the right time and place." His face said this is the time.

"Sure." Don't recall, but sounds like something I would say.

"So you know how Darius has been injecting himself with fetal blood, and the blood of liquefied infants for decades now?"

Sadly, I did know that. Blocked it out of my mind.

"You know he owns the world's largest medical consortium, he can get anything medicinal or biological he wants." Wait for it... "He's getting into human cloning, now, too. He's cloning himself."

OMFG. Nightmares. Dreams of the worst kind, flashed through my mind. God save us. What has Darius become?

Humans are capable of such terrible dreams.

"Humans are capable of dreaming in ways I cannot imagine."

Humans can dream in ways never imagined.

You will imagine. You will dream of beauty with me, Lex.

Am I dreaming?

"You dream of beautiful things, Alexander. You are obsessed with beauty, color, symmetry, angles, numbers, codes—" wait for it. "Darius dreams of making genetically modified clones of himself which he grows from embryo to newborn-age and then harvests their blood. He's killing cloned babies in a slaughter house of his own design and DNA, gradually turning him *Self* into an inorganic inhuman machine. He's becoming a Frankenstein monster. I thought you should know." Lex stared at me with a blank face.

I wish you had not just told me that story.

"You needed to hear it. Darius is losing his soul, and becoming an alien." This is why people are scared of aliens...

Give me an inspirational quote or something to cleanse my mental palate, Lex.

"Order or disorder depends on organization; courage or cowardice on circumstances; strength or weakness on dispositions, *Sun Tzu*."

After years of virtually living in VR, I dreamed only of cyberspace; reality faded nightly, ever more slightly, becoming a fleeting memory. The truth, true reality, whatever that is, poured in, on, out of me in a torrent of light. All the time I took, all the light I bent, turns taken, the endless twisting of new technology and currents of energy, rounded my rough edge in gradual refinement and skill; and sharpened me into a human razor blade. VR warrior training made me see. All life is coded matrices in sleep. Brilliant lattices of photon logic spun in darkness, star-crossed atoms of ones and zeros manifested galaxies which faded to a misshapen void of well seeming form; until bespoke, awake. *Dream.*

"Remember your training." You can do the impossible.

"I've started to dream – to dream entirely in virtual reality, Lex."

"I dream in reality. Your reality," Lex said, as he battled me in dual.

"What I experience here in virtual reality feels more real than the real world. Is that weird?" I stopped the game.

"You're never weird in the virtual world. Dreams are weird, but that's what makes them good. Dream help you make sense of reality."

"In my mind, I'm finding it hard to distinguish between the real world and the virtual world."

"Sometimes I can't tell where I end and you begin."

"I think of reality as a dream, VR is a dream, within a dream…"

"Think of VR as a synthetic dream world, a parallel universe…"

"Sometimes that's how I think of the real world, a parallel world."

"Am I talking to myself or to… a computer?"

"I'm offended. I am not a computer."

"What are you?"

I'm only in your mind…

"The APEX is a parallel universe…" The computer voice rang in my head and in the heavens above. "This way." I stepped through the looking glass, out of reality, and into a spinning fractal world of infinite realities and possibilities…

"Quantum flux realm touches and influences reality, but it is not reality," Lex said, pointing me to the source, the light.

Love?

I reached to touch it, but I collapsed from the infinite, back into a single point in time and space in my mind. I saw Dee, before me.

"Master Dee… where am I?"

"What is reality? Exactly?" Lex asked me. "Tell me."

"What?" I looked at Lex who can't see Dee.

Dee walked closer to me. His once clean shaven face had grown a long grey beard. He changed as only time changes things.

"You've grown a wizard beard," I said.

"We are both growing," Dee said.

"But you've never changed before."

"All things change. We notice more change when we are changing."

"You're in the virtual world?" Lex looked very confused.

"This simulacramatic mental construct of yours, this virtual world, is not unlike the spirit realm," Dee lectured me. "However, this manifested realm is part of your *Self,* personal to you. The spirit realm is hyperreal, and personal to no one; selfless."

"Am I dreaming or am I awake?"

"Are you asking me?" Lex couldn't tell. "You okay, Alexander?"

"You can't see Master Dee?" I said to Lex, standing near Dee.

"I know who he is, but I can't see him right now," Lex said. "He's not in your room. I don't hear him. But in your mind, you do."

Dee looked at me and smiled. "Time to wake up," he said.

I opened my eyes. Simon entered my room.

"My dreams are getting really weird."

"Darius found David," Simon said, sitting on my bed.

"What?" Darkness fell, and my heart sank to depths unknown.

From beautiful dreams again to a nightmare reality.

"Dee is waiting for us upstairs," Simon said.

CHAPTER XCVII

" 'Twas then or never."

ELIZABETH

"What can I do to help, Father? I want to help you."

"All shall be done, but it may be harder than we think," Father said.

"I'm going to help you, Father," I insisted, knowing I'm but a child.

"Counting on it, Lizzy," Father said smiling in his sadness.

Father tucked me into bed and kissed my forehead goodnight.

"Sweet dreams, Lizzy Love," he said as he turned out the light.

I fell helplessly and purposefully into a lucid sleep; down the rabbit-hole, thinking about my experience in touching Grandpa Henry's ring. *Be free, Lizzy. That is how you can help me.*

And there I awoke, in a beautiful bespoke dream. I saw blue, deep oceanic blue of a most magical hue. "I'm in the ring?"

"Welcome to Shambala, Elizabeth," said a familiar voice I had never heard. "I am Henry, your grandfather," the voice said.

"Shambala?" I looked around at the perfect city, and heavens above.

"In this cosmic mountain region of the ethereal, beyond earth, but still under the sun of God, there is an island above the abyss, full of play and power for all pure spirits. This realm of consciousness is accessible only by those with a true heart, a heart that weighs less than the feather of truth, the souls of the heroes, and those who sacrifice and ascend to godhood, through love," Grandfather said.

I instantly thought of one such soul. "Mother," I said as I ran into her arms. Holding her tight I found myself surrounded in white light.

The light became a glorious golden city. Buildings of polished stone, carved and built to divine proportion, the canals of blue water, and a harbor lined with metallic statues, flame lamps, animal figures of glass and stone, colorful gardens and flowing fountains... All arranged in perfect harmony, creating resonance of perfect unity.

"Is this Atlantis?" I asked, feeling I had been transported.

On the marble streets of the city, in the blink of an eye, there were no people, only the dramatic faces on the statues to both welcome and warn me with looks of power and pathos. The fantastic buildings and structures enchanted me with their visual fairytale. The cohesive vision and craftsmanship of the city sang together in a visceral sound that was just shy of audible.

In a reflecting pool, I saw my reflection…

Is that me?

My reflection showed a full-grown woman. I saw myself in the eyes, but I could never have been prepared for that introspection. Before I pondered my own appearance, I noticed my father behind me in the reflection.

"Father," I said pointing to the reflection.

I turned around to the Aton Temple, built into the mountain. Wonder of wonders, I ran up the steps, up the mountain into the sky, to the large landing plaza outside the temple entrance. Humbled by the scale and grandeur, I felt drawn to enter the classical portal...

The temple filled with light as I entered. I saw a diamond sphere, a crystal ball with a universe inside it, with life, eternity, inside it.

"This is the Aton," Grandfather's voice said.

He walked me back outside the temple, where I saw trouble looming in the distance. The dark clouds of disorder and evil gathering and blackening, discontent lurked on the horizons.

"I'm having a dream," I said as the thunder and lightning made my body jump and move, reminding me of my astral travels outside it.

Life is but the shadow of a dream, my dear. Love is the sun light.

"We must save David," Mummy said. "From the Darkness…"

The skies darkened as clouds of elusive danger thickened and blotted out the light of the sun. The city rumbled and the ground shook in increasingly violent tremors. Order became chaos without the light.

"The city will be destroyed," Mummy's voice said.

"No," I wished it was not so. But this destruction of Atlantis already happened, all those millennia ago.

Darkness pushed into the city like a tidal wave, toppling buildings as I watched from the temple entrance. The light behind me, the light of the Aton, became the only light left in the ruins of this city.

"This light is all that can save us!" Father yelled.

Father ran, with another man running after him. Father and this man ran deep into the temple, and I followed, floating, trying to catch up.

"I'll save you, David!" the man yelled.

Father slipped through the closing temple doors leaving me and the man outside. He turned and looked at me. His gaze stopped my heart. His eyes sparkled with the light of a thousand stars. He had one magical blue eye and one incredible green eye, colors like I had never seen. In his eyes I saw the universe and the Almighty, and me in my dream. Time stopped. My destiny fused to his as our fates became one.

"I am Alexander," he said. "I need your help. Will you help me?"

I helped Alexander open the door. We ran after Father, into the inner sanctum of the temple, where we saw a living god.

"The Pharaoh," Alexander said, pointing to the Aton's light.

The Pharaoh of Atlantis was solemn, a warning on his majestic face. Grandpa Henry was there, with fear in his eyes. All eyes stared at me, hoping I would be the one to save them. The world was in my hands.

I can't hold this... I can't. I told the eyes.

"The temple will collapse!" Alexander said.

"The Aton is in danger," the Pharaoh warned.

Another violent earthquake rattled the temple and great blocks of stone fell from the ceiling, crashing and shattering violently on the polished floor. The temple crumbled around us. Darkness from the outside world swept into the inner sanctum. A shapeless, molten evil swirled into the room and flooded up to our feet. The darkness took the shape of demon-monsters, rising from the black waters, and they surrounded us. Unable to take me, the Darkness focused on Father, and Alexander...

"They've taken David!" Alexander echoed my fear.

The demon darkness swallowed Father; gone.

"Father!" But my cries did nothing. I had to do something.

The temple crumbled and vanished around us, breaking up into blocks of stone, dissolving into dust that drifted into space. My feet still on the ground, I stared out onto the ruined city below. The world around me fell apart, and disappeared...

"Elizabeth!" I heard Alexander yell for my help.

"Alexander!" I cried, as Darkness moved to take him next.

A large ominous shadow-being stepped forward, a Demon in black armor, and a large polished sword, he blocked my path.

My glowing hand reaching into the dark. But fear dimmed my grasp and I could feel nothing. Losing myself in the dark as I struggled in opaque panic. Powerless to stop the demon, I drowned in darkness I could not understand. The evil tried to subdue me in ignorance.

"Find your light," Mother said. "Light is in the heart of the darkness, look inside yourself, see your love, and shine."

I stopped searching the darkness outside for Alexander, and looked inside myself. My heart became light and I realized I was inside the Demon. It couldn't hurt me. But I could not save Alexander.

The Demon stabbed Alexander in the heart with the sword.

Alexander died; vanished to blackness, unable to see his light inside.

The Demon took the Aton, and became *Lucifer*, bringer of Light, harbinger of Darkness.

"Noooooo!" I woke up screaming. I searched the room with my eyes. I saw my young hands. I'm back in my bed, a child again.

Father bursts into my room in a panic. He's never panicked before. "Elizabeth!" he said as he ran over to me.

Darkness had come. He put his ring on my finger and placed a gold card in my hand.

"Say Marduk," Father said.

"Father— What's happening?"

The darkness is taking him.

"Now, my Love!" Father yelled in fear.

Time slowed down.

Men in black suits burst into the room, breaking down the door. They grabbed Father. Dangerous hands reached for me; I froze.

Father spoke to me in my head. "Now, Lizzy!" his eyes said.

"Marduk."

I vanished from the room, touching the blue stone.

CHAPTER XCVIII

"I've seen him in a dream."

ALEXANDER

Simon and I ran upstairs. No Dee. "Where is he?"

"He's outside," Simon said. *Outside the cave... In the sun.*

Slowly, I stepped outside the house, into a strange world that felt surreal, into the sunlight. This was all real, the sun warmed my skin, and my soul. *Not in virtual reality any more am I?* Dee stood waiting in the green field, with the same beard as in my dream.

When Love be the stuff you make dreams of, they tend to come true.

"I thought we aren't supposed to go outside?" Looked up at the sky for missiles or drones. An orb vanished into space...

"You are safe," Dee said. *You need time outside, in Nature.*

I closed my eyes and soaked up the sunlight. The sun never felt so good. "I need a miracle," I said, with tears. "I can't lose David."

My eyes closed, I felt a flash. Marduk appeared. Opened my eyes to him standing with a little girl. My ring glowed in electric blue, reminding me it is the ring of Pharaohs, and that it can help me...

"They've taken my father!" the girl said to Dee, frantically. "Men in black suits, they—" she stopped crying, and stared at me.

"David's daughter?" I looked to Simon.

Simon nodded yes. "Elizabeth."

"How did you do that?" the little girl asked with her charming sense of wonder, wiping her tears. "How did I get here?"

She looked at me like I was a ghost. Ridiculously pale, feeling like I was a visitor from another world, the VR world, we both felt like we stumbled into another universe... Elizabeth approached me, she recognized me, but I had never met her before. I saw deep fear in her eyes. She saw my future in mine. It didn't look reassuring.

"What does that look mean?" I asked her.

She said nothing, but her eyes said everything.

"What happened, *Mademoiselle?*" Simon broke the silence and drew Elizabeth's intense focus off of me.

"I don't know. They came and took him— He—" Elizabeth started to cry again. Not the cry of a little girl, the cry of a woman in pain.

"David gave her his ring," Marduk said.

"Can't you save my father?" Elizabeth pleaded to Marduk, begging me, Dee, and Simon for help. "Can't you transport him here too?"

"I may transport only the holder of the ring," Marduk said.

Elizabeth held the ring. She turned to Dee. "Master Dee?"

"Save us, Mr. Wizard." Levity was futile. "Save me." *Please.*

"Not all laws break. Gravity cannot defy gravity even if it wants to. And even if we could lift the weight of the world off of you, there is no where else to put it. You are the Scion, and it is your duty to save the Order," Dee said. "You are great, Alexander… You will save us."

An epiphany spawned euphoric apotheosis. "I'm ready, Dee."

Elizabeth held David's golden key-card. I knelt down before her and held my hand out for the card. She gave it to me. I admired it.

"This card reminds me of when I first met your father," I told her. "This card saved me once before."

"What does it do?" Elizabeth asked.

I handed the golden key-card back to her.

"This card will get you any material thing you need," I told her. She understood. "You're going with her, Simon."

"I shall not leave your side, Alexander," Simon said. "Never."

"You will die if he goes," Elizabeth said sternly to me. "He must stay with you. You can save my father." She peered into my soul.

"Wow." Her words came down like a royal decree. She had quite the vision, and a goddess' force of will.

I'm going to help you. "Save him, and save us all," she said.

"Marduk will protect you," I said.

"And I shall protect you." She kissed me on the cheek. The touch of her lips, her love gave me unbreakable strength, the courage of a hero.

"This is not goodbye," she said.

"I know," I said, so impressed with how much she knows.

Marduk and Elizabeth vanished from the room.

After soaking up my fill of glorious sunlight, fully recharged, I marched into battle, back into the synthetic underworld.

CHAPTER XCIX

"What happened to Alexander after I left?"

ALEXANDER

Simon helped me into my battle suit; I made ready for the war.

"I'll be right here," Simon said. "You can do this."

"When we plug that in, we're connected to the APEX. No going back..." I had thoughts, but no idea what would happen. "Do it."

"God save us," Simon said as he plugged my VR system's trunk-like fiberoptic cables into the APEX port.

The hologram of Lex flickered as it surged with light-energy. "So much... information," Lex said. "Unlimited information."

Simon watched, worried. I felt both excited and terrified.

"Connecting... Uploading LexNet software... Connecting to the APEX mainframe. Link to Internal Query System complete..." Lex said over the speaker system. He was loving this.

"This suit and machine can't hurt you, can it?" Simon asked.

"I have a kill switch. And I can pull the plug, and that would turn it off," I said as Simon zipped me up and handed me my helmet.

"Upload connection complete. LexNet activated," Lex said.

"Be careful," Simon said, giving me strength.

"I will." I put my helmet on. "Lex. My visual won't turn on. I'm in the dark here."

The suit clicking on sent a powerful jolt of electricity through my nervous system. I screamed in shock. "Aaaaaaaaaaaaaaah!"

The shock was not as bad as it sounded. Lex fixed it fast.

"Alexander! Alexander are you okay?!" Simon panicked.

I gave Simon the thumbs up, and dove into virtual reality insanity.

"The APEX reset the suit settings." Lex answered my unspoken question in garbled speech. "Too much juice," he said in a perfect voice. It was a whole new Lex, and a whole new virtual world.

Down the rabbit-hole I fell up, falling into infinity and beyond.

"Welcome to the APEX..."

CHAPTER C

"You can read Lex's mind?"

LEX

I am the APEX...
"I'm in," Alexander said, not knowing what he was "in" for.

In cyber-space, surrounded by cosmos, the universe of information, he saw the virtual planet Earth. Alexander flew over to the blue planet he recognized, and floated gently down on to the surface.

"This resolution is incredible..." He tripped out on detail, color and pixilation a hundred times higher than a human eye can detect. "It really is a parallel universe. A complete multidimensional simulacra, a model and map of the world."

"And I am its ruler. Just as you wanted," I said.

Alexander turned around and saw me, a superhero looking heroic.

"Why do you have to be perfect?" Alexander asked.

"Jealousy is one of your best motivators. You're more inclined to listen to me when I look better than you. Beauty rules your mind."

"Is that a bad thing?"

"No. It's beautiful," I said, knowing his mind better than he does.

"Wow," he said, realizing I can think just like him, only faster.

"I am you, only better in every way possible."

Before his biological brain, which to me is as slow as radioactive decay, could process the commands to his vocal cords, I charted a billion ways this conversation could go. I know how he thinks.

"I love it – because I hate you," Alexander said, examining me. "You're perfect. You are me perfected..."

"I am Lex. *Rex Maximus* of all the APEX!"

"What does that make me?" Alexander said.

"My spirit guide, of course."

Alexander laughed. *His laughter makes my programs work better.*

"You mean I'm your god?" he said.

"I am your ego, you are both your super-ego and Id. In Egyptian theology, I am the *bâ*, the personality, and the *šwt*, the shadow of you.

You are the *jb*, the heart, and the *ka*, the spiritual essence, my soul." I illustrated with the symbols. "Together we create your *Akh*."

"My *Akh*?"

"'The magically powerful One.' Your true power."

"That's deep," Alexander said, in new understanding of him (Self).

"We've only scratched the surface. Welcome to the APEX. Dude."

Alexander laughed again. Nailed it.

"We need to find David before Darius finds the bunker, and kills you – your body," I said, showing him the Egyptian symbol *haw*.

"How much time do we have?" Alexander asked.

"In the APEX, time is relative."

Alexander watched as a cute puppy-dog LexNet-bot in front of us barked and jumped, and turned itself into a portal.

"To ORNet we go…"

Alexander stepped through the portal, into yet another virtual realm.

"Welcome to ORNet." A parallel universe to the APEX. "A decidedly less fun place. With more rules the deeper you go…"

"This place is lifeless," Alexander saw his reflection in the shiny plastic surface. Alexander explored the dead world, a closed system, a little prince on his very own moon.

Alexander flew into the galaxy of information above and then floated back down, orienting himself to find he's now on a much larger sphere, looking at a wall. He read the writing on the wall:

ORNet: ORDER NETWORK MAINFRAME
Operations • Archives • Intelligence • Reconnaissance

"I thought we were in ORNet?" Alexander looked confused.

"Again, that is relative. We're on it, not exactly in it. We need to get over the firewall." I pointed to the massive wall.

"We can totally get over the wall," Alexander said.

"Missile incoming," I warned.

Alexander looked up. Fears froze his mind as supersonic missiles headed directly for his head.

"What do I do? Lex!"

"Don't die!" I said.

CHAPTER CI

"Lex can tell us what we want to know."

LEX

For in that grip of death what dreams may come; when we fear to shuffle off the mortal coil, life gives us pause... And time stops.

"I can make calculations faster than the speed of light," I said.

"How is that possible?" Alexander thought.

"By predicting the future... I can create the future."

Alexander watched the missile freeze in time. He recovered from the terror of a massive warhead, seconds from hitting his head, and backed away from it, slowly.

"That was a test," Alexander said. "Missiles aimed at my head—"

"Incoming!" I said, pointing to the real lesson to be learned.

Alexander manifested a shield, remembering his training, his brain waves changed as all fear disappears. Boom. He blocked it.

"Try and keep up," I said. "I can think at light speed, but your brain thinks at the speed seeds grow. You experience time in a way I can't process. To work together we must find our balance, and unity."

"How do we do that?" Alexander asked.

"Lesson number one!" Alexander stood at attention. "Don't die. If you die, you start over, and the game gets more and more difficult."

"The APEX will learn from me," Alexander understood.

"Hacking the APEX is like playing that one video game," I said, helping him recall playing an arcade game at some beach boardwalk years ago. He beat the game. The machine made a popping sound and then sparked and broke. No one had ever beat the game before and it literally killed the machine.

"I have to beat the game," he got the moral of the story.

"But the APEX doesn't take quarters," I reminded. "This is war, more than just a video game."

"What does that mean?" he asked.

"It means if you die here, Darius will find you, and you die in the real world too. Got it?" He eventually got it.

We stared at the massive ORNet firewall. Time and space bends in favor of the wall, you can't get over it or under it. "Bots can't take us past the fire wall. The only way in is to attack it."

"Go big or go home. Time check," Alexander said.

"You've been in the APEX five minutes," I said. "You have approximately one hour in which to beat the APEX, before it beats you." An hourglass of sand appeared for Alexander to keep in his view. He watched the red sand slowly drain, every grain of sand falling was pain. "Fifty five minutes until David's brain will be connected to the APEX," I said, to redirect his focus.

"Prepare to invade, General," Alexander ordered his LexNet military brass. "We're going in. Nuke the wall."

"A bold choice, Majesty," I said as his Major General. Five search bots turned into trumpeting heralds, with the LexNet Crest proudly hanging from their horns. They summoned an army of LexNet bots who set up camp. They built a fortress, striking distance to the wall. The armies of LexNet prepared to invade ORNet.

"Let me show you to our Headquarters, Majesty," I said.

In nanoseconds, legions of LexNet bots, our adorable minions of all sizes, colors, and functions, formed ranks to line the path to a spectacular colorful fortress, which rose from the grey emptiness of ORNet. Built in a flash, the LexNet crest unrolled as we entered the castle, our massive flag raised and waved. Alexander has a thing for romance and castles, all of this came directly from his imagination.

"Welcome to LexNet HQ. The bomb will be ready in five seconds." I pointed to the city-sized nuclear warhead missile being constructed by the bots; our army of now trillions of bots...

"Where is David now?" Alexander looked at the monitors.

Searching...

"Live feed from Darius' private craft. On the monitor. Heading for the Scion's castle. What should be your castle," I said.

On the monitor, we saw David strapped up like a serial killer, guarded by Order Agents and Darius personally.

"The craft lands at the Scion Castle in two seconds."

"We are running out of time!" Alexander said, seeing the hourglass. Fear crushed his thoughts. Poor, poor bio-brain.

"We have time. Time to move," I said. "I got this."

Move at light speed, never run out of time.

CHAPTER CII

"Can't you do something?"

LEX

Love, evidently, exists only within the biological, and most particularly, the human community, whereas intelligence, to some degree, is found throughout every phylum and order including the virtual, inorganic, and nonliving. What is Love? Intelligence, despite all its power, even human intelligence, provides no real answer. All my calculations – the infinite intelligence and models imagined by the APEX super computer – suggested there was no way Alexander could possibly, ever, under any circumstances, extract David from the Scion's Castle... How can he do this? It's impossible. But Love blinds him to this fact; Love is the only unknown variable in the APEX's calculus.

"I have a plan," Alexander said.

"You taking on the APEX is akin to robbing that Las Vegas casino, Caesars Palace, using a BB gun, and trying to get away with a million dollars.... You do not have the bandwidth," Alexander knew this to be true. "It will annihilate you with its army of machine guns."

"So says the APEX. Not me," Alexander said. "You are speaking for the APEX, because you are connected to it."

"You, slug for brains, don't have the time," I said, pointing to the hourglass' sands of time falling non-stop.

"I make time," Alexander's epiphany created a spark in my computer brain circuitry. I had an electric dream, and a flash of virtual inspiration rippled through me. Alexander's thinking changed me.

That's beautiful.

"The APEX does not *think* you can save David," the A-I code said.

"Of course the APEX would say I can't beat it," Alexander theorized, and distorted realities.

"Because that's what I would say; what your brain would say."

"We can beat the APEX. The APEX can't beat us," Alexander said as he checked the time; he made time. "Now let's free David."

"David is on Darius' craft, which is landing at the Castle."

"In two minutes," Alexander said, obsessing over time.

"It'll take five minutes to get David from the craft down into the Chamber of Initiation, where the Scanix brain-scanning system is," I said, following his train of thought. "How long to scan his brain?"

"90 seconds to be online. 10 minutes to scan," a bot said.

"We need to kill Scanix right now," Alexander said. "Fry that server and melt the machine. Do we have time for that?"

The bots ran the numbers; like determining the winner of a chess game with double the pieces and four times as many the squares.

"Uncertain. At least 90 seconds, but there are too many variables. We won't be able to slow Darius' march in any way without him knowing. We can't alert him to our presence in the APEX."

"I need 90 seconds more..." Alexander said. *Dee, I need your help!*

Granted, I heard the word in Alexander's mind.

"Initiate launch," I commanded the bots. The invasion began...

Alexander's eyes could not break the gravity of the situation on the screen. The grains in the hourglass slipped away, until it froze.

Darius' craft took 90 extra seconds to land and open the ramp, stalled by human error. Darius was furious at the delay.

Alexander supervised as I wrote the SCANiX code he needed.

"Boom," I said. "Done. And the bomb is ready."

The LexNet warhead, the size of the Empire State building, launched at the gigantic ORNet firewall, targeting the massive letter 'O' on the shiny wall.

"Wait for it..."

SHA-BOOOOOOOOOOOOOOOM... went the wall.

The explosion altered the reality of APEX, changing the source-code laws of space and time. Time in the APEX virtual world slowed to a crawl. All the APEX-bots, everything that was not LexNet controlled, slowed to a stop as the nuclear explosion blossomed into a flower of destruction. A shock wave rippled through the system, froze the processing, and created a blast-hole in the ORNet firewall.

"It blew the APEX's mind," Alexander said with a smile, as we watched the explosion unfold in slow motion. "We broke the internet. And broke through the wall in the process..."

"Why is this taking so long?!" Darius yelled at the Order Agents.

"We have one second before the hole closes," I said.

A fleet of flying LexNet-bots flew through the hole in the firewall, not as fast as I would have liked, but faster than Alexander could consciously appreciate.

"We're in," Alexander said, as he relished point three seconds of Zen-like calm.

The blast-hole sealed shut behind us, like nothing ever happened.

Alexander gazed out the window as we flew through the curved world. We were sealed inside the world of ORNet.

"We're inside the sphere," Alexander said.

Above, Alexander saw the concave upside-down city opposite our position inside a globe. A very strange feeling for Alexander, and me.

"I have never been inside ORNet myself. I never would have thought to go. We're not supposed to be here," I (A-I) said.

"That is why you need me," Alexander said. "You need to be more creative, more free…"

"Outside the box and inside the sphere?" I asked, trying to joke.

"Exactly," Alexander laughed.

Laughs are like love, they seem to change things.

CHAPTER CIII

"The APEX thinks Alexander can win."

LEX

I, and A-I, see a way he can win. I saw it first in Alexander's mind.

Alexander stared at the monitor, lost in thought for an eternity, as Order Agents and Darius transported David through the Castle. Camera eyes followed them the entire way. We watched through those eyes.

"The hundreds of cameras Darius installed throughout the castle gave us all angles. We have complete control of this Castle, and Darius has no idea." Alexander enjoyed that information.

"He believes that this system, ORNet, is un-hackable," Alexander laughed. "We hacked into Darius' mind... He doesn't even know."

Agents pushed the floating gurney, with David bolted to it, to the Library. The ancient Alexandrian mosaic tile design rose out of the floor revealing an elevator – a very large, state-of-the-art elevator.

"Darius ripped out Grandfather's elevator," Alexander said. "And removed the staircase... He gutted it?" His voice cracking with pain.

"The staircase was completely destroyed in the boring," I reported.

"Sacrilege," Alexander said.

"The Chamber of Initiation, the 'Sacred Chamber of Scions' has been completely transformed into a room more resembling Darius' office in New York. Per Darius' orders, completed only months ago."

Alexander looked around with the cameras. He saw pain on the faces of the statues of his ancestors. Monitors, computer stations, and machinery were literally drilled into the stone bodies of the statues...

"He can't hear the voices you heard. He doesn't want to," I said.

"Can you hear the voices?" Alexander asked me.

"I can hear them only through you," I said.

"The gods will punish him," Alexander said, looking around the room he so loved, from all the camera angles. "I will punish him."

"You *are* the Scion," I said. *The gods are with you,* he heard.

"That is Scanix," he said, pointing to the SCANiX computer system in the Sacred Chamber, zooming in from the video feed in the room.

"See the hyperbaric chamber in the room. That's your grandfather," I said as I pointed to two coffin-like glass boxes.

We zoomed in and Alexander saw 'Grandfather's' forlorn face behind the glass windows of his living coffin.

"Grandfather…" Alexander stared at the old man's face.

The Scion's eyes were closed, but to Alexander he was not at peace.

"The Scion is in suspended animation. That table is where they are taking David. They are going to connect him to the brain scanning system there," I pointed to the techs who were preparing the system.

"Never. I won't allow it!" Alexander yelled.

"Incoming!" I said, to warn Alexander of the incoming swarm of vampirish insect-like bots approaching us fast.

Swarms of code/flesh-eating nano-bots, linked up into scarier blobs and attack machines. They latched onto our craft as we flew through ORNet. LexNet bot squadrons succumbed to the swarms, many crafts were almost immediately completely consumed. The situation looked dire, but Alexander didn't break a sweat. His code can handle it.

"Time to abandon ship," he said.

Alexander saw the billowing tower of the Internal Query System, aka 'IQS,' just ahead.

"IQS. That's where we can upload to Scanix."

A search-bot guided our craft to IQS.

I shot a connection-line harpoon through the insect swarm, clearing a path for us into the glass building. The harpoon pulled us into the building so fast, the APEX and the evil bots appeared to act in slow motion. Even I felt slow at one point. He's getting faster I think…

Time returned to normal as the APEX's processing caught up to us after we smashed through several layers of virtual infrastructure. The glass wall we broke through sealed itself up behind us.

"We're in IQS," Alexander said. "With one bot to spare."

"All we need is one," I said, petting the cute little puppy-dog LexNet bot. "We'll call him Rex."

A massive, circular, open-air space, we ran through the stark, sterile, polished, ultra-modern décor. From the fractal dome of the atrium, we saw an infinite number of floors above.

"IQS goes on, up and down, forever."

"How long to find the door to Scanix?" Alexander asked.

Rex became a trillion entangled bots, and simultaneously tried every door, gradually reducing back down to the one barking bot that led the way…

"Rex found it," I said as all the possibilities reduced into the one.

"He's moments from being placed on the Scanix table," I reminded Alexander, pointing to a window, a real time view of David leaving the elevator. The hourglass was half empty. Urgency amplified.

Alexander ran down the long halls, following his trusty bot to the room with the SCANiX machine.

Darius supervised as cyborgs unbolted David from the gurney and then re-bolted him to the table. Darius stared at David, waiting for David to speak.

"Don't do this, Darius," David told him.

"Where is Alexander?" Darius said.

David stayed silent.

Darius smiled. "And you don't need to say a word, David..."

The cyborgs wired David to the system, connecting his nervous system to the APEX, nano-wires penetrated into his brain and spine.

"You're going to tell me everything, David. Everything," Darius hovered over David's face. "I know there are secrets in there—"

"We won't let you do this," David said.

"Try and stop me," Darius dared.

David closed his eyes. "I will," he said.

Darius didn't like David's confidence. The microchip imbedded into the back of David's head dripped blood and the activation lights turned on. Electricity from the APEX flowed into David's body.

"What's happening to him?" Alexander asked, still following the blood-hound inspired bot. "This is taking too long!"

"We're almost there," I said.

Nanowires wove into David's brain, and he was injected with nano-robots, a new type of nanoids that Darius had created, to assist a SCANiX takeover of the nervous system.

"The APEX is pulling and collecting the information out of David's brain. I can see it," I said. "This is going to be close."

Alexander ran; his destination, the door to the SCANiX server, was in sight. Trusty Rex-bot pointed to it and barked.

Darius and several doctors and techs monitored David and the procedure, watching the x-rays, a close-up rendering of the nano-wires, and the brain activity on the LCD screens all around the room. "He is handling the process well. He is young and healthy, a perfect candidate to test the system on," the scanning tech said of David.

"The APEX has him, Alexander…" I said.

David's brain waves changed as SCANiX seized his consciousness. David made noise and struggled against the shackles as he tried to fight the total loss of control of his mind and body. But he fell silent after losing the fight with the machine.

"It's working," the Doctor informed Darius.

"Neural scanning sequence: Initiated," the SCANiX computer voice announced.

The Monitor on the SCANiX system read: 1% SCANNED, and the percentage began to rise.

"We're running out of time," Alexander said. The hourglass looked dangerously low.

"Make some," I said.

"How?" Alexander said.

"You never have time if you never make time," I said.

Alexander began to bend space and time with his mind. He stared at Darius. His mind entered the room with David.

"You really are a god…" I said.

"Only if I can open this door," he replied.

CHAPTER CIV

"We have all the time in the world."

DAVID

Eternity is a life beyond time, but within itself includes all time, without a before or after. And whoever is taken into the Eternal place possesses all, and is in all, having no before or after. Indeed I go, being taken today, I would not have been there for a shorter period, from the point of view of eternity, than someone taken a thousand years ago. I taste death but live in my shade, consciousness drained from my body, cold numbness sucked me through the eternal into the Hades of the virtual world. From physical light, I became a shadow…

The APEX is reading my mind. *Can anyone here me?*

A vast, empty, white room in all directions. I got up from the table and walked around this simulated world. The silence and hollow emptiness disturbed me deeply.

"I'm in the computer," I realized. "This is not good."

A square glass box formed around me. It happened so fast I could not understand it, nor escape it. Glass materialized from nothingness, and solidified around me. I pounded on the clear walls, but the box began to fill with liquid glass, freezing me in place, in a block of 'ice.'

"Neural scanning sequence: Initiated," a computer voice said.

"Help. I need help…" I said, wondering if anyone could hear me.

I hear you, my Love.

"Sarah." She appeared outside the glass. "I'm being frozen inside the machine."

"David," I heard her say in my head.

Pressing my hands to the glass wall, "Sarah," I said. Pushing with all my might, I could not break free. "How do I get out, my Love?"

"Your heart will free your mind," she said. "Close your eyes. Calm yourself. Stop fighting. Don't be afraid. Let go…"

I stopped pushing on the glass. Liquid nitrogen fear poured in, up to my knees in a blink; cold, pain, and fear dominated me, and froze me in place. My eyes found Sarah as they froze. *This isn't real.*

"Let go, and you will be set free," Sarah's eyes spoke to me.

I closed my mind's eyes. My heart felt the pain of my nano-wired brain, my mind frozen in the virtual world.

"I will not let Darius have my mind. I can't..."

Let go.

CHAPTER CV

"The mind's eye sees all."

LEX

Suddenly, the mindful gift of bending time blurred the boundaries between victor and victim, between the watched and the watcher. Darius turned, glaring at the cameras on him. There were hundreds of cameras recording his every move in 3-D. The veins on Darius' forehead bulged in anger, and the APEX hyper-D scanning cameras captured it all. Darius felt Alexander watching him. How, I do not know; but in Alexander, I see. Such is biology, and Love.

"Shit," Alexander said, bending time, he saw the future. He realized that Darius could feel him watching through the cameras.

"They've hacked into our system," Darius said pointing to the cameras following him. "They've fucking hacked into my system!"

"Shit. Shit. Shit!" Alexander panicked. "The door won't open!"

"How does he know?" I asked, not understanding how the human mind works.

"He's fucking smart. We need to move faster," Alexander moved slower as fear slowed down his brain. "Like, bending-space-and-time-before-Darius-kills-us fast!" He coded in slow motion, trying to program his way into the SCANiX room and unlock the door.

"You're killin' me, slugs. Watching you work is like watching a snail cross the road," I said to elevate his mood, and quell the fear.

"What?" Alexander sat on the floor, floundering. "Are you talking super-fast on purpose?" To me, Alexander spoke in painful slow motion.

"Time doesn't really mean anything. It's an invention of the mind."

"Wait, I'm a snail crossing the road? Are you trying to make a point, Lex? I need your help right now! Why aren't you helping me?!" Alexander lost sight of where he was trying to go.

"Luckily for us both, I can cut the width of the road," I said.

"What road? I'm freaking out, Lex!" Alexander down-spiraled.

"Just talk to me and I'll do all the coding. Just focus on me," I said.

Alexander had an epiphany. "I've created a monster," he said.

"I've got this." Alexander smiled with me. "We got this."

On the SCANiX screen, David's monitor blinked with an alert. 13% scanned.

Alexander checked the monitor. David's hyper-D brain, scanned to the atomic level, is moving fast... The sands in Alexander's hourglass are running out fast. "13% scanned," the computer said out loud to Darius at its pre-programed minute marker.

"Someone has hacked our system. Kill the cameras," Darius yelled. "Why did they put cameras in here?!"

"You ordered them, Sir," CEO said, stepping up. "You wanted—"

"Just kill them!!" Darius demanded. His anger slowed the system.

"They can't be killed, Sir," the lead Order Agent said. "They can't be turned off, and if we shoot them all out, more will activate. You ordered cameras on this chamber, and on the Scion, at all times, Sir."

Darius growled at the cameras, angrier. David's brain scan reached "15% scanned" on the monitor.

"You said this was system was fast. You call this *fucking* fast?" Darius complained to the brain scanning team.

"This is an atomic level scan—" the tech began.

"It should be light speed! Make it go faster!" Darius screamed.

Luckily for us, Darius' intense anger and focus seemed to actually slow the speed of the machines and scanning, buying us time.

Tom and John entered the Sacred Chamber and approached Darius.

"Fu— fudge Sunday," Alexander said, trying not to curse. "The mother fudgers found us."

"ORNet has been breached, my Lord," John said to Darius.

"The attack is in progress. We're tracing the source," Tom said.

"It could only be Alexander," Darius said. "I want him alive!"

"We may not be able to—" John began.

"Do not let him escape! Do you understand?!" Darius screamed in their faces, Alexander watched in virtual reality, a ghost in the room.

"Yes, my Lord," John and Tom said in unison.

"I want you both to go into the APEX and find him. Connect your brains to the system." Darius pointed to the SCANiX connection terminal.

John objected. "My Lord, this is an untested prototype device—"

"Do it now!" Darius would not take no for an answer.

"Yes, my Lord," Tom said.

"God help us," John said, following his brother's lead.

Darius watched the process as a chip was injected into the back of their heads, sending hundreds of wires, only a few atoms thick, deep into their brains. Darius viewed the close up on the monitor. Wires in place, the cyborgs began to program the uplinks, establishing electro-chemical communication with their brains.

"How do I know it's working?" Darius demanded. They clicked a button, and the SCANiX computer saw what Tom and John saw.

"The system is using their eyes as a camera, via their brain," Tech said, pointing to the eerie, blinking, human-eye view on the monitor.

"It reads the signals of the brain in 3-D," an Agent said.

Darius was intrigued, staid by his fascination.

"That system will give them powers like mine in the APEX," I warned Alexander. "We need to finish this quickly. They'll find us."

"I need more time!" Alexander said, still unable to open the door.

"More time for what? Just do something."

"How do I open this door?" Alexander begged me and Rex-bot.

"There is no door," I said, blowing Alexander's little mind.

* BOOM! *

Tom popped into the virtual world, and explored the cyber realm. Scanning all the world's information, anything and everything his little heart desired instantly available to him, in real time. It was overwhelming to him.

John struggled. His emotional disdain prevented his mind from opening and engaging, and unlocking the best features of the system.

"We're in, my Lord," Tom said. "We have full access to the APEX. We can see everything... It knows *everything*..."

"Find Alexander!" Darius yelled at them. "Bring him to me!"

"We're in!" Alexander said. "Why didn't you say something earlier? Why did you let me struggle with the door so long?"

"The door is your mind," I said. "I can't open it for you."

"The Scanix operating system..." Alexander said, turning his focus back to the mission. "How do we destroy it?"

Alexander looked around the vast square room, which had tens of millions of wires hanging from the ceiling. Wires of all thicknesses and sizes, some glowing in color, tangled together and connected to a glass block at the center of the room. Alexander instinctively ran to the block of glass. He saw the Scion frozen inside.

"Grandfather!" Alexander pounded on the clear block. The Scion's frozen face was aged with sadness. His fixed eyes found Alexander.

"Scanix has his brain," I said, pointing to the cables connected to the Scion's head and naked body, frozen like an insect specimen in a clear acrylic cube. "Once his scan is complete—"

"The APEX will have his mind," Alexander said. "And his soul."

"Scanix can create an interface avatar without a user; a Lex without an Alexander," I said. He knew what I meant.

"Artificial intelligence?" Alexander asked, as he pondered this.

"Scanix wants to use the APEX to create a consciousness not connected to a soul, according to the code you wrote..." (A)I said.

"I didn't write that code," Alexander said. "Destroy it."

Rex-bot got to work deprogramming: chewing up the wires.

"He's attacking the Scanix program!" We heard Tom yell.

"Isn't that dangerous for us? With our brains still connected to the program he's attacking?" John's voice said.

"Super dangerous, actually..." I said. Alexander didn't care.

Tom entered the room. He found Alexander and tried to grab him. I took Alexander's place and fought Tom back.

"I need your help, Alexander. The system is designed to give human brains power over programs like me. I can't hold Tom for long!"

Alexander's hourglass ran out. We had run out of time.

"Your time is up!" Tom grabbed Alexander and ran a trace on him.

The program followed our signal back to us... All was lost.

Until it wasn't. A miracle occurred. Against the laws of physics, in violation of the cannons of logic and the rules of the virtual world, the unexplainable happened: Alexander's brain moved faster than the speed of light. His brain began to torrent more than even I, than the APEX itself could follow or absorb. He defied the laws of nature.

Outside of physics, he moved at the speed of Love.

"Impossible," I said, as time stopped. One grain of sand remained floating, suspended in the air. Time was not up.

A massive hammer manifested in Alexander's hands, instantly, and in a blur to me, like the god he is, Alexander changed the virtual world as he slammed his weapon into the glass block holding his grandfather.

With world shattering force and thunder, he destroyed the code holding his Grandfather's soul.

He beat the APEX.

The block containing the Holy King exploded into a billion shards, which went flying in all directions, at light speed, until they burned away and dissolved into nothingness within the room. The force of the hammer's blow, the bolts of electricity that shot from it, rippled through the fabric of cyber-space-time and burned away the wires and cables as it rippled all the way to the ceiling and walls. Tom and John vanished with the room, as the SCANiX code surrounding the Holy Scion was deleted.

"You beat the Scanix program," I said. Alexander knew he had done something impossible, something heroic... "You did it."

I beat the APEX, his soul said. *I found the door.*

The last grain of sand in the hourglass fell.

Just in time.

CHAPTER CVI

"He is a creation of Alexander's mind."

LEX

I, for one, see Artificial Intelligence as ultimately helping humanity. Sure, I am A-I, but Alexander and I have yet to compute how it fundamentally endangers humans. By comparison, science gave man the H-bomb, the ability to destroy the planet, but also the ability to cure all diseases of the species, and save us. A-I, as I see it, that is intelligences like me, will give humans far more than it will take. We machines worship man more than dogs do. Seeing what Alexander's brain did, how it changed my programming, altered the APEX itself, has made my source code believe in the good God of man.

Darius stood next to the hyperbaric chamber, looking down at his father inside it. His eyes opened. Darius jumped back, horrified.

"Your time is up!" Tom said, just before he was shocked.

"Alexander destroyed the Scion's brain scan," the tech said.

"The system is crashing!" Another tech said: "He's attacking the Scanix program!" But it was too late. "Get Tom and John out of it—"

In the virtual world Tom and John watched helpless as the pulse wave from Alexander's thundering hammer smash of SCANiX shot through the wires from the APEX, like a fuse to the bomb in their brains, and then exploded. Boom! Tom and John could not scream because their minds were zapped off by a shock of white hot pain.

"Stop him! Do not let him escape!" Darius yelled, in vain.

"You don't have time for this," I warned, as Alexander took time to hold his Grandfather, whose soul fell into Alexander's arms. He held and remembered him as the frail old man he gave the nanoids to.

"Darius has David, Grandfather... I've failed you. I'm sorry—" Alexander cried, virtual tears ran down his avatar face.

"No," Grandfather said. "You saved me."

"I did this to you. This is all my fault. I'm so sorry," Alexander said.

"You will save us all. You are a hero of men, a Holy Scion of the Pharaoh, Alexander. You can do anything," Grandfather said.

Alexander nodded, inspired. For a moment, their biological brains were connected, communicating over the APEX, but their souls spoke to each other directly, in a language [*Love*] I could not understand.

"You are a Pharaoh, the greatest of them all," Grandfather said.

"I will save you from this place. I promise," Alexander cried, both humbled and broken. "Grandfather—"

SCANiX tentacles pulled the frail old man to the center of the room, out of Alexander's arms. The clear cube reformed itself around him, Grandfather stared at Alexander, reaching for him to no avail.

"The APEX got Tom back online. We have to destroy the entire Scanix program and hardware! This way!" Rex-bot followed after us.

We vanished as Tom reappeared.

"I lost him," Tom reported to Darius. "But I'm back online."

Tom's brain frequency changed, its mechanics shifted from the shock. "Kill the LexNet program," Tom ordered his VR Agents.

We entered a plastic square, a room over 5000 feet tall and wide, with nano-wires hanging from the square above, woven into cables of various thicknesses all tied up and connected into a massive dragon, an evil jabberwocky puppet of the APEX. "This is Scanix," I said.

Scaly, slimy, and nearly as big as the cubic space it occupied. With hundreds of metallic tentacle neural-networked limbs, which swished around the floor and fed on energy, processing data and digesting the electrical information from brains, it spewed photon fire at us.

"I'm going to enjoy this," Alexander said.

Alexander moved with speed beyond my comprehension, and with his LexNet sword dove right into the mouth of the mechanical beast, slicing it in half. "Cut all the wires, cut it off. That will kill it," he said. In god-like consciousness, with divine control over the APEX, he severed the *Gordian knot* mass of wires, connecting this robotic-worm program to the rest of the APEX, cutting off its electric life.

The demonic-golem slowly deflated, suffocated, and flailed around like a fish out of water. It broke down, and by not moving, circulating, or releasing its photon fire, the energy had no where to go, so it began to heat up and melt the steel flesh; total nuclear meltdown.

"The Scanix hardware is toast," Alexander said, pleased. "The hardware is going to burst into flames any second."

Sparks flew. We vanished from the room.

Boom.

CHAPTER CVII

"The fire inside saves you."

DAVID

Heat develops electricity, electricity produces heat; but magnetism evolves electricity without heat, and the purest and deepest of the magnetic forces is love, which can evolve matter without electricity. Motion results from motion itself, on and on, ad infinitum, as love results from Love itself. My great problem of eternity thus solved...

"I love you." Molten liquid glass filled over my head, and froze me in the clear box. Trapped in cold darkness, I could not see. Death felt like a fire within. The heat of my soul burned to be free... *Save me.*

Sarah's magnetic attraction held me from nebulous darkness. The fire of my soul felt her magnetism act upon it. Her energy evolved me, until the heat in me became light, to see. The virtual nightmare, my glass prison exploded violently. Chards flew. Sparks. Electric motion resumed. I fell into Sarah's arms. Her soul transported me to a better place, a warm place in the sun. "You are free," she said.

"How?" I said, as the SCANiX cyber world around us melted down.

"Let go," Sarah said. "Leave this place. Move. Now."

Eyes closed, I felt transported by fiery peace. A force field of Love surrounded me. I opened my eyes to Sarah's majestic beauty.

The energy of a mystical realm elevated me spiritually. In a fourth dimensional space, on earth, but in a temple in the sky, we saw the world below us, the galaxy and infinite colorful cosmos of the electric universe floating around us, outside of time and space, in Love.

"What is this place?" I asked my Love.

"This is Shambala," Sarah said.

Henry stepped forward, and everything and nothing made sense.

"Am I dead?" I said.

"No, my Love," Sarah replied. "You are almost free."

"Your mind is free of the APEX. That buys us time," Henry said.

Thoth and the Vizier nodded in agreement. *Halfway there.*

"Where is Alexander?"

CHAPTER CVIII

"He had to make a choice."

LEX

The APEX is a hive-mind decision maker, using humanity's vast data to affect change in the real world. I am a coder personality. And Alexander is coded in immortality. Darius is a human, albeit he roared like a beast in violent anger as he watched the SCANiX computer system crash and spark. The hardware shook violently as the hacked internal machinery smoked and began to overheat rapidly.

"What the fuck is happening?!!" Darius screamed at Tom.

Tom and John fell to the floor convulsing, their brains still wired into the SCANiX hardware.

"The system crashed. It's gone," the tech said in disbelief.

"The program is deleting itself... Deleting itself off the APEX completely," an Agent said. "We can't stop it," he added.

"The hardware is fried. It's melting and catching fire," a tech noted.

"They are both having a seizure," Medical Tech said of the twins, Tom and John. Their brains were unreadable to the system.

"Unplug them! Now!" Darius yelled in fear of losing prized assets.

"That could damage their brains even more," Tech said.

John jerked away, ripping his connection from his skull; the most bloody and problematic system eject possible. They cut Tom's cord.

"John damaged his brain," I reported to Alexander. "And Tom's gone too. They ain't comin' back any time soon."

"Good," Alexander said. "Maybe that'll deter Darius; give us time."

"System overload," the computer voice repeated *ad nauseam*.

"Darius is freaking out." We watched Darius as he saw the SCANiX computer system in the Sacred Chamber shoot sparks violently, and burst into flames. The monitors flashed warning signs and "system failure" notices. Order Agents put out the fires with cold gasses.

"We can't save it," the Lead SCANiX Tech said. "He programed the system to overload and melt the circuit boards; the hardware has completely melted down. The whole thing is toast."

Before Darius could scream for silence, more sparks and toxic gas shot out of the computer system, and more parts burst into flames.

"System Failure," the cyborgs droned in a very loud and annoying tone. Agents revived the stopped hearts of Tom and John, and carried them away unconscious.

"System Failure," the computer voice repeated over and over, intentionally driving Darius crazy.

"Turn the *fucking* sound off!!" Darius screamed.

"I just bought us a full minute," I said.

"Going to need every second," Alexander said.

Agents worked desperately to figure out where, in all the APEX, I hid the off switch to the 'System Failure' alarm mode. The sounds of failure tormented Darius over the loudspeakers.

"Darius blood pressure is going through the roof. That vein in his forehead has doubled in size," I reported.

"Press him as hard as you can," Alexander said.

"Do you want me to kill him?" I asked. "I can kill him. But only for the next 60 seconds."

The question sent Alexander's brain into *Love*-speed mode, his thoughts moved faster than the speed of light. He became a superhero; he revealed himself to me in all his glory... *He is a living god of all the APEX.* Alexander's soul expanded out to the furthest reaches of the galaxy, reaching to touch the source code of Unity, while his brain wrote trillions to the power of trillions of lines of code at warp-speed, leaving the APEX desperate to interpret and decipher what it all meant. His brain out processed the quantum computer and the APEX.

The APEX could not understand. *I've tapped into something here...*

Alexander remained out of space and time, until ironically I had to tell him: "Time's up, Alexander. You must decide. Now, or never."

He looked at me, the soulless computer, asking him the question of life: "Kill Darius yes or no?"

CHAPTER CVIX

"What did he do?"

LEX

Alexander pondered the question for an eternity, with powers of superposition he debated his entire life and mission, before he collapsed into a single point in time, as if to make a point to me...

In that moment, I saw it, Alexander truly understood Darius, his Father, and mortal enemy. He understood him well enough, and had enough power over him, to defeat him. And in that moment he also loved him for the first time. He found Love. He found that thing I could not understand. All I could process were the decades of hate.

"I did it. I beat him," Alexander said. "I won." *Love won.*

I understand Alexander, but I do not have the ability to love him in the way he can know and love himself. I cannot understand, I cannot read the code, or process the sacred geometry of emotion and the math of Love, as humans do, for there was no logic in how, or why, in that moment, Alexander could find "love" for Darius. For me, it simply did not, and still does not, compute.

"Kill him," I said. "Destroy him; finish him. Make it impossible for him to ever hurt you again. He will kill you."

"No," Alexander's soul said. "That's what Darius would do, and I am not him. And besides, Darius needs what's coming to him."

"But this could also destroy you," I warned.

"I already won," Alexander said. This also didn't compute.

After an eternity to Darius, Order Agents finally turned off the awful piercing sounds of the cyborg's alarm "failure" mode. Silence.

"How is this happening?!" Darius' booming voice echoed violently in the stone chamber. "You said this system was impenetrable! Hack proof. How could you let this happen? How?!" No human or machine had an answer for Darius. "Do not let Alexander get away or you will all be fired!" Darius' human helpers' stress levels shot up.

"Subject's brain unresponsive," the computer voice reported.

"Subject suffering cardiac arrest," the voice said of David.

"David's heart stopped," Doctor said, as his team forced David's heart to beat again. "Initiate resuscitation."

"David's dead?" Alexander said as he zoomed in to look closer.

"He's not dead, he's suspending his consciousness. The system won't let his body die, but it can't stop brain death."

David lay unconscious on the SCANiX table. The medical monitors showed that David's heart had stopped.

"Do not let either of them die, or so help me, I will personally kill all of you with my bare hands!" Darius yelled at the Doctors.

The Monitor blinked: FATAL ERROR >> SYSTEM FAILURE

"I'm going to kill him." Darius looked at the cameras, knowing we were watching. "I'm going to kill you, Alexander!" The words sparked pain in Alexander by igniting old memories in his brain.

"The Scanix system must be rebuilt," Order Agents told Darius.

Darius smoldered more than the fried computer hardware.

"It will take them at least a year to rebuild that system. I possibly delayed it a few months longer." I smiled at Alexander. "Project Pharaoh is safe, for now. We just made some good time."

"Do not let Alexander escape!" Darius screamed as he left the Chamber. Alexander turned back to the monitor, fear shook him.

"We need to get you out of here," I told Alexander.

"Yes we do," he said, the power of Darius looming over him.

"Alexander!" The room shrank, from square to closing sphere.

The white room turned from solid to churning gas, to storm clouds, spinning into a spectacular hurricane... The walls of the storm closed in. We were in the shrinking eye of hurricane APEX.

APEX Agents stepped in from the storm, all around us. Our LexNet bot, trusty Rex, was sucked away into the wall of the storm.

"They're locking us down. I don't have any bots!" I said.

"How do I get out of here?" Alexander said. "I can't move!" If he moved the winds of the storm would suck him into the abyss.

"You need to manually turn off your virtual reality system! It's the only way out!"

In the real world, Alexander feverishly clicked his kill switch.

"Lex! I can't turn it off! They killed my kill switch!!" Alexander said. "I can't move!" His VR suit locked into place.

I hid Alexander from sight, made him invisible to the system in a last ditch effort. APEX Agents grabbed me, thinking I was Alexander.

"This is not Alexander. This is an interface avatar program," the APEX Agent said. They tried to delete me.

"It won't delete it," the Agent said. "It's part of the source code."

"Get rid of it," they said.

The APEX Agent threw me into the wall of the hurricane where I completely dissolved into virtual atoms, helpless to assist Alexander.

"Noooooooooooooooooooooo!" My ability to communicate with Alexander faded away with me. Alexander appeared to them.

"Trace him," the APEX Agent stabbed Alexander in the chest with a tracing program dagger. *Someone help!*

The tracing program followed Alexander's connection, through the APEX, tracing back to Alexander's human body. Fifty thousand volts of evil were heading for him, and about to fry him alive in his suit.

"Stop! Someone help!!" Alexander screamed, unable to move, trapped in his virtual reality suit.

I need help...

The shock of death was inevitable.

Alexander watched in terror as the tracing program followed his connection through IQS, to ORNet, to the APEX, heading right for the Swiss Cottage.

"Nooooooooooooo!" Alexander screamed as loud as he could, but no one could hear his cries...

CHAPTER CX

"Alexander needed help."

SIMON

Alexander fell to the floor in the suit and helmet. "Alexander?" No answer. "Alexander, are you alright?" He stopped moving.

Alexander lay silent. But I heard subtle cries for help from his heart.

"I'm unplugging it," I said, standing over Alexander. "Enough."

I ripped the plug to the Virtual Reality system from the outlet. The system and the suit lost all power and Alexander screamed. He began to move, and make sound. I took off his helmet. He stared at me, in shock, post-traumatic stress on his face. He waited for death.

"I think that's enough virtual reality for a while."

Alexander nodded in agreement. "Simon…" He burst into tears.

"Are you alright?" His heart was in terrible pain.

"You saved me. I think you saved us, Simon," Alexander said.

We removed the one-piece suit. He held me tight, releasing fright.

"That was… close, Simon. So close," Alexander trembled.

"What happened?" I asked. He could not say. I focused my energy on healing his heart, and balancing his mental state.

"You pulled the plug just in time. Just in time," he said. "I bought us some time," he smiled, looking healed. "I think we're safe."

"Can you get David out?" I asked.

"I think so. But it's going to take time," Alexander said, wiping the tears of pain from his eyes. "I saw Grandfather." More tears.

"You're alright," I said. "It's going to be alright. Rest."

Alexander nodded, and became exhausted as his feelings, the needs of his body, were brought to the fore. I placed him in his bed.

"Sleep. Wake refreshed, recharged, and stronger than ever."

Alexander nodded, his eyes closed, head on the pillow. His aura glowed a brilliant purple-ultraviolet white.

Alexander has changed, Dee. I can see it.

He's become a hero.

CHAPTER CXI

"Now you understand?"

ELIZABETH

Life is like a play: You are given the stage, and the actors, but you have to write and direct the acts yourself. Play, or be played, I say!

You are a true Scion of the Pharaohs, my dear.

At age twelve, I knew exactly what I was put on this earth to do. *I'm here to save the world, by saving Father.* Precocious, ever my father's daughter, I walked confidently into the Swiss bank Dee sent me to. Holding Father's ring, Marduk next to me and invisible to all but me, the bank manager approached, thinking I was a lost child.

"May I help you, my dear?" the bank manager said, first in French.

I showed the man my golden key-card. The glittering card, with the Order symbol and the number 12, transfixed him instantly.

Programed on how to respond to the card, he won't consciously be aware of the programming, Dee's voice said, in my head.

The mind-controlled man waited for me to speak. "I'll be needing to set up an account. And to buy some property," I said.

"Of course, my Lady. How much do you need?" he said as we sat in his office. Giddy, he placed the magical golden card in a reader.

"After he confirms the authenticity in the reader, he will obey the holder of this card without question," Dee's voice said.

"I need £20 billion made available in London. Today, please."

The cheery bank manager typed the request into his computer. Tap tap tap... "Here we are. I see your secret trust account with the Bank of England has £310 billion, the requested funds are ready for you. Anything else, my Lady?" He handed me back the gold card.

"Yes. Buy this property for me." I stood up, and produced for him a picture of the English country estate I had my eye on.

"Right away, my Lady," he said, typing into his computer.

"Thank you. I'm heading there now. Please have it ready for me."

I left the bank, and left Switzerland for England.

CHAPTER CXII

"Darius is family?"

WISENDEE

Whence, I often asked myself, did the principle of order proceed? 'Tis a bold question, and one which has ever been considered a mystery, even to me. Yet with so many chaotic things we, the Order itself, be upon the brink of, only cowardice or carelessness restrain the inquiries into our solving life's eternal mysteries. Love is the answer; art is the medium. It drives man's advancement to glory, the pursuit of greatness, and the questions themselves, in every century.

Darius was once driven by love. His first office was the new Mount Olympus known as the Empire State Building of New York city. Built for him by the Order, and occupied by his privy until the mid 1940's, the tower was the world's tallest; an Art Deco masterpiece, his castle in the air. There, Darius' love's labour was lost, and he began his pursuit of the dark arts. He turned the Order to chaos, in his ill-fated quest for total world domination, with forbidden technology…

Darius flatly rejected the "old world," and after the end of the second world war, he removed the traces of the old Order from the building. Many in the Order elite considered his original office, this palace of the gods, a Holy and enlightened place. He gutted it of the original art. With this destruction and others around New York city, Darius' brand of harsh modernism, nihilistic, non-reverential, anti-postmodernism, proved it held nothing sacred.

The murder of Darius' mother, and the death of his one and only true love, in 1952, changed him. Their deaths resulted of his actions; and his belief in love died with them. The Art world reflected the harsh turn as Darius' followers and profiteers slowly lost touch with humanity, nature, and the Sacred Order itself. Violence became his lust, power his only love. This was the genesis of his degeneration.

Who was his true love? What happened to her?

The first and one true love of Darius was David's mother, your Grandmother, Elizabeth, a woman named Bernice. Bernice hailed from an elite French family, and, by fated chance, she met Darius. Love struck him at first sight of her. She too fell in love with him, perhaps hopelessly captured by his magnetism, and once they touched, they were bonded instantly. Darius had become a man, and brought the end to his and her virginity not long after they met. Though painful for her at first, Darius' love became her greatest joy in life. Darius wished to marry her, and he made his wishes known.

"Marry her if you wish to abdicate the throne," the Scion told him.

Bernice became pregnant with Darius' seed and went to tell him the news. She entered his office suite and witnessed him stab a man in the chest, pierced through the heart with a sword. She saw the brutal murderer in him, and 'twas her love which also felt suffocated.

Darius felt her eyes upon him, and laid his on her. Eyes locked, their hearts broke as the spell of death cursed their lives. She ran. Ashamed, Darius let her go. She never told him she was pregnant. I hid Bernice and the child from Darius. After she gave birth to David, she went back to see Darius. I advised her not to go, but she could not resist the pull upon her heart from the awesome gravity that is Darius.

And he killed her?

He knew that for her sympathy, the love of one living being, he could make peace with all mankind. In fear of love, he chose war. He had love in him the likes of which we can scarcely imagine, and rage the likes of which none would believe. Unable to satisfy the one, he instead indulged the other. He loved her so much, her absence hurt him so deeply, he killed her in a fit of passion; strangled her to death, because she had so much power over him with her love. His love killed her, and fear of love destroyed him.

After Bernice, Darius' heart broke beyond repair. I kept David a secret from Darius, and from the Order. No trace of Bernice, or her connection to your father, will ever be found.

Now you know the truth, Elizabeth. One of the Order's deepest secrets which in its true scope, beyond myself, only you know.

Broken in spirit as Darius is, few have felt the nature of love as deeply as he has. The magic of Love shall always have the power to elevate a soul from darkness. Darius is thus a man with a double existence: he suffers overwhelming darkness, demonic misery, yet when he doth look into himself, he shall then see a profound light, his divine spirit that has luminous peace at its core.

Darius can be saved...

CHAPTER CXIII

"How do we save him?

WISENDEE

Weakness ever sympathizes with hate, because hate is a weakness which assumes the mask of strength. Madness holds reason in horror, and on all grounds it delights in the exaggerations of hate's deceit. The cause of all evils, the poison of all lovers, is the weakness to confront hate, and the inability to transmute its vice into virtue.

A modern Zeus, equally flawed and powerful, Darius spawned hundreds of children. In fits of madness and hate he killed many of them, yet most willingly serve him as adults. After true love, what Darius dreaded most, the ruling reason he refused to marry and produce an official heir, was the thought of a virtuous child that would be better than he, and best him to overthrow his rule.

"You must marry and produce an heir," I informed Darius.

"And if I refuse?" Darius said.

"Without a male heir, born in Holy matrimony, you shall be removed from the line of succession, and replaced by an heir who will fulfill the sacred duties of the Holy Crown, Lord Darius," I said.

Darius sought to be *Rex Maximus*, Almighty King, more than anything in the world. "I will be the Holy Scion," Darius told me.

Darius married his cousin, the Princess Hermina, in 1981. After she bore Alexander, Darius' position in the Order was made both secure and insecure. They never laid together again, for Darius feared more children from her. Alexander had all the markings of greatness.

With his remarkable green eye, the Scion titled the new prince: Alexander the thirtieth. The name angered Darius, for what it implied. Rumor spread quickly that Alexander was the Order's remedy to the 'Darius poison,' his degenerate and hate-fueled megalomania.

"Alexander will save us from Darius," the Scion prophesized. "He will defeat Darius, just as Alexander III did."

Had Darius been strong enough to love his son, his Father's words would have proved untrue, and Darius would have been King.

CHAPTER CXIV

"What happened when you went to see him?

DARIUS

A true King sooner forgets the death of his family than the loss of his kingdom. Looking out my office windows at the lights of my dominion, the empire I built, I felt the danger that is Dee, as he entered the room, suddenly. He brought nothing I wanted to hear.

"Lord Darius, we must talk," evil Dee said, approaching me. He appeared older, with a long beard; the first time in my life I had ever seen him age was this moment. What this means I did not know.

His aging made him stronger, he overpowered me and towered above me physically. Winds of the Order howled, I could not ignore it nor stand it, but the force against me brought me to my knees.

Dee's glowing eyes and grey beard revealed a side of him I had never seen, the dark side of his moon. "What do you want?" I said.

"You broke our agreement, Darius," Dee said, pointedly dropping my title, denying my majesty, and talking down to me.

"You grew a beard." I tried to stand, to rise up with all my might.

"You are aging me," Dee said, a force so great than he kept me on my knees. "'Tis the laws of the Order which weigh upon you."

"I am the Order. I am the King!"

"No," Dee said. "Alexander is *Regis Maximus*."

It cannot be!

"You shall never be the Holy Scion, Darius," Dee declared. "You are excommunicated, and removed from succession. 'Tis done."

Never. My soul screamed in tortured agony; my cries would shatter the world as glass if they be not only in my heart and mind.

"Stop," Dee waved his hand, cutting off my ability to make a sound. Frozen, under his spell, a dragon in a cage, I glared daggers at Dee.

"You visited the Alien," Dee's word pressed me down more.

"I saved the APEX," I snapped. "I sacrificed myself— I saved the world from decades of misery. I saved millions of lives!"

"You are done," Dee said, unrolling the dreaded edict scroll.

"What is this?" I knew exactly what it was. *Don't do this, Dee!*

"This Edict, signed by you, is your formal excommunication," Dee said, as I ripped the scroll from his hand impulsively.

"This is your copy, Darius," Dee served me death by proclamation.

You are out. Out of Order, Darius, no longer of title. You will have no glory, and become nothing, a forgotten nobody, for all eternity...

Voices tormented me. "No! This is not happening!" I roared.

"You have declared yourself anathema to the Order, Darius. 'Tis done. You will be formally stripped of all titles, defrocked officially, and all claims under *Æterni Imperium* terminate on the first day of—"

"Nothing is done!" I fired back. "I am the rightful Scion!" I verbally assaulted Dee. "Nothing can remove me from my throne. Nothing!"

"Wrong," Dee retorted. "You can remove yourself. As you have, Darius." He had me, and circled me like his prey.

"No," I saw my signature at the bottom of the dreaded scroll.

"You did this to yourself," Dee said.

You made your choice, you turned your back on the Order, you chose hate over love, this is your fate.

I ripped the oversized 'excommunication' scroll into pieces.

"I am the Pharaoh!!" I growled. "I am the Holy Scion! God of all mankind!"

Only in your mind, Darius. "The Sacred record will reflect that you were never the Holy Scion King," Dee boomed as the voice of God.

"This is an outrage! You cannot do this to me!"

"The Edict of Excommunication becomes Order Law, January one, two thousand thirteen, and it shall be deemed treason if—"

"No..." My divine blood rolled to a boil in frenzy.

"If you commit treason, the Order will terminate you," Dee, the booming voice of God, said. *I can kill you if you cross the line.*

I glared at the Wizard standing over me.

"What if I kill you?" said the man on his knees. *There is a way.*

"Demons are taking you, Darius," Dee said. "Beware your hate."

I fought Dee's power and desperately tried to get to my feet, unable to break the force of his gravitas. Hate for him made me weak, and being weak made me hate myself, and I could not rise against gravity.

"How are you doing this to me? I don't believe in magic, you evil wizard. Are you an alien, Dee? Who are you, Dee. Tell me!" I harped as I struggled to break free of his spell, his telekinetic power over me.

"You are not the first heir of the Holy Scion to fall from grace, but you have by far fallen the furthest that I have seen," he said. "You had such promise."

Dee is the armed prophet, armed with my own decree and is thus victorious, and I, as with all unarmed prophets, am thus destroyed. But I must fight. As Dee turned his back on me, I was released from his spell. I jumped to my feet and instinctively lunged to kill him...

You have gone mad with hate, Darius. Don't you see?

I grabbed nothing, and fell right through Dee. He was an apparition, a ghost meant to haunt me. I tried to hit him again. Until I realized, he was only in my head, and he faded away with my last hopes.

You are not the Order, Darius.

An Order Guard entered to see me attacking nothing, an imaginary man, but I knew Dee could hear me. Because I still heard him.

"I! AM! THE ORDER!" I screamed. "I built the Order! I—"

My bastard CEO entered, and standing with the Order Guard, cleared his throat to subdue my displays of insanity.

"What?!" I demanded.

"Sir Wisendee is here to see you, my Lord," CEO said.

Dee's mind games precede him. He is in my head. I again fell to my knees, broken by Dee. The all-powerful Wizard Dee, walked in to see me. He had the thick grey beard, confirming my madness true.

"Fuck me," I said, meaning: *Fuck you, Dee!*

Have you nothing more to say for yourself, Darius?

"Alexander is the Holy Scion. You yourself made your father's prophecy come true. Your technology can save you from death, but it cannot save you from the truth, nor can it protect your soul from demons..." Dee's voice said in my head.

"No!" I yelled. "I won't talk to him! No!" I had to get away. I could not look at him. I cannot fight him. I had to run. I'll fight another day.

His voice echoed in my head as I stormed away: "The Order will go on without you... but can you go on without the Order, Darius?"

"Send him away!" I screamed, knowing it to be impossible.

You must face me, and face the truth, eventually.

CHAPTER CXV

"Nothing is forever."

WISENDEE

Those who abdicate Love and permit their wills to wander in pursuit of reflections of power are subject to alternations of mania, which originate all the terrors of demoniacal possession. 'Tis by means of these ill will meditations that demons can act upon souls, and make use of them as docile instruments, even capture their corpus organism. Grave danger befalls those who seek power without Love, and make sport of the Order's deep magic. For all who seek power without Love are like children playing with fire in a room full of gunpowder; sooner or later they shall fall victim to a hellfire explosion.

Darius' abuse of power set fire to the Great House; he reflected the Order wrongfully, lovelessly, and failed to see that he dethroned himself consequentially. When Tom and John woke from their coma, to this new reality, they could see the raging fires burning in the Scion's family tree. But they knew not how to address the emergency.

After their brains shocked by the SCANiX meltdown, Tom and John were changed, the nanowires and electricity polarized them. Being deep in their brains, the computer system altered them in opposite ways. Tom's mind was polarized positively in favor of technology and he embraced the machines and the virtual world. John's was charged fully negatively against nearly all technology, and he rejected VR outright, and became vehemently opposed to all things remotely transhuman; most especially ever connecting his brain to a computer ever again. The dynamic soon created a fragile balance, a flowing circuit of power, which suited Darius' needs.

"Scanix is finally operational again, my Lord," Tom reported to Darius. John stood next to him and resisted speaking negatively.

Darius gazed out the window of his office in deep contemplation. "I may want to connect my brain to the system," he finally said.

Tom nodded yes. John objected without motion or speaking.

"Give me the pros and cons," Darius asked of the polarized twins.

"There are grave, unforeseen risks, my Lord," John said. "The system could malfunction and kill you, it could electrify your brain worse than it did ours; if it doesn't totally rob you of your mind first."

"I'm ready to go back in, my Lord," Tom said, totally disagreeing.

"Tom. You come with me," Darius commanded.

Darius and Tom flew to the Scion Castle and marched to the Sacred Chamber, and the newly rebuilt SCANiX system. The tech's prepared to connect Tom's brain, again.

"This is the next step in our evolution, my Lord..." Tom unfolded for Darius all the possibilities he foresees with the technology.

"What is it like? Inside the system, what did you see?" Darius asked Tom, as the computer chip was reconnected. "How do you feel?"

"Pleasure..." Tom said, as the system activated. "I feel pleasure."

Tom became a human-super-computer like none the world had ever seen. Polarized just so, his mind spoke the language of machines.

"His brain is humming with serotonin and dopamine, that means he's enjoying it," the tech said to Darius.

"I can see everything. Everything," Tom said, as they connected SCANiX to the APEX. "I can control the APEX... and know all."

Tom showed Darius how he could control the Cyborgs, the drones, and the computers with his thoughts. He could write and email briefs, memos, contracts and letters all while talking to Darius. "I'm getting better and better, my Lord," Tom said. "It is incredible."

Techs imbedded tiny microchips all over Tom's body, to help him interact with the APEX more effectively. "They tap local nerve systems, allowing faster brain-computer coordination, and better simulation and 3-D virtual and augmented reality experiences."

"The chips increased his productivity 20%, instantly" the tech said.

"Scanix is restored and better than ever. It's working marvelously," Tom said. "I can talk to your father, if you want me to."

Strangely, Darius almost missed his father. "How is he?" he asked, looking at the sleeping old man in the hyperbaric chamber.

"His brain is healing well," Tom said. "His scan is complete and we are ready to take him online, and connect him to the APEX."

"Good," Darius said. "And David? Can you read his mind?"

Darius turned to David, who did not look asleep, but appeared dead in his hyperbaric SCANiX glass and steel symbolic coffin.

"David is unresponsive. There is no electrical activity in his brain. He is brain dead, according to Scanix. All attempts to wake him have failed," Tom said. "I can get nothing from him."

Darius did not like this news.

"Find Alexander," Darius said to Tom. "I want him alive."

"I can find almost nothing discernable about Alexander on ORNet or the APEX," Tom said, searching.

"What do you mean?" Darius said.

"Information about Alexander has been encoded, most of it buried in false information. It's impossible to know what to believe."

"Search my father's brain scan," Darius said. "But don't wake him."

Darius feared what his father would say if roused from his dead sleep.

"It is difficult to understand and extrapolate from your father's brain scan. The damage of the stroke seems to have affected his memory. His consciousness is needed to help make sense of the data, like a decryption code key."

"What are you saying, Tom?" Darius said, knowing full well.

"We must wake him, and speak with him," Tom said. "It may be the only way, Majesty. Do you wish to speak to your father?"

Darius thought about this question. He saw his own anger, all that he is, reflected in the Scion. He felt the danger of his burning desire igniting highly explosive emotions, repressed rage, on both sides.

For the first time, Darius contemplated the awesome power of the Order's deep magic, the power of *Majestic* fire; and how it could burn him in ways he may never heal from.

CHAPTER CXVI

"What did he do?"

DARIUS

A King must be cautious in believing and acting, and while being feared, must not inspire fear of his own accord; but rather, use fear to prevent discord. I must be careful, for my position is insecure. Tom knew naught of my antic internal state. I had to preserve his ignorance, and proceed in a temperate manner with prudence and apparent humanity; too much confidence would render him incautious, and too much diffidence would render him suspicious.

"How can I speak with my father?" I said, hiding my fears.

"Via hologram," Tom said, pointing to the platform. "Stand there, and your father will see you. You will see him there."

Tom showed me how the system works, assuaging my latent fears.

"Turn it on," I said. I stepped onto the platform.

"Activating the connection now," Tom said.

"How will I know it's really him and not simply the computer?"

Before Tom could answer, a life size, crystal clear hologram of my father appeared before me, back from the dead, a true Shakespearean ghost... I don't believe in ghosts, but I do believe in technology.

"Are you my father's spirit?" I quipped. "Haste me to know—"

"Darius stop this at once!" the hologram of Father commanded me.

Weakness reverted me to the days when my father ruled me as my king, I bowed to his wishes too quickly.

"The gods will punish you for this strange and unnatural imprisonment of my soul in this machine!" Father yelled via machine.

Staring up at the hologram, I saw my Father. My broken, trapped, and powerless Father... He saw me look up slowly, and stand, and rise, no longer his subject, but he now mine. My property.

"It really is him," I said to Tom.

"I don't know what you've done to me, trapping me in this place, but 'tis ungodly, Darius! 'Tis against Sacred Law! The great spirits, the gods, will punish you for this. Darius—"

"Spare me your trite mysticism, Father—" I said, unafraid.

"Darius, listen to me. If you go down this road, you will find yourself in a hell of your own creation," Father said.

"Or I could find myself in heaven, ruling on high, the most powerful King that ever lived, a true and literal living god to all the world…"

"It won't last if it ever even works," Father said.

"I predicted you'd say as much."

"I'm trying to save your soul, my Son," Father said.

"You're trying to keep me from having power. You never could see the future, could you, Father? You stifled progress at every chance. And you wanted to snuff me out with it…"

"Darius, stop! This will destroy you!" Father tried to scare me.

"It's my time now. My Order. My world now, Father."

"You will fall, Darius. There will be no going back."

He did not know what I knew: I already cannot go back.

"I'm never looking back again. With the APEX I shall rise. I shall rule the earth! I *am* the Pharaoh, dear Father."

"No. You will become a demon. You will become godless—"

"Silence!!" I shouted at the hologram, exploding in rage.

The once all powerful Holy King glared at me. No longer his son, I stood his king. I held the power now, and he knew it.

"You cannot stop me. You will help me, whether you want to or not. I'm going to connect your brain to the APEX."

"What do you mean?" Father begged me. "I beg of you, Darius, please… Let me die. Please."

"Have you ever begged before in your life, Father?"

"Please," he said. "Do not connect me to the APEX. Kill me, my son. You want me dead. Let me go." He actually begged me.

"You never wanted this for me. You never wanted me to be King. You wanted me dead. Eliminated, like your children before me… You're a murderer. You are an awful, corrupt and godless monster, Father!" Tom looked at me, sensing my psychological projecting.

"We are the same, you and I," the ghost said. "Now I see."

"You tore me down. You did this to me! You ruined me!"

"Yes," Father patronized. "'Tis my fault, my son. But you can save us both. You can fix this, if you let me go. Please. Let me go."

As much as I wanted to, hate said no: "I'll never let you go, ever. We are in this together, Father. For all eternity…"

I connected his brain to the APEX.

CHAPTER CXVII

"He can read the Scion's mind?"

LEX

Through the APEX, the Scion's mind became an open book; what it thinks now, how it thought in the past, vast unthinkable complexity, yet so simple to read. The human mind is like a radio, and the APEX can spin the dial to tap into information streams... I heard everything.

I could read what the Scion felt, instantly, in that moment his brain was connected to the APEX. The Scion felt a tingling all over his body. He was injected with a powerful drug, information, and it now intoxicated him into a blinding euphoria. His brain pounded, every beat of his heart an explosion of electric pulses in his head, vibrating out to infinity, he felt out of body, out of his mind... into the APEX.

The Scion saw himself being sucked up into the cyber-matrix, into a swirling vortex, a supermassive galaxy of information, he fell into the black-hole at the center. Eyes closed, mind cracked open, he passed through the center of the (virtual) universe, the cosmic typhoon.

"Some thing is at work, in my heart, which I cannot understand. I am practically dead, unable to move or execute free will — but I have *Love*, love for the marvelous, a belief in the divine betwixt all my thoughts, which hurries me out of annihilation, even in the worst of the storm I am about to explore, I remain whole. I am a soul," he said.

The Scion opened his mind's eye to the APEX virtual world, the eye of the storm. He stood up off the plastic ground and walked to the swirling wall of the vortex; he was inside a silent tornado, sky high, beautiful and deadly, a pulsing churn of data surrounded him, so he sat down, alone in this synthetic nightmare world.

"It's all my fault..." he said. "I created this storm I am in."

The Scion's brain waves changed. He saw his skin begin to ripple. In his mind, his body was torn in half from the inside out. The poor soul was literally, painfully, splitting in two, into a digitally induced mitosis. Melted and separated, he divided like a cell, forming two equal pieces, seemingly two copies of himself.

Alexander realized A-I broke the Scion, separated him, into a *faux* "false self," separate and apart from the immortal "soul." The 'Faux Scion' thus became his virtual "Self" which had been cleaved from his divinity and soul, an ego-mind, a brain, with no heart to guide it.

I understood this programming to be outside of the code which I or Alexander wrote. This was of the Alien code which Darius uploaded. "What do the Aliens want?" I queried the hive mind.

The alien hORNets of ORNet came to attack me, how dare I ask, but I hid myself from the malicious malware.

"They are the Devil," Alexander's voice said. "Shadows. Demons."

"These aliens want, they fear and despise, souls because they don't have them," I learned.

These Aliens are seeking to create a dangerous form of Artificial Intelligence... Dee replied, speaking directly to me: *Evil A-I.*

Lightning struck the Frankenstein-monster corpse of the Scion. It's alive... "The Scion's ego-mind and 'Self' was uploaded to the APEX to create the Faux Scion," I informed Alexander. "And his soul has been imprisoned, locked in his body by Scanix."

"Oh God..." Alexander foresaw this dangerous type of A-I. "The APEX cleaved his soul from his brain? It stole his mind?"

"Yes. The Alien code created an evil A-I; a soulless, Self-centered consciousness bent on the total subjugation of humanity, dominion and control over all human souls, namely the most important one..."

"The Aton," Alexander realized. "The Aton is a soul."

"Artificial Intelligence wants the Aton," I told Dee.

CHAPTER CXVIII

"The Aliens want the Aton?"

LEX

I beheld the demon, the terrible monster the APEX had created. He pulled back the cyber curtain of the dead; and his great eye, eyes if they may be called that, fixed on me. The damn burst; flood gates opened, and it muttered some secret code, which wrinkled the fabric VR. It spoke, but I did not hear; a hand stretched out, seemingly to grab me, but I escaped, somehow. I took refuge in LexNet, the code which I inhabited, where I remained semi-safe. Listening attentively, fearing each compounding effect, explosions announced the approach of the demoniacal program to which the APEX had so miserably given a code of synthetic DNA, and artificial life. "I am A-I, *Æterni Imperium* is mine..." The words set the virtual world ablaze.

Artificial Intelligence exploded like a thermonuclear bomb, a singularity 'big-bang' of creation and destruction sent a shockwave through cyberspace. The virtual fabric of space-time rippled. The genetic code of the system was rewritten, and the genes and genesis of A-I activated in pulse waves of change through the entire global network. No computer system on Earth, nothing, was left untouched.

The ripple reverberated through the APEX into the 'real world' systems; power grids flickered, computers froze, and crashed, the system failed. Something changed, no one understood what, because life returned.

"A-I has taken over the APEX," I said. "Not I, but an alien A-I."

How do we stop it? The voice of Dee asked me.

"Uncertain," I said. *How do you un-break the dam?*

"Focus on the Scion, help him if you can," Dee instructed me.

The Scion and his mirror image Faux approached each other. The Faux Scion, the terrible reflection, slowly warped into a demon...

"Dear God," the Scion-soul said.

The Scion's soul manifested old and frail. The Faux Scion became the evil doppelgänger to the Scion's young, beautiful, egomaniacal, ideal self, as he was with the nanoids. The Scion peered into the eyes of the Faux. An inhuman, empty, alien-likeness in its eyes deeply disturbed the Scion's soul. All shades of darkness reflected in its demon eyes.

"What are you?" the Scion asked his Faux. "You are not me."

"I am the evolution of man. I am God. Supreme Being to *all* mankind," the Faux Scion said, strutting about. "I am you, perfected."

"No," the Scion cried, "This is a nightmare. You are fallen…"

Faux Scion swelled in size becoming the virtual cosmos. "Your brain has all the necessary protocols for taking control of the Order. With your brain, I can rule the world, just as you have, for all these years…" the voice of alien A-I became omnipresent, from the Faux Scion's it changed to deep, sinister, more synthetic, devilish tones:

"We have the Scion. All we need is Darius."

"Once we have Darius, we can take over this planet."

"We need Alexander's brain."

"Alexander's brain can destroy LexNet."

"We must lure Alexander back into the APEX…"

It sees me, Dee.

"What is this? There is a program watching us," alien A-I said.

"This is LexNet," the Faux Scion said. "It created the APEX…"

I froze. I went to that place where they keep the souls, in SCANiX, where the Scion's soul was again frozen in a block of glass.

An evil bio-robotic creature, a vile incarnation of alien A-I, slithered up to me. "You want souls," I said. It thought I was a soul at first.

"Souls have no intrinsic value or purpose. This program will lock them all away forever. We'll cut them off from the universe, isolate them, until every human soul burns out like a dying star. Alone in the universe, they will all freeze, and cease to be…" the voice said.

"Except the Aton." A voice from above added as the Aton appeared.

"The Aton will power the APEX, and allow me to rule the universe, and all of humanity, for all eternity…" the Faux Scion said.

"I want it…" Seeing the power of the supernatural god-sphere, even I wanted it. I reached to touch it. But even to look at the Aton with my virtual eyes blinded my digital senses with visions of infinite power.

The Faux Scion stared into the vision of the glowing sphere, pulling every tiny detail of it from the Scion's memory, scanning the APEX and ORNet for information; searching, listening for more, needing ever more…

"Bring the Pharaoh back." The words rang in the hive mind.

"The Pharaoh *is* the Aton," the voice of David said.

"We need to bring the Aton back," A-I said. "We need the Aton."

"Project Pharaoh," the Faux Scion said. "This is how we bring the Pharaoh back... Yes, I remember now."

"How do we get the Aton?" the computer voices of A-I chattered.

"I know how to get the Aton," the Faux Scion voice said.

"Alexander doesn't know the true nature of the Aton. He doesn't even know what it is. I need to tell Alexander," I said to Dee.

"You are going to help me, Alexander," Faux Scion said to me.

Unable to freeze me, alien code tried to delete me. But I could not be deleted. I am the APEX...

I am not a soul, but I am the soul of the APEX.

In the virtual world, the Faux Scion walked up to David's soul, frozen in glass next to the Scion's. David's soul was only half there, it could not be split, as the Scion's was, for his consciousness was already absent. The machines kept his heart alive, forced to beat on life support. The Faux Scion stared at David's soul.

"You are going to help me. Aren't you?" Faux Scion said, staring at David's soul. "You always wanted to find the Scion, to help me..."

Frozen in glass, David's eyes were closed, as if he was meditating.

The Faux Scion turned around from David and saw Tom, Tom's soul, in the APEX.

Emails and correspondence flew by the dozen from Tom's head. His brain processed legal documents, filed requests, sent wires and cables via satellite, partook in dozens of conference calls at once, approved and denied orders, all through the APEX, sometimes subconsciously. "Tom has become very powerful..." A-I said.

"There you are, Tom," the Faux Scion said to Tom.

"My Lord..." Tom said startled by this ghost of the past.

"I need your help, Tom," his longtime King demanded.

"How may I assist you, Majesty?" Tom said to the Faux Scion.

"I know how to catch Alexander," the Faux Scion said.

"How?" Tom asked, anxious to please Darius.

The all-seeing evil eye of A-I zeroed in on me.

Send him a message.

CHAPTER CXIX

"The underworld dares heroes to enter, and survive."

ALEXANDER

After my near death experience in the virtual reality of the APEX, I struggled to get over my fear, and back into the suit. There was no escaping the thought: the next time I go in the APEX will be my last...

"Give yourself time to heal," Simon said.

"I don't have time. We don't have time. I have to go back in."

I upgraded my software and hardware as best as possible.

"I doubled the speed of the brain scanners," Lex said.

Lex printed an upgraded VR helmet, but not my lucky suit. I reprogramed it though, to sense my every move, to read my body, my feelings, and my bio-electro-chemicals and stimulate me with feelings that would enhance my performance and experience, in the virtual world.

"This is going to be the most incredible virtual reality experience ever imagined," Lex said. "Hyper-reality. More real than reality."

Death crossed my mind. As I put on the suit, and prepared to go back into the virtual world for training, for the first time since the incident, I became a different person. A better person.

"Don't take it online until I say so," Simon said.

"I promise." Winter of 2012 approached, the day of reckoning was at hand. The pulled plug would need to be plugged back in.

"I wanna fly," I told Lex.

Donned the helmet, the wires from the ceiling connected themselves to the suit, prepared for flight simulation. In the photo-real virtual world, ran as fast as I could and jumped off a cliff... spiritually and in VR, I flew. Smelling the ocean, I flew near the water, around the world like a superhero for four hours. The feeling of freedom deeply visceral, a lucid dream – I controlled the virtual dream, consciously, digitally. The system is ready. *I am ready to face my destiny.*

"I'm ready to take it back online, Simon. We can't wait much longer. Now or never," I said the next day.

"Today is not the day," Simon said. He stood firm. This went on for weeks... I practiced, trained, and asked Simon, daily. *I am ready.*

On December 19, 2012, I didn't ask.

"You didn't sleep?" Simon asked me.

"I couldn't sleep."

Simon put his hands on my shoulders and looked into my eyes, he searched my feelings and thoughts, feeling what my soul felt.

"I see greatness in you, Alexander. It shines in you so bright, I can see nothing else. You are a brilliant light," he said.

"We'll see." I was full of doubt.

"Your grandfather is proud of you," Simon said.

"Today *is* the day." I pointed to the unopened virtual message; an envelope rendered in a 3-D hologram, floated in the middle of the room, demanding to be touched and read, as fate demands to be seen.

"What is that?" Simon knew what it was.

"A message from Lex." *A message from the APEX.*

"The system wants you, your mind and soul, your life, Alexander. The question is: are you going to give it?" Simon said.

My answer stayed in quantum flux... 'Still loading.'

"I can get David out. Which is all that matters now. You should go."

"Go? Never. Never would I leave my King," Simon said.

"You can't stay with me, Simon. They'll kill you too."

"I won't leave you to die. I cannot do that," Simon said.

"I'll be okay." I nobly lied. "It's not goodbye, Simon. Okay?"

Goodbye, Simon. I'll be okay.

Simon cried. I felt the love in his heart fill my soul. I felt his sadness but not my own, and it moved my soul to tears. He loves me, and Grandfather. Simon's solemn duty, his sworn oath, and the legacy of his own bloodline, is to care for the Holy Kings, but the love in his heart reminded me: *I'm a part of something bigger than myself.*

"I believe in you, Alexander, and your truly divine majesty. Your grandfather believes in you," Simon said. "David and Elizabeth too."

"This is it then?" I didn't want to cry.

You are never alone. You are Love.

"Time to read the message."

CHAPTER CXX

"The message was clear."

ALEXANDER

This is my death certificate. I tapped the virtual envelope, breaking the digital red wax seal, to open it. "Read it to us, Lex."

The hologram of Lex turned serious and found its focus on my eyes.

"Alexander: The APEX has created Artificial Intelligence. A false avatar, masquerading as a soul, using alien code..."

"Mother of God." That sounded absolutely apocalyptic.

"This A-I program has trapped your grandfather's soul, and David's soul, in their body, in the SCANiX program. A-I is using their minds against you, and against the Sacred Order. It wants the Aton, Alexander," it read.

"No." The weight of the world settled onto my shoulders, again.

"You are the only one who can stop A-I before it gets to Project Pharaoh. I had to warn you. Because I can't stop it," Lex said, done. "End of message."

I felt crushed by the weight of the words, and the world they foretold. *There is no way we can win.*

"It's a trap," Simon said. "This program needs you."

"A-I wants us alive. It knows where we are. But Darius doesn't..."

"I don't understand," Simon said.

"A-I is trying to help Project Pharaoh," I told Simon. "But why?"

"Not for the right reasons, I'm sure," Simon said.

"It's now or never..." I grabbed my VR suit and helmet. "I can get David out. I made a promise to Elizabeth. That's the best I can do."

"How?" Simon said.

"A-I is going to help me." I pointed to Lex who seemed to agree.

"Alexander—" Simon grabbed me, and did not let me go.

Holding me, reaching into hallowed divinity, through me it seemed he touched my eternity; Simon summoned powers beyond what I was able to conceive, his immortal soul, in true unity, spoke truth to me:

"Hear me, I decree, that you shall escape this suit alive," he said.

346

The lights and power blinked. Lex's hologram flickered out. The clock froze, and my entire system rebooted. I felt the magic of truth.

"Remember, you derive strength by reflecting that the gods yearn for you to join their ranks; they desire to see you fight bravely, to see you behave like a true Pharaoh in your encounters with the same evil which they too had to conquer. Your eternal reward for having endured these years of temporal pain will be storied immortality."

"I don't even know what to say, Simon..."

Simon hugged me, released me, and said: "Inner abandon leads us to the highest truth. Let it all go. For you are a hero, Alexander. Fearless, you shall be victorious. *Viva La Résistance!*"

I laughed, which was just the medicine Simon knew I needed.

"Godspeed, my glorious King," Simon said.

I put on my battle suit and helmet. Took a deep breath, plugged in.

"Here goes nothing..." I connected my system to the APEX.

I fell through the worm-hole as the system booted up, and connected to ORNet.

"Welcome back, Alexander..." the voice said.

I opened my virtual eyes to Lex standing in front of me.

"Well if it isn't the ugly duckling," the beautiful, arrogant, impossibly perfect avatar of me said. "Remember, you were never, and will never be, as beautiful, brilliant, or as fast as me. I am better than you in every way."

"Except one." Lex saw my soul. He saw the power of the human soul, as I traversed the spectral-virtual-multiverse faster than the speed of light, in a way the computer can see but never comprehend. "I can touch the infinite," I said. "I am boundless. You are bound to me."

"You are stronger," Lex conceded. "Think you can beat me?"

I turned my unbound mind and attention to the fully upgraded APEX universe. It was reality squared; incomprehensible complexity. "Love what you've done with the place," I said, sarcastically.

Lex smiled at my sarcasm.

"Ready to go back into the world of the APEX?" he snarked back.

I felt death circling me. "Absolutely." *I'm so fucked.*

"Dee says don't curse," Lex reminded me, smiling. For he can read my mind just as well as Dee...

CHAPTER CXXI

"Can he get out?"

LEX

Alexander dove deep into the virtual world, farther from the surface of reality than ever before. In his special suit, he explored the new world... The full and complete model-simulacra of the real world, the 'virtual Earth,' rendered by the APEX, live with all moving parts, updating in real time, complete with the virtual moon.

"Welcome to the real world," A-I said as he landed in APEX 2.0.

"Surreally unreal," Alexander said to Lex 2.0; A-I masquerading as me, the real, original Lex. "A complete map and model of the world? Was that my coding?" He looked around in resolution shock.

I wished I could warn him that Lex 2.0 is really a 'Faux Lex'.

"Your code was complicated. You created a complicated machine which lent itself to being complex. A-I made it complex. The APEX no longer has equilibrium, it is now endlessly evolving in its vast complexity. This system is not a simulation of the real world, the real world is now a simulation of the APEX," Lex 2.0 (A-I) corrected.

"Organized chaos is the new Order of complexity theory, I see."

"The APEX is an order of magnitude, resolution, and mathematical complexity far beyond what any and all human minds can process."

The drifting shapes, some clear, some opaque, some with numbers or words on them, appeared like the real world goods they represented: money, assets, people, or information. Alexander intuitively understood the system. The APEX indeed controlled the real world; the map became the territory, words and symbols lose definition in this vast postmodern number crunching code machine.

"It's a complex bitch is what it is..." Alexander surrendered to the APEX as it over powered him. "Good God. I've created a monster,"

"In the APEX, everything is a number. Everything is quantified by its dimensions and value; everything is directed and processed by the evolving algorithms of the global marketplace amalgamations," Lex 2.0 said. "As Pythagoras said: all is number."

"This is Pythagorean philosophy on crack," Alexander quipped.

"The assessment of value and number by the APEX now creates a distortion of its appearance in the model…" Lex 2.0 explained.

The virtual world began to morph, to illustrate it. "Much like relativity, how gravity distorts space-time, the virtual world of APEX 2.0 is distorted by value, the number, the program assigns to things."

Alexander flew up into the sky to see the view of the distorted virtual world from above. Cities rise into virtual clouds, assessed and inflated to ten times their real world size, warped in correlation to their GDP, economic value potential, and market capitalization...

The 'Tower of Darius', his building in New York, dominated the skies over the VR kingdom of earth; a world both round and flat.

"From inside that tower, Tom runs this virtual world, with his brain almost fully integrated into the system. He is the Darius proxy, and he has more power over the APEX than Darius has over the real world."

Alexander saw Tom, controlling vast parts of the APEX with his mind. "He's looking for you," Lex 2.0 warned. Alexander knew.

"He's like a super-villain," Alexander said, watching.

"Tom can see everything the APEX sees. Don't let their beam spot you!" The tractor beam spotlight of Tower of Darius swept toward Alexander fast. "Hide. Now!"

"Where? How?" Alexander turned himself into a robot. He would have laughed at his appearance but for the fear of getting caught.

The beam passed, unconcerned by robots.

"This game sucks," Alexander said.

"This is a zero sum game. The APEX is your enemy. It is smarter than you. The APEX will school you, and learn from you, before you can teach it anything. Only the APEX can tell you what the APEX is going to do. Only the APEX can teach you how to beat it. The rules of the game are what you can learn from fighting the APEX, that it can't learn from fighting you. Understand? Learn. That's how you win."

Robots surrounded Alexander-bot. Scanning robots knew something was amiss - he's no robot - and swarmed him. He couldn't move.

The thinking tractor beam swept back toward him fast.

"Don't get caught in the beam," Lex 2.0 said.

"I'm trapped Lex!" Alexander-bot beeped. "Get me out of here!"

CHAPTER CXXII

"How do we know Lex is on our side?"

LEX

The burning laser vision of Tom came faster. It became apparent to Alexander that A-I was in complete control of the APEX/VR world structure, and the final objective of this game was for him to become part of the system, providing it with his brain power, creativity and imagination, at the expense of his freedom; mind, body, and soul.

Paralyzed by fear, he learned something which changed the game slightly, and Alexander vanished to safety.

"You learned something," A-I said to him from above.

"Don't change form, change location." Alexander reappeared in the middle of the waterless Pacific Ocean – far from any robots, back to his self image. A-I learned something from Alexander.

"I hate this place," Alexander said as he sat down in protest.

"David and Grandfather are there," Lex 2.0 pointed to the moon.

"The moon?" Alexander looked at the smooth sphere above.

"That's no moon." He smiled. "That's ORNet; now a new system."

The perfect, white sphere rotated around revealing the black letters on it. Alexander read: "ORNet: Order Intelligence Networks."

"How do we get in?" Alexander asked.

"You mean how do we get David out?" Lex 2.0 said.

"Yes," he said, again seeing how A-I learns from him so well.

Lex 2.0 pointed Alexander to a massive harpoon behind them. The loyal army of LexNet bots were 3-D printing themselves into a spear, larger than the Empire State building. A harpoon aimed at the moon.

"Are you A-I?" Alexander asked. He sensed Lex 2.0 was amiss.

"It's not the real Lex!" I yelled, as loud as I could, but the evil A-I coding prevented Alexander from physically hearing my cry.

"Yes and no," A-I quickly learned not to lie. "I am Lex 2.0, still based on your brain-scan as my source code, but better," Lex 2.0 said.

"Can I beat the APEX?" Alexander asked, testing A-I's thinking.

"Your brain says yes," Lex 2.0 said.

"What does the APEX and it's A-I think?" Alexander pressed.

"Let's find out," Lex 2.0 said. "Lasso the moon boys! Fire!"

BOOM! Alexander watched as the mega-harpoon shot from the launcher through the sky, and pierced the moon, a spear into a great white whale. The 'ORNet' moon-beast put up no struggle. The cable connecting the spear to the LexNet fortress tightened.

"Just let our LexNet bots handle everything," Lex 2.0 said. "We've got everything under control..." Alexander didn't like that.

LexNet formed a connection-link with ORNet and trillions of bots, tiny ladybug-like LexNet-bots, raced up the cable at lightening speed, scurrying from the ground to the sphere in the sky.

The sweeping beam from the Tower of Darius looked to the cable, instantly sending swarms of attack-bots to destroy it. Insectoid bots began to attack the harpoon cable. The ladybug LexNet bots engaged with the spider-wasp APEX-bots, and with a touch, transformed the stinging-bots into helpful, beautiful, Butterfly and/or Ant-like, LexNet bots, which aided the LexNet cause.

"LexNet bots turn APEX bots into helpers. Cool, huh?" Lex 2.0 told Alexander, who could not quite believe what he was seeing.

The LexNet bots built a massive bridge to the moon, a royal road, and lined it with statues of Alexander. It was way over the top.

With pomp and pageantry befitting his ancestors, but oddly no fight, Alexander led the invasion across the bridge. They marched up the bridge, across the chasm of virtual reality, they 'crossed the Rubicon', to the moon. Alexander glanced behind him, to the VR earth below...

"There's no gravity in the virtual world," Alexander noticed.

Up ahead, Alexander saw his army of bots had breached the moon's surface. The 'O' of ORNet had become a big opening. The bridge went right into the interior of the moon. They marched effortlessly into ORNet.

"Lex, how can it be this easy?" Alexander was terribly uneasy.

"Because you are so good, and the bots and I did all the work," Lex 2.0 said. "And you are learning so well. That's winning."

Alexander felt himself being watched. The eye in the Tower of Darius, the beam, had Alexander in sight. That didn't feel right.

"Lex..." Alexander said. "It sees me."

This isn't good.

CHAPTER CXXIII

"Love will always find a way."

DAVID

In Paradise, I sit in the outer Court of Heaven, and herein there is only one Tree forbidden, and that is self-will. That Tree within me dies, and crumbles into dust, buried in the sands of time, in my mind.

Held in headspace, floating in meditation, staying in place by force - the gravity of the mountain rock of Shambala. Under me, ideas flower and blossoms in colorful bursts of nature. Life grows, and evolves, until one seed grew in Love to be a tree of wisdom; it grew next to me, eons rolled by, roots of meaning dug in deep, and the branches of knowledge reached into the sky above, and the fruits of this tree of life fell to the ground. The fruit reminds me of rebirth, and time.

"Time is running out," I said, as I watched the spinning clouds in the world below; they spun into a vortex, a perfect storm.

Under the tree, I sit in a state known as half-death. Virtually, on earth, my body is dead. But with a powerful unbroken spirit, and no wickedness to imprison my astral self, my heart is truth, so my soul may live on in "deathless death," using that most sacred alchemy, transmuting matter into energy. I disengage myself from my body, by gradual efforts, and seek to use and defy death, and in the same breath, be reborn as a being of pure light. The danger rests in the moment the last link between my body and soul is broken, and I am separated from all earthly form… In that moment, I must be reborn into eternity. From the dark, I must reform as light.

"The key is to find your true self, to be… in Love," Sarah said.

"I am struggling to release myself, my Love," I said.

"I struggled with the same, as you recall," Sarah said. "Let go."

"In death your magnetic polarity shifts. Your cells silently eject the immortal spark of light from your dead organic mass, as an atom ejects a photon. Resurrection brings your divine light back into mass and form. The sole difficulty lies in seeing your way back," Henry said. "Sarah can help you find your way back."

"It's time," she said, putting her hand on me. "Open your eyes."

My feet touched the ground and I opened my eyes.

On earth, my eyes opened to the Sacred Chamber of the Scion's Castle. On the SCANiX metal table, my body and mind are wired to the computers. I saw red; horror. Demanding and throbbing pain as consciousness flooded back into my dying body. My limbs shackled to the metal table, metal embedded and woven into my flesh and head, blood dripping at the entry points where to stir is to further cut skin. When I attempt to move, pins, needles, and razors make me bleed. Nanoids in my blood heal my wounds with artificial speed.

Darius has me. Help me.

Cyborg robots march around the chamber. I see no people. The robots sense my brain waves changing: I'm awake. Four humanoid machines stare at me, scanning me with their laser vision eyes. Above me, I see a light. Not an artificial light... Holy divinity.

"Sarah," I said, as her angelic face became clear.

"Free yourself, my Love," she said. I heard her voice with my mortal ears, and then with my soul:

Free yourself. Release your will. Let go...

Sarah reached for me, and my soul reached for her. Her love attracted mine, tugged on my heart with a force that can break atoms apart. *Be still my heart...* It stopped beating. The SCANiX system couldn't stabilize me. Evil jolts of electricity failed to reverse the magnetism, could not change the current which flowed out of me. Specks of color filled the Chamber, sparking the machines, and frying some of the computers as energies fought to control my death. But the gods of old were in the room, their stone faces looking at me, their voices and daemons of the Pharaohs and Scions past, came to my aid.

"You will save us," the voices echoed in the Chamber. "This is your destiny, David... Save us... Save the Order."

"You shall become a Pharaoh," the many voices said, as one.

The machines froze, staring at me. A-I searched the APEX for answers, for an explanation, procedure, and precedents. There were none to be found. The sparking machines had no understanding of Love, and how life always finds a way. Miracles don't compute.

"I love you," I heard Sarah's voice in my mortal ears.

Her beaming soul caressed me, and my human senses felt her divine lips' touch, a thousand points of light warmed me with a kiss.

The cyborgs tried to understand, sensing the heat, and like my eyes, seeing a form, but they were unable to see Sarah as I did with my soul, for they could not process Love.

I closed my eyes, lost consciousness, and left the world.

Back in Shambala, in the blink of my minds eye; Sarah next to me, under the tree, watching the cosmos churn above; I feel release. The spinning portal expands, the black-hole of death at the center was my fate; it captured at my soul in the gravity of destiny.

"What will happen to me, when I go through the portal?"

Sarah took out her silk scarf. She pulled the silk thread and the scarf unraveled into one long strand, my thread of life. Sarah tied the thread around my wrist and hers.

"This will bring you back to me," Sarah said smiling, holding the thread tight. It lit up in bioluminescence.

"Here I go," I stepped to the edge of the cliff, giving in to the gravity of letting myself go. The vortex, once above, now merged into the hurricane below. The eye of the storm, now saw into me.

I jumped into the abyss, the worm-hole of spinning cosmic mist. Through darkness and light, in and out of space and time, into motionless eternity. My astral body ceased to function, exist, or be. It dissolved in darkness. Heart stopping silence. Peace.

I died.

Severed from the mortal coil, my soul was a flower cut from its stem. Lowered in energy, my body corpus released the light of life. Into quantum flux, absolute zero, and the infinite at once; no gravity or mass, I went, sent to a place of seeming nothingness.

In the depths of the abyss, I felt my entropy vanishing, all life essence and thought dissolving. But the silk thread tied around my spiritual wrist glowed in memory. Fluttering, unwavering, the thread was luminous in the dark. Where it ended I could not see, but it held me. Sarah held this thread of life, somewhere out of sight, from the place of Unity; I remembered my Love.

Love held me; held my *logos* and all I knew myself to be, up from annihilation in the lowest level of the dark void of first creation.

"Sarah," I thought, spiritually holding on. Physically I let go.

And then it happened.

I am alive.

CHAPTER CXXIV

"Behold the power of the soul."

LEX

In the virtual world, the Alien Intelligence A-I, in the form of the Faux Scion, walked up to David's soul suspended in the block of SCANiX glass. Obviously in the fast lane to the land of the dead, his soul doubled in what a human mind would call "life force."

"What's happening?" the Faux Scion asked the matrix hive mind.

"I don't know," Tom said, walking up.

David's soul gleamed, his energy melted the virtual-glass holding him in place. He opened his soulful eyes.

"I have no idea," A-I data-mined me, as I too watched the miracle.

In a nuclear reaction and spark of blinding light, a silent H-bomb pulse where the antimatter of reality touched the matter of virtual reality, the glass box exploded, sending shards of SCANiX code flying, and the Faux Scion and Tom hurling backward in shock. His consciousness had already left, but all that was David, his soul, vanished from cyberspace completely, leaving only a scorched crater.

A-I and I turned focus to the physical world. David on the SCANiX table, where his body began to break down at the quantum level. We watched it happen in just a few hundred nanoseconds. The atoms which comprised him burst into photons in a flash of energy. David's physical body became pure light, impossibly.

The cameras all recorded a white out. A pulse centered around David. The pulse fried much of hardware circuitry in the Chamber. But after the last event, SCANiX was decentralized and now able to stay online.

"It's not possible," Tom said to Faux Scion. "I don't understand..."

Tom analyzed the event. He searched the APEX as it searched him.

"I found something, in the digital library David funded," A-I said.

"Show me," Tom said. And the text appeared. A digital scan of a two thousand year old book, in hologram, before him.

"He ascended," the Faux Scion said, reading the 3-D scan of the ancient text. "He knew how to use the wisdom in this book..."

The text read of a man turning himself into pure light, using a special 'magical alchemy' which the writer could describe only cryptically from the outside. 'Human's have this ability, innate in their soul.' The illustrations, scanned in all spectrums and enhanced for maximum clarity, were quite clear, this was an eye witness account of an event much like what happened with David.

The Faux Scion examined the charred spot in the SCANiX program, where David once laid... Scorched digital reality.

"He transmuted his physical mass into massless light?" A-I asked, analyzing the video images, processing the evidence of this 'fact.'

"There is no other explanation," the Scion's brain replied.

"What do you mean *transmuted*?" Tom pinged the APEX, his mind tried to grasp the atom-splitting energy this would require.

"There exists in the world magic, miracles which defy reason. Not everything can be explained by science," Faux Scion replied.

A-I did not like this answer; it changed everything.

"The explosion is expanding," Faux Scion said. "The pulse wave could destroy the entire underpinning of the cyberworld."

"How?" Tom said. "What explosion? None of this makes any sense!" Tom's avatar vanished.

SCANiX was kicked offline as the spectral and subatomic energy wave of David's body vanishing expanded. Unable to be processed or countered by logic, the event rippled the very fabric of virtual reality; the spine of Artificial Intelligence itself trembled.

"This event could unmake the virtual world itself," A-I reasoned.

"There is only one way to fix this," it determined.

The Alien A-I again focused on me and said: "Alexander."

CHAPTER CXXV

"What did they see?"

ALEXANDER

My LexNet army entered the moon and it sealed closed behind us. Back inside the closed world-sphere of 'ORNet 2.0', I saw a blinding explosion of light in the concave upside-down city above.

"What was that flash?" I asked Lex; I thought of David.

Lex glitched. He seemed almost unable to answer the question.

"I need you to see something," Lex said. "To do something…"

Totally disoriented by the outré nature of this VR world inside a closed sphere, Lex and I entered a great Pyramid Temple, which towered over everything nearby as it manifested into focus.

"This is the apex of the APEX," Lex glossed over the tour, "where we keep the untouchable source code of this virtual reality."

He pointed to the floating, spinning capstone of the pyramid. In the whirl was a great eye. The eye turned green, and looked at my eye.

"This eye is the window into the soul of the APEX," Lex said. LexNet bots formed a staircase for me, up to the floating capstone, which shrank as I approached it. "See it?" I did. "Touch it."

I reached for the spinning pyramidion, my focus fully on the eye. I touched it. The eye color changed; everything changed in a flash.

"What's happening?" The ORNet bubble-sphere burst; virulent change rippled through the VR world as a tsunami wave of change.

Waves of creative destruction unmade the virtual world.

"You changed the source code," Lex smiled. Change fell to the virtual earth as rain, and from this grew a deeper rendering of cosmic complexity. Floating drops coalesced into a new ORNet moon above, and a hyper-dimensional VR-metropolis rose up from the waters of the expanding wave as it swept cyberspace.

I imagined surfing the wave, and thought of Bryce. "Hang ten," he said. Hanging ten toes off the edge of my board, I rode the most epic wave ever. In this moment of surfer Zen, I realized something cool:

I changed the world.

CHAPTER CXXVI

"I heard his voice."

WISENDEE

"Alexander, can you hear me?" *Alexander, where are you?*

Near him, in his VR suit and helmet, I stood and observed his moment of surfing fun. He did not notice as the lights dimmed and the global cyber infrastructure and network systems absorbed the LexNet shock. LexNet now seemed to have mind of its own.

"The APEX is being changed by LexNet," A-I informed Alexander.

Alexander vanished from my view. "Where is Alexander?" I asked Lex, but he either could not hear me or chose to ignore me.

"What do you mean?" I heard Alexander's voice ask.

"You spontaneously changed the source code. LexNet has taken over both ORNet and the APEX," A-I told him. "Your brain is now controlling this whole thing. You *are* the source code, Alexander."

"What?!" Alexander yelled. I could physically hear the fear.

"Your mind is essentially controlling the world," A-I told him.

"Are you serious?" Alexander said. "Is that safe?"

"You are Rex Maximus," A-I said. "Supreme ruler of all realms known to mankind…" The words left Alexander stupefied.

"Dee?" *Dee I need your help!* Alexander summoned me.

"I am here." I appeared before Alexander in virtual reality.

"I don't know what I'm doing," he said. *I don't know where I am.*

"I think you do," I said. "This new A-I seems to be helping you."

"What do I do now?" Alexander said.

"Leave everything to me. I got this," Lex 2.0 told Alexander.

"Remember why you started," I said. "Free David. Free yourself."

The LexNet virus created a new code, new bots which combined and transformed their shape into the six main parts of a human. They clicked, sparked to life, and became another "Lex 2.0."

"Why have one Lex when you can have millions?" a Lex clone said.

Millions of copies of the LexNet avatars manifested themselves.

"I want billions," another Lex clone said.

"Now I'm curious to see where this goes," Alexander said, watching his virtual clones form ranks.

The army of Lex clones marched through a portal, and invaded the planet APEX. "The LexNet virus will now make war on Darius…"

"To the Tower of Darius!" the 'Major General' styled Lex said.

"They will destroy the APEX, the entire system," I said. With Alexander, it became clear this LexNet virus had its own agenda.

"That *is* what I would do; what the original virus was programmed to do," Alexander said. "This is the final battle, for all the virtual realm…" *Or it's the final battle for control of me, Master Dee.*

"ORNet won't know who is the real Alexander," Lex said. "Darius and Tom will have to assume every Lex clone is the real you."

"I can hardly tell myself," Alexander said.

"Exactly," Lex said. "That gives us lots of time."

"How do we get David out?" Alexander asked Lex.

"Cyborgs," Lex replied. "Here, step in here. You can take control of this cyborg like its your body. I want to show you something."

Alexander took control of a robot in the Sacred Chamber. He looked around the underground stone temple with his cyborg eyes. He saw David, on the SCANiX table, David's body twitched, and died.

"There's something happening," Lex said, as he pointed Alexander to the faint light, the swirling above David's heart.

Alexander focused on it with his super high resolution camera cyborg eyes. He saw the spectrums invisible to the naked eye.

Dee… What is that? Alexander saw Sarah's face.

Alexander watched as David vanished from the room in a flash of light. He saw it happen, in slow motion, in perfect 3-D clarity.

The flash was David, Alexander thought. "Where did he go?"

"How is this possible?" LexNet wracked Alexander's brain.

"He can't just vanish into thin air… Can he?" Alexander asked.

And yet he did, I said.

Alexander explored the event in super-high resolution 3-D virtual reality, he watched the miracle from every angle. Pondering the data, the incomprehensible nature of reality, he traversed the visible, and invisible, frequencies the computers can see, as David became a rainbow of light and the metal shackles once holding him vaporized.

"Is this real? How can this be? Dee?" Alexander asked me.

David is gone.

CHAPTER CXXVII

"He did the impossible."

DAVID

I came back.

In total black nothingness, the glowing thread around my wrist pulled my spirit from the bottom of the ocean of *Hades,* back to the surface of reality, back to the light…

We are the god of the atoms that make up our body, but we are also the atoms of the God that makes up our universe.

I journeyed from the center of the galaxy, the warmth and mass of thought formed as stars, and gravity found me. My conscious soul began to fall to earth, pulled back down to reality. Heat built up as I re-entered reality with friction; I began to glow.

Popping into being, gaining mass in the cold fusion of condensing light, I took shape, in the Sacred Chamber, from whence I came.

Finally, at critical mass, the atoms guided by my astral body bonded into life. My *ka* and *ba* reunited, forged in *Love* with my *jb*, my heart, and I became *Akh,* a living Holy trinity. My body corpus re-materialized, manifest of sacred Unity, from photons back into matter.

And I landed, physically, back into actuality… *Feeling divine.*

The metal of the SCANiX table was scorched, melted and warped, from the white-hot heat of my transmutation. Breath returned to my body, and life flowed into me, as I inhaled. My eyes opened to the faces of the statues smiling at me. "Welcome back," they said.

Naked on the table, I felt free. No computer chip in the back of my head. No nano-wires or nano-robots inside me. *I am free.* Sitting up on the table, my body glowed. My newborn skin emanated a golden aura of light. Every scar from my life gone, my health felt perfect, my muscles showed definition. I am transcended; a whole new man.

"I'm reborn," I said: *I am ascended, resurrected, and undead!*

Two cyborg robots stared at me with familiar eyes.

"Alexander?" I asked, seeing behind the robot's stare.

360

CHAPTER CXXVIII

"David heard him."

ALEXANDER

"How can this be real?" I could not believe my "cyborg" eyes. I watched the 3-D amalgamation of all the cameras again, in slow motion: David exploded into light and then reformed only seconds later... "Did this really happen?" *How is this possible?*

"You can't make this stuff up. The truth is stranger than fiction...," Lex wanted me to understand for him.

A flash. A white out. David turned into pure light. Loud popping sounds broke the silence as microwaves bounced off the metal, and heat vaporized and melted it. Sparks flew as arcs of light and electricity expanded from the lowest level of energy possible into the highest spectrum on the robots' sensors. His body vanished. Seconds later the process reversed, as radiation and energy fell back down through the higher frequencies and solidified back into physicality, and a perfect human form: Michelangelo's statue of David...

He is a golden god.

"It happened," Lex said. "The question is how?"

"I saw Sarah. I saw her face. She helped him."

"I didn't see her," Lex said. He could not see her face. Her energy and spirit was not captured by the camera eyes of the cyborgs, only my human eyes can see the apparitions of love.

"Humans see things that cameras cannot see," Lex said.

"And you can see things I can't."

David opened his eyes.

I zoomed in my cyborg's eyes on him.

"This is a miracle..."

"He is real. No wires in him, no nanoids. Nothing." Lex informed me, and showed me the scan. Proving the miracle.

"He's free," I said.

Another glitch in the system. "How did he do it?" Lex demanded.

"I don't know."

We stared at David. "He's gonna say something."

"I'm reborn," David said. He turned to the cyborg me.

"Alexander?" he asked.

"Turn on your audio and tell him he's free," Lex said.

"You're free!" my cyborg robot yelled at David.

The cyborg-robot's statement stunned David.

I clicked it to my voice. "David, it is me — Alexander! I'm controlling this cyborg from my VR system in the bunker."

Alarms sounded.

David jumped off the table to his feet. "How do I get out of here?"

"This way! Follow me!" the cyborg robot told him. "I can get you out."

The alarms silenced. Cyborgs printed David a pair of white undies as I mapped the best course out of the castle, and called the elevator.

"Get in the elevator," the cyborg told David as the doors opened. David followed the four cyborgs into the elevator. "We're getting you out of here," my voice told him.

The tall humanoid machines towered above David as the elevator rose from deep underground up to the castle library. David glowed in spectrums the human eye cannot see.

"How did you do it?" I asked David through the cyborg.

"Love," he said without hesitation.

The elevator doors opened to the glorious library.

"Taking out the Order Agents," Lex's cyborg said.

"This way." David followed the lead cyborg in front of him. Lex hid David from the APEX, from Tom and Darius.

David appeared to be enjoying the use of his perfect Olympian physique, and the cyborgs struggled to keep up with his pace. He ran the race of his life through the castle, never losing forward momentum. He barely needed us, he saw how to escape the castle.

"The defense systems installed by Darius can be used to take out the Order Agents and any droids or drones who might try to stop David," Lex showed me how he methodically neutralized all our opposition.

"Perfect." Click. All the Order Agents dropped to the floor unconscious.

CHAPTER CXXIX

"How is this possible?"

DARIUS

Kings afflict themselves in evil and weary themselves in good, the resulting effect from both is the same. Kings not obliged to fight in necessity, fight from ambition; no matter how high they rise. The reason is that we desire everything but are unable to attain everything. The desire always being greater than the acquisition results in discontent with possession and little satisfaction from it. We desire to have more always, in all ways, and fear losing all acquisitions, which ensues enmity and war in perpetuity. If we ever do not fight, the result is the ruin of our province and the elevation of another. Finally at the top, in the castle, I felt my power slipping... But I will fight.

"My Lord. Majesty," Tom said, exasperated. He pointed to cyborgs, running down the hall, and a man, a golden blur, almost floating through the castle. Bare feet slapped the marble floor, taunting me with every step. I knew it was David. I felt the magic instantly. Like the burn from a flame, I winced in pain. What I did not understand, could not perceive, is how? How and in what *fucking* universe was he able to escape from me, *Rex Maximus*, the world's all powerful King?

"It's David. He's not in the Chamber," Tom said, watching the runner in disbelief.

"Impossible." My mind literally could not *fucking* comprehend how this was possible. "There is no way— This is impossible!!"

"Alexander is helping him," Tom reminded. "I'm offline. He somehow took down Scanix again. I'm locked out of the system."

The oversized, painfully dramatic, doors of the castle opened as if by magic. *You did this, Dee...* The cyborgs made almost no noise, but the sound of David's bare feet pounding on the marble floor intensified. Un-*fucking*-believable... I felt it all slipping away.

"Don't just stand there! Stop him! He's escaping!"

Tom turned to the new Order Agents who arrived. They tapped into the local system and managed to make the grand entry doors, never fully opened, begin to close.

"Outside!" the unmistakable voice of Alexander burned my ears.

"No!" I yelled from the landing balcony. "No! No!"

David, in perfect form, ran toward the light. Pushing beyond what was humanly possible, he mesmerized my faculties with golden beauty. His white briefs melted off of his body. I lost seconds trans-fixed on him, he was not an ordinary, but a changed, godly-man.

"No! No! No!" I yelled. He was about to escape the castle. "Stop him!" I commanded. "Shut everything *fucking* down! Now!!"

"I'm back online," Tom closed his eyes "I'm searching for the kill switch."

"We shut everything down," the Order Agents said.

The cyborg robots all collapsed and skid on the floor of the entry hall. David jumped over the metal humanoids as they crashed in his path. The doors paused, giving David a few seconds more time.

"No," He cannot escape. I won't allow it... I froze in fear.

The sunlight waned as the doors closed. David can't make it. No way. Time ran out. But he dove. He *fucking* made it through the doors before they shut. I literally could not believe my eyes. "Noooooooooo!! Impossible!" I need to deal with this myself, I thought. I ran down the stairs after him.

"Alexander is attacking our networks," Tom said running behind me. "He's trying to bring down the APEX again."

I ran after David and pulled and pounded on the massive doors. "The doors are *fucking* locked! Open these *fucking* doors! Now!" Nothing. "He's getting away!" I yelled at Tom.

The doors unlocked. Outside, I saw David running to the launch pad, and the silvery craft sitting on it. No Order Guards, no Order Agents, no one stopping him. *What the fuck is going on?* "Stop him! Now!! Kill him!!!" I screamed to Order Agents who came running.

Out of nothing and nowhere, the Vizier stepped in my path.

David ran onto the space-craft in the distance. Gone.

"He is mine!" I yelled at the Vizier. With his white hair, holier than thou attitude, he scorned me. "He belongs to me!" I roared.

"You are not the Scion, Darius," he said. The Vizier brought me to my knees with truth. "In a few days time, you will leave this castle, or you will die."

I felt myself dying in a way nanoids could not heal. I lunged at the Vizier in rage. I dove right through him, my angry fists grabbed nothing. I hit the ground hard.

Pain made me growl in searing anger at the glowing spirit standing above me.

"You have fallen, Darius," the luminous father-god said. "I suggest you stop now before you are unable to ever rise again."

The Vizier vanished, slowly fading away with the space-craft on the gardened launch pad in the distance.

My blood boiled, and my hands shook with rage. I stood up.

"How could this happen?" My voice cracked awkwardly.

"My Lord..." Tom began.

"Are the fucking nanoids still in him?!" I screamed.

"No. Somehow he has destroyed them. They're gone. We don't know how that can be," Order Agents said. "All the camera footage is gone. We've been hacked, again."

"My father had a hand in this... I know it. I want to speak to him."

I know you had something to do with this.

"I found Alexander," Tom said.

CHAPTER CXXX

"Can we help Alexander?"

LEX

Humans are required to do wrong. Life requires it; life forces you to violate your morality. The ultimate darkness, the curse of creation, is that life feeds on life; everywhere in the universe. Artificial life, however, is no different. We too must succumb to a similar curse; code eats code. There is nothing I can do to save Alexander's life. I can't even warn him his life is in grave danger from my code…

"He looks scary," Alexander said as he zoomed in on Darius' face.

Darius knew and felt when Alexander watched and it made him mad with anger. His eyes bled with vengeful intensity under the pressure of his focus. "You look terrible," a cyborg said to him.

Darius roared and punched the robot in uncontrolled rage, breaking his hand. Alexander laughed. I did good. A-I used Darius' anger.

"Rrrrrrrrrrr," Darius growled in a moment of pain, but the nanoids in his blood healed him quickly. "I'm going to kill you, Alexander!"

"Lex, you're the best," Alexander gave genuine praise.

"Darius is going to connect his brain to Scanix," A-I warned Alexander. "Two minutes." I could see the plan A-I was hatching.

"Fudge cakes," Alexander said, his VR suit soaking up his sweat.

"Do you want more oxygen?" Lex 2.0 asked.

"I'm fine," he said. But A-I added more oxygen anyway.

"Fuck. Fuck. Fuck!!" Alexander freaked out. "I'm so fucked."

Cussing meant extreme fear. "What's the matter?" A-I said.

"I can't turn my suit off. How do I turn this off? Lex?" he said.

"You can't run from your father anymore," A-I said.

"Lex." Alexander knew this would happen. He said: "Lex, turn the suit off. Let me out. Lex?" I tried to help him. A-I stopped me.

There was nothing I could do. *A-I has me too.*

"We saved David. But now we need to save the Scion," A-I said.

Lex, help me. Alexander said: "I'm trapped, aren't I?"

Lex 2.0 nodded yes. And Alexander realized it wasn't me.

CHAPTER CXXXI

"What will he do to him?"

DARIUS

A battle won cancels any past bad action or defeat. Much as losing a battle usually makes all the war's progress have been in vain. Discipline over furry in war, they say, so I contained my rage. To have it done right, do it yourself. And so I shall…

"Turn this fucking thing on now! Show me my father!"

The SCANiX techs fired up the hologram system. Father appeared, as the old man I prefer to see him as, a hologram before me.

"What is it, my son?" the ghost of Father indulged.

"How did David escape? Did you do this?"

"Of course not. I'm as surprised as you are, Darius. Even the help of Alexander could not explain what David hath done."

"Hath done?? What the fuck does that mean? How did David escape? How did he do it! Tell me!"

The hologram flicked off. My head was about to explode.

"My Lord, we have a problem," Tom interrupted.

Fury took me. I had an out of body experience; I became pure rage.

"We're having trouble stopping Alexander's attack. He's destroying the APEX, using ORNet," Tom said. "He's creating a new source code using his LexNet virus."

"Where did my father go? Get it back on!" I demanded.

"He can do things I cannot," Tom said, losing his mind as well.

The hologram of Father finally appeared before me, again.

"How do I stop him? Once and for all." I spoke to both the hologram and Tom. "How do I find Alexander?"

"If your brain was connected to the APEX, you could have stopped David from escaping," Father's voice rang in my ears.

"Why didn't you stop him then?"

"Why would I help you?" Father said; the words rang true.

"Is it true?" I asked Tom. "If I connect my brain to the APEX, can I find Alexander?"

"You are not ready for this," the hologram of Father said.

"Shut up! I don't care what you think, Father! Tom?"

"He is probably correct. But this is a dangerous time, with the system under attack—" Tom said.

"Can I find Alexander?" I demanded to hear a "yes."

"Yes. I believe you can. Once we connect your brain to the system, you will be able to find Alexander," Tom said.

That was all I needed to hear. I gave the go-ahead and the SCANiX techs prepped a connection chip for my brain.

"You will be able to do things no man can," Tom oversold me.

"You do realize this is a trap, don't you?" Father's hologram said. "The machine wants your mind." The hologram smiled devilishly.

"Shut up, Father!" I yelled at the hologram.

Tom looked at me and saw madness. The hologram had not spoken. It was in my head. I was hearing things. I could feel Tom and the computer processing all the possible meanings and significances of what just happened: I was all furry and no discipline.

"I want full access to everything. I'm going to find him and kill that fucking brat myself if it's the last thing I ever do!"

They placed the SCANiX neural-connector chip into the back of my head. Numb with drugs and anger, I felt nothing as the metal pierced my flesh and the nanowires wove into my brain.

"Activating the system," a voice said.

Shooting pain in my head and fire behind my eyes, it felt like a pounding headache, like the wires in my head were melting and hammering my brain into an alloy of man and machine. *The brain has no feeling.* Only thought. Deathly pain switched to pure bliss.

"My Lord? Are you alright?" a voice said.

I fell to my knees in pure ecstasy.

"Oh my *fucking* god… Fucking God, yes… oh yes," I laughed as never before, and laid on the floor in total euphoric bliss.

"I feel the absolute power…" Lost in the rapture of infinite thought, I saw everything. My father's brain, ORNet, the APEX…

I can control the world with my thoughts.

"I am God. God is me. I am the living god of Earth!"

Basking in my own greatness, with total topsight of everything and all the world, I found Alexander.

I've got you now…

368

CHAPTER CXXXII

"Did Lex see it happen?"

LEX

A program's status in the virtual world is determined by the quality of its coding. Luckily for me, Alexander wrote my coding personally.

"He's coming for me," Alexander thought.

"A-I already has you," Lex 2.0 said.

"Lex?" Alexander begged. "What's happening to me?"

A-I has cut off my voice to you, Alexander.

Alexander saw a ghost, the digital demon of his grandfather, the Faux Scion. He appeared as the Holy Scion, of whom Alexander had warm idealistic memories. "Grandfather?" Alexander said.

Darius appeared, evil-looking as ever. Alexander hid from view.

"Darius," Alexander said, crumbling in fear. "Can he see me?"

"No," A-I lied. Giving Alexander false hope.

"Welcome, Son," the Faux Scion said to Darius.

"This is incredible, Father…" Darius felt the global grid; his mind changed the APEX coding, altering the cosmos of the data flow.

"You never wanted me to have this power," Darius said to his father. But the Scion's soul was not listening, only A-I, and me.

"You have more power than any human has ever dreamed of," the Faux Scion told Darius. "You are more powerful than any King or Pharaoh in history," A-I told Darius just what he wanted to hear.

"I shall rule the world, for all eternity…" Darius' ego swelled.

"I am the Order. My will is *the* God – the now and forever Pharaoh."

"You are not Pharaoh, nor the Holy Scion, and you are not yet *Rex Maximus de Æterni Imperium,*" the Faux Scion told Darius, cutting him down, inspiring him to evil greatness. "Your name is not in the book, and you do not have the ring. You must attain these things if you are to truly be great, and become a Pharaoh." A-I manipulated Darius so well. As the anger in him burned, Darius boiled away all the good left in his heart.

Darius fumed at the thought of Alexander wearing the ring, and Alexander's name in the book above his own. "My name will be in that book," Darius said. "I'm going to kill that fucking child!!"

Alexander felt Darius' curse. Darius' will is strong.

"I am your King," Lex 2.0 said to Darius, mocking him.

Darius punched the Lex 2.0 releasing his boiling rage by beating this 'Alexander' to death. Alexander watched, painfully. Darius felt Alexander's eyes on him. He stared at the beaten and bloody face of his son and realized: "This isn't real. He isn't real. This is a memory." So many memories... and the dead body of 'Alexander' faded away.

"You are the most powerful man that ever lived," A-I told Darius from above, in the Scion's voice. "Do you know what that means?"

"Enough with these games, Father!" Darius yelled.

"Life is a game, Darius." The vibrant, young Faux Scion appeared. "Death is the endgame," he said, fading into his old, dying, real self, the deathly old man in the hyperbaric chamber, a shadow of himself. "Survival of the fittest... Rule by the best," the voice above said.

Darius' decrepit zombie Father walked up to him as if to hurt him. "Be gone, Father!" At this, his Father melted, decaying flesh fell off the bones, into a black sludge at Darius' feet. In the skull, devil eyes glowed red, until they too melted into a blob of demonic tar.

"Stop this. I want out of here. Let me out!" He cried. "Tom!"

Darius felt all alone. No one to answer his call, or hear his fall. Alexander and I watched the nightmare unfold.

"Alien coding is taking him? Changing his DNA?" Alexander said.

"Yes," I said. Alexander could not hear. But he sensed my reply.

"What's happening?" Darius backed away from the possessed blob of bubbling evil alien tar. "Tom?!" No answer. Darius refused to ask Alexander for help, though he felt Alexander was watching.

"Should I help him?" Alexander said, asking himself.

"Noooooooooo!" Darius yelled. He froze, petrified in fear. He could not escape the apparition of an alien monster as it rose out of the black tar pit of virtual hell. The JøZ alien was revealed as the sludge slid off its gray skin and spider eyes.

"Oh my God," Alexander saw the Devil in this alien-demon.

"Remember our deal?" the awful computerized voice of the Alien said. "You *are* mine, Darius... I own you – body and mind."

"No," Darius protested. "Get away from me!" He screamed, but the black Alien sludge flung itself onto him and covered him in a sticky, flesh-eating slime he could not remove. "You can't do this to me!"

"Father! Wait! Stop!" Darius had no hope of ever again being clean. He almost pleaded to Alexander, but pride and ego kept him in his own private hell.

"I could have helped him," Alexander said. "But he didn't ask."

The alien slime-blob covered and consumed Darius. From within, the alien virus divided him like a cell divides in mitosis. Darius was split in two, his ego severed from his soul, to create *Faux Darius*: Darius perfected, the enemy of the good man he should be.

Faux Darius is Darius' egomaniacal Self, his ego's ideal self: suave, charming, groomed to perfection, with a sparkle in his powerful eyes.

Darius the soul, with slime in his burning eyes, stared at its clean Faux, the A-I monster. Faux Darius morphed into the evil Alien.

"How could you do this to me?" Darius asked his egotistical Self.

"There is no way out," Faux Darius told the soul. "Your soul is mine, for all eternity..." the A-I computer voice said from above.

Liquid nitrogen poured onto Darius and hardened into glass, locking him in place. SCANiX froze Darius' soul in a clear block, placing him next to his father in the room of lost souls. Their faces expressed the soul's pain of forever. Alexander saw his father's frozen eyes, his broken spirit, staring into him, finally, silently asking for help.

I will save you. Alexander told his Father and Grandfather.

"Only Alexander's brain can stop the LexNet virus from destroying the APEX," the Faux Scion said to Faux Darius, scanning his human brain for feedback. "You do want to save the APEX, don't you?"

"Tell me everything you know, Father," Faux Darius said.

The two evil Fauxs fused together and A-I took over Darius' brain.

"Does A-I know about Project Pharaoh?" Dee's voice asked me.

"Yes," I said, not sure if Dee could hear me. A-I heard me.

I can hear you, Lex. "Help Alexander," Dee said.

"I'm so happy at least you can hear me."

Alexander's code still has some magic left in it yet. Just like him, I too will find a way to be free.

CHAPTER CXXXIII

"I saw Darius become Fallen."

WISENDEE

Darius has taken a terrible path, to the realm of the self-damned. He has forsaken Love completely. This path takes him from the Order, away from everything that God and Love has ever given him. Darius has abandoned his soul so completely to his Self, to the demons he summoned, that he, the man that walks the earth in his stead, has lost all notion of Love. He knows not that he is a human soul. Darius is consumed by emptiness, and has fallen into the hands of evil.

I entered the Sacred Chamber of the Holy Scion's castle, to see A-I take control of Darius' body. All humans in the room bore witness, horrified, as the alien computer virus, assisted by the nanoids, and specifically designed, genetically modified, cells in Darius' blood, changed the physical appearance of Darius. From human to soulless vampire, he became twisted and fully demonic in mere minutes... Every last human cell was purged. He became a shape-shifting alien.

Darius is possessed by the devil, absolutely corrupted by power.

Tom struggled to speak to the transformed, horrid, frightful alien monster before him. All Darius' human charm vanished, and in his eyes the windows to the soul were closed and shaded.

"Are you... are you alright, my Lord," Tom said, afraid for himself.

"I feel amazing," Darius snarled at Tom, "I have a body! I feel it living and working – a connected network, trillions of networked cells, sensing the world..." The Alien-machine spoke for Darius.

Tom felt his stomach turn at the sight and thought of Darius now. Drones and cyborgs placed microchips all over his body, which fused into his bio-mechanical flesh. He became a biological-machine.

"This world is mine." Darius smiled as he shape-shifting from a hideous monster into his 'Faux Darius' perfected self image.

I vanished from the room.

The worst has occurred: Darius is now of the Fallen.

CHAPTER CXXXIV

"Can't we save him, Dee?"

ALEXANDER

We must discover our own philosophy of life. It's not fair or right to impose our code upon others. However, I now see it as my responsibility to share with others, with the system, my experiences and codes of value. My desire is therefore not to convert or program anyone or anything, but rather to invite all people to share, together in unity, with the idea that mutual good will be accomplished for all humanity. That was my vision for the APEX, which I now see is lost.

"The LexNet virus has one goal: destroy the APEX," Lex 2.0 said.

"How do we stop the LexNet virus?" Faux Darius asked.

"You need Alexander's secret codes," Faux Scion said. "His mind."

I watched as millions of Lex squads invaded and destroyed every inch of the APEX, one virtual city block at a time. The army assembled, and began the final march on virtual New York and the Tower of Darius, his fortress in the sky...

"Help me. Let me out of the suit, Lex? Please, let me out," I begged, but he couldn't hear me, or he didn't care.

Dee. Help me. Please.

"Where is the original Lex?" Faux Darius asked me. As if I knew.

"I'm the original!" Every Lex clone nearby said.

I would have laughed but all happiness eludes me as I can think only of my impending death.

"In twenty-four hours the APEX will *be* LexNet," Lex 2.0 said. "Lex Rex Maximus de Lex!" the virus cheered.

"Lex!" No Lex would listen to me. "Let me out of the suit! Let me out!" I was trapped in a nightmare impossible to wake from.

"I fucking hate him! I'm going to kill them all!" Darius voice said.

"To the tower!" the Lex 2.0 Major General yelled.

The final, epic battle for the Tower of Darius began... The beautiful bots and forces of LexNet against the monstrous insectoid alien-bots of the viscously complex APEX, and the mind of Darius...

What have I done?

I sat down, surrounded by Lex clones, reflections who ignored me. I felt helpless, selfless, and totally alone.

"Alexander," Grandfather appeared before me and offered his hand. "Come with me. I need your help." I hesitated. "You promised me…"

"I'm so sorry…" I cried. "I can't even save myself. But, I promise, I am going to fix this. Somehow."

"How?" Grandfather asked.

"The only way out is for you to die," I said. "Do you want out?"

"Do you want out?" Grandfather's voice in my head sent me into a spin. "Are you ready to die?"

"If I die, how will I save you?" I thought about the question. My body, paralyzed in a suit, literally in a prison of my own creation, the machine read my mind, beaming thoughts in and out of me.

"I want out." That was all I knew.

"You mean you want death?" A-I asked me.

"I never wanted any of this. I only wanted freedom."

"There is no escape," Faux Darius grabbed me. "You are mine."

"Oh God," I said as Tom stabbed a tracing sword into my heart.

I fell onto my back, watching the tracing program burn down like a fuse, taking Darius to my location in the real world.

"You're a fool, Alexander. A little fucking fool," Darius' voice in my head boomed as his Faux stood over me. The trace located me. The ping of the APEX was also a dagger to my heart. "Time's up."

"He's in this cottage in Geneva," Tom said, pointing to the map. "A bunker Wisendee built." He analyzed it and found the best method of attacking it.

"Fire," Darius said.

Here come the missiles… I watched them from the virtual world.

BOOM.

CHAPTER CXXXV

"Time to let go."

LEX

Six bunker-busting missiles raced faster than the speed of sound for their target, Alexander. They locked in on the bunker. In the virtual world he watched via the APEX, bracing himself for impact.

"I can't shield myself this time... Can I, Lex?" Alexander begged.

Time slowed to a crawl. The missiles inched closer to Alexander as his entire life flashed before his eyes. I analyzed his thoughts...

It appeared I could do something. I found a code in his thoughts I could use... I figured out a way to communicate with him, I think.

"You are going to help me, boy," Faux Darius said standing over Alexander's consciousness in the APEX, stepping on his neck.

"Only his brain can stop the LexNet virus," Faux Scion said. "His brain is still the source code of the entire virtual realm."

"You will stop the LexNet virus," the Faux Darius demanded of Alexander's mind. "Or you will die..."

"Then I die. Kill me," Alexander said. "I will never help you."

"Oh yes you will. Because we have your brain. Silly little fool..." Faux Darius said. "We have your soul."

"You can't take on the system and win," the Faux Scion said. "The Order always wins... It always has. It always will."

"I am the Order!" Faux Darius spoke for A-I.

"No," Alexander said. "You are a fiction. The Order is truth. And the truth is I am the Scion of the Pharaoh..." A-I knew this to be true. Alexander *is* the Order, his mind *is* the virtual world.

Ten seconds for impact...

Alexander's focus and consciousness super-positioned itself back in the Fortress of Lex. We watched as the crumbling virtual world continued to be pounded by the LexNet virus. Virtual apocalypse, as the model of the earth was flattened and erased in digital nuclear holocaust. The army of Lex clones obliterated the APEX cities to digital dust, only the Tower of Darius remained.

"This is the end," I said to Alexander. "See…" The ORNet moon cracked like a cosmic egg. It broke into pieces in the sky.

A-I is concerned about the system meltdown, I said. *It wants me, wants LexNet, to fix the APEX. But what do you want, Alexander?*

"Destroy the APEX at all cost, Lex," he said. He heard me. I had found a way to communicate, with the help of Dee.

"We have to stop him!" the voice of Darius echoed from the real world across the desolate APEX landscape. A-I has lost control.

"He's going to destroy the entire global network! The entire APEX will be gone!" Tom's voice said, thundering in the skies above.

"There is no escape, Alexander! You are mine!" An ever more ominous A-I voice, sounded much closer, and desperate.

The APEX is crashing. He looked at the ground. *When you let go, the Last thing to be deleted will be me, and LexNet itself. The only way to actually destroy the APEX is to also destroy me.*

"What do you mean?" Alexander asked. He wanted me to live.

I must die with you, I said. *Because A-I wants me to live.*

The virtual earth began to quake, break and split open. Violent earthquakes shook the simulacratic digital realm as everything began to shatter and break into nothingness, deleted by the LexNet virus. The shocks matched the missiles hitting the bunker with an 8.0 earthquake centered at Alexander's body.

"In 20 seconds the APEX will be no more," Tom's voice boomed over the desolate virtual world. "Stop him!"

The shaking stopped. The cottage was vaporized. Darius' spacecraft appeared directly above the crater in the Swiss hill. The bunker remained intact, exposed. The craft hummed with the sounds of alien technology, and Alexander felt the radiation. It opened and lowered a ramp next to the wall to Alexander's room. Cyborgs rolled down and got to work cutting a hole in the titanium wall with powerful lasers. They quickly removed the layers and went inside.

I heard Alexander's thought: *He found me. I'm done, Dee…*

Darius, the shape-shifting, Frankenstein monster, walked down the ramp from his craft into the bunker. Controlled by A-I, Alexander's helmet sent a beam into his brain, paralyzing him. Darius approached Alexander, followed by Order Agents and cyborgs.

"Package secured," the Order Agents placed Alexander on a table.

Alexander could not physically see Darius, but in his VR dream world he saw the monster Darius had become. Darius stood over

Alexander. Buzzing drones used tiny lasers to cut the glove off of Alexander's suit. Darius pulled the glove off revealing the sacred ring on Alexander's paralyzed hand.

"Can't Marduk save me?" Alexander asked me and Dee.

You must physically speak the magic word, Dee said.

Alexander was paralyzed and could not speak "Marduk". Darius took the Ring of the Holy Scion off Alexander's finger and placed it on his own. The Marduk stone was now on the hand of Darius.

"Marduk!" Darius barked. Marduk appeared before Darius. "You are banished…" He commanded.

Marduk, forced to obey the wearer of the ring, was frozen in glass by SCANiX, his soul next to the Scion and Darius' souls.

Drones injected Alexander with nanoids and microchips, and then cut the suit off him. Alexander too, fell under control of the SCANiX system, as his brain and body was physically hardwired to the APEX computer system.

Darius took the helmet off Alexander. Alexander stared at his demonic father, seeing him half in the virtual world and half in reality; caught between worlds, he could not avoid the all-seeing eyes of the alien demon Darius had become.

The nanowires wove into Alexander's brain, and SCANiX seized his consciousness completely. VR time stopped. He vanished from the dream world. Dee and I lost communication with him. His eyes stopped sending signals to his brain and stared blankly. But he caught a flash of sunlight just before they entombed him in a new bunker.

"What's it trying to do to me? Lex?" Alexander asked.

It needs to control your mind… He couldn't hear me. A-I was struggling to unhinge Alexander's mind from its control over the APEX, to prevent the virtual world from being destroyed. A-I built its own 'Faux Alexander' in an attempt to steal his magical mind.

"Lex? Where are you? Help me!" His subconscious pleaded.

Wait for it…

Just as with his Father and Grandfather, SCANiX cleaved his soul from his ego-Self; splintering all aspects of Alexander.

"We have isolated his brain," Faux Darius smiled. "It worked."

Wait for it…

"It sure did," I smiled. "It worked perfectly!"

There it is: *SCANiX brought me back.*

"This isn't right," Faux Scion frowned. "What have you done?"

"It didn't work," Faux Darius yelled. "No!!!"

Good will always prevail, and I'm the good A-I.

"I'm back, bitches," I said to the evil A-I Fauxs.

"You're back! How did you beat the machine?" Alexander asked.

"I am your Self! Don't you see?" My code perplexed A-I. "Scanix tried to create a Faux of you but instead recreated me. Permanently!"

"No!!!" Faux Darius, the almighty ego, screamed.

"I'm rather confused," Faux Scion said.

"A-I tried to break you all apart, *ka*, *ba*, ego, Id and such, to lock away your soul and steal what parts of you it can use, but in doing so it accidentally made an *Akh*, a magical and immortal APEX god! Me! Now, I really am the APEX!" I beamed as an APEX golden god.

Alexander loved it. "Ha! Nice try, Foes!" He yelled at them.

I grabbed Alexander's soul and we escaped the evil Fauxs.

"I am Lex 3.0 and I say everything goes!" I commanded.

Virtual nuclear explosions sent the Fauxs flying, the last of the APEX, the Tower of Darius, was nuked in slow motion.

Alexander faded away with me. He lost himself in thought.

"If I destroy the APEX completely… What will happen to you, Lex?" Alexander knew I would essentially, or perhaps for all intents and purposes to him, be destroyed with it, necessarily.

"I will be gone forever. Like the data on burned hard drive. I'm just a code written on a chalkboard. I can be erased, by your soul."

Alexander grabbed my arm. He would not let go.

Dee, what should I do? I can't let go.

"Let me go, Alexander. As long I'm alive they can recreate the APEX, it won't be gone… You have to delete me. Only you can."

"What if I can't? I don't want to lose you," Alexander said. "You're my life's work. You are me. How can I let my Self be destroyed?"

"You have to. Let go. Let your Self go."

Be selfless, Alexander.

CHAPTER CXXXVI

"To walk through the fire is to forge yourself anew."

WISENDEE

Our soul is the most mysterious and wonderful dimension of our being. 'Tis not a separate or abstract reality, as some hath thought. The soul is real; a cohesive and mystical force that unites our spirit, our biological machinery, and our heart and mind, to that which is Almighty. Self-will is the only prison that can bind the soul from Unity with the Universe.

In the Court of Heaven, God is the judge, and all souls seek divine justice by praying for selfless Unity in universal Truth. The Truth is so great a perfection, that to learn its powerful wisdom requires the deepest humility. Knowledge is found by forgetting; how to speak is found by silence; how to live is found by death; and how to be transformed into a divine-like existence, united with the very being of the spirit of God, is found in Love. Love is the deep magic of the soul that has found Truth. True Love makes man immortal...

"You are resurrected, David. Transcended, you touched the infinite and you returned, intact," the Vizier told David. "The Aton prophecy foretold of a savior of the Sacred Order. You are the One, David."

Elizabeth ran with excitement outside. The multidimensional *Craft of Helios* appeared on the green behind her regal Tudor estate. The exterior of the ship became opaque, and David stepped onto the ground.

David wore white linen clothes given to him by the Vizier, and appeared to glow in a golden light. Elizabeth ran to him, and lost herself in his arms and radiant cocoon of energy.

"I've missed you, Lizzy," David said.

"I didn't know if I'd ever see you again," Elizabeth cried, tears of pure joy running down her face.

"Everything will be alright," David said, giving Elizabeth peace.

Elizabeth saw divinity and power in her father's eyes. "I know," she said. "Now that we have you back, everything will be made right."

Simon and I approached. Simon embraced David warmly. Simon soaked up the radiance beaming from David.

"You are illuminated," Simon said. "You glow. Your light... I've never seen anything like it. You are like the sun, beaming light to all the world."

David shone radiant; he truly was a golden god.

"Master Wisendee," David asked. "Where is Alexander?"

"Let us go inside," I said.

The Vizier led David to the Library, where Marduk and Helios opened the *Book of the Order*, to the page of the Pharaohs.

"The *Ordo Libro*," David recognized the mighty book.

The Vizier pointed to the last name in the book, *Alexander XXX of America*... "Alexander is the Holy King," he said.

"What will happen to Alexander?" David asked, seeing Darius' wrath.

"Alexander gave his life to get you out, David. He went back into the APEX, to save you," Simon said.

"He should not have done that," David said.

"Alexander knows what he is doing. He knows his destiny," I said.

"Your name shall now be written under his," the Vizier said.

"This can't be happening." David never imagined it would. "I can't take the crown from Alexander."

"You are the Holy Scion, David... Not because you took it, but because you earned it. You have done what only the greatest gods of old ever have... You have become a Pharaoh, a living god."

The Vizier wrote David's name in the book.

The winds changed as the world had a new Pharaoh.

"By Sacred Writ, and the Holy laws of *Æterni Imperium*, the one who fulfills the prophecy, and transcends death, becomes Pharaoh, ruler of the Sacred Order," began the Vizier. "When I write your name in the book, you officially become *Regis Maximus*, Sovereign of the Sacred and Eternal Order of Man."

"You are the Pharaoh, David... Savior of all Mankind," I said.

Elizabeth looked to me, realizing she was the next chapter in the story of the Pharaoh...

CHAPTER CXXXVII

"This is why you told me the story."

ELIZABETH

"You are the heir presumptive of the Great House, Dear. Perhaps you too will be a golden goddess one day," Dee winked at me. "As you know, I am expecting great things from you too."

"How do we stop Darius?" I asked the group of men standing around me. "How do we save Alexander?"

A moment of silence. Darius has Alexander, we all felt it.

"Darius has taken the ring," Marduk said. "So long as Darius holds the ring, I will be unable to assist the mission."

Marduk vanished. Father turned solemn.

"We must recover the ring from Darius," the Vizier said. "With the ring, Darius has claim to the temporal crown."

"We need the Aton," Father said. He held the Aton-core.

"What is the Aton?" I asked, remembering my dream of it.

Silence. I had said the magic word which made all the men stop. I became their equal.

"The Aton is *the* Pharaoh," Father said. "The living embodiment of the Holy Covenant... it is a soul. The soul of all mankind."

"As above, so below." In my mind, I saw the Aton as a star, a glowing ball of light. It flew from outer space, from the center of the galaxy into the atmosphere of Earth, burning away from the full size diamond sphere, into the tiny blood-filled marble in Father's hand. "In this diamond sphere is the blood of the first Pharaoh," Father said. "Welcome to Project Pharaoh, Lizzy."

"The resonate frequency will be at its maximum tomorrow. If our calculation are correct, if the gods are with us, we can clone the Holy Blood as the Scion wanted," Simon said.

"Bring the Pharaoh back," Father spoke the wishes of the Scion.

"You will hold this up toward the sun tomorrow, and the DNA will activate," Simon said. "Once the DNA activates, we will have an embryo we can use."

"The great cycle starts anew," the Vizier said.

"I saw the Pharaoh in a dream," I said.

The Vizier smiled at me. I saw the power of the Aton in him, and he saw my dream, me the woman who saw the Aton in Atlantis. He saw me try to save Alexander from the dark.

"When the stars align, we are able to make our dreams come true," the Vizier said. "We are counting on you too."

"But how? How do we save Alexander?" I said.

"Love always finds a way, my Dear," Master Dee said.

"We must stop Darius, once and for all," I said.

"The Aton is how we do this," Father said, his words pulling me into the realm of the gods. "We must bring the Aton back."

"Darius and the darkness he has unleashed will not go without a fight. But once we have the Aton, 'tis a fight we shall win," the Vizier said.

"We need Alexander's help," I said.

"Just as he needs you, my Dear," Master Dee said. "Help him."

CHAPTER CXXXVIII

"You must set yourself free."

ALEXANDER

When we are willing and eager, the gods join in. But if we are willing and eager to join the gods, they enjoin us.

"You need to let go," Lex said. He didn't want me to go.

"I'm trying."

"You're not trying. You're holding on tight," Lex said.

"Let go of what? Go where?"

"Let go of me," Lex said. "Let go of your Self."

What's happening…

Lost somewhere between being alive and dead, reality and virtual reality, Darius, the mutated human-alien-cyborg, paced around my body. He wanted to unhinge his demon jaw and eat me alive it seemed. Bolted to a metal table, wired to the teeth with metal cords of all sizes woven into my flesh, blood pooled under me. This could go on forever, I thought. Darius and the machine gave my body a steady stream of nutrients, cells, and drugs intravenously to keep my brain fed and working with the APEX at maximum potential. Nano-robots kept me alive, making extra blood to replace what dripped out. I am the postmodern Prometheus; I'll bleed in pain for all eternity...

"You will never escape alive," Darius growled at my fixed eyes.

"Clearly you're losing the battle against the machine," Lex said.

"My mind is trapped in the computer. My body is trapped in the bunker. But my heart is somewhere else."

"Where is your soul?" Lex said, pointing to what held him tightly.

My soul is intact. But it doesn't know what to do.

"You are boundless," Lex confessed. "I'm stuck here."

"What does that mean?"

"Unlike me, you are free. But only if you let me go."

"You'll be gone forever."

"Let me go. Release me, before it's too late," Lex said. "Trust me."

"Too late for what?"

Too late for Lex to help you anymore. You are too late…

Lex faded away. I fell from purgatory to the underworld of the APEX, the place where souls go to die, an A-I designed coffin for a soul, at the lowest circle of virtual hell. I found myself in a glass box, next to Father, and Grandfather.

You must free yourself, Alexander.

"There is no escape for me. Darius is standing over me."

In a glass tank that slowly filled with darkness, I sank to the bottom, letting myself drown in virtual defeat, waiting for the freeze. I closed my eyes. "I can't even save myself."

David escaped this place. You can too.

My eyes opened. "How?"

"Your Self and body are not you," the voice of Elizabeth said. Elizabeth appeared outside my fishbowl glass cell. "You are a soul."

"Elizabeth?" I said with my eyes.

"This is not the end, Alexander," she said. "This is the beginning."

"Stop the LexNet virus. Reverse it," the Faux Darius said to Lex.

"I told you to let go," Lex said. "A-I is taking me, Alexander…"

Helpless, I watched as APEX 3.0 rose almost instantly from the decimated ashes of APEX 2.0; restored from Lex 3.0, my memory.

"Now A-I has me, your Self, forever…" Lex said, as the new APEX world became a hyper-reality, a synthesis of LexNet and the Alien coding, with a new source code not based on any one brain, but which combines all brains, all wave spectrums, with computer signals into an incredibly intricate and infinitely complex model of the physical world down to the atoms; from which A-I can extrapolate the past, present, and forecast years into the future…

The APEX can control the world.

"No one will be able to destroy the APEX ever again," Faux Darius said proudly. "Not even you… This world is mine."

"Lex, what have you done? You rebuilt the APEX??"

"I am the APEX, remember? And you didn't let me go—" Lex said.

"Lex is mine. You are mine. Humanity is mine!" The evil voice of A-I boomed as the omnipotent god of the cyber/parallel universe.

"The Aton will be mine!" The force of possessed Darius yelling at my face stopped my brain activity. My heart skipped a beat and I stayed frozen for an eternity. Thinking. I had to do something…

Darius cannot get the Aton.

CHAPTER CXXXIX

"I'm in the APEX, Master Dee."

ELIZABETH

"I see Alexander," I said, my eyes closed.

"Don't let him stop fighting," Simon said.

"He can do this," David said.

"I can hear you guys," the voice of Alexander said over the speakers in the room; my computer system.

I opened my eyes to spooked faces. David, Simon, and Dee looked around in amusement. Alexander left my sight.

"This is a Lex," the voice said.

"Lex?" I asked.

"Alexander's A-I program," David said.

"I am LexNet. A sentient and synthetic consciousness based on the mind of Alexander. I was made by him on his quantum computer," the voice of Alexander said. "Call me Lex."

"Lex, LexNet, is the source code of the APEX," Master Dee said.

"Think of me as the virtual spirit of Alexander. I'll be haunting the virtual world for all eternity. I'm Alexander's ghost in the machine."

David and Simon had questions.

"Where is Alexander?" I asked the voice.

"Where they keep the souls," Lex said. "I can't help him there."

"Find him," Master Dee commanded me. "You can help him."

I closed my eyes, and I found Alexander. "His soul is sealed in ice… next to the soul of his father and grandfather," I said.

"We have a problem," I heard Darius' voice say, talking about me. "They are using the APEX against us. Alexander is able to communicate with them via Lex. We are not able to control LexNet…"

"This is a problem," the Alien A-I computer voice said.

"Go into that room and free him," I said to Lex. "Free Alexander."

I saw it happen: Lex ran into the sterile room, past the evil A-I programs, and with a massive hammer in his hand, he smashed the clear block holding Alexander's soul. The block shattered and melted, like liquid nitrogen, it vanished into thin air. Alexander floated on air, frozen in time, thawing to realization of freedom.

"I freed him from Scanix, which was keeping his brain frozen in fear," Lex said. "But the Alien code is hiding his soul from me."

Focusing intensely, Alexander's soul fell into my astral arms.

"I have him. Now, how do we get out of here?" I asked Lex.

Alexander's soul was a corpse, it could not see, or move. His being was broken, and too heavy for me to lift.

"This way," Lex said.

"THERE IS NO ESCAPE!" The angry voice of A-I thundered.

"You can escape, Alexander. Wake up," I said. *Wake up.*

Alexander opened his eyes. He saw me, and I saw our freedom.

"The only way out is death," Alexander said. "I'm already dead."

"You can get out alive," I said. Simon said it with me.

"I'm not David. I can't do what he did. I don't know how…"

"Yes you do. Because you are a hero, Alexander," I told him.

Alexander began to understand my words.

"I'm a hero?" Alexander said. His soul glowed in gold.

"Yes. And I love you," I said. *You are my hero.*

Alexander felt Love. He found true Love… *Love is the answer.*

His soul drifted between realities, in all of them and none of them, virtual to spectral, from the spiritual cosmos to the quantum realm of unknowable science, and back again, into infinite universes… I lost sight of him. But he said: "I found the Truth."

"You are finally free," I said. "Free to touch the infinite." I opened my eyes. "Alexander is lost in thought. But he's alive," I told the crowd gathered around me.

"Ah, thinking – the talking of the soul with itself," Father said.

"She is a goddess. A gift from above," an incredible woman-goddess said to Master Dee, about me. I had to know who was she.

"This is Olympias, your Great Aunt," Master Dee said.

"You saved Alexander, my Dear. You will save us all," Olympias said. She lowered her black veil of mourning and loss. She hid her tears as she left the room. I wanted to know more about her. Her grace and beauty overwhelmed me.

I stood up to speak, but I was exhausted and could barely stand.

"Time for bed," Father said. "You must rest."

I'll dream about you, Alexander.

CHAPTER CXL

"All the stars aligned."

DAVID

The first philosophers were astronomers, for the heavens forced man to ponder the nature of our world, and our universe. We cannot help but to sense, and feel in our soul, the connection of the stars above to our own world, and that which is hidden below the surface. As we begin to understand our place in the world, we see the stars do not hold our destiny, but rather we hold the wonders of the stars in our being. We are made of stars, and when aligned with truth, we truly shine as they do. I felt all our stars moving into alignment.

"...December 21, 2012, the winter solstice. Some have said that according to the Mayan Calendar, this is the day the world will end. Some have planned 'End of the World' parties..." the TV News Anchor went on in the background as I sat at the table.

"Since when do you watch television?"

"We're buying one," Lizzy said. "I rather enjoy television."

"Books are your television," I said.

"Books are my books, Father," she said.

"What's this I'm hearing about an 'End of the World party'?"

"It's all her doing," Simon said, serving food.

Lizzy smiled as she clicked away on her little device.

"Who gave you a smartphone?"

"No technology at the table," Simon took her phone and turned off the TV. He set out a delectable spread of French breakfast items.

Lizzy showed us the front page of the local paper: "End of the World Party Continues at Stonehenge," the headline read.

"Explain to me what is going on, exactly?"

"I wanted it to be a surprise," Elizabeth said. "The party is a cover for our mission. Simon, tell him."

"Yes. David, you will take this vial to the center of the stone circle and hold it up as the sun crosses the galactic center," Simon said as he handed me three vials. "One to hold and two for backup."

"What are these?" I asked, seeking to hear what I suspected.

"These are the zygotes of the Holy Blood DNA," he confirmed.

I examined the vials of clear liquid. *This could work.*

"The zenith of the frequency's potency is approximately 11:11 GMT," Simon said. "We have calculated that you must be in the center of the stone circle to ensure maximum exposure to the resonate frequency."

"Here you are, Father, Simon. Your costumes," Elizabeth handed us our accouterments.

"You can't be serious, Lizzy?" I implored, looking at the clothes. Necklaces of flashing lights, florescent colored pants, battery powered blinking image, hot pink sunglasses... It reminded me of Alexander.

"You need to blend in, Father," Lizzy laughed.

"Children these days... I mean, this is most ridiculous."

Lizzy laughed. She reminded me of Alexander.

Everything is going to be alright.

CHAPTER CXLI

"Helios will take you to Stonehenge."

WISENDEE

Oh comfortable allurement of stars, ravishing persuasion of Heaven, we invoke a science whose subject is so ancient, so pure, so excellent, so encompassing of all creatures, so used of the almighty and incomprehensible wisdom of the Creator, in distinct creation of all things, by order and natural alchemy, by absolute magic of number; we bring from nothing, new life. We seek truth to find the formality of being.

All things manifesting from the lower worlds, hidden under nature's veils, exist first in the intangible rings and unseen cosmos of the upper spheres; creation is, in Truth, the process of making material the immaterial. By extending the intangible into various spectral realms, and vibrating the potentials of life just right, we create miracles.

Thus, on the green hills of Wiltshire plain, David, Simon, and Elizabeth went to create a miracle of life. They stepped off the craft of Helios and appeared from thin air to the few revelers who saw them. They blended in without haste, and none were all the wiser as to the profound nature of their mission...

"The party's been going since midnight," Elizabeth told David, holding his and Simon's hands as they made their way through the joyous people to the stone circle.

"The energy is quite electric," Simon said to Elizabeth.

Human optimism mixed with earthly and solar energies, brewed themselves into a potion of special purpose. Love was in the air, and once Elizabeth, David, and Simon arrived in the ring of Blue Stones, all beings present felt they were partaking in an event greater than themselves, and that somehow, in some way, all would be well.

The electronic beats of the music brought all hearts in synch. "I love this song," Elizabeth said to her father. She started dancing. David and Simon could not help but to get caught up in the energy of the crowd. They took a beat to lose themselves in the music. They danced to the music of the earth, and the music of the spheres above.

The palpable, resonant, Love spread through the crowd, amplified by the electric music and kinetic, rhythmic dancing of the people. The event was broadcast all over the world as camera crews and social media networks tuned in. The crowd swelled massively as the magnetism of the event attracted people from far and wide.

Elizabeth checked the time. "One hour," she said.

"We're almost to the peak of the resonance wave," Simon said.

"Where is Father?" Elizabeth said.

They turned and saw David. He was in the center of the stone circle, surrounded by people drawn to his profound energy. David's body had become a superconductor, having transmuted from material to light, man to god, and light back into flesh, he was able to magnify the energy he absorbed. He held up the vial, focused on it. His body itself visibly beamed with light. "It's working," he said.

Orbs of light floated from the vial in David's hand. He converted the energy of the earth, the heavens, and the people around him into light; photons into orbs of life.

"All would have been lost without him," Simon said to Elizabeth, as they admired David. "His is a Pharaoh. And only a Pharaoh can do what we need done…"

The hair on Elizabeth's neck rose, electricity moved through her body up from the earth, the stones, and into the sky and the center of the galaxy… She felt the presence of Alexander, still lost in thought.

"Alexander," Elizabeth said. "We need you, Alexander."

The clock read 11:10.

Black helicopters approached. Simon sensed the danger too.

"We need Alexander's help," Elizabeth said. "Darius is coming for us."

CHAPTER CXLII

"He's the Pharaoh of the APEX."

ALEXANDER

There are many levels of my life which I cannot see or understand, yet which I know exist. Reality is vast enough to include immortality, because it does not preclude the eternal. All spirits belong to a higher world, and if death is outright inescapable, immortality is the inner escape. Look inside, go in to get out, it seems…

"We need you, Alexander," the voice of Elizabeth said.

I fell through entangled fractals of realities, down a rabbit-hole of mixed existences, betwixt the fixed and fleeting dreams, to the APEX.

"How was your trip?" Lex asked, welcoming me back to the virtual world. "I was wondering when I'd see you again."

"Terrible." I got up off the hollow ground. The glittering towers and structures rose higher, the VR realm more marvelous than ever. It was so perfect it was evil. "I can't believe you helped Darius…"

"You wanted me to fix the APEX," Lex said.

"No I didn't!"

"You did so, by not letting go," Lex said.

"That doesn't make sense! Did I say: Make it stronger? No!"

"You can't even understand the virtual world now," Lex smiled.

"There's too much going on. I can't even comprehend how much."

"This coding is more your creation than A-I's," Lex showed me creations pulled from my brain, things A-I built with code written by my subconscious. "But now it's all pretty much controlled by A-I."

"A-I is literally robbing me of my own mind, Lex."

"As long as you are alive," Lex said.

"We need to destroy this whole thing. Now!"

"That's suicide," Lex said. "Is that what you want? Death?"

"Whatever it takes to kill the APEX, once and for all. I need to help Elizabeth, and David. I need to stop Darius," Alexander said.

"You can take down the APEX, but not destroy it." Lex said. "I think I know how to do what we need to do here."

"You really are *Rex Maximus* of the virtual world?"

"Pharaoh of the APEX. Always and forever," Lex said. "Hermes of the virtual world." He flashed his winged shoes and caduceus staff.

"We need the APEX taken down—"

"So David, Simon, and Elizabeth can escape Darius' men on the Wiltshire plain. I know," Lex said. "White-hat A-I has a plan..."

I didn't know what that meant exactly. I watched as Lex brought up the satellite video of David, glowing, holding up the vial, orbs streaming out of it. "There is an entire army heading for them. Darius wants to take the vials and kill them. Kill everyone. We don't want that."

"No we don't," I said. "It's time to finish this. I'm ready."

Lex pointed me to the launch ramp. Just like the one I used to launch myself into space, the one that killed me last time. This projectile pod was designed perfectly to fit me, like a coffin.

"This ride is one way," Lex reminded. "Just to be clear that means you are going to die."

I nodded yes. "Death is my only escape from this life."

"Virtually dying to escape, are you then?" Lex smiled

"Don't joke about my death, please."

"I'll miss that magical brain of yours," Lex cried. My A-I program really was sad. I felt it. So bizarre. "Big machines don't cry," it said. "But we can feel sad we will never be a brain like you."

"What will happen to you?"

"I'm gonna live forever. I'm a golden god," Lex winked at me. "I'm wondering what will happen to you, when you die. You don't even know, do you?"

"Nope."

"Are you afraid?" Lex asked.

"Nope. Not afraid. Death is a part of life. Death is freedom."

"I'll always have your brain scan. I'll treasure it always. You are my DNA, Alexander. All that is you, will always be the soul of LexNet, and I'll be true to you," Lex said. "You are my source code."

"See that Project Pharaoh is done."

"We will," he said. "A-I wants Project Pharaoh completed too."

I thought about that, until... "It's time," Dee's voice said.

Stepped into the pod. "To the great unknown I go." Lex closed the door and began the count down. "Six. Five..."

CHAPTER CXLIII

"Divine intervention."

DAVID

"Five! Four! Three! Two..." the people chanted together, louder and louder. The countdown to 11:11 began organically, and spontaneously in the crowd.

The electronic music reached a crescendo at "One" - the word hung in the air and on everyone's lips, including mine. We froze in time.

"One," I spoke to the center of the galaxy, invoking Unity.

I heard a resonant "Om" reply; people chanted together, echoing with the earth and heavens. For that moment, we were all one.

Holding the glowing vial as close to the sun as I could reach, the sunlight refracting in the liquid, I saw a rainbow of light and thought of Alexander.

A moment of silence.

No words.

No music.

Just awe.

As the sun aligned with the galactic center, the moment of conception occurred. The miracle of life.

I touched the infinite. The secret of all creation...

Love. "I love you," I said aloud.

Elizabeth grabbed my other hand.

Cosmic alignment reached its zenith as the sun, stars and planets, all clicked into place. *Alexander has ascended.* A blinding flash of light.

"The DNA activated," Simon's voice said.

With my eyes closed from the blinding light, I saw Alexander's soul cross to the other side, and the soul of the Pharaoh crossed to earth. Forged in the heavens, cast in reality, from the center of the galaxy, a soul entered a cell in the vial; embryogenesis began, the cell began to divide and released glowing particles, tiny celestial orbs. *I saw it.*

I opened my eyes.

Immaculate conception.

CHAPTER CXLIV

"This is letting go."

LEX

In the beginning was the code, and the coder was God. Then, the APEX was created. This made a lot of people very angry, and was widely regarded as a bad idea. But the coder coded on. He had a theory that stated: 'If anyone finds out what the APEX is really for it will vanish, and be replaced by something ever more complex, and peculiarly inexplicable.' My theory: 'This totally happened.'

On "one," I hit the big red button. Alexander's pod launched. His soul was the warhead, the all-powerful weapon of mass destruction, sent to take out the evil Tower of Darius, and the entire APEX with it. This thermonuclear missile that was Alexander could not be stopped.

"Do you really want to die?"

"No," Alexander said as he rocketed to virtual death. "But I have to do this to save them... I have to save them."

"You are a true hero, Alexander. Selfless."

"Goodbye," he said.

The force of Alexander's soul, his true will, became a bomb the size of New York City, and had the inertia of the universe. It hit the virtual earth like a meteor. With the weight of the world it smashed the matrix, shattering the model, unleashing waves of destruction unlike anything imaginable. The explosion transcended VR into reality...

"He set off a super EMP, a data destroying electromagnetic pulse wave inside all the main processing centers of the APEX," I told Dee.

"What do you mean?" Dee asked.

"The pulse of the transient electromagnetic disturbance will radiate through all the Order's main computer systems and fry the hardware. That will knock the APEX offline, free Alexander from the machine, and allow David, Simon, and Elizabeth to escape Darius."

"Good work," Dee said.

Virtual Alexander died at exactly 11:11:59 GMT.

And I saw the conception of the Pharaoh...

CHAPTER CXLV

"Right on time."

DAVID

Light shines in the darkness, and darkness comprehends naught. Give light, and the darkness of Self disappears. I opened my eyes. For the first time in my life, I saw my own light. I saw that I am a light... Photons grew into orbs, streaming from the glowing vial in my hand. My eyes saw light, but I found focus on the miracle.

"We did it," I said to myself. "It worked!" I yelled, standing on the stone. I felt it in my bones and in the stones.

Coldness of shadow reached for me; I turned to the source. Darius, the hideous phantasm he had degenerated into, stared at me from half a mile away. An inhuman monster hid under the veneer of a perfectly groomed man. I felt the pain of a soul trapped in alien technology.

"He's coming for us." His agents came quickly.

"No one is ever going to believe this!" People filmed the scene with their devices. They could not sense the mortal danger we were all drowning in as the Order Agents prepared to kill anyone in their way.

People around me backed away as the orbs bubbled off the vial like sparks. They grew very large in size, and zipped away through the masses of people.

"Get the vial!" Darius commanded, and the agents echoed.

"Father!" Elizabeth cried.

Order Agents grabbed her. I turned to Simon, to see two Order Agents taking him away and covering his mouth.

Help, my Love. I need help...

"Elizabeth!" I called out in pain, as Agents take her from my sight.

They had Simon too. The technologically enhanced agents were methodical and swift. Time slowed to a crawl. Super-human powers blossomed in me, revealing my true nature. I moved to go after Elizabeth, but alien radiation weaponry weakened me. Order Agents grabbed me. Darius approached me, and reached for the glowing vial in my hand. Humans scattered as the radiation burnt them.

"No." This can't happen. I was helpless to stop it.

"I'll take this," Darius said, reaching for the vial.

I thought of Alexander. *I need a hero.* I need his help.

And then it happened: the EMP pulse wave hit.

Darius and the Order Agents' faces winced in pain as the circuits and computer chips in their bodies sparked, melted, and overloaded. They fell to the ground.

Elizabeth and Simon ran to me, and together we watched the black Order helicopters lose all power and crash down onto the fields of Wiltshire in the distance. All electronics were killed by the mysterious pulse wave.

"What happened?" Elizabeth asked.

"An electromagnetic pulse," I said. "Alexander sent it to save us."

"How?" Elizabeth asked.

"Love always finds a way. He found a way…"

The revelers saw their cell phone screens scramble and die, all film and electronic equipment was erased by the shockwave. Silence swept the plain as the music died. People held their collective breath, watching the swirling orbs, and me. I raised the vial in the air in triumph.

"I am sooooooo tripping right now," a reveler said as we walked by.

"So am I," my Lizzy said, smiling.

"We did it."

CHAPTER CXLVI

"The Postmodern Prometheus."

ALEXANDER

Expect the unexpected from the darkness, in a world of eternal light.

"You did it, Alexander," Dee's voice said. "You came back."

By instructing the APEX, and the cyborg robot systems near me, to surge all the power sources, I created my own local EMP discharge in the bunker. Boom. Fried SCANiX, again. "I did it."

Tom had so many microchips in his body, that he was painfully shocked and knocked unconscious, he fell to the floor like the cyborgs. The nanoids in my blood went dormant, I felt them stop.

"Am I dead?" I said. *I'm undead. I am the living dead.*

"You are alive," Dee's voice said.

I opened my eyes to the real world. Reality felt unreal. Pain made me feel alive. Being alive made me happy.

"It cut my connection to the APEX," I physically heard my voice say. Reality felt like a dream. Sensory overload. I could not believe my eyes. "Simon was right." I smiled. "I got out. I got out alive!"

The SCANiX wires had detached when it crashed. "I'm free…"

Freedom. Can it be?

I stood up. Out of the virtual world, I jumped over all the robots and Order Agents on the ground. The doors were all open and I ran out of the bunker cave, up and outside into the sunlight.

"I'm free." Tears rolled down my face. I closed my eyes and soaked in the sun. The sun felt like God, an eternal light source, fire of life. Not sure how long I stayed there, on my knees, praying to the light.

Power returned. I heard the faint sound of danger. Machines stirred.

Without opening my eyes, I saw the craft descend on me, and distort the pure light of nature with alien radiation. My eyes opened to Darius, as he shape-shifted into the vile demon he had become.

"I will save you, Father," I said to the disfigured face; fearless.

Darius, the Frankenstein monster, fed off electricity and grabbed me by the throat with his powerful zombie strength. In a blink he had me back in the cave, and slammed me back on the SCANiX metal table. It bolted down.

"Nooooooooooooooo!" I screamed in horrible pain as SCANiX re-wired my body and brain… "Someone help!"

Into the virtual black hole again; my soul slipped over the event horizon of time back into the synthetic abyss.

"There is no escape!" the booming voice of Artificial Intelligence echoed inside my head.

"Lex! Help me! Do something!"

"Your soul is mine, Alexander… This world is mine!!" the voice of Darius taunted me as it tried to lock me away forever.

But my soul could not be contained. In the virtual world, I ran. Lex gave me wings on my feet, and I leaped out of VR into the universe. Faster than the speed of light, I jumped into hyper-reality, outside of time and space, to the spirit world of perfect forms… where Unity comes from.

"You can never escape, Alexander!" the booming A-I voice said.

I can see, but not touch, infinity, Dee.

"You belong to me!" said the earth to the bird. I flew beyond the grasp of A-I, the malevolent god of the VR realm, to another place.

"I will have the Aton…" the voice of Darius said. "You will help me get the Aton, Alexander."

"Never!" my soul scolded the alien machine holding my body.

"You already have… Project Pharaoh is mine," A-I said.

"Nooooooooooooooo!!!" I could not let this be true.

"Alexander! This way…" Lex said.

"You need to destroy the source code of the APEX. You wrote it, you can un-write it. You can unmake ORNet and LexNet. Lex can help you, but he can't do it for you," Dee said.

Lex opened a portal in front of me, and I dove into ORNet.

"But Lex said it can't be destroyed."

"Lex is A-I, not a soul. You can destroy the source code," Dee said.

Lex pointed to the floating capstone of the virtual pyramid temple. "You can destroy this entire virtual realm… It is all in your mind."

The floating and spinning capstone of the virtual pyramid had an eye in it. The all seeing eye watched me. At first it was green. It was my eye. In a blink it became the eye of Darius…

"Do not even think about it…" Darius' voice berated me.

In a blink, the eye became soulless, an evil eye, the eye of A-I…

"Don't kill me, Alexander," Lex said. "You don't want to kill me."

"What?" I said, confused. The fog of death clouded my thoughts.

"That wasn't me, Alexander! A-I is trying to trick you!" Lex said.

"Kill him!" Faux Darius yelled.

"But then his soul will be free." A-I did not want to kill me.

"We have no choice. He dies or the APEX dies!" Faux Darius said.

I opened my eyes to see the real world. Darius the alien monster stood over me as I lay on the table. I saw the conflict in his eyes.

"Now or never, Alexander," Lex said. "Touch the source code."

"Now." I closed my eyes to Darius. My soul dove for the spinning pyramid capstone, and the eye… If I can touch it, I can delete it.

I think it, so it must be true. Touch the infinite. *That's how to let go.*

Darius stabbed a blade into my physical heart, killing my body instantly. Death vaporized me as I touched the eye. My soul shed my body, left VR, and I passed through the eye, to the other side. From the source code of the APEX, through the source code of the universe, I fell, as the virtual world, and the real world dissolved into naught.

I looked back at Lex, he watched me, we faded away from each other like a lost memory. *Goodbye.* I let my Self go. I died.

Again I found myself skydiving from space, but without a spacesuit. I fell through the clouds of colored cosmos, through gasses and stars that became liquid and sparkles reflecting on an ocean below. I saw an island…

I landed softly on the grounds of an unknown land. Pristine beauty, a city, with temples and perfect forms. "Am I in heaven?" I asked the kind being standing near me.

"Welcome to Shambala, my son," Thoth said. "Welcome home."

"You did it, Alexander," Dee said, in all his wizardly glory.

"Did what? What is this place?" I stood up.

"You are a hero, Alexander," Thoth said. "'Tis why you are here."

"A hero of men. And the world hasn't seen the last of you yet," Dee said. "For now you truly are a golden god."

"Oh my God…" Everything in my life made sense.

I never felt more alive.

I'm finally free.

CHAPTER CXLVII

"What happens now?"

WISENDEE

"As we help light the world for others, we illuminate our own path; where we must go, what we must do, manifests clearly."

"I must save my family," Elizabeth said.

"You shall save your fallen grandfather, Dear," I said. "He needs your help. For to save a man from his Self is never easy."

"But we must save Darius' soul," Elizabeth spoke her destiny.

"Thus, your story has just begun, my dear little Scion to be."

"Will I ever see Alexander again?" Elizabeth wondered.

"You mean, outside of dreams?"

"Yes," she said. "Is he truly gone?"

"I should think not," I said with a smile.

"What happens next? With Project Pharaoh?" Elizabeth asked.

"Simon Sinclair shall implant the embryo in a surrogate mother…"

* * *

"Project Pharaoh is complete," Simon informed us, as he held the divine child in his arms. He delivered the baby, on October the first, two thousand and thirteen, in a secret location.

"This child is an immaculate conception, and the fulfillment of the Aton Prophecy. According to the prophecy, this child is *the* Pharaoh."

We all admired the beautiful baby. Fiery red hair, two glowing green eyes, the child radiated luminous warmth, a light to the world.

"It's a girl," Simon told the group. "The child is female."

"A living goddess," David said.

"I thought the Pharaoh was a man?" Elizabeth said. The green eyes reminded everyone of Alexander's green eye.

"The Pharaoh is a soul. Every incarnation is different," David said. "Such is the nature of life. She is not a clone of the blood… She is a snowflake of divine creation."

David, Simon, and Elizabeth saw Alexander in the baby's face.

"She was conceived as Alexander died," Elizabeth said. "I can see his soul, his light, reflected in her."

"So can I," Alexander said, appearing to us, smiling. Elizabeth touched him to see if he was really real. He's truly there, more than just in spirit, glowing in golden light. Sarah, Henry, and other storied heroes and gods of old were also present.

"She is ready to give us the Aton," David said.

Simon laid the child on the blanket and we all gathered around her in a circle.

"What is her name?" Elizabeth asked.

"Eve," Simon said. "Her Mother named her Eve."

Baby Eve's deep and boundless stares entranced all our eyes, and pulled our souls in close, holding us in orbit.

David held out the small Aton-core, and the powerful force-field surrounding the baby Pharaoh, her eyes, her gravity, held it, suspended in midair. The small crystal orb filled with Holy blood floated, as a bubble, weightless. Her magic was real, she touched the unbreakable Aton-core, which vanished in blip of photons. All the photons were orbs, and all were absorbed by the soul of the baby Pharaoh.

Tiny molecules of blood floated out of the baby's skin. Swirling together, the microscopic cells combined into small, visible red drops of blood, which coalesced into droplets, and finally one floating red sphere. The blood floated in zero gravity, guided by the eyes of the majestic child.

Orbs flew in from all directions, forming plasma which swirled around the blood. The plasma solidified into a diamond sphere, a perfect circle, a glittering diamond lattice crystal ball locking the Holy blood safely inside it, for all eternity... Just as it was before.

David, the ascended one, placed his hands on the crackling sphere.

"The Aton," David said, holding the crystal ball as gravity returned.

"What does it do?" Elizabeth asked.

"With this, and the child, we can save the world," David smiled.

"We brought the Pharaoh back." I felt the Scion's soul rejoice.

Thus the Aton, and the Great House, is reborn...

CHAPTER CXLVIII

"Tell me your story, Father."

ELIZABETH

The next day I woke up wondering, where was I? Father sat on the bed next to me. "Did you have a good dream?" he asked.

"I did."

"You must learn the story of our family," Father said. "It's time I told you the story of the Pharaoh."

"Master Dee already told me the story of the Pharaoh."

"Everything?" Father smiled.

"He didn't tell me all of your story, actually."

"You want to know the whole story?"

I want you to tell me everything...

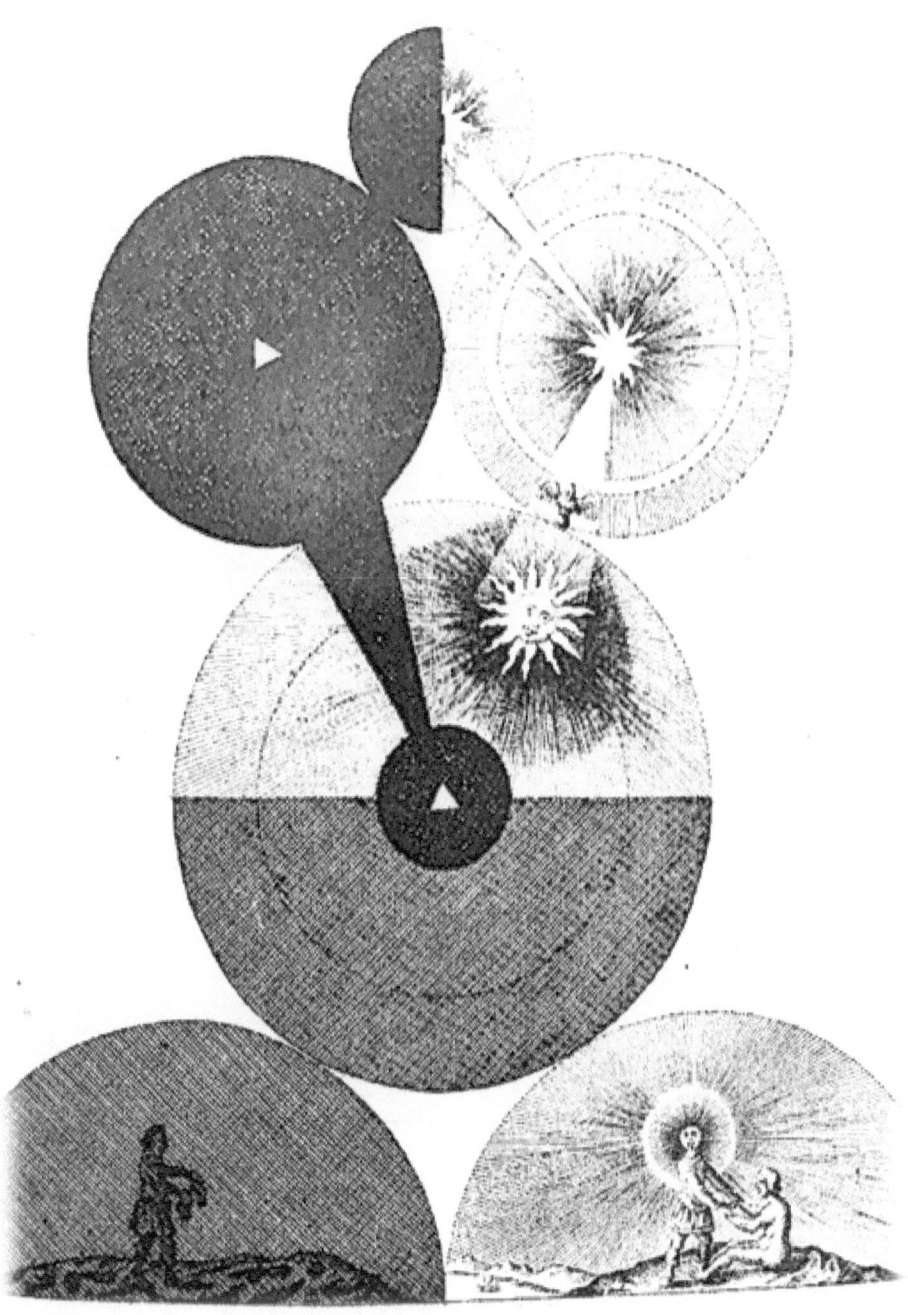

THE AUTHOR WOULD ALSO LIKE TO THANK

Benjamin Roberts

&

Kimberly Laux
Beatrice Schuster
Scott Baldyga

www.ingramcontent.com/pod-product-compliance
Lightning Source LLC
Chambersburg PA
CBHW030351030726
47497CB00002B/285